Bite Marks & Brken Hearts

TJ Rose

Contents

Welcome

Bite Marks & Broken Hearts is an adult paranormal MM romance suitable for mature readers only.

Content advisories:

- explicit adult content, including CNC/roleplay

- reference to grandparent dying of cancer

- reference to homophobic grandparent

- reference to losing a parent as a child

- very brief reference to historic suicidal thoughts

- blood *(shock, horror!)*

- mild gore

Thank you for reading and I hope you enjoy Flynn & Seb's story. This new world was an absolute blast to create!

Note: This book is written in British English.

– TJ Rose

I desire the things which will destroy me in the end.
Sylvia Plath

I

Sebastián

London's forgotten churches held many secrets, but the dead girl sprawled across the altar wasn't supposed to be one of them.

Moonlight filtered through the broken rose window, casting fractured colours across the chapel's crumbling walls. Blood pooled across weathered flagstones, seeping between the cracks in a crimson constellation. Too late. *Again.*

Above her, the cambion—the most foul sort of lesser demon—crouched on a fallen beam, perfectly still in its human male form. Dark energy harvested from the corpse crackled around it like static electricity, raising the hairs on my arms. The demon's presence made a mockery of what little sanctity remained—though after five centuries, I'd seen enough to know how hollow that had always been.

"You're too late, vampire," the vile thing hissed.

I adjusted the sleeves of my knee-length black coat, brass buttons clinking. "I can see that."

I'd tracked the cambion for the last three nights, always one step behind. Another dead human because I hadn't been fast enough. The familiar weight of failure pressed against my chest. I smoothed down my fitted trousers, brushing away debris from the decrepit pews I'd vaulted over in my pursuit.

The cambion shrieked—an almighty, ear-deafening sound that shattered what remained of the stained glass, sending a kaleidoscope of coloured shards raining down around us.

Honestly, it was a miracle my coat had survived over fifty years of this abuse.

The beast launched itself from the beam and I sidestepped, my movements precise despite the glass crunching beneath my shoes.

"Magpie," I snapped into my comms earpiece as I ducked under claws that would have taken my head off. "Location of the others?"

A burst of anxious typing filled my ear. "Boss! Peacock and Terrier are in the parish house across the courtyard. About two minutes from—"

I didn't hear the rest. The creature slammed me into a stone pillar, decades' worth of dust raining down with the impact. A sharp tear pierced the air. *Ah!* There went my waistcoat.

I lunged forward, my hand closing around its throat. In one fluid motion, I hooked my foot behind its leg and spun us both, slamming the cambion against the pillar. Stone cracked. The impact would have crushed human bones, but the creature merely wheezed out a laugh.

The cambion's human glamour was slipping, revealing scaled skin beneath. Its eyes blazed with stolen power as it lunged again, but this time I was ready.

"Who are you working for?" I demanded. Blood from my split lip trickled down my chin, the copper taste filling my mouth. "Tell me, and I'll show mercy by making your death quick and painless."

"The old powers are stirring, vampire." Its voice grated like rusted metal before a forked tongue flicked out, tasting the air. "They remember what you forgot."

The cambion's words struck deep. *What you forgot.* The familiar fog rolled through my mind, memories slipping away like smoke whenever I tried to grasp them. Faces without names. Places without context. Centuries of existence, reduced to fragments and whispers.

Sweat slicked my palms, and in that moment of distraction, my grip slipped against the creature's scaly flesh—a fatal mistake.

The creature's tail manifested, whipping around to slam into my chest. I flew backward, crashing through rotting pews. Wood splintered. Pain lanced through my ribs as I rolled, barely avoiding the cambion's follow-up strike.

The creature pressed its advantage, driving me back across the chapel floor. Each blow carried supernatural strength, fuelled by its recent kill. I drew my silver dagger from my hip, its ancient Spanish metalwork gleaming sharply.

Moonlight caught the cambion's scales as it lunged. This time, I didn't dodge.

I let its momentum carry us both down, using its own weight to drive the blade deep into its throat. "*In tenebris te dimitto,*" I snarled, the Latin falling from my lips like muscle memory.

The effect was immediate. Where silver met flesh, the creature's skin began to bubble and dissolve. Holy oil mixed with quicksilver—an old recipe, effective against demons and the damned alike. The cambion's scream echoed through the derelict chapel, its human glamour completely shattering as corruption ate through muscle and bone. Sulphur filled the air, its rancid stench burning my nostrils.

Delightful. This was exactly how I'd planned to spend my Thursday evening.

Rapid footsteps approached from outside. *About bloody time.*

The chapel doors burst open, wood groaning in protest. Kit's massive frame filled the entrance, his gun trained on the dissolving cambion.

Behind him, Rory bounced on his toes, his usually chaotic blond hair housing a thick layer of grey grime. "Aw, you had fun without us!"

"Shut up," Kit growled at his brother, lowering his weapon. His eyes scanned me for injuries, then flicked to the pile of ash and scales that had been the cambion moments before. "You unharmed, boss?"

I wiped blood from my split lip with my sleeve. "Peachy."

"That coat is going to need a good wash again." Priya stepped around them both, adjusting her oversized purple scarf. "Are you hurt?"

My ribs ached, but they could wait. "The girl first."

We approached the altar together, forming a small circle around the body. She couldn't have been more than sixteen. Dark hair fanned out like a halo against the stone.

Her white shirt was torn, jagged edges revealing frost patterns spiralling across her chest in intricate whorls, spreading outward from her heart.

"Identical markings to the other victims," Kit said.

I sighed. We'd now exceeded ten bodies, but were little closer to discovering what malicious entity was behind this gruesome operation: seeding dark magic inside a victim, harvesting it once it had been cultivated.

I traced the air above the frost patterns, feeling the residual cold emanate from them. "The cambion said something cryptic about old powers stirring... but nothing actually useful." Ignoring the protest from my ribs, I straightened. The slow speed at which the injury was healing was a stark reminder that I needed to feed. I'd have to drink the rest of my meager supply of blood when I returned to the hotel.

"Priya, document everything. Kit, coordinate with Felix for cleanup. Rory—"

"Yeah?"

"Try not to touch anything."

"That was *one* time—"

"Three times," Kit corrected. "Last month alone."

I tuned out their bickering, my gaze returning to the dead teenager. The frost patterns on her chest caught the moonlight, throwing strange shadows across her pale skin.

Another body. Another failure. And somewhere in London, evil was already choosing its next prey.

2

Flynn

There was a guy eye-fucking me from across the street, and he wasn't even pretending to be subtle about it.

Lounging against the brick wall of Wilde Card's smoking garden, he was all sharp angles and dark leather, watching me like a starved wolf tracking a wounded deer. The brutal October wind whipped between the buildings, carrying the thrum of music each time the bar door swung open, but he didn't seem bothered by the cold.

Conversely, I stood shivering in my new jumper. I'd purchased it with my first paycheck—gorgeously soft, a crocheted criss-cross of tawny wool with holes in, revealing a pattern of my bare, pale skin. Extremely risqué, for me.

But tonight was about change, about transforming from someone who tiptoed around his own town, afraid to be seen, to someone who *wanted* to be seen.

I checked my phone again. 21:47. No new messages from Emma. *Perfect.* Seventeen minutes late and counting, leaving me to hover alone on this shadowy corner. The neon signs above the bar painted everything in alternating splashes of pink and blue, including the growing queue of people waiting to get inside.

My fingers hovered over the keyboard. Should I message her again? No. Three texts in fifteen minutes was already edging into desperate territory.

My phone vibrated with an incoming call. Not Emma, but Tom. My stomach twisted into familiar knots—guilt, anger, longing—all the feelings I'd been running from. I jabbed the reject button before I could change my mind, shoving the phone deep into my pocket as if I could bury the past along with it.

I glanced up. Mystery man hadn't moved, but his head was tilted now, a slight smile playing at the corners of his mouth. The pink light caught the sharp line of his jaw, the leather jacket stretched across broad shoulders. A silver chain glinted at his throat. What did he want from me?

This was exactly why I'd wanted Emma here. I didn't know what the fuck I was doing.

Earlier, we got talking at the end of our shift at the bakery, and I let slip that I'd lived in London for three weeks without a single night out. She'd flicked her dirty drying towel at my head and begged me to come to her favourite gay bar that evening. Of course, I jumped at the chance—anything was better than another night alone in my shoebox room, hiding from my weird new housemates. To have finally made a "friend," even if it was the loosest definition of one.

And the chance to potentially hook up with some random guy. Random *hot* guy. Random hot *nice* guy. Hopefully.

21:48. Still nothing. Was Emma coming? She didn't seem the type to bail without warning...

The top of my phone burst into life with an incoming message, and my heart lifted.

Tom

> **If you're not going to answer my calls, at least reply to my messages. Or your sister's. This isn't fucking funny. Everyone is so worried.**

And there went my heart, free-falling back down into oblivion, painfully squeezing itself for good measure. Katie's messages were the hardest to ignore—each one a reminder of how I'd abandoned the sister who'd helped raise me after Dad died.

I quickly swiped Tom's message away, but the damage was done. I could almost feel the rough wood of the pier beneath my hands from that night, when Tom had casually announced he was leaving for the yachting circuit.

Escaping Braymore.

Leaving me behind.

One impulsive moment on that beach had shattered a decade of friendship. I'd known Tom was straight, had spent years carefully guarding my feelings, until that final night when everything fell apart.

The kiss had been a mistake—a desperate, last-ditch attempt to make him understand what he meant to me.

Everyone is so worried.

The worst part wasn't even leaving—it was knowing I'd abandoned Katie and my mother to deal with the aftermath. They'd supported me through everything, and how had I repaid them? By disappearing in the middle of the night like a coward, leaving them to sort out the mess of Seabreeze Sailing in the wake of my grandfather's death.

I wish they could have seen that staying would have killed me slowly—crushed under the weight of family legacy, the business I never wanted, the suffocating expectations. Every morning I'd wake up to another piece of myself drowning in that endless sea.

I couldn't go back. Not yet. Not when the mere thought of those narrow streets and watchful eyes made my chest constrict, when every memory of that beach felt like another anchor trying to drag me under.

That didn't make the guilt any easier to bear. Tom almost undoubtedly thought I'd fled from Braymore that night because he'd rejected me, but that wasn't the truth. Not the whole truth, anyway.

It was what happened an hour later with Connor that was the nail in the coffin.

Before my thoughts could spiral into absolute oblivion, I looked up again. That man had shifted position. Both hands in his pockets now, but still watching. Still smiling that knowing little smile that made my stomach flip.

I couldn't help it—stealing repeated glances at the gorgeous stranger who'd apparently decided I was the most interesting thing on this entire street. Though, to be fair, my competition was a lamppost.

Several other guys had noticed him, standing there alone—not surprising, given that he was six feet worth of pure hotness. But he seemed hellbent on ignoring them to stare at me.

I checked behind my shoulder.

Nope.

Nothing.

Should I... smile? Wave? Run for the hills?

Fuck it.

Back home, I was known for my stubbornness. *Like a tide against a cliff face*, my grandfather often said, when my freezing stiff fingers fumbled with the last knot. Katie called it infuriating, my sheer bloody-minded persistence.

Besides, I most certainly didn't come out tonight wearing this cute-as-fuck jumper just to stand on a roadside.

Twenty-five years old and still a virgin—that's what happens when you spend your youth in a tiny tourist town where everyone knows your business. But London was different. Here, I could finally be myself. Tonight was about new beginnings, about finally living my life on my terms.

My feet carried me across the road before my brain could catch up. A car passed in front of me, and when I looked back into the smoking garden, the man had disappeared inside. I joined the queue, the memory of that stranger's gaze still following me, prickling across my skin like static electricity.

A hen party laughed ahead of me, while theatre performers chatted behind.

Everyone seemed to be part of a group. A team. *Something.*

And here was me all alone, Billy No Mates.

I shrank further into my jumper. What was I even doing here? Emma clearly wasn't coming. I should just go back to the flat, take a long hot shower until the water ran out, pretend tonight never happened—

The bouncer waved me forward. Though butterflies exploded in my gut, I flashed my ID, paid the charge, and stepped into another world.

Wilde Card spread before me in a sprawling maze of levels and alcoves. Rainbow strobe lights swept across a dance floor that pulsed with a sea of brightly coloured bodies surging and swelling as one, a tide of laughter and joy.

The crowd here dwarfed anything I'd seen back in Braymore, even when the tourists descended en masse to the historic seaside town, often searching for their Irish roots. But this—hundreds of strangers pressed together, each caught in their own private moment—made me feel more alone than any empty street back home ever had.

Circular booths lined the walls, upholstered in deep-purple velvet. To my left, the bar stretched the entire length of the wall. Three bartenders danced between stations. One of them—tall, with close-cropped, dyed silver hair—caught my eye and winked.

Suddenly the air tasted of sweat, artificial fog, and... *possibility*.

I wasn't sure what I'd imagined a gay bar would be like inside, but watching everyone move so freely, so *goddamn* comfortably in their own skin...

It made my chest ache with something between envy and hope.

The back of my neck prickled, and I knew—I just *knew*—it was the staring, smoking-hot dude before I even turned around.

I spun, and there he was. Close. Way, *way* too close.

I stumbled backwards, catching my foot on absolutely nothing. His hand shot out, steadying my arm, and every nerve ending in my body decided to focus on that single point of contact. Long fingers wrapped around me, warm through the gaps in my jumper.

Up close, he was *beyond* ridiculously attractive. I almost wanted to snap a picture for evidence. Thick dark hair fell across one eye in an artful sweep. A thin scar curved up from the corner of his mouth, somehow making him even more attractive, the bastard. And his eyes... In this light, they weren't just dark; they were *black*. No distinction between iris and pupil.

Those dark eyes reminded me of the deep, unfathomable ocean—pulling at me like the tides ever seeking to claim what lay upon the shore.

"I've been waiting for you."

"Uhh..." What the fuck did anyone say to that? "Thanks?"

He stepped closer, and I caught a whiff of something earthy. "What are you drinking?"

An alarm bell went off at the back of my head—what if this guy spiked my drink?

Stop that.

Here was an incredibly attractive guy who had chosen *me*, out of everyone in this bar, to flirt with—and I was going to ruin it with para-noia.

Heart hammering, I batted my eyelashes at him. "Whatever you want to buy me," I purred, aiming for a semi-seductive voice but achieving something closer to a seagull with laryngitis.

Yet my boldness earned me a raised eyebrow and a slight widening of that crooked smile. He looked me up and down, gaze lingering on the patches of exposed skin. "You look like a whiskey sour sort of guy."

"Uhh... why not?" I said, too brightly, digging my nails into my palms.

"What's your name, handsome?"

"Flynn."

"Flynn," he echoed, licking his lips as if savouring the taste of it. "Where are you from, Flynn?"

Resisting a sigh, I said, "I was born in England, but I've lived in Ireland for the last ten years."

I'd found myself repeating that same sentence again and again since I'd moved to London. It was usually followed by some comment about how pale I was, or my subtle accent.

"That explains your unique accent," he said with a smile.

Called it.

"What's your name?" My voice was already strained from shouting over the pounding music.

He smiled at me, pausing before finally saying, "Damien." He leaned in, boldly tucking a lock of my dirty-blond hair behind my ear. His face came closer and closer, his hot breath tickling my skin. "And I look forward to hearing you screaming that name many, *many* times later."

Holy shit.

If I had any lingering doubts about this guy's intentions, they catapulted straight out of my mind. My skin buzzed with anticipation, and though part of me wanted to bolt for the door, a far larger part wanted to follow that dangerous smile wherever it led.

As Damien weaved through the crowd toward the bar, the shadows near the pillar shifted, resolving into a man I hadn't noticed before.

His formal attire made him stick out from the crowd—precise angles and sharp tailoring, from his waistcoat to his sleek skinny tie—certainly a bizarre choice for this bar. One arm held a bulky black coat. His dark eyes followed Damien's every move, burning into him with an intensity that made my breath catch.

My stomach clenched. Of course someone else would want him. Everyone probably wanted him. But *I* saw him first. Sort of.

The overdressed guy locked eyes with me, spearing me with a glare that could have frozen Hell itself—deep frown lines etched themselves across his forehead. He folded his arms as if I had annoyed him somehow.

I pointedly looked away from him, and Damien returned, pressing a cold glass into my hand—amber coloured, smelling strong enough to strip paint.

"Cheers." I clinked my glass against his and knocked back half the sour contents in one go. It burned my throat, but the warmth spread through my chest, settling my nerves. When I lowered the glass, pillar guy was *still* staring over—his entire body radiating a possessive tension that screamed "back off."

Tough luck, mate, I thought, even as doubt niggled at me. Did they have history? That would make sense. But did he really have to go out of his way to make me so uncomfortable?

Screw this.

Let the angry bloke at the pillar stare all he wanted. I hadn't escaped one suffocating town just to let another stranger's disapproval cage me in. Maybe it was the alcohol, or maybe just three weeks of crushing loneliness in a city of millions, but Damien's attention felt like a lifeline. Something real and tangible in this sea of strangers. And if his interest came with an edge of danger? Well, anything was better than another night alone with my thoughts, drowning in memories of home.

I drained the rest of my drink, grabbed Damien's hand, and tugged. "Let's dance."

His eyebrows shot up, but he followed me willingly enough onto the crowded dance floor. Sweat-slicked shoulders and swaying hips enclosed us, a sea of bodies and sound and movement that made the rest of the world feel distant and unreal.

But the gorgeous man I turned to face was very, *very* real.

He smiled at me, and his attention felt like drowning in the sweetest way—the kind of surrender I'd imagined on nights when the Irish Sea had whispered promises of peace beneath my boat. But unlike those gentle waters back home, there was something sharp and hungry in the depths of Damien's smile, like jagged rocks waiting beneath a calm surface.

The bass thrummed through my veins like liquid courage. I let my body move with it, years of private bedroom dancing finally paying off. In a strange moment of disconnect, I became both dancer and audience, watching myself dance circles around Damien. Watching the confident way I commanded attention, half wondering who this fearless stranger was and half thrilled to discover it was me. Watching how I teased him with almost-touches until I finally caught his hands, guiding them to where I wanted them—one on my hip, one splayed across my lower back. I pressed myself against him, grinding as hard as I dared.

"Someone's eager," he murmured against my ear.

Over Damien's shoulder, a flash of movement caught my eye. That fucking guy from the pillar, now storming through the crowd like an angry thundercloud, shouldering people aside. His face was a mask of fury, gaze locked onto us.

Shit. I didn't know why this guy thought he had a claim over Damien, but I wasn't going to hang around to find out.

"Why don't we get out of here?" I blurted, tugging at Damien's sleeve.

Damien's laugh rumbled against my chest. "You read my mind." His fingers threaded through mine, and he pulled me toward the exit.

As we weaved through the crowd, I risked a glance back. The man had reached where we'd been dancing, his jaw clenched so tight he could shatter his teeth.

Damien yanked on my hand, leading me in a winding path through the club, past the main bar, then ducking into a service area. We left through a fire exit, into a narrow alley behind the building. The music became muffled, replaced by the distant sounds of traffic. A single security light cast everything in harsh shadows.

My breath left my lungs as Damien backed me against the rough brick wall. My fingers curled into his shirt as he pressed closer. Our bodies aligned nearly perfectly, the slight difference in our heights creating just enough space for him to look down at me with those dark eyes.

His fingers tangled in my hair, tugging my head back to expose my throat. Soft lips traced a burning path up my neck, each kiss sending sparks through my body.

"God, you're gorgeous," he murmured against my skin, his breath warm. "I wish I had more time with you."

What?

My hands roamed across his broad shoulders, feeling the solid muscle beneath his leather jacket. The spicy scent of him filled my senses, making my head spin. Or maybe that was the whiskey. Either way, I didn't care.

His mouth moved higher, closer to mine, and my breath caught. I wanted—no, *needed* him to kiss me. To replace that last devastating kiss, to overwrite the memory that had destroyed me. To make me forget, even for just a moment.

But his lips stopped at my jawline, his hands sliding down my sides, fingers catching in the holes of my jumper, brushing against bare skin. I arched into his touch.

"Your place?" I gasped between ragged breaths. No way in hell did I want him in my dingy flat, with its paper-thin walls and nosy housemates.

He sighed as if something deeply pained him. "No need. This won't take long at all."

My hands froze against his shoulders. The bar for my first time wasn't particularly high, but getting fucked in this dirty alley was possibly a step too far.

Before I could respond, Damien's fingers curled into the front of my jumper. With one sharp movement, he ripped it straight down the middle. The wool tore with a sickening sound, exposing my bare chest to the cold night air.

"What the fuck?" I shoved against his chest, rage flooding through me. "Dude, that was expensive!"

He didn't budge an inch. His smile had transformed into something predatory—sharp edges and dark promise. The security light above us flickered, casting strange shadows across his face. And *fuck*, his eyes! The black of his irises bled outward, swallowing the whites whole.

My pulse skyrocketed. Every instinct screamed that something was deeply, terribly wrong. The brick wall scraped against my back as I tried to push him away, but his grip was like iron.

Damien's palm pressed flat against my chest, right over my thundering heart. The touch burned ice-cold through my skin, and I gasped. It felt like he was stabbing me with an icicle.

"Hold still, sweet thing," he murmured, almost soothingly. "This will only hurt for a moment."

All those nights I'd lain awake back home, dreaming of escape—and now here I was, about to become another statistic, another cautionary tale. Katie would never forgive me. Mum would blame herself somehow.

Dread constricted my throat, and a horrible whimper escaped me before I could swallow it back. That burning cold spread through my chest like frost across a window, almost like something inside me was beginning to crack.

"Stop!"

The shout echoed off the brick walls. My head snapped towards the sound—it was that guy again. The man from the pillar. He stood at the entrance to the alley, holding something that glinted in the security light.

My brain struggled to process what I was seeing. Was that... a *gun?!* I'd never seen one in real life before.

"Get away from him. *Now.*" The man's voice carried deadly intent, his aim unwavering.

Damien's hand remained pressed against my chest, that bone-deep cold spreading further across my skin. He turned his head towards the newcomer, that horrible smile still fixed in place.

"Ah. Right on schedule." Damien's voice dripped with amusement. "No matter. I'm finished here anyway."

Damien pushed away from me, sending the back of my head cracking against the brick. One moment he was in front of me, the next he was halfway up the wall, climbing it like some sort of demented spider creature.

With a gurgled yelp of shock, I scrambled away from the wall just as a soft *pfft* sound cut through the air—the muffled cough of a gun. Brick dust exploded beside Damien's shoulder. The man cursed and re-aimed, but Damien had already reached the roof, disappearing over the edge with a mocking salute.

I am going mad.

I am going certifiably insane.

Wait. The drink. The whiskey sour. Damien must have done something to it—spiked it—and now I was experiencing a very real-seeming hallucination.

Hysterical giggles erupted out of me, and my knees nearly gave out. I slumped against the wall, clutching the ruins of my jumper.

The stranger in his skinny tie and brass-buttoned long coat strode towards me, weapon lowered. I stared at him. He looked like he'd stepped straight out of a vintage magazine from the mod era—all smart, sharp lines and careful precision.

Time suspended as we locked gazes, my breath hitching in my throat. His eyes were incredibly dark brown, a swirl of burnt caramel, deep enough to drown in.

Shadows played across his warm golden-olive skin as his eyebrows knitted together, his face hardening into a harsh frown. "Let me see your chest," he practically barked at me.

"Stay back!" I scrambled sideways, holding my hands up, my eyes unable to leave his gun. "Don't come any closer."

I'd already been violated once in this hallucination. I didn't need a repeat.

He stopped, those dark eyes fixed on me with an intensity that made my skin prickle. "I need to see your chest. Show it to me."

"*Why?*" My voice cracked, and I threw my arms around myself protectively. "What the hell are you talking about? Just leave me alone."

He took another step forward. I pressed myself flat against the wall, heart hammering so hard it could burst. The security light caught the man's face properly for the first time—tight dark curls framed devastating cheekbones and full lips that might have been beautiful if they weren't twisted into a glower. His long coat hugged broad shoulders that spoke of contained power, and even through my panic, I caught myself wondering what he looked like underneath all those fancy clothes.

But criminally attractive or not, I didn't want him anywhere near me. I wasn't about to make the same mistake twice.

His lips parted as he drew closer, and I caught a glimpse of white teeth that seemed a touch too sharp.

"I said stay back!" My voice came out as an embarrassing croak.

"Listen, y—"

"Get away from him!"

Emma's voice rang out from the entrance of the alley. My tiny colleague stood there like an angry sparrow, her cropped dark hair spiked with sweat, brandishing her phone like a weapon. The screen's glow illuminated her face as she shouted, "I'm calling the police right now, you freak!"

He clicked his tongue, eyes darting between Emma and me. His jaw clenched, and something dangerous flickered across his face, like he might just call her bluff. But he tucked whatever weapon he'd been holding into his long coat and backed away, maintaining that intense eye contact with me until he disappeared around the corner.

Emma sprinted towards me, her trainers pounding on the concrete. On her phone, I caught a glimpse of the tracking app she'd added me to earlier that day. She threw her arms around my waist, nearly knocking me over with the force.

"Oh my god, Flynn! Are you okay? I'm so sorry I was late. The Tube was delayed and I had no signal—" She pulled back, holding me at arm's length. "What happened to your jumper?"

I glanced down at the torn wool hanging off my shoulders. "I... There was this other guy. Before that guy, I mean. He—" The words stuck in my throat. How could I possibly explain what had just happened? I wasn't even sure myself.

"Let me see." Emma's hands hovered over my chest. "Did he hurt you?"

"I don't know. It feels like... like ice. Right here." I pointed to the spot where Damien had pressed his hand, which still felt wrong somehow, like someone had replaced that patch of skin with frozen metal. "Can you see anything?"

Emma squinted, phone torch aimed at my skin. "No marks or anything. Maybe you're just cold?" She shrugged off her denim jacket and draped it over my shoulders. "Here."

The jacket was far too small, and did nothing to combat the chill, which seemed to come from inside my chest rather than the night air.

"Can you help me find the nearest hospital?" My voice came out small and pathetic, and I cringed at myself. This was surely not the way to make friends. "Please?"

"Of course." Emma wrapped an arm around my waist, steadying me.

She guided me towards the street, away from the pulsing music of Wilde Card and the shadows that seemed to writhe at the edges of my vision. I took one last look back at the wall that Damien had scaled with impossible ease. Though I felt stone-cold sober, that tosser *must* have spiked my drink—it was the only explanation.

Well, it was safe to say my first night out in London was an epic fail.

I was supposed to solidify my friendship with the only person who'd shown the slightest interest in getting to know me, and distract myself from constant thoughts of home and Tom and Connor by hooking up with a cute stranger.

Instead, my jumper looked like it had been mauled by a bear, and I'd almost been shot at by some deranged psycho who made murder look unreasonably attractive.

At least the night couldn't get any worse.

Though judging by the strange burning chill still spreading through my chest, I had a horrible feeling I could be wrong about that.

3

Flynn

"**W**hat do you mean, there's absolutely nothing wrong with me? I'm telling you, it feels like there's a shard of ice stuck inside me!"

The doctor peered at me over her wire-rimmed glasses, tapping her pen against the clipboard. Four hours, two blood tests, a chest x-ray, and an ECG later, and this was what I got? A pat on the head and directions to the nearest psych ward?

"Mr Carter, we've run every test we can think of. Your vitals are normal, there's no sign of any foreign substances in your system, and nothing is visible on your chest under any of our equipment."

I pulled my torn jumper aside, jabbing at the spot where Damien had touched me. "Look, I know how this sounds, but—"

"Have you considered that this might be anxiety related?" The doctor didn't hide her patronising tone. "You mentioned you've recently moved to London. Big changes can trigger physical manifestations of stress."

Right. Because anxiety explained how that bastard had climbed a vertical wall like Spider-Man.

"Fine." I stood up, gathering what remained of my dignity. "Thanks for your help."

The doctor held something out. "Here's a leaflet on counselling if you'd—"

I snatched the paper and stuffed it in my pocket, already heading for the door. The fluorescent lights of A&E made my head throb, then outside, the pre-dawn air was a slap in the face. I checked my phone: 03:47. Public transport wasn't running, and a taxi was way over budget.

Fucking brilliant.

I pulled up maps and started the long walk home, hugging Emma's tiny jacket to my chest in a futile attempt to combat the chill. Thank god she'd finally agreed to leave—at least she hadn't been there to see the doctor laugh at me.

Each step brought fresh waves of mortification.

I'd brought this all upon myself by foolishly believing that Damien was interested in sleeping with me.

You fucking idiot. Your first night out in London and you broke every single basic safety rule. Don't accept drinks within five minutes of meeting someone. Don't follow them down dark alleys.

Don't let yourself become a human ice lolly was a new one, but apparently it needed adding to the list.

I'd wondered earlier why Damien had selected *me* out of everyone in that crowded bar.

The answer was now glaringly obvious—easy fucking prey.

Not for the first time, homesickness washed over me. If I'd stayed in Ireland, I'd be safely tucked away in my cosy little room at Barbara's house right now—my dear, sweet old landlady.

The empty streets echoed with my footsteps. Each shadow stretched longer, darker, more menacing than the last. The ice in my chest pulsed with renewed vigour.

Time stretched like treacle as I walked, my thoughts cycling between self-recrimination and panic. Three miles had never felt so far. The occasional rumble of a night bus or distant siren only emphasised how alone I was.

My pace quickened. The familiar outline of my tower block loomed ahead, its brutalist concrete edges stark against the sky.

Nearly home. Nearly safe.

Something scraped against the pavement behind me.

Don't look back. Don't run. Act normal.

The hair on my neck prickled. Footsteps suddenly perfectly matched my rhythm.

I sped up. They sped up.

Shit shit shit. My throat tightened at the thought of Damien's cold hands on me again.

My mother's voice rang in my head... *Keys between your fingers, love. Like brass knuckles.* She'd taught us both that trick years ago in our kitchen, Katie and I laughing until Mum made us practise properly. Katie's face had turned deadly serious as she punched the air, and I'd never forgotten the look in her eyes—the same protective glare she'd given any boy who'd ever bothered me at school.

I fumbled in my pocket, wrapping my fingers around the cold metal. The weight felt reassuring, familiar.

Twenty metres to the door. Fifteen. Ten.

The footsteps grew closer.

My hand shook as I reached for the security panel. Just one more step into the fluorescent light of the entrance—

A vice-like grip clamped around my arm, yanking me backwards. I spun, keys raised, ready to slash—

Another hand seized my wrist, stopping my attack mid-swing. The grip was iron, immovable.

A gasp of surprise left my lips as I found myself staring into dark eyes framed by tight chestnut curls.

The guy with the gun.

The guy with the gun had *followed me home.*

"Don't panic," he said, voice low and controlled. "Listen, I just need—"

I *screamed*, the sound echoing off the concrete walls.

His hand clamped over my mouth, muffling my cries, the touch of his skin ice-cold against my lips.

No! I'd already been easy prey once this evening. I refused to go down a second time without a fight.

Pure instinct took over. I bit down hard, my teeth meeting resistance like I was trying to bite through marble instead of flesh. His grip loosened for a split second—just enough time. I drove my knee upward, connecting with his groin with every ounce of strength I had.

"*¡Joder!*" He stumbled back, doubling over. "*Hijo de—*"

I didn't wait to hear the rest of whatever curse he was spitting. My fingers flew across the keypad, punching in the code. The lock clicked. I yanked the door open and bolted down the corridor.

My heart hammered against my ribs as I rounded the corner, nearly slipping on the polished floor. The lift was too risky—he could catch up while I waited. Instead, I crashed through the fire escape door and took the stairs two at a time.

The ice in my chest burned colder with each step.

Should I call the police? But what would I say? Some bloke—"*who shot at another man spider-monkeying up a wall, officer*"—followed me home and grabbed me? After the doctor's dismissal, the last thing I needed was another authority figure treating me like I belonged in a padded room.

No. Better to get inside, lock the door, and pretend none of this had happened.

You're getting rather good at that, aren't you?

The thought hit like a punch to the gut. I pushed it away, focusing on the four flights of stairs. My fingers trembled as I fumbled with my keys, dropping them twice before managing to get the right one into the lock.

Inside, I slammed the door shut. The chain slid into place with a satisfying click. My legs gave out. I slumped against the door, sliding down until I hit the floor with a thud.

I held my breath, straining my ears.

Nothing.

I should have felt safer once I was home, but this cramped flat still didn't feel like *home* after three weeks.

I forced myself to stand up on my jelly legs, then fled to my bedroom. I jumped into my waiting bed, curling into a ball. My breath came in waves, each one pulling me further from shore. I pressed my back against the wall, trying to find an anchor point as memories of Damien's smile and then my assailant's grip threatened to drag me under.

You're okay. You're inside. He can't get in.

But then the memory of Damien scaling that wall flashed through my mind, and I jerked my head up to stare at my bedroom window.

Fourth floor. No fire escape. No ledges. Just smooth concrete and glass.

Even Spider-Man would struggle with that.

A hysterical laugh bubbled up in my throat. I choked it back down.

My fingers traced the spot where the chill radiated, like my blood had been replaced with liquid nitrogen.

I pressed my palm flat against my chest, willing the sensation to fade.

Please, just let me wake up and let this nightmare be over.

4

Sebastián

8th October 2025 - Daily Report

Terrier - Followed up on the Finchley Road case. Three victims found drained. Confirmed rogue vampire. Forensics matched dental records to previous attacks in Manchester. Suspected new recruit of Marcus Vale's expanding clan.

Poodle - Infiltrated meeting between West and South London wolf packs in Greenwich. Growing unrest about territory boundaries.

Noctule - Intercepted attack at Wilde Card. Target: human male, mid-twenties. Target suspected to have been—

The scratch of my fountain pen halted at footsteps down the corridor. I sighed and set it down on my mahogany desk. It had travelled with me through five countries before finding its home at Killigrew Street Hotel. One of life's few constants.

A loud series of sharp knocks—Kit's, for certain—dragged me to my feet.

"Seb." Kit's broad frame filled the doorway, his expression as rigid as his posture. Even after all these years, his military bearing hadn't left him. Sometimes that stance of his triggered hazy impressions of other soldiers in other lives. "We've located the target."

I gestured for him to enter, closing the door behind him.

"He left his building?"

"Affirmative. At seven this morning. Travelled half an hour north to some bakery. Surveillance confirmed he entered through the back entrance. Staff access." Kit pulled a crisp printout from a manila folder.

Flynn Carter, twenty-five years old, a list of addresses spanning his life: born in England, moved to Braymore Bay, Ireland at fifteen, registered as a resident of London just a few weeks ago.

"This is him," I murmured, touching the ID image. He was younger in the photo, and though his dark blond hair was similarly dishevelled, this Flynn had no dark smudges under his eyes. He gazed fiercely into the camera, a slight tilt of his lips indicating he was trying not to smile. I'd seen that smile last night—not aimed at me, of course, but at that foul demon, minutes before the attack. Flynn had smiled at the monster with such warmth and trust, without any inkling he was dancing with death.

It had infuriated me, his lack of basic self-preservation.

"Seb?"

My head shot up. "What?"

"You were staring at the picture funny."

"I certainly wasn't," I snapped back. "Do we still have eyes on his apartment?"

"Priya's still watching." Kit shifted, his wolf's restlessness showing through as he paced. "Permission to speak freely?"

"When have you ever needed permission, Kit?" The man had a habit of speaking his mind with or without my consent, just like his brother, Rory.

"He's spooked. After what you said happened last night..." Kit's jaw tightened. "The lad's barely holding it together. Jumped at his own shadow the whole way to work."

I studied the picture again, the weight in my chest growing heavier. "Time to go spook him some more."

"We could send Felix. He's far less intimidating than you or me."

I barked a laugh. "Felix would probably just stare at Flynn for several hours until he filed a restraining order."

When Kit clicked his tongue instead of laughing, guilt pricked at my conscience. Though he treated Felix like the rest of the team, his protective edge towards the shy tech expert—our newest recruit—betrayed his soft spot for the boy. He always did have a habit of picking up strays.

"No. I'll go," I said, throwing on my coat. "He can't run away from me in broad daylight."

"Though perhaps you should send someone else," Kit mused, a smirk playing at the corners of his mouth. "Given how your last encounter went." He eyed my sorry genitals, still sore from Flynn's assault.

Groaning, I straightened my coat lapels, and tried to maintain what dignity I had left. "The boy was frightened. It was a natural reaction."

"Natural reaction?" Kit's eyebrows shot up. "Well, you did grab him from behind on a dark street. What did you expect? A friendly handshake?"

"I expected him to listen when I told him to."

"Ah yes, because that always goes down well with terrified civilians." Kit's Scottish accent grew thicker with his amusement. "Face it, boss. You deserved that knee to the balls."

I pinched the bridge of my nose. "Are you quite finished?"

"Not even close." Kit grinned, all teeth. "Should I assign you a protective cup for this mission? We've got spare gear in the weapons room."

"I'm leaving now."

I shut the door hard, yet Kit's muffled chuckle still carried through.

Five centuries of existence, and this was what my dignity had come to. Being mocked by a wolf over getting kneed in the groin by some human who didn't even seem to possess the most basic of common sense in his pretty head.

By the time I'd reached Rising Dough, the weather had taken a turn for the worse—the sun had decided to make an appearance, and I hadn't bothered to bring my umbrella. As luck would have it, there was a large tree on the pavement outside the bakery, offering some protection from the blasted rays.

Through the window, I watched Flynn Carter work the till. It was remarkable how different he looked in the daylight. Gone was the cornered animal from the alley, replaced by someone who moved with easy grace, who smiled freely at customers. Only the bruised shadows under his eyes hinted at last night's events. His fingers danced across the register as sunlight caught his hair, spinning it into glittering gold.

The same woman who'd interrupted us yesterday—Emma, her name tag informed me—stood beside him, both of them sharing quiet laughs between customers. When Emma hung up her apron and headed out back, the queue quickly spilled out onto the pavement. *Fascinating.* What made this particular establishment's bread so compelling? The scent wafting through the door was pleasant enough, but hardly extraordinary.

As I inched closer to the counter, I instinctively tracked Flynn's heartbeat—a pleasant, gentle rhythm. Then his gaze finally landed on me. The steady thrum exploded into a frantic percussion, blood rushing through his veins hummingbird fast. Colour drained from his face, leaving him ghost-pale. His eyes darted to the back door. I had a mere moment before he bolted.

"One bread, please." The words tumbled out before I could stop them.

Flynn's eyebrows shot up. "One... bread?"

"Yes. I mean, one *loaf*." I scanned the displays, filled with various loaves that surely would taste identical. "Whatever you'd recommend."

"Right." He cleared his throat, his fingers tapping against the counter. "The sourdough's our best seller."

"Perfect."

Flynn offered me the card machine, blinking when I placed the exact change on the counter instead.

"And might I trouble you for five minutes of your time?"

Flynn's shoulders tensed as he glanced at the clock. The tiniest bead of sweat formed on his brow. "What do you want?"

"To talk," I said, subtly opening my coat to prove I was unarmed.

"Well, I don't really want to talk to you."

"It's important. It's about last night. I want to help you."

He looked at me for a very long time. His teeth sank into his bottom lip, worrying it. "When Emma returns from her break, I can take mine," he said slowly.

I claimed a table by the window, setting down the paper bag. I'd take the bread back to Killigrew Street, and Kit and Rory could fight over it. My gaze soon returned to Flynn Carter, unable to stop tracking him as he moved behind the counter. He had this curious habit of tucking a rogue strand of hair behind his ear, only for it to spring loose again seconds later.

Flynn seemed hellbent on not looking my way, until he turned to glare at me, red-faced, to mouth, "stop staring at me" rather aggressively.

Blinking rapidly to show my surprise, I then pretended to try the sourdough he'd sold me, ripping a tiny chunk off and placing it on my tongue. I let it dissolve, experiencing a muted sensation of texture without flavour. My curse had dulled my ability to taste to a mere *suggestion* of what it once was. It hardly mattered. While I swallowed food to keep up appearances, my sustenance flowed from a rather different vein entirely. Still, I found myself missing the taste of fresh bread, a memory so old it felt more like a story I'd once been told.

The bell above the door chimed. Emma breezed back in, unwinding a scarf from her neck. Flynn's hand shot up, beckoning her over with sharp, urgent movements. I tensed—this plan could quickly unravel, should the small woman decide she didn't trust me after what she saw last night.

After a quiet, hurried exchange, Emma's eyes darted to me, then back to Flynn. She gripped his forearm, but Flynn shook his head, already untying his apron.

When he slid into the seat opposite me, his lips were pressed in a grim line, and his hands disappeared beneath the table. The chair scraped against the floor as he positioned himself as far from me as the small table allowed.

"Right." Flynn's voice cracked. "What do you want?"

I leaned casually back in the seat, trying my best to appear non-threatening. A pulse fluttered visibly at Flynn's throat, panic-rapid, yet he held my gaze with stubborn determination, chin raised in defiance.

"You're very brave." The words slipped out unbidden, and I stiffened, my fingers curling against the leather armrest.

My companion's mouth fell open, his eyes widening, and for a moment the carefully maintained rhythm of my false breathing faltered. Because Flynn's eyes were the kind of blue that belonged in cathedral windows, sanctified and untouchable. As blue as the spring sky over Toledo had been, all those centuries ago.

"Are you going to hurt me?" Flynn said, so quietly I almost didn't catch it.

The accusation struck me like a physical blow. "What makes you say that?"

"You stalked me to my flat, then attacked me!" His fingers grabbed the edge of the table, knuckles white. "I thought—" He swallowed hard. "I thought you were going to kill me."

Kill me. The words ricocheted around my mind, stirring memories from the shadows. Some were screams I couldn't quite place, faces I couldn't fully remember, the weight of deaths I knew were by my hand even if the details remained mercifully blurred.

Flynn was right to fear me—I was a killer. Yet for some reason, the thought of this bright young man seeing only the darkness in me twisted like a knife between my ribs.

"You're very quick to assume my malicious intent, yet you happily followed a strange man into a dark alley after knowing him for all of five seconds." I couldn't stop the sharpness of my tone, but in all honesty, he needed to hear it. "Is your sense of self-preservation usually so compromised?" *What was it about that cambion that made all common sense fly out the window?*

A blush bled across his pale cheeks. "Look, I'm not usually that much of an idiot. I... haven't been thinking straight recently."

"Clearly." I should have stopped, but I could not resist the urge to press the matter. "What was it about him that entranced you so?" The question wasn't entirely fair—the demon may well have used some level of compulsion.

"I don't know..."

"He must have done *something* to get you to follow him so easily." *Surely.*

Flynn sighed. "I guess he made me feel... wanted. 'Special,' or whatever. God, did you really have to make me say that out loud?" He twisted his hands together, staring down at the table. Regret flooded through me—I didn't want to wound him further. "I guess sometimes when you're running from everything else, any direction looks like the right one."

He lifted his head to hold my gaze, and I caught a glimpse of something raw beneath his carefully constructed smile. The kind of pain that made people reckless. Made them run. Made them end up in places they shouldn't be. Made them do stupid things like follow strangers into dark alleys. Not that any of this was my business.

"Though to be fair, I did eventually realise something was off with him. If you hadn't arrived with your *gun*..." He hissed the word. "I would have removed myself from the situation."

I stared at him, my eyes falling to where his lips pressed into an angry, determined line.

"*Removed* yourself? And how would you have done that?"

"Well, a knee to the balls certainly did the trick with you, didn't it?"

Touché.

I held up my palms. "Fair point. And I apologise for scaring you. I... certainly learned my lesson." My raised eyebrow hopefully communicated the degree of the damage he'd done. "But I only wished to talk with you."

Flynn barked out a laugh, harsh and brittle. "Well, talk now then!" He dropped to a fierce whisper to say, "What's so bloody important?"

I leaned forward, keeping my movements slow and deliberate. "That man. Before I got there, did he touch you?"

Flynn's face flushed an even darker scarlet. His mouth opened and closed several times before he found his voice. "I— What? I'm not sure how that's any of your business, pal." His volume rose to a worrying level. "It's hardly your concern! If anything like that happened, obviously I'd go to the police, not you! Who the fuck are you, anyway?"

What in all hells...?

I studied his flustered face until the penny finally dropped. "*What?* I didn't mean—" I pinched the bridge of my nose. "Not in that way. *Jesus!* Your chest! Did he touch your chest?"

Flynn stared at me as if I'd grown a second head. "Oh." He sank lower in his chair, clearly mortified. "Right. Yes. Yes, he did."

Something in the way Flynn held my gaze as he placed his hand on his black shirt over his heart told me everything I needed to know.

"Can you tell me what it felt like?"

Flynn bit his lip again, then shuffled his chair as close to the table as he could. The movement stirred the air between us, and his scent hit me like a physical force—an intoxicating mix of sea salt and cinnamon sugar. It was the same combination that had clouded my mind for a moment last night, when I'd had him pressed against me, his pulse thundering beneath my hands.

"I went to the hospital," he said, as if confessing. "They told me I was mad."

Something compelled me to reach across the table. My fingers wrapped around Flynn's bare forearm, and to my surprise, he didn't pull away. His skin blazed beneath my touch, a furnace compared to my chill. The blood beneath his skin sang to me, a siren's song that made my gums itch. That ancient, feral part of me stretched and purred, drawn to his vitality like a moth to flame.

I snatched my hand back, disgusted with myself. *Get it together, Sebastián.* Twenty straight years of immaculate control meant nothing if I couldn't keep myself in check around one random human.

But there was something about this Flynn Carter...

"You're not mad, Flynn. But you are in danger."

Flynn leaned closer. "What sort of danger?"

His proximity hit me like a slap. That scent—salt and sugar and *life*—wrapped around me, drawing me in. My throat burned with sudden, vicious thirst. *You fool.* I should have drunk before leaving Killigrew Street. How long had it been? Twenty-four hours? More? The hunger clawed at my insides, sharp and insistent.

"Are... are you alright?" Flynn's face swam into focus. He'd moved even closer, close enough that I could count each individual eyelash, see the subtle variations of blue in his irises. His features held such open concern, such sweet innocence, that my dead heart clenched.

"I am fine."

"Am I going to die?" The question fell from his lips, soft and frightened.

My fingers twitched with the bizarre urge to cup his face, to promise him everything would be fine. His question—those exact words—echoed through the centuries, spoken by countless voices I could no longer put faces to. I gripped the edge of the table, anchoring myself against the wave of protective fury that swept through me.

I couldn't lie to him. Not when the demon, its master, and god knows how many more monsters were still out there, waiting. "You need to come with me."

Fear flashed across his face, and I ground my teeth together. Maybe I *should* have sent someone else to do this job after all. Social graces were not my forte, as Rory was so keen on reminding me.

"Please," I tried, making my voice feather soft. "The doctors didn't believe you, but you're not going mad. There *is* something inside your chest. They can't help you, but I can. Let me help you, Flynn."

He continued to study me, clearly weighing up my words and his remaining choices. I recognised the irony in the situation—I'd lectured him on running off alone with strangers, and now I was demanding he do just that.

But there was little other choice.

"After last night, you might find this hard to believe, but I promise you that you're completely safe with me. But if you don't let me help you, Flynn, that feeling in your chest..." I trailed off. The implication was clear.

Our gazes continued to bore into each other.

Then, to my immense relief, he nodded.

I offered him my hand to shake, and if I was being honest, it was mainly so I could feel the warmth of his skin once more.

"Sebastián Salazar," I said, allowing the Spanish accent I'd lost a hundred years ago to resurface. "Go get your things."

5

Flynn

What kind of idiot follows their armed stalker to an unknown location? Oh, right—me.

Clearly, last night had taught me nothing.

Sebastián Salazar either enjoyed walking in silence, or had nothing to say to me. Given that he'd basically demanded I walk out of my shift to go to some undisclosed place with him, his lack of communication soon grated on me as we navigated street after street. He kept wanting to cross the road and then back again, seemingly in a bizarre, random pattern, until I finally realised he was favouring the shadier sides. He must have been hot in his stupidly thick coat.

Here I was, trailing after this strange, oddly dressed bloke like a lost puppy. He was wearing another skinny tie today—this one a dark grey—though it hung slightly looser than last night. I suppose I had to admit his outfit *did* sort of suit him—the navy-blue tailored trousers hugged his legs in a way that did not escape my notice. I forced my gaze elsewhere. Getting distracted by a potentially dangerous stranger's ass wasn't going to help my situation. I'd experienced that first-hand yesterday.

"Can you please just tell me where we're actually going?" I eventually blurted, and he turned to me with obvious surprise, freezing in his tracks.

I peered up at him, though he wasn't much taller than me. I couldn't decide how old I thought he was—late twenties? Thirties? Last night he'd appeared terrifying, but now his face displayed only confusion as he lifted his hand to run it through those tight curls of his. They bounced right back into perfect ringlets, shiny and soft-looking.

"Killigrew Street," he said, like this was a perfectly acceptable answer, then proceeded to keep walking.

"Right. And what's on Killigrew Street?"

No response. Just the click of his fancy boots against concrete as he strode ahead, still clutching that paper bag with his bread in.

Great. Perfect. Following a complete stranger to a street I'd never heard of. Got it.

Killigrew Street was a slice of nineteenth century London that time had forgotten. The cobblestones inclined gently, past terraced houses in faded pastels and old-fashioned street lamps that hadn't changed in a century. A quaint florist's shop caught the late afternoon sun, its windows a jungle of greenery and colour.

But it was what waited at the top that made me stop dead in my tracks.

The street opened into a circular courtyard, dominated by a behemoth of Victorian architecture. Four storeys of weathered stone and elaborate cornices stretched skyward, its countless windows staring down at us like hollow eyes.

"Here we are," said Sebastián. "Welcome to Killigrew Street Hotel."

My mouth fell open as I stared at the building, our apparent destination.

The place was a wreck.

Even worse than the old lighthouse on the edge of Braymore, where we all snuck in with bottles of cheap cider as teenagers—until Tom nearly went through the rotting floorboards one night.

Thick tangles of ivy crept up the once cream walls like grasping fingers. Many of the tall windows were either boarded up or smashed, leaving jagged teeth of glass in their frames. What remained of the original paintwork had chipped and peeled away in great flakes.

A rusted wrought-iron gate blocked our path, secured with a chunky padlock that looked far newer than its surroundings. Behind it, more weeds had claimed the small front garden, creating a jungle of brambles and nettles. The front steps leading to massive double doors were crumbling. Above the entrance, elegant lettering spelled out "KILLIGREW STREET HOTEL" in faded gold paint.

A massive "FOR SALE" sign hung crooked on the gate, its red letters sun-bleached to a dull pink.

"This is where you wanted to bring me?" It came out as a choked whisper, and my stomach clenched as my mind calculated every horrible thing Sebastián might do to me once he'd locked me in his dungeon.

The man chuckled, a hint of a smile threatening one corner of his mouth. "It's nicer on the inside."

I'd rather not find out, thank you very much.

I opened my mouth to tell him exactly where he could stick his "nicer inside," when that now familiar icy sensation gripped my heart. The cold spread through my chest, tendrils of frost creeping outward until my whole body seized.

My legs wobbled. The horrible memory of Damien pressing his palm against my chest crashed over me, and the world tilted.

Sebastián's hand shot out to steady me, but he didn't quite touch me. His fingers hovered near my elbow, waiting. The gesture was oddly considerate.

"Come on."

No. No, no, *no.*

"I think I'm just going to go home now," I whispered, backing away very slowly. My hand slid into my pocket, ready to hit the emergency call button.

"Flynn." Sebastián's voice cut through my rising panic. Shifting the paper bag under his arm, he lifted both hands, palms out. "I know how this looks."

"Like you're about to murder me in an abandoned building?"

"If I wanted to hurt you, I could have done it last night. Or this morning. Or on our walk here."

Fair point. But still. "That's not as reassuring as you think it is."

"Look. I run an organisation. From this hotel. We handle... unusual cases."

"What do you mean, unusual?"

"The cold sensation you keep experiencing? That's not normal. And it's not going away on its own." His eyes bored into mine. "I can help you understand what's happening."

I glanced between him and the decrepit building. Everything screamed at me to run. But that cold feeling in my chest hadn't completely faded since Damien touched me. The doctor had dismissed it. Even Emma thought I was being dramatic, I could tell.

But Sebastián knew about it, without me saying anything first.

"You promise I can leave whenever I want?"

He nodded once, firmly.

"And there are... other people in there?"

"Yes. My team."

Are they more normal than you?

I took a deep breath. "Fine. But I'm keeping my phone ready to call for help." *9-9-9, I've willingly followed my armed stalker to a haunted hotel, can you help me please?*

"Understood." A ghost of a smile touched his lips. "Though I should warn you, the reception in here is terrible."

With a resigned nod, I followed Sebastián as he veered left, circling around the side of the decrepit building to a narrow path. A thick bush pressed against the iron fence—except as Sebastián pushed its branches aside, I spotted where several bars had been bent outward, creating a gap just wide enough for a person to squeeze through.

"After you," he said, holding the thorny branches back.

I ducked through the gap, stumbling slightly as my trainers hit uneven ground on the other side. As Sebastián led me to a weathered wooden door—a side entrance—I took a long, deep breath, then another, stuffing trembling hands into my jeans.

Sebastián produced an ornate copper key from his coat pocket, its elaborate handle carved with swirling patterns.

The key slid into the lock with a satisfying *click.*

My chest still pulsed with an icy chill, and half of me still expected Sebastián to whip out an axe, but...

With a sigh, I stepped into the hotel.

This side door led to a narrow corridor, its walls lined with faded Victorian wallpaper. My footsteps echoed against an intricate mosaic floor—thousands of tiny tiles arranged in geometric patterns of blue and gold. Despite the building's derelict exterior, this hallway appeared... clean. No cobwebs, no dust, just the musty scent of age-old wood and stone.

"Home sweet home," Sebastián murmured behind me.

I almost choked on my own spit. "You *live* here?"

"Not technically." He let out a low chuckle. "Well, I'm not supposed to. According to my own rules."

What the fuck?!

The corridor stretched ahead, lit by wall-mounted brass lamps that cast a warm glow across the mosaic tiles. My feet moved of their own accord, following Sebastián as he strode past me.

"We're heading to the basement. It's just down here."

The basement?! Why?!

The passageway opened into what must have once been the hotel's grand reception. Tall windows stretched up toward an ornate ceiling, though most were now covered by heavy velvet curtains. My gaze swept across antique furniture—plush armchairs, gilt-framed mirrors reflecting our movements. Everything looked... preserved. Like stepping into a time capsule.

Sebastián walked straight to the reception desk—a massive mahogany counter that curved along one wall. I trailed after him, my attention caught by the brass bell and ancient leather-bound guest book still sitting open.

"Dolly, any messages?"

I looked up, expecting to see another person, and jumped backward with a yelp.

"Jesus Christ!" My heart hammered against my ribs. "What the *hell* is that?"

Behind the desk sat what appeared to be a life-sized porcelain doll. Her painted face smiled serenely, glass eyes staring creepily at me. She wore a high-necked Victorian dress, complete with a lace collar and cameo brooch. Her blonde ringlets were arranged perfectly around her face, hands folded primly on the desk before her.

"That's Dolly." Sebastián remained completely serious. "Our receptionist."

I stared at the doll's fixed expression, fighting the urge to run. Her painted smile seemed to mock me.

I turned slowly back to Sebastián, once again seriously questioning my choice to follow him here. "You're having me on."

"Dolly's been with us for years. Very reliable employee. Never takes sick days." He winked at me.

"Ha... *ha?*" If he thought his odd humour would make me relax, he was severely wrong.

Sebastián continued down another corridor, and I jogged to catch up, glad to get as far away from Dolly as possible.

The corridor ended at what looked like a bank vault door—gleaming steel with a digital keypad mounted beside it, which stuck out like a smartphone at a Victorian tea party against the aged wallpaper. *What the fuck was in the basement, and why did it have a state-of-the-art security system?*

Sebastián tapped in a code lightning quick. The keypad chirped, a green light flashed, and the massive door released with a pneumatic hiss.

"After you." He gestured toward the darkness beyond.

My feet refused to move. "You know what? I think I'll pass."

"Flynn." His voice softened. "I promise you're safe."

Right. Because following a stranger into a basement was the epitome of safety. Every horror film ever made screamed at me to run.

Sebastián waited, patient and still, while my mind conjured increasingly gruesome scenarios. A dungeon filled with torture devices. A blood-spattered operating theatre. Chains dangling from ceiling hooks, ready to—

"I can hear you catastrophizing from here."

Heat crept up my neck. "I'm not—"

"You are." He stepped through the doorway first, flicking a switch. Fluorescent lights flickered to life, illuminating a concrete stairwell descending into the bowels of the hotel. "Better?"

I stared at him, my feet glued to the floor.

"We can keep this door open," he said. "There's a brick around here somewhere..."

He located said brick, wedging it in the doorframe. Then he descended without looking back.

Last chance to run.

I pressed my hand against my icy chest, resigned myself to my fate, and followed him downwards.

The air grew cooler as we descended, raising goosebumps along my arms. The stairwell opened into a vast underground space. More fluorescent tubes buzzed overhead, casting harsh shadows. Computer monitors lined one wall, their screens displaying various camera feeds, some of which I recognised from the walk here. A large table dominated the centre of the room, covered in maps and papers.

Curious.

There was a notable lack of a metal examination table with thick leather restraints, so I crept into the middle of the room, wrapping my arms around myself.

"What is this place?"

"Our command centre."

Just as I was about to question "our," thundering footsteps echoed down the stairwell, accompanied by shrieks of laughter. Two people burst into the space—a smaller pale bloke with chaotic blond hair and more ear piercings than I could count, followed by a striking woman in a vibrant purple dress, her long dark plait swinging as she chased him.

They skidded to a halt when they spotted me. The woman's hand flew to a pendant at her throat, while the guy's eyes went comically wide.

"Seb!" His voice splintered with disbelief. "What the actual fuck?"

"This is Flynn Carter," Sebastián said, as if that explained everything.

The woman stepped forward, her rich brown skin glowing under the harsh lights. A small tattoo peeked out from beneath her sleeve as she tilted her head, studying me with intelligent eyes. "The one from last night?"

Sebastián tossed his paper bag onto the table. The smell of fresh sourdough filled the room, and both newcomers pounced on it like they hadn't eaten in days. The blond one actually ripped the bag apart, sending paper flying.

"Oi, save some for me!" The woman elbowed him aside, grabbing for a chunk of bread.

"You had the last muffin earlier!" He shoved some into his mouth, speaking around it. "Besides, I deserve this after that thing with the—"

"If you mention that one more time—"

"It was literally *massive!* Like, the size of a Range Rover!"

I'd been completely forgotten. Almost hilariously so. I didn't know whether to laugh or cry.

They squabbled over the sourdough, weighing up how much they could eat before someone called Kit arrived to take it all for himself.

And I stood there, ignored, feeling like I'd somehow stumbled into a very strange dream. Sebastián pinched the bridge of his nose, muttering something under his breath.

"It was a labrador, Rory."

"A *possessed* labrador! That thing was proper demonic!"

A loud clatter broke through their bickering. I spun around to find another dude frozen in the doorway. He looked like he could be Korean, or partially at least. A puddle of liquid spread around his feet from a dropped energy drink. His oversized hoodie swallowed his frame. Dark eyes darted between me and the others.

"Felix!" Rory said brightly. "Want some bread? Hopefully no."

Felix's mouth opened and closed without sound. His eyebrows drew together in what looked like rising panic.

Because it seemed like nobody else was going to move, and because I didn't want to keep standing there like a lemon, I crossed the room and scooped up Felix's can, pressing it back into his hands.

"I... um... thanks." His voice was barely above a whisper as he scratched the back of his neck.

Rory sniggered for a second before clearing his throat.

The woman in purple stepped forward, extending her hand with a warm smile. "I'm Priya. I'm sorry about everyone else—they haven't been properly socialised." Her handshake was firm, the faintest scent of lavender following her. As I tried to withdraw my hand, she twisted it, bringing my palm towards her face. Her dark eyes traced the lines etched across my skin with intense focus.

"Well, *that's* rather unexpected. Have you ever had your palm read? These life lines suggest—"

"Right, that's enough." Sebastián's command caused Priya to drop my palm before she could announce whatever fate she'd seen written there. *Thank the stars.* I didn't want to know my future. "Don't you all have work to do? But first, Priya, can you bring Flynn one of your chamomile teas? As soon as possible, please."

"The kettle's already boiled, so it'll be just a sec!" she said brightly, skipping up the stairs.

The other two also vanished somewhere, and Sebastián guided me to a corner of the basement, where an L-shaped burgundy sofa wrapped around a scarred coffee table, creating a makeshift living area. I perched on the end of the sofa while he slung his massive coat on a hook.

A sleek coffee machine sat on a sidebar. Someone had taped a note to it reading "OUT OF ORDER (Kit, stop trying to fix it, nobody wants you to)" with several angry faces drawn underneath.

I gestured to the note. "So... Kit's not great with repairs then?"

Sebastián's lips twitched. "Oh, he's not bad at all, actually. He served in the military for a couple of years and picked up many handy skills.

It's that the others don't want it fixed. They like the excuse to go to that coffee shop on Killigrew Street we just passed. Kit claims it's 'highway robbery.'"

I found myself grinning, despite everything. "My mum says the exact same. Says she can buy a whole jar of coffee."

Sebastián laughed—a rich, velvety sound that seemed to chase away some of the basement's chill. He lowered his voice to a conspiratorial whisper. "Don't tell Kit this, but after the last time he fixed it, Rory snuck down in the middle of the night and attacked it with a butter knife."

The mental image made me snort. "Seriously?"

"Felix caught him on the security cameras. He was wearing all black, an official coffee machine saboteur." Sebastián's eyes crinkled at the corners. "We have the footage saved somewhere. For leverage."

As I sank back, the sofa cushions molded perfectly to my body, and I felt... almost *cozy*. Like I'd walked into someone's slightly chaotic family home rather than a secret underground lair. My shoulders began to un-knot, even as my brain screamed that this was definitely how horror films started—luring you into a false sense of security before the chainsaws came out. "Dedication to the cause. I like Rory's style."

Priya burst back into the basement like a whirlwind of purple fabric and jangling bracelets, a steaming mug clutched between her hands. The scent of chamomile and something sweeter—honey, maybe?—wafted toward me.

"Here you go." She pressed the warm ceramic into my palms. "My own special blend. This will make you feel amazing," she tossed over her shoulder, already heading back towards the stairs.

My fingers curled around the mug gratefully, the heat seeping into my skin as I inhaled the aromatic steam. When I took a sip, warmth bloomed across my tongue, spreading through my chest like liquid sunshine, chasing away the last lingering traces of that horrid ice in my chest.

I looked pointedly at Sebastián, waiting for him to start talking. As if finally preparing to get down to business, he cleared his throat and began rolling up the sleeves of his crisp white dress shirt. The fabric was so perfectly pressed, each fold created sharp lines as he worked methodically up his arms.

My mouth went dry.

The movement revealed rather lovely tanned forearms corded with muscle. Thick veins traced paths beneath his skin, rising and falling over prominent tendons that flexed as his fingers worked each precise fold. A light dusting of dark hair highlighted the sculptural quality of his arms—like something carved from bronze, all clean lines and sharp angles.

Christ. What was in this tea? I forced my gaze away, though the image had already burned itself into my brain. The room abruptly felt far too hot.

"So," Sebastián said, settling further into the armchair opposite me. He ran his hand down the length of his tie. "I'm sure you're thinking, 'What exactly is this strange establishment I find myself in?'"

Actually, I was fantasising about licking your forearms while simultaneously sort of still pondering if I'm going to die, but sure, let's go with that.

"Sure."

Sebastián leaned forward, resting his nice elbows on his knees. His white shirt pulled taut across his shoulders, and I forced myself to focus on his face. Which was also rather nice.

"You may have already guessed this, but what that man did to you... it wasn't..." He paused, considering. "Natural."

The cold sensation in my chest flared at the memory. I wrapped my arms around myself, trying to hold in whatever warmth remained. "Okay..."

"I suppose some people would say, it was *super*natural."

I blinked at him, and he pinched his nose again, sighing.

"Kit is always so much better at this than I am."

My brain stuttered over his words, trying to process them. *Supernatural? Like... ghosts and shit?*

A hysterical laugh bubbled up in my throat. "Right. Of course. Makes perfect sense. So what was he, then? The bogeyman?"

"A demon, actually. A lesser one. Often referred to as a *cambion*."

The matter-of-fact way he said it made me laugh harder. The sound echoed off the concrete walls, wild and unhinged even to my own ears.

"Oh, a *lesser* demon." I mimed wiping fake tears from my eyes, just to be dramatic. "No need to panic, then. But sure, why not? And I suppose next you'll tell me your blond friend upstairs is secretly a werewolf?"

Sebastián's lips parted. "Well, we don't use that terminology... but yes. How did you know?"

My laughter died instantly, leaving a hollow silence. The look in his dark eyes sent chills down my spine. Either this was an elaborate prank, or... "You can't be serious."

"I assure you, I am."

The gravity of the statement hit me like a rogue wave—the kind that appears from nowhere and sends you sprawling, capsized in unknown waters, with no means to tell which way was up.

"Prove it."

The words left my mouth before I could stop them. Sebastián's eyebrows rose slightly, and something flickered across his face. Hesitation? Fear?

"Flynn." His eyes held mine, utterly serious. "What did you feel when he touched you?"

The memory alone made my breath catch painfully in my throat. "Cold. Like... death cold. And everything went sort of... grey." My fingers pressed against my sternum, phantom pain ghosting through my chest. "And the sensation keeps coming back."

Sebastián's expression changed almost imperceptibly.

"And... his eyes..." A tremor ran through my words. "They were wrong. They went completely black. But... I thought I was seeing things."

"You weren't. Did you see the way he scaled the wall? No human could have done that, Flynn, you know that."

The room seemed to tilt, and I gripped the edge of the sofa to steady myself. "This is mental."

"Is it?" Sebastián crossed one leg over the other. "Is it really so hard to believe there might be more to this world than what you've been told?"

I opened my mouth to argue, then closed it again. The events of last night played through my mind... No, it wasn't impossible to believe. Not impossible at all.

"That guy Rory can really turn into... a wolf?" I whispered. My voice sounded small, childlike with fear. For some reason, this is what my brain was stuck on. Maybe it didn't want to think about what exactly the "demon" had done to me.

"And his older brother, Kit." My eyes moved to the note taped to the coffee machine. "They're from a Scottish Highland pack."

"There's a whole *pack* of them?" I pressed a shaking hand to my mouth, fighting another wave of hysteria.

"Just those two, here. But there are dozens of packs in England, yes."

"Can I... Can I see him? As a wolf, I mean?" I winced at my high-pitched voice.

Sebastián appeared amused. "That's not really a priority right now."

"Right." I nodded. "Demons and stuff. Ice in my heart." I swallowed hard, the cold in my chest seeming to spread at the mere mention of it.

I glanced around the basement again. The space felt oddly homey—there were cushions on the sofa, a few potted plants struggling under artificial light, and a collection of mugs by the broken coffee machine, each decorated with terrible puns.

"But... like, what is this place, though? A place for wolves?"

Sebastián laughed—properly *laughed* for the first time—and the rich sound made my stomach flip. "Kit and Rory would love that. But no." He shifted forward, his expression growing more serious. "Killigrew Street is a specialist response unit. We monitor and manage supernatural threats in London—everything from rogue demons to dark magic practitioners who cross lines. Think of us as... an unofficial taskforce keeping the peace between worlds." His lips quirked. "Everyone here is part of my team."

"Christ." I pressed my palms against my eyes until spots danced behind my lids, my breaths coming quick and shallow. "This is absolutely barking. I've gone mad, for sure."

"Well, you're not mad alone, Flynn. We're all a bit... *barking* here."

When I looked up, the corner of his mouth had curved upward slightly. The tiny smile transformed his whole face, softening the sharp angles into something almost... charming.

I was definitely losing it.

"You saved me." The words tumbled out of my mouth. "You saved me from a demon. *You saved me.*" Gratitude hit me like a wave, washing away some of my earlier panic. "I'm sorry I... um... kneed you. In the..." I gestured vaguely at his balls.

But his almost-smile had vanished. "Don't thank me, Flynn. Because I wasn't fast enough to save you."

"What?"

"You're not the first victim of these lesser demons." He moved towards me, shadows deepening the hollows of his face. "And yesterday, you were marked before I could stop it."

The cold in my chest seemed to pulse in response, as if acknowledging its presence. "Marked me?"

"It's more like... a seed. The demon plants it in the victim's heart, and it grows. Feeds. Gets stronger."

A wave of nausea rolled through me. *Nope, this doesn't sound good at all.*

Sebastián's fingers brushed his own chest, the movement so quick I almost missed it. "We suspect something else is at play here, with cambions at their bidding, marking humans for them. We've found ten bodies so far. All drained, all with the same frost patterns under their skin. But by the time we find them, it's too late. The dark magic's already developed, already been... harvested."

My lungs seized. A rushing sound filled my ears, drowning out everything else. The cold in my chest exploded outward, a freezing blast that seemed to reach my fingertips. "What are the symptoms?"

"It starts small. The victim feels cold, no matter how warm it is. They have weird dreams. Ice. Darkness." His gaze grew distant. "But they also feel... more. Everything becomes intense. Emotions run higher. It's like the magic amplifies everything they feel, makes it stronger, richer..." He trailed off, troubled.

"But I feel fine!" The words burst out of me—too loud, too desperate. "I mean, emotionally. Normal." Apart from the overwhelming terror currently clawing at my insides, and the occasional panic attack and crushing anxiety.

Sebastián's dark eyes met mine, and I found myself holding my breath.

"This is just the beginning."

"So I'm going to die?" I choked out. "Like the others?"

The cold in my chest spread, tendrils of ice wrapping around my ribs like skeletal fingers. My breath came in short, painful gasps that didn't seem to deliver any oxygen. I was drowning on dry land. *No, no, no.* After everything that had happened, after running all this way from Braymore Bay, this was how it would end?

Three weeks in London, then *boom,* dead at the tender age of twenty-five. I wasn't even sure what to do with my life yet. Just a burning desire to keep breathing. Funny that.

Fuck, I really needed to call my mother now, before she saw my face on the news. And Katie—Christ, she'd probably want to arrange my funeral flowers herself.

The sofa dipped beside me. Cool fingers wrapped around my forearm, anchoring me.

"Flynn. Look at me."

I raised my head with effort, feeling as though my neck could barely support its weight. This close, I could see tiny flecks of amber in Sebastián's eyes, like dying embers in the depths of night.

"I won't let that happen." His grip tightened, firm enough to ground me. "We have time. And I promise you, I will do everything in my power to save you."

My supposed saviour's presence radiated a strange sort of calm—the conviction in his tone steadied my breathing, though my heart still raced like a trapped animal.

"Thank you." The words felt inadequate. I searched his face, seeing only steadfast determination, and in that moment, I felt safer than I had in months. My gaze landed on his full, plump lips, slightly parted.

Without thinking, my free hand reached for his other arm as some magnetic pull drew me toward him, urging me closer. My fingers barely brushed his sleeve before he jerked away, putting three feet of space between us as he retreated to his armchair.

Heat flooded my cheeks. *What the fuck was I doing?* The man had just told me demons were real and I was dying, and here I was, practically throwing myself at him.

"I'm sorry," I mumbled, studying the concrete floor. "I didn't mean to..."

"It's fine." His voice had gone carefully neutral. "The mark... it might make you act... impulsively."

I wanted the sofa to swallow me whole.

Right. Blame it on the demon magic. Much better than admitting I'd been about to make an advance on the mysterious, beautiful man who'd saved my life. *Almost* saved my life.

I had to take what I could get.

Sebastián rose and strode to a wall panel. "Everyone to the basement. Now."

A crackle of static: "Oooh, is this about our new friend? Has he fainted yet?" Rory's voice echoed. "Five quid says he's fainted."

"Rory." Sebastián's tone was pure warning.

I hugged my arms around my middle, trying to stop the trembling that had taken over my body. Footsteps thundered above. Priya and Rory appeared first, the latter bouncing down the stairs. Felix skulked in, retreating behind an armchair, eyes darting everywhere except at me.

Heavy boots announced another arrival. This had to be Kit—Rory's brother. Though larger, the family resemblance showed in the sharp jawline and proud nose. But where Rory was compact energy, Kit was pure predator. A thin scar traced through his left eyebrow, his movements controlled and deliberate.

Kit's gaze swept the room, softening at Felix's hunched form. "Felix. Come sit properly."

Felix's head snapped up then down again. He inched around the armchair but remained standing.

Kit sighed and settled into the chair. "Right, then. Flynn Carter, aye?" His Scottish accent was more pronounced than Rory's. "Well, you don't look quite as scrawny as Rory reported."

Ouch.

I glared at Rory, annoyance overriding my fear. I raked my eyes over his small frame. "Right, because you're clearly qualified to judge physical proportions."

Rory's mouth dropped open, and Kit barked out a laugh. I tried not to look smug.

Sebastián stood, commanding attention without speaking a word. "As I suspected," he began, voice grave. "Flynn has been marked by a cambion, the very one we received information about weeks ago. The symptoms match our previous cases." He pulled over a corkboard covered in photos and documents, with Damien's grainy CCTV image at the centre.

"He's called Damien," I offered.

Rory snickered, but Kit's hand shot out, catching him across the back of the head with a solid *thwack*.

"Aye, but that's not likely his real designation, Flynn," Kit said, giving me a patient look.

"Oh." I shrank back into the sofa, feeling foolish. "Right. Of course..." Did lesser demons even have real names anyway?

"We'll call him Damien, then," Sebastián said, glowering at Rory. This time, I couldn't resist shooting him a smirk. "From now on, Flynn will be under twenty-four-hour supervision."

I inhaled sharply. "*What?*"

"Whatever is controlling these cambions might come to collect Flynn at any moment. We can't risk leaving him unprotected. We'll need to establish a protection detail."

Collected? By what? The cold spot in my chest pulsed. *Twenty-four-hour supervision?* At work? Back at my flat, even while I slept? I felt about five years old. I sank deeper into the sofa cushions, wishing I could disappear entirely.

Sebastián continued outlining plans—something about schedules and security protocols—but his words faded into background noise as my thoughts spiralled.

"—use him as a lure?" Priya's voice cut through my panic.

My head snapped up, adrenaline flooding my system.

"No," Sebastián said firmly. "Absolutely not. We're not risking—"

But I'd already lost track again, my pulse pounding in my ears like war drums. *A lure? Bait? They wanted to use me as bait?*

A collective groan pulled me back to the present.

"Everyone is to use the underground entrance until further notice," he continued. "The cambion saw my face. We don't know if Killigrew Street has been compromised."

"But how will we get to Fat Cat's?" Rory whined.

I stared at him in disbelief, a hysterical laugh threatening to bubble up again. The café? They were worried about coffee shop access while actual demons were apparently hunting me down?

"If you must, you can take turns making the longer trip," Sebastián replied, pinching the bridge of his nose yet again. Honestly, it was a wonder he wasn't grey, dealing with this lot. What was he thinking when he hired them?

Kit's eyes drifted toward the broken coffee machine. "Maybe it's time to—"

"No!" Rory and Priya shouted.

"Don't take this one thing away from us, Kit," Priya added.

"Just let them have their coffee, Kit," Sebastián cut in, his tone final. He turned to me, and something in his expression made me tense. "Flynn, you'll stay here tonight. We have rooms upstairs. Obviously. It's a hotel. We'll collect your things from your flat."

No, no, no, no, no.

My throat constricted painfully. The walls of the basement seemed to close in around me. Demons were real. Werewolves were real. Magic was real. And I was marked—*dying*—with some kind of supernatural parasite feeding on my heart. And now this strange man wanted me to just... what? Pack up and live in this decrepit Victorian hotel with a bunch of people who apparently weren't even *human* and a creepy porcelain doll?

My pulse raced wildly as claustrophobia gripped me. My gaze darted to the concrete walls, the fluorescent lights of the basement. Were the rooms upstairs even liveable?

"Hang on—" I started, my voice thin with panic, but Sebastián had moved on.

I ground my teeth to keep from shouting. My fear was morphing into something else—frustration, anger at being so completely powerless. Nobody had even asked my opinion between discussing using me as demon bait and debating coffee.

Priya and Rory celebrated their coffee victory. Felix typed furiously on a laptop. Kit watched over them all with barely concealed fondness.

And Sebastián... He stood apart, outlined against the harsh fluorescent lights, all sharp angles and quiet authority. As if sensing my gaze, he turned, those dark eyes meeting mine. Something passed between us—a spark of... *something*. Then he looked away, leaving me with only the memory of amber flecks in darkness.

What the actual fuck had I got myself into?

6

Sebastián

I closed the diary with a snap.

I'd kept these leather-bound volumes for centuries, though the earlier ones had faded to ink-stained fragments of lives I could barely remember living.

The antique clock on my desk showed almost 11:00 p.m. Only an hour remained until my meeting with Greaves.

I only ever needed a few hours' sleep, and I tended to catch them just before dawn. These days, room 204 had become my sleeping quarters, though I remained steadfast in my rule against overnight stays for the rest of the team. Hypocritical, perhaps.

At least for now, Flynn's presence would provide the perfect excuse.

I'd placed him in room 208, a few doors down from mine. It was one of my favourites. The corner suite boasted original Victorian features—ornate ceiling roses, a marble fireplace, and tall sash windows that always caught the evening sun. I'd seen dozens of architectural styles come and go, but this craftsmanship held a particular charm. Perhaps because it reminded me of... *something*. The memory slipped away like smoke.

What was Flynn doing in there? Had he managed to find sleep in his new surroundings? Perhaps I should knock, just to check if he needed anything—

No.

Best to leave him be. The poor soul had endured enough upheaval for one day without me hovering like some gothic horror at his door.

I leant back in my chair, the memory of Flynn's earlier gratitude washing over me. The way he'd gazed up at me, those fatally blue eyes filled with such trust. "Thank you," he'd said, quiet and sincere and bloody hell—my dead heart had actually skipped.

And now, the image refused to leave me in peace.

My phone buzzed.

Kit

5 mins away for Flynn duty. I hope you're not still working, boss.

Right. Time to focus on getting to Greaves. I quickly tidied room 210, my office come diary room, and stepped into the corridor—

Thump.

A warm body collided with mine. A startled squeak pierced the air as Flynn stumbled backwards. Pure instinct had me reaching out, my hands finding his waist to steady him.

"S-sorry!" Flynn gasped.

My fingers brushed against bare skin where his pyjama top had ridden up. The flannel hung loose on his frame, red chequered pattern stark against his pale complexion. That strip of exposed flesh felt like fire under my touch—gloriously warm, impossibly soft.

I snatched my hand back as if burned. "Do you need something?"

Flynn shifted from foot to foot, his hand rubbing the back of his neck. "Actually... I'm a bit hungry. Haven't eaten since—" His stomach growled, finishing the sentence for him.

Bloody hell. *Food.* Of course he needed food.

"Ah." Heat crept up my neck. "I should have thought—" I barely paid attention to my team's mealtime routines, and as for my own...

"It's fine, really." Flynn offered a small smile.

"I'll remind you where the kitchen is. The others always keep food there." *The others.* I tensed—would Flynn pick up on my odd phrasing? This would probably be an ideal time to mention my own eating habits, and well, the whole undead vampire thing.

But something seized my vocal cords.

I *could* have pretended to myself that I didn't understand why I kept silent. But that would've been a lie.

I didn't want Flynn Carter to see me as a monster. Not when he looked at me with such raw, unguarded trust—like I was some kind of saviour who could piece him back together.

The truth about what I was would surely shatter that illusion.

I'd just keep it going for a *tiny* bit longer, until Flynn felt safer with us.

As we walked to the kitchen, Flynn hummed a soft tune to himself—possibly some sort of sea shanty—seeming fairly content in what must have been very strange circumstances. I delivered him to the door, explaining that he should help himself to anything he could find in the spacious hotel kitchen. When I bid him farewell, I had to drag my feet away, fighting the odd urge to stay with him, to make sure he found food. To watch him eat.

Because that wouldn't be creepy at all.

The basement's cold air distracted me from my thoughts. From Felix's side room, three monitors glowed blue, displaying CCTV feeds as he scanned footage near Wilde Card, hunting for any trace of "Damien."

"Go home, Felix," I said, spooking him—he near enough jumped out of his desk chair.

"Five minutes," Felix promised.

"Kit is taking over from me in a moment. You don't want him to catch you here."

Felix grimaced and began meticulously reorganising his workspace, though there was hardly anything out of place. His fingers twitched as he aligned his keyboard perfectly parallel to the edge of the desk. I'd once opened a drawer to find a collection of USB drives arranged by size and colour.

During my very first meeting with Felix, he'd nearly had a panic attack. I'd cornered him on the street after he'd hacked into our apparently mediocre system. A year later, though still skittish, his genius had transformed Killigrew Street's digital security.

His mother—the first female CEO of Korean quantum computing giant QuByte—thought he worked IT support. Dr Chŭng had expected her son to follow her meteoric rise, not waste away at a help desk. According to Felix, family dinners were just thinly veiled career interventions, full of comments about wasted opportunities at her company.

If only she knew how brilliant her son was—how he'd crafted the most sophisticated security system in London.

Or so Rory and Kit reassured me, anyway. I hadn't a single clue about it all.

"I've set up automated AI tracking," Felix muttered, more to his keyboard than to me. "If anyone matching Damien's description shows up on any CCTV..." His voice trailed off as he noticed a cable slightly out of place.

"Go home, Felix," I said again, before I strode towards the bookcase that dominated the far wall. My fingers found the brass spine of *The Picture of Dorian Gray*—which always gave me a chuckle—and pulled it forward. With a soft click, the entire bookcase swung outward to reveal the gleaming security door behind it.

"But it's *always* behind the bookcase," Kit had protested when I'd installed it three years ago. "It's like something from a shit B-movie."

"Precisely why no one will expect it," I'd replied.

I typed the sixteen-digit code into the keypad. The door slid open with a hydraulic hiss, revealing Kit's broad frame on the other side.

"You're late." Kit folded his arms.

"By two minutes."

"Still late."

"I was ordering Felix home."

As expected, Kit's expression softened. I descended the narrow stairs into the tunnel network. LED strips cast clinical white light along the passage. Strange to think of London churning above—the buses, the revellers, the constant pulse of the city—while I walked these silent corridors. I'd known them as war bunkers once, and before that... Well, the city had always held secrets beneath its streets.

The tunnels now connected Killigrew Street to various points across London. Tonight's exit lay a quarter-mile ahead.

My footsteps echoed off concrete walls. Kit had lectured me about structural integrity when I'd first shown him, but these tunnels had survived a hundred years. They'd outlast us all.

The final door opened into a brick-vaulted railway arch, walls thick with graffiti. A purple octopus wrapped around the word "DEEP" marked the metal exit. I found the hidden lock.

The hospital lay thirty minutes away. The night air bit cold as I wound through narrow streets. A cat yowled ahead, echoing off brickwork. Once, I thought footsteps matched mine, but when I paused, only silence followed. The skin between my shoulders prickled.

Three streets from the hospital, something moved in the shadows ahead. I stopped dead. There, beneath a flickering streetlight—no, it couldn't be. The creature was too large for a dog, its sloping back and powerful shoulders unmistakable even at this distance. A hyena? In London? *Impossible.* The beast turned its head, eyes reflecting an unnatural yellow in the darkness. For a moment, our gazes locked, and the sensation of being observed became overwhelming. Then it quickly slunk away between the buildings.

I shook my head, trying to clear it. Hunger must be affecting me more than I'd thought if I was now hallucinating impossible creatures. Arriving at last, I favoured the shadows as I crept toward the underground garage for hospital staff.

Dr Alistair Greaves was already waiting for me in his car, and his face pulled into his typical frown as I slid into the passenger seat. The forty-something pathologist didn't like me very much, but he *did* like my money. Almost as much as I liked the blood he stole for me.

Greaves shifted in his seat, refusing to meet my gaze. "I've only got five bags tonight."

My fingers dug into the leather of the seat. "Five." The word came out as a hiss. "We agreed on ten at the very least."

"Look, it's been a difficult week. Most of the bodies came in too late—"

"I don't care for excuses." The hunger gnawed at my insides, sharpening my tone. "You're being paid handsomely for this arrangement."

Greaves fumbled with his briefcase. "I don't choose the bodies I'm assigned. You're aware that the blood clots if I don't get to them quickly enough. Can't exactly push past police cordons when they've got a suspicious death on their hands. Sometimes the bodies sit upstairs for hours before anyone even notifies us there's been a death, and by then…" He shrugged helplessly. "Well, you know how it goes with coagulation."

The metallic scent of blood wafted from his case as he retrieved the cooling bag. Even through the medical packaging, the aroma made my throat burn.

"Five hundred per bag," I said, keeping my voice level. "That's far above market rate. If you're unable to meet my requirements, perhaps I should seek alternative arrangements?"

His head snapped up. "No, no. I appreciate the business. It's just been—"

"I don't pay you to make excuses. I pay you to deliver." I pulled out my wallet, counting out crisp fifties. "Two thousand five hundred."

His hands trembled slightly as he passed over the blood. "Next week will be better. I promise."

"It had better be." I unfolded a canvas bag from my pocket. "Ten bags, Greaves. Not nine, not eight, and certainly not five."

"Of course." He cleared his throat. "Though if we're talking about raising quantities, perhaps we could discuss adjusting the price—"

"The price stays exactly where it is." I let my lip curl, just enough to flash my slightly extended canines.

"Fine, fine. Five hundred is… Five hundred is perfect."

"Wonderful." I opened the car door. "Same time next week. Ten bags. *At least.*"

The night air hit my face as I stepped out, carrying the precious cargo. *Five bags.* I only had one left at Killigrew Street. That meant six bags—less than a bag each day this week.

It was going to be tough, especially with this cursed hunger riding me so hard lately.

I couldn't deny it—this endless rationing was slowly destroying me.

The memory of Flynn reaching for me earlier, the column of his neck so easily accessible, flashed through my mind, and my fangs ached.

Blood had pulsed so temptingly in his neck, his heart rate spiking with every breath. My heightened senses picked up the rush of it beneath his delicate skin, that steady thrum calling to the predator within me.

The scent of him lingered in my nose, even now. Clean sweat, traces of cinnamon sugar from the bakery, and beneath it all, that intoxicating hint of *fear*. God help me, but the monster inside me had tuned into it like a shark scenting blood in the water.

I'd spent centuries learning to control these urges, to master the beast that dwelled beneath my skin. But the vile creature that I was, I couldn't help imagining sinking my fangs deep into that tender flesh, drinking down his essence until—

No. *No.*

But the thought had already taken root. Of course, that led me to imagine what Flynn's moans might sound like, as the euphoric pleasure hit him. That blissful high that came with a vampire's bite, the way victims melted into it, surrendering completely...

My fangs pressed hungrily against my gums. The canvas bag of blood felt impossibly heavy in my hands.

God help me.

I could not allow myself to fantasise about drinking from anyone, let alone gorgeously innocent blond men with warm smiles.

If the few times—those dire emergencies—where I'd drunk from Kit had taught me anything, it was that centuries of being a vampire still hadn't granted me the iron control I pretended to possess. The bloodlust owned me, no matter how I tried to cage it. Each time, the hunger had nearly consumed me, and I always took too much.

The last time—the *very* last time, I'd vowed—Priya and Rory had to use their combined strength to wrench me off Kit, who took one wobbly step away from me before fainting.

The memory of fresh blood—rich, intoxicating, *alive*—made my tongue tingle in anticipation.

No. Flynn would never know that side of me. I refused to let him see the monster that lurked beneath this carefully constructed façade of control and civility.

He was a guest in my hotel, under my protection.

Six blood bags. I'd make them last.

I made my way back through the tunnel network in record time.

Voices from the kitchen drifted down across the ground floor as I climbed the basement stairs—Felix's hesitant tones mixed with...

Flynn's? At this hour? My hearing picked up their conversation with perfect clarity.

"And then the whole system crashed." Felix's voice carried none of its usual nervous energy. "But I'd already copied the data, so..."

Flynn's laugh, sweet as honey, rang through the air. "Oh my god, that's brilliant. Did they ever find out?"

"N-no. But I felt so bad, I sent them an anonymous email explaining the security flaw."

"Of course you did." Another laugh.

I paused outside the kitchen door, frowning. I'd never heard Felix speak so freely. The boy barely managed two sentences in team meetings, yet here he was, chatting away like they were old friends.

"Want another tea?" Flynn asked. "I found some proper loose leaf stuff in this cupboard."

More tea? Shouldn't they want to sleep?

"Yes, please. Though technically that's Kit's private stash..."

"I won't tell if you won't."

Another easy laugh rolled forth. Something tight coiled in my chest. What sort of magic had Flynn worked to draw Felix out of his shell so effortlessly? The rest of us had tried for months without success.

"So, how long have you worked here?" Flynn asked.

"About a year. After I hacked their—"

I didn't quite realise I'd barged in until both of them jumped at my sudden appearance. Felix's mug clattered against one of the vast stainless steel workbenches, while Flynn nearly dropped the kettle.

"I thought I told you to go home, Felix." The harsh words escaped before I had time to censor them. "I mean, you should be at home resting, Felix."

Felix hastily dumped his mug in the sink. "S-sorry, I'm going." He practically fled past me.

Flynn's shoulders hunched inward, his earlier warmth vanishing as he busied himself with the kettle. The sight of him shrinking away from me felt like a knife to the gut.

"I didn't mean to..." I cleared my throat. What was even my excuse for being here? "I was actually looking to see if any of that sourdough made it to the kitchen."

Flynn's hands stilled. "Oh. No, it's all gone. Never seen people eat bread so fast." His lips twitched. "Or violently."

"Ah." I shifted my weight, hyper-aware of how I must appear to him—lurking in doorways, frightening everyone. "Well, perhaps you could bake some more for us?"

What? I cringed at myself. I needed to leave before I suggested indentured servitude.

Flynn's laugh filled the kitchen, but this time it held a nervous edge. "God no, I can't bake to save my life. I just work the till." He fiddled with his mug. "Been there two weeks now. Took me an entire week to find work in London, actually."

I shifted further into the hotel's kitchen, past the wall lined with industrial ovens to lean against the dumbwaiter system, now sealed shut.

"What did you do before?" Really, I shouldn't have encouraged conversation, not when the hunger gnawed at me like this. But since our first encounter at Wilde Card, my curiosity about him had only intensified with each passing moment, each laugh, each fidget of those restless hands.

"Back home, I spent ten years working for my grandfather's boating company." Flynn's expression clouded. "Well, *dead* grandfather's boating company. Think it's in Mum's name now..."

The words trailed off, weighted with unspoken pain. I recognised that look—the careful way people stepped around sharp memories, like avoiding broken glass.

Flynn moved suddenly, reaching past me for the sugar pot on the counter behind. His shoulder brushed against my chest, and the scent of him hit me like a tidal wave. Cinnamon and warmth and *life*, coursing just beneath that delicate skin.

I should have drunk one of those blood bags on the way back. My fangs pressed against my gums, desperate to extend. The predator in me fixated on his pulse point, so tantalizingly close.

No.

I gripped the edge of the counter, willing myself to stay perfectly still as Flynn retrieved the sugar and stepped away.

A draft whistled through the spacious kitchen—our old building had terrible insulation. Flynn visibly shivered. Unsurprising as his pyjamas appeared paper thin.

"You're cold."

He blinked at me in surprise. "I'll be okay. I didn't pack many jumpers when I left Ireland."

"What about that one you were wearing yesterday?"

The memory of him in that crocheted garment was one I wouldn't forget in a hurry—the holes had revealed tantalising glimpses of delectable skin, like some kind of torturous connect-the-dots puzzle. That damned jumper. Professional duty had dictated I concentrate on the supernatural threat at hand, yet I'd been thoroughly compromised by that strategic arrangement of holes and skin.

"Though I have to say," I continued. "It was more decoration than defence against the cold."

He grimaced, two pleasant pink dots appearing on his cheeks. "Damien ripped it. To shreds."

"Oh, that's a shame." And it was, though perhaps not for the purely practical reasons I should have been concerned with.

"Is it?" Confusion swam in his eyes. Or was it... a challenge? His tongue darted out to wet his lower lip, and I found myself tracking the movement with minute precision.

"So you've just moved here?" I redirected.

He stirred his tea, the spoon clinking against china. "To this hotel? Yeah, pretty sweet rates." His mouth quirked. "Thought I'd save on rent."

His humour caught me off guard, and dormant muscles in my face formed what might have been a grin. "Where did you say you lived?"

"Braymore Bay." Flynn's shoulders tensed. "Little tourist trap on the Irish coast. One of those places that's packed in summer, dead in winter. Lots of fancy holiday homes owned by rich Dublin folk who show up twice a year. We moved there from England after my dad died when I was fifteen. That's when I started at the boating company—fishing trips, seal watching tours, that sort of thing." His fingers tightened around the mug.

"And what brought you to London?"

The question hung in the air. Flynn stared into his tea as if it held answers, the steam rising between us like a barrier.

"It must be very different here," I said, to fill the silence.

"Yeah." He scrunched up his nose in the most adorable way. "So, you were at Wilde Card last night watching Damien? Did you know he was...?"

"A cambion?" I leaned against the counter, folding my arms. "The product of a demon coupling with a human."

Flynn's eyes widened. "That's... possible?"

"More common than you'd think." I watched his reaction carefully. "Many end up in service to more powerful entities—demons, various...

other creatures. Their mixed blood makes them particularly... susceptible to influences."

"Service?" Flynn frowned, leaning forward. "You mean like slavery?"

"Not exactly. Though some would argue it's not far off." His captivated interest loosened my tongue more than usual. "There's an ongoing debate about their nature. Some claim they're soulless beings, caught between two worlds. Though personally, I find theological arguments about souls rather tiresome."

"And last night... you were what, just hanging about, waiting for Damien to attack someone?"

"We'd been tracking his movements for weeks. Yesterday, I was conducting surveillance."

Flynn let out a sharp laugh. "*Surveillance*? You were doing a terrible job of being subtle about it. Kept glaring daggers at us from across the room. I thought you were Damien's jealous ex or something."

"Well, you weren't exactly helping matters, throwing yourself at a complete stranger with absolutely no sense of self-preservation. You practically handed yourself to him on a plate."

Flynn's eyes flashed. "Excuse me? Are you actually victim-blaming me right now?"

I opened my mouth, then closed it. My words had emerged far more judgmental than intended. And god knew that I'd certainly indulged in my share of carnal pleasure throughout the centuries. Perhaps twenty years of self-imposed solitude had made me forget what it was to be young and desperate for connection.

"You're right." I forced myself to meet his gaze. "That was... unfair of me. Please forgive me. I understand the urge to seek comfort in the wrong places."

Flynn raised a challenging eyebrow. "Do you?"

The way he looked at me—defiant, curious, perhaps even a touch flirtatious—sent a jolt through my lifeless heart.

Before I could reply, Flynn broke the moment by darting his gaze around the kitchen, landing on the small altar in the corner. "What's that?"

The shrine sat on a worn wooden table beside the pantry—exactly where Issac used to perch when we gathered here. Fresh oranges nestled among incense and dried flowers. A worn leather jacket hung on a hook above, its sleeve touching a collection of photographs.

The familiar scent of leather and citrus carved a fresh wound through the pain I was trying my best to fossilise. Beneath it lay the cloying sweetness of incense—a scent that still made my skin crawl after centuries, dragging with it half-formed memories of stone chambers and desperate prayers. Of confession boxes and judgement halls, where I had served the Spanish Inquisition with misplaced devotion. But I endured it, here in our kitchen. For Issac.

"That's for Issac." His name still caught in my throat, every time I went to say it. My fingers curled into my palm, nails biting skin. "We lost him last year."

"Oh." Flynn shifted closer to examine the shrine. "The fruit?"

"He used to juggle them when he was thinking." My smile wavered, the memory both sweet and sharp. "Drove Kit mad, watching perfectly good fruit being tossed around."

Priya had built the shrine the day after we lost him. She refreshed the offerings regularly—fresh fruit, burning sage, new photographs. The rest of us contributed too. Even Kit, who claimed he didn't believe in "spiritual nonsense," left small tokens.

Flynn's fingers hovered over a photograph—from that last Christmas, Issac balanced on that very table, his face split in a wild grin as he pelted Rory with paper chains. That laughter echoed in my memories, a ghost of happiness that would never return.

Life at Killigrew Street divided neatly into two chapters: before and after. Before was all noise and chaos and badly-juggled fruit. After was hushed voices and empty spaces and the weight of words we couldn't bring ourselves to say. Some days the difference had felt like a physical thing, heavy as the hotel's foundations. But slowly, carefully, we were learning to write a new chapter—one where Priya's tea flowed freely again, where Kit's grumbling had regained its fondness, where Rory's laughter, though different now, still brightened our halls.

"Just a warning..." I swallowed hard against the lump in my throat. "Rory hasn't quite accepted that he's gone. Don't bring Issac up with him when Kit's in the room. It causes... the kind of conflict that leaves scars."

I could see the question on Flynn's lips—*so how did Issac die?*—and my muscles tensed.

"But anyway, back to lighter topics. Are you enjoying London, at least?"

Flynn's laugh was as brittle as frost. "You want the truth?" His fingers worried at a loose thread on his sleeve. "People back home always say the same thing about cities, and it's true. I've never been more surrounded by people, and I've never felt so bloody alone."

The words struck a chord deep within me. Our eyes met across the dim kitchen, and something electric passed between us. His gaze held such raw honesty—a mirror to my own centuries of isolation. The weight of endless nights spent watching the world change while I remained frozen in time pressed against my chest.

In that moment, I saw past his youth, past the warmth of his blood calling to me. I saw someone who understood what it meant to be adrift in a sea of strangers.

"I understand that more than you might think." The truth of countless solitary years.

Flynn's expression softened. "At least you've got this place, though. Everyone here seems so... connected. Almost like a proper family."

If only he knew how temporary it all was. How there had been different teams before them. How this now, as wonderful as it was, would all be over in a heartbeat. Kit and Rory's wolf's blood might grant them a slightly extended lifespan, but eventually everyone would grow old and grey while I remained unchanged.

They were all shooting stars, burning brilliant but brief across my eternal night. And like all the others before them, they would leave me behind, either by choice or by death's inevitable hand.

Just as Issac had.

Just as everyone always did.

The weight of that knowledge pressed against my chest like a stone.

It was at times like these that I was grateful my memories prior to the last half a century were hazy at best. How many people had I lost over the course of my lifespan? How many names had I carved into my memory, only to watch them fade into history?

"Sebastián?"

It was the first time Flynn had said my name, and the tentative, unsure way he rolled the word across his lips sent a visceral shiver through me. The Spanish lilt he attempted was imperfect, hesitant, yet somehow extremely intimate.

"Are you okay?" The words ghosted between us, gentle as a feather, and he closed the small space separating us.

The predator in me purred at Flynn's proximity. His scent wrapped around me like a physical caress. My fangs pressed harder against my gums, desperate to extend. His pulse beckoned, calling to me like the tide pulls the moon, and my throat burned with need. The vein in his neck jumped with each heartbeat, and I tracked the movement like a cat watching a mouse. The hunger clawed at my insides, demanding satisfaction. If I just leaned forward slightly...

"I'm fine." The words came out rougher than intended, my voice thick with barely contained need. I gripped the counter edge, hard. "Perfectly fine."

Flynn stepped even closer, concern etched across his features. Sweet, innocent Flynn, who had no idea he was drawing nearer to a starving beast. The monster inside me stretched, reaching for him with phantom claws. *Just one taste,* it whispered.

The sound of footsteps made Flynn shuffle back from me, consciously or unconsciously.

Kit poked his head in, glaring at us. "If you don't mind, I'd like to head home now."

Ah. I'd forgotten to tell him I'd returned.

"Of course. Go home, Kit. Thank you."

Flynn looked between us. "I should get some sleep too."

Once they'd both left, I sagged against the counter. The canvas bag, containing the bags of blood wedged between ice packs, sat waiting by my feet.

I retrieved a glass from the cupboard, hands trembling slightly as I tore open one of the medical bags. The blood was chilled—which always tasted worse—but I couldn't wait any longer. Not after being so close to Flynn, breathing in his scent, hearing his pulse...

The first swallow hit my system like lightning. My fangs extended fully as I drained the glass, and then another.

One bag already gone.

The desperate hunger dulled. For now.

My hands itched to tear open a second bag, but I restrained myself.

It would have to be enough.

7

Flynn

"So, Dolly... how's your morning going so far?"

The life-sized Victorian doll perched behind the reception desk fixed me with her painted-on smile.

"Oh, that bad, huh? Well, let me tell you, I bet it's not as bad as mine." I slumped against the desk, chin propped in my hands. "First off, I woke up in this bizarre hotel where I'm practically a fucking prisoner. I mean, sure, there's the whole 'we're protecting you from demons' thing, but still."

Her porcelain face maintained that unnervingly cheerful expression.

"Then I spent ages wandering these empty corridors looking for any sign of life. You'd think in a place this size there'd be someone about, but no. Just creepy noises coming from half the rooms." I drummed my fingers on the worn wooden desk. "And the cherry on top? I can't even go down to the basement because I don't have the code. So I'm stuck up here on the first floor, talking to—"

I paused, giving her a slight smile.

"Well, at least I've got you, Dolly!"

The doll didn't even blink. *Rude.*

"Flynn! Get down here!"

Priya's voice screeched down a corridor, making me jump. I shot Dolly an apologetic look.

"We can see you talking to Dolly on camera. I'm glad the two of you are getting to know each other," she shouted.

Heat crept up my neck. Brilliant. Not only had they caught me chatting with a bloody doll, but they'd been watching me do it. Still, after wandering these empty corridors like a lost ghost, even the prospect of mockery seemed better than more silence.

The basement door finally opened, and I bounded down the stairs two at a time, nearly tripping over my own feet in my eagerness for actual human contact.

The team lounged across the collection of mismatched sofas, all eyes fixed on me as I entered, which slowed my pace somewhat. The rich scent of coffee filled the air, and everyone except Kit clutched paper cups adorned with an orange tabby cat logo reading "Fat Cat's."

"Here." Priya offered me a steaming cup. "We guessed latte, one sugar."

I stared at the cup, oddly touched. Maybe using me as demon bait was firmly off the table after all.

Sebastián cleared his throat, and every head swivelled towards him like a well-oiled machine, mobile phones slipping into pockets.

Leather-bound notebook in hand, Sebastián began rattling off updates. His voice had a smooth, commanding tone that washed over me like warm water, oddly soothing despite the formal setting. My gaze drifted to his perfectly pressed button-down shirt, the way his skinny black tie lay flat against his chest, how the collar sat just so against his throat.

My attention scattered further as Sebastián mentioned places I'd never heard of, throwing around terms like "Class B entities" and "metaphysical anomalies." I caught something about increased activity in Hackney, and Kit muttering some sort of moan, but it wasn't until I heard my own name that my ears pricked up.

"Rory, you're with Flynn today."

Before I could even get a proper look at my newly assigned minder's reaction to that, words tumbled out of my mouth. "Hold up. I need to lay down some ground rules."

Felix let out a snort of laughter that died the moment Sebastián's eyes flicked his way.

"First off, am I going to be locked in this creepy hotel all day, every day?" The coffee cup trembled slightly in my hand. "Because that's absolutely not happening. And..." I set my jaw, determined to get this out. I'd just started building a little life in London for myself, and I'd be damned if I'd let it all burn without a fight. "I'm supposed to be at work tomorrow. Rising Dough. I *have* to go in."

"Out of the question," Sebastián said, fingers idly trailing down his tie as if straightening an already perfect line.

"No, you don't understand. I need this job. Emma—" I swallowed hard. "I can't just disappear on them. I won't."

The silence stretched as thin as spider silk. Sebastián's dark eyes bored into mine, and I forced myself not to look away. This was my life they were mucking about with, demon or no demon.

Finally, Sebastián's shoulders dropped a fraction. "Someone will accompany you to supervise." He consulted his notebook one more time, then barked, "Right. Meeting adjourned."

I took a half-hearted step towards Rory, pausing when Sebastián blocked my path, hand outstretched. "Give me your phone."

"What? No." I clutched it to my chest like a shield. "Why can't I have it? I promise I won't go posting about demons all over the internet. Who would believe me anyway?"

"Flynn—"

"Please." My voice cracked. "There are people I need to stay in contact with." *Or, more accurately, people I* should *be staying in contact with, whom I'm merrily ignoring, but still.*

Sebastián's expression softened, and he held out his hand again. "I just want to put my number in it."

"Oh." Heat flooded my cheeks as I fumbled with my passcode. "Right. Sorry."

Sebastián's fingers brushed mine as he took the phone, and a shiver trilled up my arm. He stood so very close, and his scent washed over me—a dark, spicy cologne. Like the siren song of deep water at midnight, it pulled at something in my chest: beautiful, intoxicating, and carrying that same warning of danger. I watched as he typed at a snail's pace, trying to ignore how my heart had picked up speed, and the ridiculous side of my brain started thinking of something witty to say.

But this wasn't flirting. This was purely professional—him making sure his demon bait didn't wander off and get eaten.

"There." He handed the phone back. "Call if anything feels wrong. Anything at all."

I stared at the new contact: Sebastián Salazar. Had I been expecting anything else?

He checked his watch—a sleek vintage-looking piece with a leather strap—and I tried my very best not to get distracted by his forearms again.

"I've got my weekly call now," Sebastián said, as if I had any idea what he meant. Then, with a final, lingering look my way, he walked towards the stairs, pausing to whisper something in Rory's ear.

Judging by the way Rory rolled his eyes, it was about me. *Brilliant.*

"Right, let's go!"

I scrambled after Rory. He reached up to a high shelf on a bookcase, and my jaw dropped as it swung away from the wall to reveal a safe door like this was some sort of bloody Scooby-Doo episode.

A burst of laughter escaped my lips before I could stop it.

"Tactically unsound, isn't it?" Kit called across the basement. "Tell Seb that, would ya?"

Down more stairs, the tunnel stretched ahead, illuminated by strips of LED lights that cast everything in a clinical blue glow. Our footsteps echoed off the damp walls as we wound through what felt like half of London's underground. We finally emerged into a small private car park tucked between two buildings.

Rory beeped his keys at an ancient Ford Cortina that looked like it had been salvaged from a scrapyard. The thing was more rust than car, its once white paint now a patchy mess of orange and brown.

"Your chariot awaits." He yanked open the passenger door with a horrific screech of metal.

I slid in, trying not to think about the stains on the seats.

Rory might have noticed something on my face, because he said, "I've been telling Seb I need a company vehicle for ages, but he's refusing to buy me a nice car until I go a whole month without a speeding ticket." Rory shot me a scowl. "He's rich as fuck, so he's just doing this to be spiteful."

"He's rich?" I asked. I'm not sure why I was surprised, with all his fancy clothes. Maybe it was the whole "squatting in an abandoned hotel" thing.

"*Filthy,*" Rory replied. "I'd have him for my sugar daddy in a heartbeat, but I couldn't cope with the brooding, you know? Can you pass me my water? It's in the back."

I twisted to find Rory's back seat buried under clothes—jeans, T-shirts, and jackets strewn in chaotic piles. I located the bottle, my heart thumping a bit harder as I turned back around, very aware I was alone in a car with someone who could apparently sprout claws and rip me to shreds.

"Nice wardrobe back there." My voice came out high--pitched.

He shrugged. "Well, never know when I might need spare clothes."

"Because..." I swallowed, lowering my voice. "Because of the whole wolf thing?"

"No, for my five times a day outfit changes." Rory rolled his eyes. "Yes, because of the wolf thing."

"So you *can* change into a wolf?" The words tumbled out before I could stop them. It wasn't every day you got the opportunity to grill a supernatural entity on their existence. "Does it hurt? Do you do it all the time? Oh, and what about the whole full moon thing? And the silver bullets? Oh, god, am I being offensive?"

Rory burst out laughing as he pulled out into traffic. "Mate, you need to chill! Right, so yeah, it hurts like a bitch. Can't do it as much as I want because London's literally the worst for finding space. Full moons are proper mental. And yeah, silver's not the vibe. But listen." He shot me a sideways glance. "If you're asking whether we look anything like those janky CGI wolves from Twilight, I'm gonna have to throw you out of this car."

My cheeks burned. I'd definitely watched those films more times than I cared to admit, though I'd been more interested in the dudes without shirts on than the wolves they turned into.

I sank back into the worn leather seat, my mind whirling. Were-wolves—or whatever they called themselves—were real. Actually real. And I was sitting next to one in a rusty Ford Cortina, driving through London like it was the most normal thing in the world.

"Actually, we're heading to see a whole pack right now. Lucky you!"

"*We are?!*"

"Yeah, Dale and Mags—they're from this pack we're tight with—keep dragging us into their territory drama. Hope you've got snacks cos it's gonna be properly boring."

Rory's phone, attached to the dashboard, burst into life, its screen lighting up with "Detective Dickface." Rory's knuckles whitened on the steering wheel as he glared at the device like it had personally offended him.

The phone kept ringing.

And ringing.

My fingers twitched. The tension rolling off Rory in waves made the car feel smaller by the second. Just as I couldn't take it anymore, Rory hit the button.

"What?" he barked into the speaker. "Why are you calling me?"

"There's been a development," a male voice replied. "I know that Killigrew Street likes to know these things as soon as possible."

Rory's jaw clenched. "Why are you calling *me*?"

"Noctule isn't picking up his phone."

I tilted my head at Rory.

"Seb's code name," he muttered to me before speaking back into the phone. "He's probably still on his weekly call."

"There's another body."

The transformation in Rory was as swift as sunshine swallowed by thunderclouds. His entire body went rigid, and before I could blink, he'd yanked the steering wheel hard to the left. Horns blared as we cut across two lanes of traffic, the car swinging around in a U-turn that had me gripping my seat.

"Your usual station?"

"Yes."

"I'll be there in twenty." Rory hung up without waiting for a response. "Change of plan. Though I don't think letting you see a dead body was part of Seb's orders." Rory drummed his fingers on the steering wheel, a mischievous glint in his eye. "You should probably wait outside the room. Right?"

I rolled my eyes at Rory's tone. He wasn't really asking—just like no one had asked if I wanted to be locked in the hotel, or have my whole life turned upside down.

I stared out the window, watching London blur past. No one had actually told me how they planned to help me, yet, or what exactly would happen to me. Just vague promises and dire warnings.

"Right. Yeah." The words tasted bitter.

But then... maybe seeing this body would tell me something useful. If this was what the demon mark did, shouldn't I know exactly what I was facing?

My fingers drummed against my leg as we drove. The closer we got, the more my resolve strengthened. Everyone kept making decisions about my life—my safety, my future.

"Actually," I said, straightening in my seat, "I want to see."

Rory's eyebrows shot up. "Seb will actually murder me if he finds out I let you—"

"Let me?" I cut in. "I'm not a child. This is happening to *me*. I deserve to know what I'm up against."

A slow grin spread across his face. "Fair point. Just... promise you won't faint on me?"

I scoffed, but made no verbal promise. My heart was already racing—partly from nerves, partly from finally taking some control back.

Rory weaved through traffic with surprising skill given the state of his car, taking corners at speeds that had me gripping the door handle. "You've certainly made quite the impression on Felix," he said, changing lanes. "He was gushing about you to Priya earlier."

"He's nice." I sat up straighter. "You need to be nicer to him."

Rory's eyebrows shot up at my boldness, but his smile widened. "Noted."

"What's with the whole Noctule code-name thing?" I gestured to his phone.

"We all use them. They're all animals and *I* made them all up." He preened slightly. "Seb's is Noctule. It's a type of bat." He grinned at me like it was the most hilarious joke in existence.

"Right," I said, pretending to get it. "And what's your code name?"

His smile morphed into a scowl. "Terrier. It was revenge for Kit's being Poodle."

I burst out laughing, the mental image of the intimidating Kit being called "Poodle" too much to handle. "You're joking!"

"Kit literally threatened to end me, but everyone loved it too much. Even Seb smirked. Slightly."

The idea of these dangerous supernatural beings running around with ridiculous code names was possibly the best thing I'd heard all week.

The Cortina screeched to a halt in a definitely illegal parking spot outside Southwark Police Station, the engine's rattle dying with a wheezing cough.

"Come on." Rory hopped out, not even bothering to lock the car. "Round the back. Just so you know, Detective Dickface and I have a bit of history. And by history, I mean I properly can't stand him. Long story."

"Okay..." I wasn't particularly surprised. I'd only met him yesterday, but Rory already seemed like the sort to attract a few enemies here and there.

"I'll try and rein it in, because you're here, but no promises. Oh, and I should probably warn you, he's a telepath."

I stopped dead.

"He *says* he doesn't go poking around in our heads, but I wouldn't trust him as far as I could throw him. Which, given he's built like a brick wall, isn't very far. But you get my point."

I followed him down a narrow alley that stank of rotting rubbish and stale piss. We emerged into a small courtyard where industrial-sized bins dominated the space.

A tall Black man in glasses and a slightly rumpled suit leaned against the wall. Even with his tie askew and his wave-patterned fade growing out at the sides, he somehow radiated authority. His gaze locked onto me immediately, his eyes narrowing.

"For fuck's sake, Rory." The man pushed off from the wall. "Who the hell is this?"

"None of your business, Teddy Bear." Rory's whole demeanour had shifted, tension radiating off him in waves.

"It absolutely is my business when you bring random civilians along like it's a school trip." The detective's voice dropped dangerously low. "What were you thinking?"

"Oh right, because leaving him to wander around London by himself when there's a bloody demon hunting him is a much better plan?" Rory stepped closer, squaring up despite being nearly a foot shorter. "What would you rather, Detective—another corpse to add to your collection?"

"Another case?" The man's eyes snapped back to me, something flickering across his expression—sympathy? He stared just a touch too long. Was he trying to read my mind?

To distract him, I stuck out my hand. "Flynn Carter."

The man's grip was firm. "DI Maxwell. Theodore Maxwell."

"Otherwise known as Teddy. Teddy Bear." Rory beamed at me, and Theodore sent him a look that could have frozen Hell. "He's one of our police links."

"Let's go. But Rory?" Theodore's jaw clenched. "Next time, follow proper procedure."

"Proper procedure?" Rory's laugh was sharp enough to cut glass. "That's rich coming from you."

The air crackled between them, laden with heavy history. I shifted awkwardly.

Clearing his throat, the detective appeared to ignore the jibe. "We're lucky this one was in our borough," Maxwell said, guiding us through a back entrance. He swiped his ID badge at least three times before we reached the morgue.

The temperature plummeted at least ten degrees, and our shoes squeaked against the polished floor. A clinical smell of disinfectant burned my nostrils.

Rory lowered his voice to ask, "You sure you're up for this?" and I automatically nodded.

Then, as I took in the body-shaped lump under the white cloth, my stomach twisted with the sudden realisation that maybe I wasn't up for this after all.

Theodore drew back the cloth with a flourish.

Time seemed to stutter, like a skipping record. The woman looked to be in her forties, her dark hair fanned out across the metal slab. My brain tried to process what I was seeing while simultaneously insisting this couldn't be real—couldn't be a person. But it was. She was.

"Third one this month." Theodore's voice echoed off the tiled walls. "Same markings."

Her skin had an unnatural grey tinge that caused bile to rise in my throat, but it was her chest that was the most horrific part of it all. An intricate pattern spread across her chest like creeping frost, radiating outward from her heart. The design seemed to shift and move under the harsh fluorescent lights, though that was possibly my imagination.

The sight dragged me back to Dad's funeral. I was fifteen, staring at his too-still face in the open casket, while Katie—barely twenty and just starting her floristry career—fussed with the flower arrangements she'd insisted on doing herself. She'd filled the whole church with sea lavender and white roses, determined to make something beautiful out of something so awful. But here in this stark morgue, under harsh fluorescent lights, there was nothing gentle or beautiful about death.

"Oldest victim so far," Theodore said, reading from a notepad. "The others were all under thirty."

"Seb won't like that." Rory crossed his arms, tilting his head to one side. "Goes against some of his incubation theory."

I took a step closer, drawn by a morbid fascination with the frost-like markings. As disturbing as the thought was, they were almost... beautiful. Like the phosphorescence that sometimes painted the waves on midnight crossings—except these patterns spoke of death, not life. My gaze traced each crystalline line, and the reality of my situation began to sink in, like the slow, horrible realisation of a ship taking on water. These same marks would spread across my skin, turn me into this hollow thing before me. I'd seen enough waterlogged corpses pulled from the harbour to know death had many faces, but this... This was something else entirely.

I felt my grip on reality slipping, the rising tide of panic threatening to pull me under.

The cold hit me like a punch to the chest. My fingers went numb, ice spreading through my veins. The room tilted sideways.

"Whoa!" Rory caught my arm as my knees buckled. "Shit, shit, shit. I'm such an idiot." He guided me to a plastic chair in the corner, crouching down in front of me. "Put your head between your knees. That's it."

"I'm fine," I mumbled into my legs.

"You're not fine. I'm the world's biggest moron." Rory tapped my back in awkward pats. "I should never have let you in here. What was I thinking? I never think."

"Rory." I lifted my head. "I'm okay. It's mostly just my chest again." *Just* my chest again. Just this demonic ice creeping through my veins until I was like that woman, dead on a table.

Rory bit his lip. "Listen, when we get back… please tell Seb you waited outside? He'll properly murder me if he finds out you had a panic attack."

"This isn't a panic attack!"

Well, I was *sort of* panicking, to be fair.

"Take your pictures and notes and let's wrap this up," said DI Maxwell, though not unkindly.

I remained seated for the rest, as Rory busied himself around the body, he and Maxwell making snide comments at each other like it was a sport.

"For fuck's sake, will you back off?" Rory snapped, typing furiously on his phone. "I swear to god, if you lean any closer…"

"This is my case. I want to see what you're writing."

"No, this is a Killigrew Street matter. You're just…"

A silence stretched between them, and I wanted to sink into the wall.

"Wow." Maxwell stepped away, shaking his head. "I can't believe you."

"Stay the hell out of my head!"

I blinked. *Huh?*

"It's hard when you're shouting abuse at me. *Pet cop?* Really? After everything I do for Killigrew Street?"

Holy shit. I fought the urge to apologise to this random guy on behalf of Rory.

Maxwell's face darkened. "You know what? Fuck you. After all my hard work, after the *risks I take for you*, this is how you treat me? I've had enough of your—"

"My what?" Rory stepped closer, tilting his chin up. "Come on, say it."

"Your childish attitude." Maxwell's voice dropped dangerously low. "Your complete disregard for protocol. Your inability to follow even the most basic—"

"Oh, that's rich coming from you!" Rory jabbed a finger at Maxwell's chest. "Mr By The Book until it suits you not to be."

"That was over a year ago now! I've already apologised. There's nothing else I can do. But that whole situation was completely different!"

"Different how?" Rory's laugh was bitter. "Because you got to play the good little copper? Because you got to prove your loyalty to your precious force?"

"I did what I had to do to protect—"

"To protect what? Your precious badge?" Rory's voice rose. "While we were locked up like animals during a full moon?"

I eyed the door, just ten paces away. Perhaps now would be a great time to actually wait outside. The morgue felt smaller by the second, the fluorescent lights harsh against their angry faces.

"You broke into a secure facility!" Maxwell's composure cracked. "What was I supposed to do?"

"Your job was to protect our secret!" Rory's hands balled into fists. "Instead, you chose to protect your reputation."

"You know that I—"

"Stop!" Rory's snarl was laced with emotion that wasn't entirely anger. "Just... stop. I can't deal with your excuses right now."

I watched them bicker like it was an increasingly aggressive tennis match, my head swivelling between the two. The tension crackled, so thick you could cut it with a knife.

"Fine!" Rory shoved his phone in his pocket. "I'll email it all to you later. Happy?"

"Ecstatic," Maxwell deadpanned.

We left through the same back entrance, Rory practically vibrating with rage. The moment we were out of earshot, he exploded.

"That absolute wanker!" He paced in tight circles, running both hands through his already chaotic hair. "Can you actually believe him? The nerve of that self-righteous prick, going on about proper procedure when he—" Rory cut himself off with a sound that was distinctly inhuman, and I flinched. Was he about to wolf out on me? "He arrested both me and another shifter. Threw us in a holding cell during a full moon, of all fucking things. Ruined our investigation, just to make himself look good at the station."

"Hey." I caught his arm, the muscles under my fingers coiled tight as springs.

I stumbled back at the sound that ripped from Rory's throat—a deep, rumbling growl that sent every survival instinct in my body into overdrive. My heart leapt into my throat as his eyes flashed, something wild and decidedly not human flickering across his face.

"Shit, sorry." Rory's expression softened instantly, the anger draining away. He ran a hand through his hair again, messing it up even further. "I didn't mean to... Sometimes I forget how new you are to all this."

New? As in, yesterday?

My pulse gradually slowed as we walked back to his car in awkward silence. The moment we rounded the corner, Rory stopped dead.

"Oh, fucking great." He yanked a parking ticket from under his windscreen wiper, threw it on the ground, and kicked the front tyre with enough force to make the whole car rock. "Don't tell Seb."

He and I were quickly amassing a long list of things I wouldn't tell Sebastián about.

As we climbed into the Cortina, my chest twinged. I pressed my palm against my sternum, where the ice-cold sensation had thankfully started to fade. *For now.* The marks on that woman's body... Would that happen to me? Was I going to end up on a metal slab while Rory and Detective Maxwell argued over my corpse?

My phone buzzed in my pocket, making me jump. I pulled it out, my stomach doing an odd little somersault when I saw Sebastián's name on the screen.

Sebastián

> **Just heard you were at the police station. I sincerely hope you weren't caught in the crossfire between our resident wolf pup and 'Detective Dickface's' eternal feud. Their sexual tension gives me migraines.**

I snorted, then quickly tried to hide it as a cough when the wolf in question glanced over from the driver's seat. I stared at the message, finding my heart curiously pounding at the surprisingly friendly, conspiratorial tone.

> **I'm fine. Though I think I now understand why you pinch your nose so much.**

The reply was instant:

> **They're like children. Extremely dangerous, supernatural children with access to firearms and magical abilities.**

I bit my lip to stop from grinning. What could I say to make the conversation continue?

For entertainment purposes, of course. It could be a long car ride, after all.

> **That detective seems… intense.**

> **That's one word for it. I prefer 'human embodiment of a Monday morning.'**

A laugh escaped before I could stop it.

"What's so funny?" The driver's eyes narrowed suspiciously.

"Umm…" I shoved my phone away, probably a touch too quickly. "Just a friend."

He didn't look convinced. My phone buzzed again. I couldn't resist immediately checking it.

> **Don't let our puppy drive too recklessly. That car is held together with prayers and duct tape.**

I glanced at the dashboard, which did indeed have several strips of silver tape holding various bits in place.

> **Too late. NGL we've already broken about 15 traffic laws.**

Sebastián

> **NGL? But wonderful. I do so enjoy dealing with the police paperwork.**

The sarcasm practically dripped through the screen. Before I could reply, another message popped up:

> **Stay safe. And Flynn? Next time Rory takes you to see a dead body? Please message me first so I can murder him myself.**

Heat crept up my neck. Right. Of course he'd heard about that too.

My mind drifted back to that cold, clinical room, to those frost-like patterns that had spread across her chest like a poisoned spider's web. A map of my future, laid out in crystalline lines across someone else's skin. The image of my own body, grey and hollow on that metal slab, threatened to drag me under again.

Then I remembered the fierce grit in Sebastián's eyes when he'd promised to help me, the way his jaw had set with unwavering resolve. A thread of warmth unfurled beneath my ribs at the memory, chasing away the lingering chill.

I could picture him now, probably sitting at some fancy, organised desk he had, straightening his tie with those precise fingers as he fired off these messages. Something magnetic pulled me back towards Killigrew Street Hotel. Back to that steady gaze, that resolute promise. Because whatever this curse was trying to do to me, surely Sebastián's determination burned hotter than any demon's ice.

8

Sebastián

I scrolled through the barrage of messages I'd sent Flynn. The screen's blue light cast shadows across my desk, matching my darkening mood.

Maxwell's call still rang in my ears—his clipped tone describing how Rory had waltzed into the morgue with Flynn in tow. That audacious little wolf. I'd explicitly told him to keep Flynn away from anything he shouldn't see or hear. A corpse definitely qualified.

Three dots appeared, disappeared, then appeared again. Then nothing. The conversation was obviously closed.

So why was I still staring at the screen like I was desperate for one more sentence?

I shoved the phone into my coat pocket. I needed to focus on actual work, not obsess over Flynn. He was with Rory. Despite his many, many faults, Rory wouldn't let anything happen to him.

Kit was waiting for me by the bookcase, ready to accompany me to the family of the woman in Maxwell's morgue.

"Did you see my message about the bus?" Kit asked, adjusting his denim jacket.

I grunted, grabbing my umbrella from its stand. "It will beat an hour's walk in the sun."

The sun blazed through the hotel's grimy windows, mocking my existence. Even in autumn, its rays still burned my sensitive skin. Not enough to kill me, but enough to make me wish I could throttle whatever cosmic force decided vampires should be allergic to sunlight.

At least my coat didn't draw strange looks in October. The same couldn't be said for the umbrella on this cloudless day, but I'd learned to ignore the stares.

The bus journey stretched into an endless parade of stopping and starting, packed with an overwhelming number of people. I'd witnessed countless innovations in human transport, yet somehow we'd ended up here—still cramming ourselves into mobile metal boxes like sardines.

"Your delightful brother has been up to mischief this morning."

Kit scoffed. "So I heard. He left me a ten-minute voice message ranting about his favourite detective. Accidentally slipped in that he'd brought Flynn in to see the body. He's a prat. Sorry, boss."

"Don't apologise for him."

When Rory had followed Kit to London, Kit had warned me against giving him a place at Killigrew Street. He was too young, too impulsive. But I could also see that look in his eye—the worried brother look. The worried brother who would secretly be relieved at having Rory under his nose each day.

A few years later, Rory was less young, but no less impulsive.

The bus jolted to another stop. A wave of perfume from a new passenger made my nose twitch.

"One day he'll learn that actions have consequences," I said.

"And I can only hope I'm there to see it." Kit's laugh was tinged with warmth. "I'll take a picture for our wall."

The slightest twinge of longing shot through me, razor sharp. The brothers might scrap tooth and nail—Kit's exasperated growls a daily symphony in the halls of Killigrew Street Hotel—but their unwavering loyalty remained as constant as the moon that ruled them.

How nice it must be, I mused bitterly, to have someone in your life who remained steadfast, ready to catch you when you fell. The thought carried the weight of five hundred years of watching families grow old and fade. Of a sister's face growing increasingly distorted by time and guilt.

I pushed Magdalena's image far from my mind.

Not presently, thank you very much.

I still had a handful of days before October 31st, when it was time to open my chest once again. The stack of leather-bound journals from my human life sat there, waiting. My stomach twisted at the thought of those yellowed pages, filled with a handwriting I barely recognised as my own.

Every ten years, on the anniversary of my sister's death, I forced myself to reread them, to re-solidify the memories of that distant time. By this point in the cycle, they were hazy, smoke-like things, impressions of images rather than sharp-edged certainties. Only the guilt remained constant, a lead weight in my chest that grew heavier with each passing century.

Kit and I finally reached our stop, then a short walk later, a quiet suburban street. Identical semi-detached houses lined both sides. Number 47 had a collection of wind chimes hanging from a twisted apple tree, their gentle tinkling at odds with the gravity of our visit.

I closed my umbrella as we stepped into the shade of the porch. Kit's knuckles rapped against the red painted door, and a middle-aged man opened it, his eyes puffy and red-rimmed.

"Mr Ashworth." Sarah's—the dead woman's—husband. "Can we trouble you for a moment of your time?"

Kit and I flashed our fabricated ID badges at him. As expected, he barely glanced at them. People rarely did, especially in times of grief.

He frowned, shoulders slumping further, but wordlessly stepped aside to let us in.

The actual police had left around ninety minutes ago, according to Felix's monitoring of the Met's digital network.

Mr Ashworth led us to the kitchen table, where an elderly lady sat with an untouched mug of tea. I reached out to shake her hand.

"Detective Morris," I said smoothly, reciting the name on my badge. "And this is Detective Allan."

"Margaret. Sarah's my daughter. Was my daughter." She glanced at a family photo on the wall, where Sarah's smile beamed back at them. "Is there another update already?"

"We've just been sent to clarify a few points, ma'am."

"Let us start by offering our condolences," interjected Kit.

I nodded, leaving a slight pause. "We intend to work tirelessly to find out what happened to Sarah."

"The police just said they suspect it could be a rare poison. A toxic agent," said Mr Ashworth.

"We're hopeful the toxicology report will provide answers, and you'll be the first to know," Kit promised them.

"So what else can we help you with?" Margaret asked.

"Did Sarah mention any new people in her life recently?" I leaned forward slightly. "Perhaps someone through work, or even just a stranger who caught her attention?"

Margaret and Mr Ashworth exchanged glances before shaking their heads.

"She kept to herself mostly," he said. "She liked to be home as much as possible."

"In the weeks or days before her death, did Sarah complain about feeling unusually cold? Or perhaps experiencing vivid dreams or night-mares?"

Mr Ashworth's brow furrowed. "Nightmares? What's that got to do with it?"

"Some toxins can cause sleep disturbances," Kit explained. "It could help narrow down what we're looking for."

Margaret's hands tightened around her mug. "Now you mention it... she did call me last week. Said she couldn't sleep. Something about... about shadows moving in her room."

I caught Kit's eye.

We worked through our prepared questions methodically. Was she spending time in any new places? Had she changed her usual routine in any way?

The answers painted a picture of a woman whose life had a comfortable routine. Same route to work. Same supermarket. Same weekly call to her mother. Until the nightmares started.

Kit jotted down notes in his little black notebook, but we now both knew the truth—this was no poisoning. Sarah had been chosen by a cambion—possibly the same one that had marked Flynn.

I leaned forward in my chair, an old familiar posture that seemed to surface from somewhere in my bones. "And you're absolutely certain Sarah never mentioned feeling extremely cold?" I pressed. "Particularly around her chest area?"

Mr Ashworth shook his head. "No, nothing like that."

This made no sense. Every other symptom matched perfectly—the nightmares, the timing, the marks found on her body. The freezing sensation was always the first sign, the demon's mark spreading its poison through the victim's chest. Until they were ready to be harvested, just like Sarah had been.

And just like Flynn would be, in a matter of weeks.

My tie suddenly felt like a noose.

"Are you quite sure?" The words came out sharper than intended, my control slipping. "Think carefully. Even the smallest detail could help us." The cadence of my voice had shifted, taking on the measured tone of one who'd now spent centuries extracting truths, though not always for the right reasons.

Margaret flinched at my tone, and Mr Ashworth's face hardened. "Yes, of course I'm sure," he snapped.

Kit shot me a warning glance, and I realised I had risen slightly from my chair, looming over the grieving husband.

"What my colleague means," Kit cut in. "Is that sometimes people mention things in passing that might not seem significant at the time. We're just trying to build a complete picture of Sarah's final days."

I forced myself to step back, swallowing hard. These people had lost their daughter, their wife. They didn't deserve my frustration.

This is why Kit tended to take the lead when talking to humans. Five hundred years of witnessing humanity's grief had stripped away my ability to handle it with complete grace. Death had become a ledger entry, a problem to solve.

Perhaps that was my punishment—to spend eternity investigating deaths when I had once dealt them out so freely. The memory surfaced like a drowning man: dark robes, the scratch of quill on parchment, recording confessions in a dimly lit chamber. I had been so certain then, so righteous in my role as Inquisitor.

"We'll be off now," Kit said, and handed the man a business card. "But call this number if anything else comes to mind."

We showed ourselves out. Clouds were now hiding the sun. I pulled my coat tighter around me, but it couldn't protect me from Kit's icy stare.

The walk back to the bus stop stretched in silence. Kit's shoulders were tense—a sure sign he had something to say but was weighing his words carefully.

"Don't let Flynn Carter's residency at Killigrew Street compromise your judgement, boss."

I almost stopped walking. "What?"

"Seven years I've served at Killigrew Street. In all that time, fewer than five individuals have been granted quarters upstairs."

"And?" It had made the most sense to me, after witnessing how little regard he spared for his own safety, to place him at the hotel.

"You're showing concern for the lad, that's all. Checked your mobile twenty times during transport, and you typically despise the device."

He wasn't wrong. My mobile phone confounded me with all of its silly features.

"And last night, in the kitchen—"

"It's my job to protect him. To save him." I fought to keep my voice level. "And yours, for that matter."

"You're normally unfond of random humans, but you're different around him. And the way he regards you..." Kit's lips twitched. "Have you noticed?"

"What do you mean?" I asked cooly.

"Most civilians fear you initially. Or at minimum show proper caution. He... well, he doesn't. Even after the firearms discharge and that failed extraction outside his residence."

"What's your point?"

"Just watching your six, that's all." Kit's expression shifted into something I couldn't quite read. Something knowing, tinged with concern. "We might *not* be able to save him, you know."

The thought speared ice through my own chest.

"That's hardly a helpful attitude," I snapped, before storming ahead. Which wasn't childish at all.

Kit jogged to catch up. "Aye, understood," he conceded. "I apologise for raising the matter. Don't mistake me—he seems a decent lad. Sweet, even."

He was sweet. Cinnamon-sugar sweet. As well as disarmingly earnest and rather attractive.

I banished the thought immediately. Flynn was under my protection, and I was more than capable of maintaining professionalism.

Even if he was the most exquisite temptation.

Even if every fibre of my being ached to taste him.

The scratch of my fountain pen against paper was the only sound in my blissfully quiet office. Well, that and the soft hum of the laptop that Felix had foisted on me—the laptop that now displayed nothing but a frozen screen mid-sentence.

Annoyance swirled inside me.

"Felix," I barked into the intercom system, holding the button for his tiny room. "Your stupid machine has frozen again."

It crackled back, and for a moment all I heard was laughter.

"What?"

I could barely hear Felix's voice over the raucousness.

"What's going on?"

"Oh, it's just Rory and Flynn."

"What?"

More distorted laughter.

"Huh? What was that?"

My annoyance curdled into anger.

"Felix, have you considered telling them to be quiet so that you can listen to the instructions of your superior?" Before he could attempt to reply, I said, "I give up. I'm just going to bring it down to you."

I disconnected the machine, gathered my possessions, and stomped down to the basement.

By the time I'd gotten down there, Felix must have tipped Rory off to my mood, because he was sitting on the sofa, blond hair chaotically disheveled, typing away on his own machine, face perfectly straight.

Flynn sat opposite him, eyes darting between Rory and me, biting down on his bottom lip.

Rory didn't glance up, not even when I moved to stand right in front of him.

I glared at Rory, who continued typing with exaggerated focus, his fingers tap-tap-tapping away at his keyboard. The sound instantly grated against my nerves.

I coughed.

Tap-tap-tap.

I coughed again.

Tap-tap-tap.

Flynn shifted in his seat, his gaze bouncing between us in time with his hands twisting in his lap.

"Rory."

Tap-tap-tap.

That was it. I tolerated a lot from my Killigrew Street team, but outright insubordination was too much.

"Rory, go and wait in my office. Now!"

"Wait!" Flynn burst out. "It's not his fault!"

I turned to him, brows drawing together. "What?"

"The dead body thing." Flynn's voice wavered. "He didn't want me to see it."

I narrowed my eyes.

"It's true!" Flynn leaned forward. "I insisted that I go in. I felt like... like I deserved to know what might happen to me." He touched his chest, and I couldn't help but soften slightly.

"Even if that's true," I said. "Rory shouldn't have allowed it."

Our younger wolf *finally* turned his head towards me. "You're right. I was out of line. I'm sorry. It won't happen again."

I paused, awaiting some sort of punch line.

"I promise. And Flynn's totally lying to cover my ass."

Flynn groaned softly, hiding his face with his hand.

"I'm aware," I snapped. "I'm not a complete fool."

Behind me, Felix coughed, holding out his hands for the laptop stowed under my arm. I wordlessly passed it to him.

"You've tried turning it on and off again, yeah?"

Oops.

I held out my hand to take it back.

A snort of laughter from the sofa—I pivoted to find Flynn with his hand over his mouth. "I can probably help him, Felix, if you have work to do."

Felix appeared relieved and scurried away, and Flynn shuffled across the sofa, patting the space beside him. My throat tightened—I hadn't drunk yet today, and the proximity would be... challenging. But his expectant look made refusing impossible, so I lowered myself onto the cushion, maintaining a careful distance.

I passed him the laptop, and Flynn reached for it, his fingers—soft, impossibly soft—grazing mine in a way that I could have sworn seemed deliberate. He kept his hand still for just a fraction of a second, and the warm touch sent an electric current through my cold skin.

Then it was over, and he swiftly opened the laptop, staring intently at the screen. I tried to watch what he was doing, but the warmth radiating from his body was incredibly distracting. As was his scent. And his soft fingers dancing across the keyboard.

I clasped my hands together, focusing on anything else—the tap of keys, the whir of computer fans, Rory's continued presence on the other sofa.

A few clicks later, and the screen flickered back to life.

"There we go." Flynn's smile lit up his whole face. "Just needed a restart."

"But why can't they make them so they don't freeze? We've sent men to the moon, for Christ's sake!"

His laugh burst forth—rich and genuine, starting deep in his chest before bubbling up into something lighter, more musical. It transformed his features, softening the subtle lines adorning his forehead. His knee shifted, pressing against mine, and the contact sent tingles shooting through my leg.

"You remind me of my grandfather."

The insult shouldn't have sounded flirtatious, but paired with the way his eyes crinkled at the corners, the slight bite of his lower lip, and that deliberate press of his knee against mine...

"Ha!" Rory's voice made me flinch. "Flynn, make sure you don't use text speak if you ever message Seb. He refuses to learn even the most basic of acronyms."

"I do not *refuse to learn*," I seethed. "I simply refuse to give in to the ridiculous notion that we can't type in full sentences!"

Flynn's leg *still* remained glued to mine, his whole body shaking with suppressed laughter. The warmth of his thigh burned through the fabric of my trousers, each tiny movement raising every hair on my body. His scent—sweet, alive, intoxicating—filled my lungs with every breath.

I couldn't focus. My thoughts scattered like leaves in a strong wind, replaced by base instincts I fought to suppress. The hunger clawed at my insides as my gums tingled.

"I can make you a little chart, like I made my grandpa," Flynn said, shoulder bumping mine as he closed the laptop.

The casual touch threatened my control. I gripped the edge of the sofa, wood creaking beneath my fingers. "As delightful as that sounds," I said, forcing my voice to remain steady. "I've witnessed the evolution of countless languages, so deciphering whether LOL means laugh out loud or lots of love is, quite frankly, beneath my level of intelligence."

Flynn laughed then—louder this time, a booming sound that lit up his whole face, his head tipping back in ecstatic joy. The sight struck something in me. My eyes fixed on the vulnerable curve of his throat, that delicate patch of skin where his pulse fluttered like a trapped bird. The urge to taste him there, to feel his laughter vibrate against my lips, crashed through me with devastating force. To press my mouth to that spot and drink in the sound, the life, the warmth of him...

I forced my gaze away, my fangs threatening to extend. "How's your chest?" I asked, mostly to remind myself of why he was here, in my hotel.

Flynn's hand went straight to his heart, fingers playing with the material of his oversized green jumper. "It's... alright now. There was another episode, though, back in the morgue."

"Was it the same severity?" I shifted to face him properly, ignoring how the movement brought us closer together. "The same length?"

Flynn's fingers twisted further in his jumper. "I... I don't know. Maybe? It's hard to think about all that when it's happening."

"You need to start logging these episodes." I patted my coat for a notepad, but found none. "Time, duration, severity. Text it to me every time, and I'll write it all down. Every detail matters."

"Right." Flynn's voice trembled. "Because if they get worse, that means..."

"Don't think about that." The words came out sharp.

His blue eyes met mine, wide and vulnerable. "But there's no point—"

"We're not letting it get that far." I fisted my hands into balls, lest they reach out to comfort him. "I need you to record everything. Even the smallest twinge. Can you do that for me?"

Flynn nodded, but his face had fallen further into a frown.

Thump thump thump

My eyes fell straight to Flynn's chest. His heart rate had quickened, along with his breathing, his chest rising and falling rapidly. His hand pressed harder against his sternum.

"Is it happening now?"

Another nod, more frantic this time.

"Look at me." I caught his chin, tilting his face up. "Focus on my voice. You're safe here."

His pulse raced beneath my fingers, but his eyes locked onto mine with startling intensity. The fear in them slowly gave way to something else—trust, perhaps. Or hope. The change was subtle but profound, like watching dawn break over dark waters.

"I'm going to die, aren't I?" The words were barely a whisper.

"No." I kept my voice firm, certain. "I won't let that happen."

The tension in his shoulders eased slightly. His breathing steadied, syncing with my performative exhalations. That look remained in his Delft-blue eyes—complete faith that I could, *would*, save him.

"Okay," he whispered.

It hit me like a freight train. The weight of his trust. The responsibility of it. The way he looked at me like I was his salvation.

Saving lives was my job, the very purpose of Killigrew Street—my penance for all the lives I'd taken. So why did this feel different?

Something about his trust cut deeper than duty, past my carefully constructed walls.

I'd saved countless lives, yet none of them had ever looked at me quite like this.

This beautiful, fragile human who was looking at me like I could protect him from each and every darkness this cruel world might throw at him.

It made me want to be worthy of that look, more than anything.

9

Sebastián

I couldn't stop staring at him.

It was like he was a magnet and I was a helpless piece of metal being pulled towards him.

This was exactly why I'd sent Priya to the bakery to watch Flynn for the last two days. Then, this morning, I'd found myself announcing it was my turn.

The bakery buzzed with the usual weekday crowd. The scent of fresh bread hung thick in the air, almost—but not quite—masking the intoxicating smell of Flynn's blood.

"*You?*" Flynn had said in the morning briefing. "Don't you have... um... more important things to do?"

Yes. Yes, I did.

I'd brought some work with me, but the bakery was proving to be fairly distracting.

Flynn was proving to be fairly distracting.

Why was it that his blood sang to me so sweetly, unlike his friend Emma's, who worked alongside him? Or any of the customers, for that matter—sat far closer to me than he was.

Despite not actually being allowed to bake the bread, Flynn's apron was dusty with flour. He scratched his nose, brushing a thin white layer onto it, and I smiled. Glancing up, he caught my eye, and quickly looked away. A blush crept up his neck.

My fingers tightened around my pen as I forced my attention back to my notepad. Yet every few seconds, my gaze drifted back to Flynn as if drawn by an invisible thread.

The way he moved with such careful precision, the slight furrow in his brow as he concentrated on his work, the curve of his neck when he bent to check the oven...

His gentle patience with flustered customers. The way he did this little shimmy dance between the counter and kitchen when he thought nobody was looking, somehow managing to rescue Emma's forgotten timer while plating his own orders.

Warmth poured from him like the sun—the dangerous, devastating sun—from his bright eyes, his infectious smile.

After two decades of control, I'd thought myself immune to such base attractions. Yet here I sat, reduced to an infatuated teenager, unable to tear my eyes away from a human who'd stumbled into my world a handful of days ago.

Again, I forced my gaze down, but a shadow soon fell across my papers. The scent of freshly buttered toast wafted towards me, mingling with Flynn's unique aroma. I glanced up.

Flynn stood there, plate in hand, a wicked glint in his oh-so-blue eyes. "Sir, these seats are for paying customers. I'm going to need you to buy something, or I'll have to kick you out."

The corner of my mouth twitched.

I reached for my wallet, making a show of eyeing the toast with exaggerated scrutiny. "But that's not what I ordered!"

Flynn blinked a few times before he quickly recovered. "Oh, silly me. Please forgive me, sir." The menace then batted his eyelashes at me, and I had to force myself not to react. "What was your order?"

"One cinnamon roll."

For a moment, I expected his eyes to widen—for him to have read my mind.

Because I didn't want a cinnamon roll to eat it, of course.

The truth was far more pathetic—I simply wanted something that reminded me of his scent. Something I could take back to room 210 and keep on my desk to indulge in privately, letting the aroma wash over me while pretending I wasn't behaving like a lovesick fool.

"Huh." His head tilted to one side. "I didn't peg you to have a sweet tooth."

"Flynn!" Emma shouted. "I need you." She glowered between the two of us. I wasn't quite sure how Flynn had managed to explain my presence.

"Sorry," he said to me, flashing a grin. "I had to tell her you're weirdly obsessed with me, and that's why you're back again."

Ah. Not far from the truth, then.

I groaned. "I'm surprised she hasn't tried to kick me out."

"I've had to make a show of loving it," he replied. "I've been quite convincing so far."

With that, he twisted on one foot, returning moments later with my cinnamon bun. I waited until he went to the kitchen before I wrapped it up for my bag.

The day dragged by like treacle. After several more cups of coffee I sipped at, I left before closing to let them clean in peace. The ancient oak tree across the street provided decent cover while I waited, its branches casting long shadows in the setting sun.

It was blissfully dark when Flynn finally emerged from Rising Dough, pulling his corduroy jacket tight against the autumn chill. He crossed the street, heading straight for me.

"Look, Emma saw you creepily hanging out under this tree watching us, and now she's even more freaked out. She didn't believe me when I tried to convince her I was wrong about you firing a gun that night before she arrived. Anyway, she was insisting she had to walk me home, so I've had to tell her you're taking me on a date." He wrung his hands. "I have to message her every hour to prove I'm alive."

My chest tightened. *A date.* The word hung between us, loaded with promise. "And what made you choose that particular excuse?"

He shrugged, not meeting my eyes. "It fit with you lurking in the bakery all day."

"It was hardly lurking."

"It absolutely was. Especially with your brooding expression."

I ignored the jab. "Well, I was actually going to suggest we take a longer route back to Killigrew Street. There's a pleasant spot not far from here that you probably haven't seen yet."

"That wouldn't be difficult." Flynn kicked at a loose stone. "Mostly, all I've seen of London is my creepy apartment, the bakery, and your hotel. Which is also creepy."

The hairs on the back of my neck suddenly prickled. That sensation of being watched—so similar to the other day—crept over me again, making my shoulders tense. Across the street, in the gap between two buildings, I caught a glimpse of that impossible creature again. Even in the poor light, I could make out its distinctive silhouette—the sloping back, the massive head. The hyena stood perfectly still, a darker shadow among shadows. Those unnatural yellow eyes fixed on me with uncanny intelligence.

"Seb?" Flynn said, hesitant, unsure.

I blinked, and the beast was gone. Was I finally losing my mind? First at the hospital, now here... I forced my lips into a smile. "Follow me."

I led Flynn through the winding streets, him filling the silence with chatter about his day. He stopped abruptly as we passed a darkened florist, its windows still displaying the day's remaining blooms beneath the glow of a street lamp.

"My sister would love this place," he said softly, reaching for his phone. His fingers hovered over the camera button, screen illuminating his face in the darkness. Then something shifted in his expression—a flicker of pain—and he shoved the device back into his pocket. "She's got her own flower shop, back home. Nowhere near as posh as this, mind, but..." He trailed off, shoulders hunching as he stepped away from the window.

As we neared our destination, tension coiled within me. Going to my tiny secret marina had seemed great in theory—the perfect spot to show him a different side of the city—but with each step closer, doubt gnawed at my insides.

I'm a fool. A complete and utter fool.

Flynn had moved here from Braymore Bay. A coastal town. With boats. And here I was, dragging him to look at more vessels in the dark and cold like some inconsiderate ass.

"It's just around this corner," I managed, my voice tight. Perhaps we could turn back, find somewhere else...

But Flynn had already rounded the bend. He halted abruptly, and my dead heart plummeted.

The marina stretched before us, its waters dark and still. Lights from the surrounding buildings and boats reflected off the surface like scattered stars, creating mirror images that danced with each ripple. The old warehouse conversions loomed above, their windows warm and inviting.

I opened my mouth to apologise, to suggest we leave, but Flynn's face lit up.

"Wow, this is gorgeous. And so quiet. It's perfect." He moved closer to the water's edge, peering at the boats. Then he stopped dead, his breath catching. "Oh my god, is that... that's a Hallberg-Rassy 40C."

The reverence in his voice made me pause. I followed his gaze to where a sleek vessel bobbed gently in its berth, its navy-blue hull gleaming under the marina lights. Even to my untrained eye, there was something distinguished about it—an elegant marriage of craftsmanship and purpose.

"She's my dream boat," Flynn breathed, taking an unconscious step forward. His fingers curled around the railing. "Well, one of them. But she's the perfect offshore cruiser. You could sail anywhere in her. Absolutely anywhere." He gave a soft, self-deprecating laugh. "Obviously, she's absolutely out of my price range. We're talking half a million, easy."

I blinked, caught off guard by his enthusiasm. "Really?" That seemed steep. "I know nothing about boats." I knew I'd travelled to England on a ship, hundreds of years ago, but that was mostly from my diaries, not a concrete memory.

"Nothing? Well, you see that..." Flynn's voice washed over me like waves against the shore as he explained the intricacies of navigation systems and hull designs. His hands moved animatedly, painting pictures in the air as he spoke. The marina lights caught in his hair, turning the messy strands to silver, while shadows danced across his face.

"—and see how the stern swoops down? That's because—"

"Mmm?" I leaned against the railing beside him, closer than was strictly necessary.

The excitement radiating from him was intoxicating. His whole being seemed to light up, and I found myself captivated not by the boats, but by the way his eyes sparkled when he described their features. The slight Irish lilt in his voice grew stronger with his enthusiasm, and my chest ached with a warmth I thought I'd buried long ago.

"—which means you can handle pretty much any weather—" He paused mid-gesture, his hand dropping. "God, I'm sorry. I'm boring you to death, aren't I?"

"Not at all." I shifted to face him properly. "It's delightful to see someone so passionate about something."

"But you haven't understood a word I've said."

"That's irrelevant." I smiled, hoping to ease his sudden self-consciousness. "I may not follow the technical details, but I understand the feeling behind them. The way you describe these boats... it's like poetry."

Flynn ducked his head. "Anyway... I must say, I won't miss cleaning the decks with sand and oil each summer. Though nothing beats the satisfaction when you're all done and it's gleaming."

"So, you didn't leave Braymore to get away from all the boats?" I said it with a jesting tone, but in truth, I found myself more and more curious about Flynn and where he'd come from.

Flynn's smile turned wistful. "The boats were never the problem." He leaned against the railing, gazing out across the dark water. "Being out at sea... There's nothing like it. The way the world just opens up around you. No walls, no boundaries. Just endless horizon in every direction." His voice took on a dreamy quality. "Sometimes, when the weather's perfect and you catch the wind just right, it feels like you could sail forever."

An endless abyss sounded fairly horrific to me, but I appreciated his passion.

"But..." He trailed off, shoulders tensing. "Some things happened back home. All at once. And I needed to get away. Quickly."

The sharp buzz of his phone cut through the peaceful atmosphere. Flynn pulled it from his pocket, grimacing at the screen before silencing it.

"They all keep calling me about it, actually." He shoved the phone back into his jacket. "I just can't bring myself to deal with it. I know that makes me a coward, running away like this."

"No." The word came out sharper than I intended, and Flynn startled slightly. I softened my tone. "Running away and choosing to remove yourself from a harmful situation are very different things."

God knows I'd done enough running in my centuries of existence to recognise the difference.

"I didn't say it was a harmful situation," Flynn said carefully, gaze locked onto mine. The marina's lights caught the vulnerability in his eyes before he could mask it, like moonlight breaking through storm clouds.

"You didn't need to." I could tell from the tight set of his jaw whenever his reason for moving came up. "And sometimes distance is exactly what you need to heal. There's nothing cowardly about protecting yourself."

Flynn's eyes met mine, searching. Whatever he found there made his shoulders relax slightly.

"You sound like you're speaking from experience."

"Perhaps." I offered him a small smile. "But we're talking about you right now."

Eyes widening, Flynn stepped towards me, and his scent hit me like a tidal wave. The cold night air had chilled his skin, but his gloriously warm blood still sang beneath the surface, sugar-sweet and tempting. My fangs ached. I gripped the railing harder, willing myself to stay perfectly still.

"Well, I want to hear more about you," Flynn said, moving closer still.

My body threatened to betray me, threatened to lean towards him like a flower to the sun.

Panic clawed at my chest. What had I been thinking, bringing him here? The setting that bordered on romantic, the intimate conversation... I'd created the perfect atmosphere, planting more seeds in Flynn's head for something that could never be.

The metal railing creaked under my grip. I forced my fingers to relax before I left dents in it.

This was selfish. Cruel to him, but also to myself, getting closer to him when our orbits were so temporarily aligned.

But it was hard to remember that when Flynn's proximity sent electricity crackling across my skin. His warmth radiated towards me like a beacon in the darkness. My gaze dropped to Flynn's lips, and centuries-old hunger stirred deep in my gut. Not just for blood, but for connection. For touch.

Though twenty years wasn't nearly long enough to forget how thoroughly love could destroy you. For over twenty long years, I'd starved myself of any human touch, intimacy, or sex. After James... I'd sworn that was the end of anything like that for me. The pain of loss had carved too deep a wound. I'd told myself I could live without those things—*had* to live without those things.

The hunger gnawing at my insides was proof enough of why. That monstrous part of me wanted nothing more than to sink my teeth into Flynn's throat, to taste what I'd been denying myself.

Flynn didn't even know what I was. Didn't know that every time he stepped closer, my fangs threatened to descend. Didn't understand that the hunger I felt wasn't just intense physical attraction, but something far more dangerous.

"Well?" Flynn said, his voice warm like melted honey, sweet with promises. His fingers found my tie, smoothing down the silk with a touch so light it was almost reverent. "Tell me about yourself, Sebastián Salazar."

Oh, Flynn. You deserve so much better than lies.

I gripped the railing tighter, steeling myself to put some distance between us before my control slipped completely. The phantom warmth of his fingers against my chest was already too much.

"I think we sh—"

Something darted at the edge of my vision—my only warning. Before I could react, a figure launched itself at Flynn from the shadows, slamming into him with inhuman force.

Flynn let out a strangled cry as he was wrenched backwards, the assailant's arm locking around his throat. His head snapped back, hair gripped in a vicious fist, exposing the creamy column of his neck.

Fangs glinted in the dim light, poised to tear into Flynn's flesh.

It took me a disorienting second to recognise the fledgling vampire restraining him—Eliza, a reckless newborn I'd been monitoring. One of Marcus Vale's clan. A constant thorn in my side, they were a group of feral vampires who rejected my ideals of civilised existence. I'd still never met Marcus Vale, only dealt with the fallout of his actions.

"Why are you allowed such pretty things when you claim the rest of us should suffer?" she hissed at me, her words slurred with frenzy. "Tell me!"

Eliza's grip tightened on Flynn, her gaze wild and unfocused. She nuzzled against his throat, panting like a rabid animal scenting its prey.

The scent of Flynn's fear cut through the night, sharp and cloying. My fangs descended instantly, the predator in me roaring to life at the threat.

Time seemed to grind to a halt as my gaze locked with Flynn's. Terror flooded his eyes, raw and visceral, as he took in the full sight of my extended fangs, his heart pounding like a captured rabbit.

The world ceased to exist beyond the two of us.

In that infinite moment, I saw every flicker of emotion play across his features—shock, confusion, dawning realization. Eliza's grip was an iron vice around his throat, yet Flynn remained perfectly still, paralyzed by the monster I had become in front of him.

My own reflection stared back at me from the depths of his eyes—a twisted, inhuman thing. A predator, poised to strike. The truth about what I was had never felt so real as it did seeing the naked fear etched onto Flynn's face.

Well, he'd already seen the truth of it now.

I had nothing left to hide.

In a blur of motion, I launched myself across the marina's walkway, crashing into Eliza with enough force to send her reeling. Her sharp nails raked across my cheek as she lost her grip on Flynn, but I barely registered the sting.

Flynn crumpled to the ground with a cry, scrambling back against the railing. His eyes were wide, one hand clutched to his throat as if he could still feel Eliza's grip there.

"Flynn!" I barked his name, the sound tearing from my chest with more desperation than I intended as I stepped in front of him. "Stay there." I couldn't have him running off—Eliza's associates could be waiting around any corner.

I didn't dare look at Flynn again, focusing every shred of my being on the threat before me.

Eliza whirled, lips peeled back in a snarl, every muscle tensed to attack. "Well, *Black*?" She spat the name I used when dealing with her kind. "Wait until I tell Marcus about this! You strut around London telling us to control ourselves, trying to suggest we drink from *bags*, to deny our nature, while you keep a pretty pet for yourself? I'm still waiting for your answer! What makes you so special that you get to feast while the rest of us starve? Or do rules only apply to the rest of us *lesser* vampires?"

"Eliza!" I snarled, unable to control my anger. How dare she manhandle Flynn like a ragdoll, and how dare she tear away any chance for me to tell him the truth in my own way? "You need to calm down. That man is an innocent human. He knows nothing of the world of vampirism, and you're scaring him."

"Innocent?" She looked behind me to Flynn, then her eyes locked challengingly on mine. "You expect me to believe you haven't had a taste? Or are you saving him? Keeping him fresh?" She laughed maniacally, the sound awakening an urge to rip out her tongue and end her taunts permanently. "Maybe I should show you what it's like to have something precious taken away. To be forced to watch while someone you care for is slaughtered."

Jason. That was the true reason for her rage tonight. She was grieving her fledgling lover who'd torn out a homeless man's throat just two weeks ago. I'd been forced to put Jason down while she watched in the corner, restrained. I'd given Jason two warnings about controlling his bloodlust, more chances than I usually allowed. But the third victim... I remembered finding the body, blood painting the warehouse walls. There had been no choice after that. The weight of signing his execution order still haunted me, as did Eliza's screams. Now here she was, wild with grief, revenge, and hunger, threatening to make me understand her loss.

"We're done being controlled by you, Black!"

I moved before she had the chance. One second I stood across from her, the next I had her pinned against the railing. She struggled, so I slammed her head into the metal, her skull smashing it with a *crack.*

She only grinned, thrilled by the show of violence.

Keeping her restrained with one hand, I drew my wicked dagger from my coat and pressed the silver blade to her throat. As a fledging vampire, she was blessed with incredible strength, but it was no match for mine.

"Don't give me no choice but to end you," I snarled, so close I could smell the lingering traces of her last victim on her breath.

For a stretched moment, Eliza stared back at me, lips still twisted in that mocking smile.

Then Eliza went slack in my grasp, her mocking smile fading. She raised her palms in a gesture of surrender.

Relief coursed through me as I inched back, lowering the blade slightly. Perhaps she'd finally regained some semblance of control over her feral urges. I opened my mouth, ready to order her to leave the area before—

My thoughts were cut off by Flynn's squeak of terror as Eliza struck like a viper, lunging towards him. He tumbled backwards onto the ground, Eliza's weight slamming on top of him as she pinned him down.

"No!" The anguished cry tore from my lips.

Eliza leaned down, her fangs extended towards the tender skin of Flynn's throat as he thrashed beneath her.

In that moment, all restraint, all control, fled me. A crimson haze of fury descended as the predator within raged at the threat to what was *mine*. My fingers found purchase on Eliza's throat, wrenching her back with all my strength.

She didn't even have time to react before I snapped her neck with a sickening crunch of bone. Her body went limp in my grasp, but it wasn't enough. I had to be sure.

I slashed the silver blade across her throat in one vicious stroke, her head lolling to the side as I severed her spinal cord. Thick, cold arterial blood sprayed across my face and coat, but I barely registered it through the haze of wrath consuming me.

It was over in seconds, though it felt like an eternity. Silence descended once more over the marina as Eliza's body crumpled to the ground.

I stared at my bloodied hands, the dagger still clutched in one fist. Slowly, far too slowly, the red haze receded from the edges of my vision.

Flynn. I had to get to Flynn.

I whirled to find him still sprawled on the ground where Eliza had tackled him, his eyes wide with a mixture of shock and terror. For twelve beats of his terrified heart, we simply stared at one another across the distance, the night air crackling with tension.

Then Flynn scrambled up and backwards, boots scuffing against the concrete until his back hit the railing behind him. He stared at me—the monster I had so dramatically revealed myself to be.

"Flynn..." My voice faltered as I took a halting step towards him. "I... I need to explain... But please don't run, it's not safe."

He flinched back violently, curling in on himself. I froze in place, something inside me shattering at his reaction.

Of course he would recoil from me. What human wouldn't after witnessing such savagery?

As much as I wanted to attend to him, to focus only on *him*, I had a rather pressing problem on my bloodied hands. With one arm, I wrenched Eliza's body up, while with the other, I jammed the speed-dial button for Kit on my phone, that Felix had installed for me.

I easily lifted Eliza's corpse and held it aloft, her head slouching sickeningly to the side.

"There's been an incident," I barked into my phone. "I need a body bag at my location immediately. Bring Terrier and the van."

"On it."

Kit hung up, and I turned my attention back to the body. I studied her face—the first time I'd seen it at peace rather than twisted with rage or hunger. A pang of sadness pierced through the storm raging inside me.

Eliza had been newly turned, just a fledgling struggling to adapt to her heightened senses and ravenous appetites. It was only the vaguest impression of a memory, but I could understand her torment from my own turbulent beginnings.

The thirst, the confusion, losing identity and purpose—it drove many new vampires into fits of violence and depravity before they learned control.

If only Marcus Vale cared enough about his loyal clan of worshippers to actually teach them...

No. I couldn't dwell on what-ifs now. Eliza had made her choices, had refused my attempts to teach her restraint. Threatening an innocent human, *my* human, was unforgivable.

My human.

I forced the possessive thought away. *The product of bloodlust and adrenaline.*

A flicker of movement in my periphery drew my attention. A couple further down the marina promenade, walking this way. I had to act quickly. As gently as possible, I flung Eliza's body over the railing and onto the deck of the nearest yacht.

She hit the boat with a slap, the waves lapping against the vessel as it rocked in the water.

I was absolutely covered in Eliza's gore. As disgusting as the idea was, if Flynn wasn't there, I might have been tempted to lick some from my ruined clothes. While not as substantial as human blood, it would certainly do in a pinch.

And I *was* starving, the kind of gnawing emptiness that couldn't be ignored, as much as I wished to.

My gaze flickered to where Flynn huddled against the railing, arms wrapped tightly around himself. He was staring at the mangled corpse facing upward on the deck, a look of abject horror etched across his features.

The couple drew closer, and I had to resist snapping at Flynn to act natural. If they noticed anything amiss, I'd have to resort to my psychic influence—a subtle mind trick that would alter the last few minutes of their memories, compel them swiftly on their way.

Thankfully, Flynn seemed to register the approaching couple through his shock. He mechanically adopted a casual position, though his eyes remained glazed and distant.

Once we were in the clear, he let out a ragged, choked sound that seemed torn from somewhere deep within him. His entire body trembled visibly, his knees appearing to barely support his weight.

"I think this time, I might actually have a panic attack," he whispered.

"Flynn..." I took a tentative step forward, hands raised in a pacifying gesture. I wanted nothing more than to go to him, to wrap him in my arms and shield him from this nightmare he'd been plunged into against his will. To reassure him that despite my horrific actions, I would never allow harm to come to him. But one look at the way he cringed from my approach told me that any attempt at comfort would only backfire. "I know that was... a lot to take in. But I need you to stay calm and let me explain—"

"You're—" he began, then stopped, swallowing hard. His gaze kept darting between my face and the bloodied corpse on the yacht, as if unable to fully process either sight. "Why didn't you tell me?"

The question shocked me into silence.

Because I didn't want this very reaction, not when I was enjoying the way you smiled at me so often.

"I was… getting around to it," I suggested, the sentence sounding weak to my own ears.

"You told me about Kit and Rory." Hurt leaked into his words. "I thought you were a human, like me!"

Yes, but they turn into fluffy wolves and I'm a bloodsucking monster.

"It wasn't necessary for you to know."

Ouch. That sounded harsh to my own ears. I bit the inside of my cheek, panic rising.

"Right." Flynn laughed hollowly.

"Please…" I half rasped, hands trembling at my sides. What was I so afraid of? "Let me take you back to Killigrew Street, once Kit arrives to help. We can talk more there."

Flynn didn't respond immediately. His gaze remained locked on the grisly mess on the yacht, his expression vacant, as if part of him had retreated somewhere far away from this horror.

After what felt like an eternity, he gave the smallest of nods. I wanted to collapse with relief, but held myself rigid.

Through the reek of Eliza's blood, another scent cut through—sweeter, more tempting. The forbidden fruit, a mere metre from me.

"You're bleeding," I whispered.

For one horrible second, I thought Eliza might have succeeded in getting her fangs into him, but then he turned to face me, tilting his face up. Across one side of his chin was a light graze.

"I…" he started, then seemed to lose his train of thought, his hand rising to touch the wound as if just becoming aware of it. "It's just a scratch."

I couldn't help it. My hand shot out, my thumb gently swiping across the length of his wound. I half expected him to flinch away from me, but instead he kept quite still.

The blood on my thumb sang to me, a siren's call. The hunger coiled within me like a serpent, hissing and ravenous, desperate to be sated.

I shouldn't have even considered it. I should've wiped it on my coat. Flynn had just witnessed me tear another vampire apart. His heart still thundered with fear, his breath coming in short gasps. What would he think of this?

But the droplet called to me like nothing ever had before.

My thumb drifted towards my mouth of its own accord. Flynn's eyes tracked the movement, his pupils blown wide. The scent grew stronger as I brought it closer, making my head swim.

I dragged my tongue across the pad of my thumb.

Fuck.

Flavour exploded across my tongue—rich, complex notes I'd forgotten existed. Heat bloomed in my chest, spreading through my limbs like wildfire. This wasn't just blood. This was *ambrosia*.

There was something else too—a peculiar undercurrent that made my tongue tingle, like tasting lightning. Something... *different*. Though the thought dissolved as quickly as it came. After so long surviving on cold, lifeless sustenance, of course fresh blood would feel electric.

My fangs raged at me, demanding I pierce flesh rather than settle for this meagre taste. Every cell in my ancient body screamed at me to take more, to feast properly.

Why did he have to taste this extraordinary?

A hot rush of need surged through my lower half, and to my absolute horror, I felt myself... *responding*. *No.* Not here, not now, not while I was covered in Eliza's blood and Flynn was on the verge of a panic attack.

But my body betrayed me, my length hardening against my will as Flynn lingered on my tongue.

Mortification crashed over me as I saw myself through his eyes—a monster with blood still coating my clothes, getting aroused from a mere taste of his essence. What must he think of me? How could I have let myself lose control like this?

I jerked my hand away from my mouth, shame burning through me. "I... apologise. That was... inappropriate."

Flynn stared at me, his expression unreadable. Something flickered in his eyes—not fear, exactly, but something deeper, more complex. For several long moments, he remained utterly still, as if trapped between conflicting impulses.

"Are you okay?" Flynn stepped towards me, deep crevices splitting across his forehead. "Are you... *hungry?*"

"Yes," I quietly admitted. *Always.* "But please believe I will not hurt you."

He moved closer still, his movements slow and dreamlike. He reached for my thumb, still wet from my mouth, his hand trembling visibly.

"What are you doing?" Though I'd sooner throw myself into the water than harm him, his proximity was torture.

I watched, transfixed, as Flynn's fingers traced over his graze with deliberate intent, pressing to draw more blood. My throat constricted at the sight, hunger clawing at my insides with renewed ferocity.

When he rubbed my thumb over his chin, bloodying it as much as possible, then pushed it towards my mouth, I should have resisted. Should have shoved him away, explained that this was dangerous, reckless. Instead, I remained frozen as he brought my hand to my parted lips, his eyes meeting mine with a mixture of fear and fascination.

The second taste was even more intoxicating than the first. A soft moan escaped me before I could contain it, the flavour overwhelming my senses.

"Flynn, you need to stop." The words came out rough, strained.

"Why?" he asked, with a clear hint of defiance.

His eyes held mine as he reached for my hand again, guiding it back to his face. Every fibre of my being screamed to let him, to take what he was so willingly offering. It took everything—*everything* I had to step away from him.

"You can have it," he whispered, voice thick with something I couldn't quite place. "You can have as much as you want."

My head spun wildly, reality blurring at the edges. This couldn't be happening. Flynn—lovely, lovely Flynn—offering himself to me like this, after witnessing the violence I was capable of mere minutes ago. It had to be shock, or trauma, or the product of adrenaline.

But the look in his eyes spoke of something else entirely. Something that made my heart attempt to stutter in my chest.

Flynn stepped closer, movements cautious yet determined, his fingers working at the zipper of his jacket. The fabric parted to reveal the pale expanse of his throat, moonlight casting shadows in the hollow of his collarbone. My gaze fixed on the spot where his pulse beat strongest, where the blood would flow hot and sweet across my tongue.

I inhaled sharply, catching the heady mix of his cinnamon sugar-sweet scent mingled with traces of fear and... something else. Something that made my hunger twist into an entirely different kind of desire.

"You don't know how much I want that, Flynn," I said. "But please, keep back from me. I'm begging you."

The words felt like they were being torn from my throat.

But I couldn't.

I *wouldn't* break the vow I'd made to myself.

Understanding finally dawned in his eyes, and he took a step back, readjusting his jacket with unsteady hands. Relief and disappointment warred within me as he created distance between us.

"Who was she, exactly?" Flynn asked, jerking his head towards the railing.

I sighed, then tentatively filled him in on the circumstances that had led her to our path tonight—explaining that Marcus Vale had spent the last six months building a cult of desperate fledglings. He'd been turning vulnerable humans and teaching them to hunt recklessly through Brixton's nightlife. His followers had already left multiple dead bodies in their wake. Victims who survived were often left with fractured memories, their minds ravaged by amateur compulsion.

Throughout my explanation, Flynn listened with tense attention, nodding at intervals, his eyes flickering between me and the spot where Eliza's body had fallen, clearly struggling to process everything.

By the time I'd finished, Kit and Rory had arrived, grim-faced. Kit took one look at Flynn, then my blood-drenched clothes, and then my face, twisted in self-loathing.

He pulled me into a rare crushing embrace, his familiar woodsmoke scent wrapping around me. Over his shoulder, I caught Flynn watching us intently.

"You okay, boss?"

I managed a nod against Kit's shoulder, allowing myself a moment of comfort before pulling away. There was work to be done.

"One of Marcus Vale's vampires attacked us. She had to be dispatched."

Kit's eyes flicked behind me. "Where is she now?"

"On one of them." I jerked my thumb at the boats.

"I'll help clean the yacht," Flynn offered, his voice surprisingly strong.

"Absolutely not." The words came out harsher than intended. "You shouldn't have to deal with this."

"It was part of my old job, remember?" Flynn's chin lifted stubbornly, and his hands were clenched at his sides. "And I want to help."

Rory was already hauling cleaning supplies out of a bag. "Don't listen to him—course you can help. Otherwise I'll be stuck doing it all myself. Here, I've got all the stuff we need."

I opened my mouth to protest again, but Flynn cut me off. "Please. I need to do something useful." There was something almost desperate in his tone—he needed to regain some control after having it so violently taken from him.

"Fine. But be careful. Don't fall in the water. It's freezing."

Flynn attempted a smile that didn't quite reach his eyes. He opened his mouth, perhaps to mock me for my concern, before snapping it shut.

It took a while, but Kit and I managed to get Eliza's body into the bag while Rory and Flynn tackled the wobbly deck. We loaded the body into the van, and I insisted Flynn sit up front with me. The drive to the tunnel access point was silent save for the engine's rumble and Flynn's slightly elevated heartbeat, which I seemed permanently attuned to.

I kept sneaking glances at him, searching for signs of shock. He sat quietly, his gaze fixed on the passing lights outside the window. His fingers occasionally drummed against his knee. Once or twice, he opened his mouth as if to speak, then closed it again.

We paused at a red light, and all of a sudden I couldn't stand the silence. "Are you alright, Flynn?" I asked, the question feeling wholly inadequate.

Flynn turned to face me, and to my surprise, concern flickered across his features. His eyes searched my face with an intensity that made me want to look away. But I held his gaze, caught in the depths of those sea-blue eyes.

"No." He paused, considering his words carefully. "But I will be, soon."

The smile he offered me was small but genuine, a gesture of reassurance I didn't deserve.

He hesitated for a moment, then reached across the space between us. His warm hand squeezed my arm briefly, the touch sending electricity through my cold flesh. The gesture was quick, almost shy, but it left me reeling.

We'd have to talk properly about everything that happened tonight. About what he'd offered me. Why I had to refuse, as kind as the offer had been.

Though I was under no illusions—I'd surely shattered Flynn's trust this evening, and that caused a deep, profound ache to bloom in my chest. Would I see a flicker of fear in his eyes tomorrow, and each day after that?

Though perhaps that was for the best. The events of tonight had shown, in no uncertain terms, why emotional entanglements with humans were dangerous.

I was a monster. I was a creature of darkness, and I had no right to drag Flynn into my shadows.

10

Flynn

I closed the door behind me, sagging against it with an exhalation of visceral relief. My Killigrew Street room would finally offer a sanctuary from the absolute madness outside. My hands still trembled as I crossed to the bed, sinking into the plush duvet.

My few possessions lay scattered about—a duffle bag of clothes spilling onto the floor, my laptop perched precariously on the bedside table, and the worn photo of Mum, Katie and me at Giant's Causeway propped against the lamp. The familiar items did little to ground me to reality.

Blood. There'd been so much blood.

And those fangs. That woman's—no, that *vampire's*—fangs, sharp as razors, an inch away from my neck.

Vampire.

The word ricocheted through my mind like a stone skipping across water.

Seconds before the attack, I'd been drunk on my own daring—fingers trailing down Seb's tie, mind racing with thoughts of pulling him closer. What else could a nighttime trip to a romantic moonlit marina mean, right?

Then *boom.* The fragile moment between us had exploded like a storm surge, dragging everything I thought I knew into its depths.

I couldn't stop seeing it—that moment Seb's eyes had locked with mine, his lips curling back to reveal fangs just as lethal as his attacker's.

How had I not known he was a fucking *vampire* this whole time?

My lungs constricted. The walls of my room pressed in, suddenly claustrophobic. I needed air, needed to run, needed to hear something *normal*. Needed to hear a voice that didn't belong to this world of monsters and blood and death.

My phone felt heavy in my hand as I pulled it from my pocket. Before I could overthink it, I pressed Mum's number and held my breath.

"Flynn?"

Her voice, soft and lilting with that familiar accent of home, hit me like a punch to the gut. One syllable carrying years of shared history, worry, and love.

"Hi," I choked out.

"What's wrong?"

A laugh bubbled up, hysteric and raw. "How did you know?"

"What's happened? Are you okay?"

"Yeah. I am. I just wanted to hear your voice."

"Well, it's about time! Are you... missing us?" The hope in her voice mixed with confusion, cutting deep. After all, I'd left nothing but a hastily scrawled note on the table before disappearing. That night, every second had felt like drowning, and I was too much of a coward to face the horror in my mother's eyes when I told her I was abandoning her. "Are you coming home?"

"No, Mum. I live here now."

Her sigh crackled through the phone. "I didn't know you hated it here quite so much, you know. You hid it so well."

"It wasn't like that."

"Then explain it to me!" Her voice rose sharply, and I tensed, waiting for the explosion. "Your messages have been so short and vague. You never once mentioned to me that you wanted to leave, never complained about the boats—and now you're suddenly in London working at some random bakery? You don't know how worried we've all been, Flynn! It's all your sister can focus on, and Tom keeps ringing her every other day."

The mention of Tom and Katie made my teeth grind together. This was a mistake, ringing home. I couldn't deal with talking about it, especially not after everything that had just happened.

"And you told Barbara to rent out your room to someone else? What if you change your mind? You'll never find another room here. You'll have to move back in with me!"

"I'm not going to change my mind." Demon marks and vampire attacks aside, London was slowly becoming home in its own way. Sure, the loneliness gnawed at me most nights, but at least here I could breathe.

She heaved her great heavy sigh—the one that meant she was deeply disappointed in me. "You could have just told us you didn't want to do it, you know. It didn't need to become... this massive deal. Not worth you leaving home over! Moving to another country, for Christ's sake!"

It was no mystery what she was referring to—taking over *Seabreeze Sailing.* The company my dead grandfather founded when he was just sixteen, with only a single penny in his pocket. If the tale was to be believed.

After he'd been diagnosed with terminal cancer earlier this year, he'd spent months trying to hand everything over to me. It made sense to him—I'd worked there under him since we moved to Braymore.

"I don't understand why you didn't talk to me." Raw hurt trembled in her words, another twist of the knife in my gut. "We all thought you loved Seabreeze. That you loved the boats. The water."

"I did. I *do.* It wasn't that, Mum." A small sigh slipped out. "It wasn't *just* that. I'm sorry. I can't explain it, but I just... needed to leave." *To escape.* She wasn't entirely wrong. The weight of expectation had been like a rope around my neck, drawing tighter with each sympathetic look at my grandfather's funeral. "Is Katie helping you with the company at least? I thought Mack might step up to run it?"

A pause. "We've decided to sell it."

"*What?*"

"Flynn, you know it's impractical for me to take it over." The metallic click of her wheelchair brake being set made me picture her exactly:

probably by the kitchen window, looking out at the dark garden I usually tended for her. "And Katie's got her own life. Her own career."

Did you not stop to think that I might have wanted that too?

"But you can't sell it," I whispered, remembering Grandad teaching me my first bowline knot. Katie had been rubbish at knots, preferring her flowers to the sea, but she'd still kept me company during quiet mornings.

The sea was in my blood—I loved the gentle rock of waves, the salt spray, those quiet moments before dawn. But taking over Seabreeze felt like watching my life stretch out on unchanging tracks, leading nowhere new. I'd be trapped by duty and expectation, watching others live while I stayed frozen in place. I needed more than that. Needed to know what lay beyond our coast.

Needed a chance to find someone who'd understand all the parts of me I'd kept hidden in Braymore's shadows.

"It's already decided, Flynn. Connor is helping us with the sale."

At the mention of my sister's husband, my stomach lurched. The room spun, and I gripped the edge of the bed.

What happened with Tom—the mess I'd made of our friendship that night—the taste of whiskey on his lips, the way his hands had pushed me away... That would have healed. Time smooths most wounds.

But *Connor.*

The memory hit with the force of a breaking wave, pressing against the edges of my mind like a dark tide threatening to drown me. Me, huddled alone on the beach, shoulders shaking, the kind of crying that leaves you hollow. Connor's shadow had stretched across the sand towards me, and I think I'd known somehow, even before he'd reached me, that whatever came next would destroy what little I had left.

And it did. He lit the fuse that would blow my whole life apart, sending me running for the last bus to Dublin.

My throat closed up. The room felt too small, too warm.

"Flynn?" Mum's voice crackled through the phone. "Are you still there?"

Bile rose in my throat. I swallowed hard. "I... I have to go."

"Will you come back for the festival at least?"

"Maybe," I said. If I wasn't dead already by then, I supposed I could attempt to make it.

We said our goodbyes, with me promising to call weekly from now on, then I stared at my phone.

Connor. Just the name made my skin crawl, made me want to scrub myself raw until the memory of his touch disappeared.

Him, finding me that night on the empty beach, salt-streaked tears mixing with the sea spray as I sobbed into my knees. The rough scratch of his wool jumper as he wrapped his arm around me, Katie's husband playing the role of concerned brother-in-law. His calloused thumb catching my tears, a gesture that should have been comforting but felt wrong, so wrong. I'd frozen, stone still, like a rabbit caught in a snare, unable to even breathe. And that's when he'd kissed me. The taste of beer on his breath. The scratch of his stubble. The nauseating realisation that this was my sister's husband, that he'd destroyed what little stability I had left in one selfish moment.

The urge to scream built within me.

Sleep. Sleep would help. Or at least, lying in the dark would give me space to process everything without anyone watching me fall apart. I yanked off my clothes, letting them fall where they landed, and pulled on my soft chequered pyjamas.

My phone lit up on the bedside table.

Sebastián

Come to the kitchen.

Please.

If you want to talk.

I'm here alone.

My thumb hovered over the screen. I touched my graze absently, remembering the gentle press of his thumb, the hunger in his eyes as he'd lifted it towards his mouth. The intimate tension of that moment made my cheeks flame even now. Facing him after that felt impossibly awkward.

Another message appeared.

> **But I could call someone else here as well, if you'd feel safer.**

Something in my chest tightened at those words. I didn't want him down there thinking I was up here terrified of him.

Because I wasn't, truly.

> **I'm coming.**

My feet dragged against the floorboards, each step feeling heavier than the last. Then I hesitated at the doorway, my hand gripping the frame. Through the gap, I spotted Seb standing by the counter, arms folded across his chest. He was wearing fresh clothes—another tight shirt, rolled up to reveal those magnetising forearms of his, though no tie for once. He'd showered, and his dark curls were damp, clinging to his face in a way that made him look younger, softer somehow.

When I finally pushed through the door, Seb's eyes widened before he cleared his throat. "Sorry. I didn't expect you to be in those pyjamas again."

"Well... it's nighttime..." I gestured vaguely at myself, trying not to notice how different Seb looked out of his usual coat. His new burgundy trousers still hugged his legs in a way that—*nope. Not going there.* I forced my gaze away and made a beeline for the kettle.

I avoided looking at him while I filled it, staring at the white glazed tiles on the walls, and their spiderweb cracks.

"So..." I pushed the kettle to boil, finally turning to face Seb. "You're a vampire."

"I'm a vampire."

A giggle escaped me before I could stop it. "How did that happen?"

"I was turned by another vampire. A very long time ago."

"How long ago?"

He paused. "Almost exactly five hundred years."

"Holy shit." I spun away from him, pressing two hands on the counter. I'd thought him thirty-five at most. "Holy *shit*."

Five hundred years.

I tried to wrap my head around the number, those centuries stretching out like an endless horizon where the sea meets sky. While I'd spent my adult life measuring time by tides and seasons, he'd lived through entire eras, watching empires rise and fall like waves against the shore.

He'd lived through the Renaissance, through wars and revolutions, while I'd barely managed to survive twenty-five years of existence. No wonder he carried himself with such quiet authority—he'd had centuries to perfect it.

"Are you okay? Your chest—"

"No. Not right now. I just..." I swallowed hard. "It's hard to process. Five hundred years. It's a lot. It's... a lot of years." I pressed my lips together to stop my burbling.

The kettle clicked off. I poured water into two mugs, added milk, and handed one to Seb.

"I remember very little about my human years, and my diaries from that period detail little aside from my descent into religious fanaticism. But I can tell you I was lucky enough to be born into a minor noble family in Toledo, Spain. But there's about where the luck ran out."

"So..." A million vampire questions danced on my tongue. "What about sunlight? Does it hurt you?" I couldn't help but stare at him like he was a science exhibit.

"Sunlight..." He traced the rim of his mug with one finger. "It won't turn me to ash, if that's what you're thinking. But still, it's... unpleasant. Like a severe sunburn that happens very quickly. We can tolerate it briefly, with proper precautions."

That explained that beloved heavy coat of his.

"And garlic?"

"A myth." His mouth curved into something almost like a smile. "Ironically, it's one of the few herbs I can taste, just about. In large doses."

"What about holy water? And crosses?" The questions tumbled out before I could stop them, memories of the small St. Christopher medallion my grandfather always wore while sailing flooding back.

Seb flinched—a tiny movement, but I caught it. He seemed lost in thought for a moment. "Sorry. No, technically, a cross has no effect on a vampire. But I personally can't stand the sight of them." He paused, as if weighing his words. "I came of age when Catholicism was more than faith—it was law. The Spanish Inquisition." His voice had gone quiet, distant. "Some scars last five hundred years."

"The Spanish Inquisition? Like... the witch hunts, and the mass executions? Were you... tortured?"

Seb's laugh was harsh, like glass breaking. He set down his mug with enough force that tea sloshed over the rim, spreading across the counter like a dark stain.

"No." The word came out sharp, brittle. His eyes fixed on some distant point. "Not myself, I—" He cut himself off, jaw tight. "It's not something I discuss. Those memories are... unclear. Like looking through murky water."

Something in his voice made me wish I could take back the question. There was more there—something dark.

Staring at the tea spilled on the counter, it suddenly occurred to me he hadn't had a single sip.

I sighed. "You can't drink tea, can you?"

He chuckled. "Darn. I thought I was going to get away with that. I'll have a few sips, as you made it for me. But no. As you may have gathered, my dietary requirements are rather more... haemoglobin-based."

My fingers tightened around my own mug. "How much do you need? Like, per day?"

"Two bags, ideally." He took a performative sip of tea. "I exist solely on bagged blood, usually from hospitals. It's more... ethical than the alternatives." His eyebrow raised meaningfully.

The steam from my tea curled up between us. The memory of him tasting my blood rose sharp and clear—his tongue against his thumb, those eyes blazing with something wild and hungry.

"Though lately, my supply has been... unreliable." His jaw tightened. "Which has made things rather difficult."

Was that why he always seemed so tightly wound? Living on the edge of hunger, controlling not just his strength but his very nature? The thought made my own throat feel tight with sympathy.

"And," I said, heat creeping up my neck. "Does it taste nice?"

His dark eyes fixed on mine, and time stretched between us like the moment before a storm breaks.

"Not quite as nice as feeding directly, no."

I swallowed hard and took another sip of tea, focusing on the warmth spreading through my chest rather than the weight of Seb's gaze.

Movement caught my eye. Seb had pushed away from the counter and was walking towards me with measured steps, each footfall deliberate. My muscles locked in place.

"What are you doing?"

He didn't answer. The space between us shrank until mere inches remained. This close, his scent soon washed over me—something floral like jasmine, from his shampoo, but underneath lay something wilder.

His hand reached out. I suddenly forgot how to breathe as his fingers caught the hem of my pyjama top, which had ridden up slightly. With careful precision, he tucked the fabric into my waistband.

My skin blazed where his knuckles had brushed against it. I *tried* not to focus on the proximity of his hand to my groin, but my cock took no notice of me, and heat rushed south.

"Why did you do that?" I said, embarrassingly hoarse.

"That strip of skin was tormenting me."

Blood rushed in my ears, my pulse a wild drum against my ribs. The kitchen felt too small, too warm, the air between us charged like the moment before lightning strikes.

"Why?"

His eyes, dark and intent, locked onto mine. "Because I find you incredibly attractive, and your blood is the sweetest thing I've ever had the pleasure of having in my mouth."

Everything stopped—my heart, my breath, time itself. Warmth flooded my face and spread down my neck, across my chest.

The mug slipped from my fingers.

Seb's hand shot out, snatching the mug from mid-air before it could smash against the floor. He placed it on the counter with impossible grace, as if catching falling objects was as natural as breathing.

I cleared my throat, willing my racing heart to slow. "Huh. And here I was worried that you were actually straight and this was all in my head."

His mouth quirked up at one corner. "I've had lovers of each and every persuasion over the centuries."

My mouth went dry. The casual way he dropped that information—as if centuries of sexual experience were nothing remarkable—made me feel impossibly young and naïve. Here I was, at twenty-five, with almost the exact opposite sexual history.

Here was this immortal being who'd probably seduced his way through history—artists in Paris, dancers in New York—while I'd barely managed a few fumbled blow jobs with sunburnt tourists behind the boat shed.

"Are you trying to perform a mental calculation, to see how many people I might have slept with?"

I shot daggers at him. "No. I don't care about that at all."

"I imagine the number is high. Very high." His eyes sparkled with amusement. "My diaries inform me I had quite a lot of fun in Europe in the late eighteen hundreds."

"You don't remember?"

Seb's face clouded over, his shoulders tensing. He shook his head, a strand of damp hair falling across his forehead. "My memory is tragically awful. Much worse than the average vampire's. I think it might be because—" He pressed his lips together. "Anyway, they get fuzzier the further back I go. Only the last thirty-odd years are clear, and then things begin to get murky. I have over a thousand diaries in room 210. They help me to remember things when I need to."

I shifted my weight, trying to sound casual. "So, when was the last time you were with anyone?"

"Twenty years ago."

"Twenty *years?*" The words burst out before I could stop them. "What happened?"

"James." His voice went soft around the name. "I suppose you could say that he broke my heart."

"Did he... die?"

"Not yet. He lives with his partner in a cottage in the countryside. They have this dog..." Seb trailed off, and I stared at him. How did he know about all this? Was he having them watched? "Their children have almost grown up now."

I bit my lip, trying to infer what he wasn't explicitly saying. "Did he know you were a vampire?"

Seb burst into laughter, brightening the kitchen. "Yes. He knew. We were together for years. And we wanted... *more.* But that wasn't something he was prepared to do. Nor I."

Do? And more what? More time? So many questions lined up on my tongue, but I forced them down.

"After he left, I experienced a... rough patch, let's just call it."

The vulnerability in Seb's expression tugged at something in my chest. Without thinking, I took a step towards him, wanting to offer comfort but unsure how. His shoulders had slumped, and those somber eyes held such ancient pain it made my own heartache from Tom's rejection feel small in comparison.

"And I made a few *mistakes.*"

My breath caught. The weight behind those words, the careful way he'd chosen them—ice slid down my spine as possibilities bloomed in my mind. Had he lost control? Gone on some kind of blood-soaked rampage through London, driven mad by heartbreak? The image of him earlier tonight, throat stained crimson, flashed through my mind. How many others had met similar ends?

"I made myself vow I'd never drink from a human again. And to never get... *entangled* with one either."

The words hit like a punch to the gut. I thought of our late night chats, of the edge of devotion in his eyes when he promised to save me. I thought of his thumb against my chin, the heat in his eyes when he'd tasted my blood. What he'd said about my exposed skin, all the smiles he'd given me—the secret ones when no one was looking and the gentle ones that softened his whole face.

"But you've been flirting with me."

His eyes narrowed. "I most certainly have not!"

I might have had limited experience with relationships, but I wasn't about to get gaslit by him, centuries-old vampire or not. "Really? What about 'I find you incredibly attractive and your blood is the sweetest thing I've ever had in my mouth?'"

His lips pressed together. "That wasn't flirting. Those were simply... observations."

I glared at him.

"I... shouldn't have been." He ran a hand through his hair. "Flirting, that is. If I was."

My heart skipped at his hesitation, at the way his fingers tangled in those dark curls. And maybe it was the late hour, or the lingering adrenaline from earlier, but something about his uncertainty made me brave. Made me want to chase this feeling, consequences be damned.

I eyed the brass fastening at Seb's collar, imagining the satisfying *pop* as it came undone. Of what Seb's chest might feel like under my fingers—smooth and firm and forbidden, like touching a precious treasure.

Maybe it was stupid, maybe it was reckless, but I was tired of playing it safe. Tired of watching opportunities slip away like tide water between my fingers.

I stepped closer, his scent—jasmine and that wild, dangerous undercurrent—wrapping around me like smoke.

"Maybe I don't mind the flirting." My voice came out lower than intended, almost sultry. "Maybe I've been enjoying it."

Seb's jaw clenched, and the temperature in the room seemed to drop several degrees as his eyes fixed on mine with an intensity that made my skin prickle. "Have you not been listening? I just explained that after James, I killed people. Many people. So I made a vow. No humans. No relationships. No exceptions."

I tilted my head, studying the tension in his shoulders, the way his hands had balled into fists at his sides. Had he really condemned himself to spend the rest of his life alone because of one incident? All those years stretching ahead of him, empty of touch, of connection—the weight of that self-imposed isolation felt suffocating even to imagine. "That's stupid."

"Stupid?" Seb's eyes flashed, and suddenly he was right in front of me, his hand resting just above my collarbone, as if to grip my throat. Not squeezing, but holding me in place with inhuman strength. "You think my control is a joke?"

Oh dear. I definitely could have phrased that better. I immediately wanted to claw back the word, seeing myself through his eyes—young, immature, *stupid*. My heart hammered against my ribs. His face hovered inches from mine, those chestnut eyes burning with predatory intent.

"Let me explain." His voice dropped to a growl that vibrated through my chest. "If we had sex, I could drain you dry. Not because I would want to, but because I couldn't stop myself. For me, like most vampires, bloodlust and sexual desire are intertwined. The moment I lost control, my fangs would sink into your throat, and I would drink and drink until your heart stopped beating."

I couldn't breathe. Not from his grip—which remained loose enough to allow air—but from the raw honesty in his words.

"Would you want to risk that?"

I watched, transfixed, as his lip curled back in a slow, deliberate motion. What happened next made my breath catch in my throat. His canines *lengthened*, extending like twin ivory needles until they tapered to wicked points. These weren't the cheap plastic fangs from Halloween—they were elegant, lethal weapons that gleamed in the dim light. My mouth fell open at the sight. Each an inch long, they looked sharp enough to slice through flesh like butter.

"Risk dying in my bed while I feast on your blood like some rabid animal?"

The raw danger in that moment, the predatory grace of those fangs, sparked a confusing cocktail of terror and want. "I—"

"Because that's what could happen. Especially with me being permanently half starved." His fingers tightened fractionally. "I could kill you, Flynn."

He released me and stepped back, and I gasped, releasing the tension I'd been holding. The kitchen spun slightly.

"So no." His voice was ice. "Nothing. I won't risk it. Not to mention you're supposed to be here under Killigrew Street protection."

"You're right. I'm sorry." I slumped forward onto the counter, resting my forehead against the cool surface, letting my mortification seep away somewhat. My heart still raced from his display of power, from those lethal fangs. "That was a *beyond* stupid thing to say. I wasn't thinking. It's been a long night."

"Are you alright?" Seb's voice had lost its edge. "I don't wish to hurt your feelings. Genuinely. I just... need to keep you safe."

"No, it's fine." I traced circles on the countertop with my finger. "I just need a moment. Besides, I'm getting accustomed to rejection these days. I'll get over it quickly."

"What do you mean, *accustomed?*"

I kept my head down, not wanting to see his expression. "After my grandfather's funeral... it was my friend Tom's last day at home. He was leaving me—well, leaving Braymore—to work a season on the yachts." The words spilled out freely, as if desperate for escape. "And I kissed him. And he... did not take it well. Not in a horrible way. He was quite nice about it, considering."

My memories of that day were tragically crystal clear: Tom by my side all throughout my grandfather's service. He'd known exactly how to make me smile, how to comfort my mum as the tears spilt down her cheeks.

Then after, we'd walked to the beach, our elbows brushing as we slipped across the sand to the pier.

Tom telling me his news. Saying how it was bad timing, but he'd be back in a couple of months.

My chest had constricted, panic clawing up my throat like the incoming tide. Everything I'd ever wanted to say to him crashed over me at once—how he'd been my anchor through so many storms, how his laugh made the whole harbour brighter, how I couldn't bear the thought of him sailing away.

The words wouldn't come. Instead, I'd lurched forward, my trembling hands finding his jacket, and pressed my lips against his. For one suspended moment, everything else fell away—the pier, the funeral, the weight of expectations. There was just Tom, and the desperate hope that maybe, just *maybe*...

Then, it was Tom's face shifting, crumpling into that gentle, devastating look of sympathy. Even now, I could still feel the softness of his lips, taste the salt from the sea air, hear his soft, "Oh, Flynn," that had shattered me.

Seb remained silent, but I could feel his presence beside me, listening.

"I thought I loved him." My voice wavered. "But now I'm not so sure. We were super close for years, and I think I just wanted desperately for *someone*." Heat crept up my neck. "I mean, I've reached twenty-five and I'm still a virgin. It's embarrassing."

I clearly wanted to dig the shard of glass in deeper as I forced myself to look up at Seb, bracing for pity or mockery. Instead, his eyebrows had shot up towards his hairline, genuine shock written across his features.

"Flynn—"

"Don't." I straightened up, forcing a smile. "Don't try to make me feel better about it. I know it's pathetic. It's humiliating."

"It's... surprising." Seb's eyes roamed over my face, down my body, and back up again. "You're so confident, so warm to everyone, and—now, this *isn't flirting*—quite frankly, very attractive. I'd have thought you'd have people fighting over you."

Heat bloomed across my cheeks at his words. The way he said it—so matter-of-fact, like he was stating the sky was blue—made it impossible to dismiss as empty flattery.

"I had a few flings with tourists," I mumbled, fiddling with my empty mug. "I'm not a complete born-again saint or whatever. Just... nothing serious."

"Why not?"

I sighed, memories of Grandpa's disapproving scowl rising unbidden. "My grandfather, I guess. He was... well, quite homophobic would be putting it mildly. Proper old-school Catholic. Half the town was."

"Did he know about you?"

"Yeah. I made Mum tell him, actually. Couldn't bear the thought of hiding it forever." I traced the rim of my mug. "She told me to ignore him, said he was from a different time and all that usual bullshit. But she fully supported me, honestly. My sister, Katie, too."

Seb leaned against the counter, expression considering.

"The thing was..." I swallowed hard. "It was his house we all lived in. My mum, Katie, and I moved in with him after my dad died. Living under his roof, seeing him every day... I think it might have stopped me—subconsciously, you know?—from pursuing anything real. He was everywhere in Braymore Bay. Local celebrity, practically ran the town council. Everyone knew him, respected him."

The words tasted bitter. It was complicated, how the same man who'd given us a home, who'd taught me to love the sea, had made me feel so small.

"Hard to risk bringing someone home to that. Wouldn't be fair to them. So yeah. Tourist flings were safer. They'd be gone in a week anyway."

Seb's expression darkened, a shadow crossing his features. "Your mother should have done more to support you."

"No." The word came out sharper than I intended. "You don't understand. We *needed* to live there."

His eyebrows drew together. "Needed?"

"My mum. She uses a wheelchair." I gripped the edge of the counter. "Has done since the accident that killed Dad. The house—it was perfect. My grandfather had already modified it years ago for Gran before she died. Wide doorways, ramps, accessible bathroom. Everything she needed."

The anger slightly melted from Seb's face.

"And Katie and I were still in school." I shrugged. "Mum's disability benefits barely covered the basics. Grandpa... he provided for us. Made sure we had everything we needed. Food on the table, clothes for school, birthday presents."

"At what cost to you?"

"Better than watching my mother struggle to survive on her own." The words came out with a snap. "What was I supposed to do? Tell her we should leave because he made me feel bad about being gay? Force her to try and find somewhere else accessible on next to no money?"

Seb remained quiet, his gaze fixed on my face.

"She did her best, okay?" My voice trembled.

The weight of everything crashed over me at once—my phone conversation with my mother, the guilt that I'd abandoned her, my icy demon heart, Eliza attacking me, Seb's firm words. A sob tore from my throat before I could stop it. I turned away, pressing my palms against my eyes, but the tears kept coming.

"You're crying." Seb's voice held a note of alarm.

"I'm fine," I choked out. "Don't mind me. This isn't because of you." *Oh god, please don't let him think that.* "I'm just a bit homesick. And I feel fucking awful for leaving her. My mum, I mean." I couldn't look at him, couldn't face the judgement in his eyes. "Her carers are amazing, and she's so independent. She's got Katie. She doesn't *need* me. But I didn't even say goodbye—I was such a fucking selfish coward. I hate myself for it."

Self-loathing flooded through me, drowning out even my mortification at falling apart in front of Seb like this. My shoulders shook as I tried to contain the sobs. Everything felt too much, too overwhelming. Like being caught in a riptide, each attempt to surface only dragging me deeper. The kitchen tiles blurred through my tears.

"Can... I hug you?"

The uncertainty in his voice caught me off guard—this powerful vampire, this dangerous man, asking permission to comfort me. As if I might shatter at his touch.

I let out a watery laugh. "In a non-flirty way?"

The joke fell flat, my voice breaking on the last word.

Seb tutted. "In whatever way you need right now."

Before I could respond, his arms wrapped around me from behind. The coolness of his body pressed against my back, and I stiffened for a moment before melting into his embrace. His touch felt like pressing against malleable marble. The sensation grounded me, pulling me back from the edge of hysteria.

I turned in his arms, burying my face against his chest. His expensive shirt would probably end up stained with tears and snot, but he didn't seem to care. One of his hands came up to cradle the back of my head, fingers threading through my hair.

"You shouldn't hate yourself, Flynn. Not even slightly." His thumb traced soothing circles against my scalp. "I can already tell you aren't the sort of person who hurts others deliberately. Sometimes we make impossible choices to survive." His other hand moved to my back, steady and firm. "Sometimes it takes more courage to leave than to stay."

"I'm ruining your shirt," I mumbled against his chest.

He scoffed, his other hand rubbed soothing circles between my shoulder blades. The gentle motion, combined with the solid presence of his body against mine, helped my sobs gradually quiet to hiccups.

Still wrapped in his firm embrace, a thought struck me. The silence between us felt different, missing something crucial. I pressed my ear closer against his chest, confirming my suspicion.

"You don't have a heartbeat."

His arms tightened fractionally around me. "I'm sorry."

The weight behind those two words hit me—he wasn't apologising for his lack of pulse. He was sorry for being what he was, for all the barriers it created between us.

I pulled back slightly, suddenly self-conscious of my tear-stained face. Wiping my cheeks with the heel of my palm, I drew in a deep, shuddering breath. The cool air helped clear my head, though my eyes felt raw and heavy.

Seb still slowly slid his feather-light fingers across my back, continuing his gentle pattern. Each sweep of his fingers left trails of warmth in their wake, despite the coolness of his touch. I barely dared to breathe. Nobody had ever touched me like this—so tender, so careful—as if I was something precious that might shatter. My body trembled with the effort of staying still, terrified that any sudden movement would make him stop. That this moment would slip away like smoke between my fingers.

The quiet stretched between us, comfortable and charged all at once. My tears had dried, but neither of us moved to break apart. As my breathing steadied, I became aware of how perfectly we fit against each other. Time suspended like that moment between waves, where the world holds its breath before crashing back to shore. My body felt heavy and light all at once, exhausted from crying, yet hyper-aware of every point where we touched. The shift came so gradually I almost missed it, but suddenly I was drowning in a different kind of sensation—the gentle circles he traced between my shoulder blades had shifted from comforting to something else—something that made my skin prickle with awareness.

When he spoke again, his voice was low and rich. "For what it's worth, if things were different..." He pressed his mouth to my ear, and even though I'd just been sobbing my heart out, my cock hardened so fast it made me dizzy. Heat pooled low as his breath ghosted across my skin. "I'd carry you up those stairs, throw you on my bed, and give you *exactly* what you deserve."

I pulled my head back, arching an eyebrow at him. "I think you and I have very different definitions of flirting, Sebastián."

"That was simply another—"

"Observation," I finished for him, glaring pointedly as his lips twisted into a smile. I cleared my throat, painfully aware of how thin my pyjama bottoms were. "Well, your... *observations* have left me with a rather obvious problem that these flimsy pyjama's you're so fond of aren't going to hide. So I should probably head upstairs before I embarrass myself further."

His eyes flickered downward for a fraction of a second, then snapped back to my face. The tips of his ears darkened—*could vampires blush?*

"Right. Yes. Absolutely." He stepped back, running a hand through his curls. "That would be... wise."

"Wouldn't want to tempt you with any more *observations*." I backed towards the door, fighting a grin despite my predicament. "Purely out of respect for your noble vow, of course."

"Flynn." His voice held a warning note that sent delicious shivers throughout my entire body.

"Going!" I threw my hands up in mock surrender. "Though I must say, for someone who doesn't flirt, you're remarkably good at—"

"Goodnight, Flynn."

The steel in his tone brooked no argument, but I caught the ghost of a smile playing at the corners of his mouth as I slipped out the door.

Climbing the stairs to my room, I touched my fingers to my chest. How could someone without a heartbeat make mine race quite so fast?

II

Sebastián

The silver crucifix lay heavy in my palm, its familiar weight a burden that transcended mere metal. Dark stains marred its surface—blood that had refused to fade. I traced the ornate edges with trembling fingers, fighting the wave of emotions that always accompanied this compulsive ritual: guilt, grief, an overwhelming sense of betrayal.

Even now, centuries later, the blood seemed to mock me. A permanent reminder of choices I could never undo.

I kept this crucifix wrapped in silk, locked away in the chest that held my most guarded possessions. It was one of only a few items I had from my human life. Though the sight of it filled me with poisonous darkness, something compelled me to keep it.

The crucifix had been a special gift from *him*. Padre Rodrigo. The priest who'd turned me into a monster. Even thinking his name made bile rise in my throat.

It was cruelly unfair. My human memories were a fog of half-formed shadows. Even Magdalena, my sister, only came to me in fragments, like a painting left out in the rain. But him? Padre Rodrigo remained crystal clear: those dark, hungry eyes that followed my every movement during confession. The way his black cassock would brush against stone floors as he drew too close, the stark white of his collar. His voice, honey-sweet and venomous, as he whispered promises of salvation into my ear.

Some memories, it seemed, refused to fade, no matter how desperately I wished they would.

I rewrapped the crucifix with sharp, angry movements, forcing it back into its silk prison. The chest clicked shut with quiet finality.

My gaze drifted to the rotary phone on my desk. I'd come up here to make a call before finding myself distracted by the cursed object.

Sitting in my chair, my fingers touched the cold brass rim. I forced my thoughts to shift to a much more recent memory: Flynn, and the events of last night. His vulnerability, his tears, the way he'd opened up. How marvellously warm he'd been when he'd wrapped himself around me, pressing his head to my chest.

The cinnamon bun I'd purchased from his bakery now rested beside my ink pot, taunting me with its intoxicating smell.

My fingers stopped their idle wandering and gripped the handset with newfound purpose.

Our next call wasn't due for days, but I was going to call White, regardless.

In the twenty years I'd known her—since that night she rescued me from my darkness, offering me purpose beyond the blood-soaked mess I'd been after James—I'd met her face-to-face only a handful of times.

Our calls were always brief, impersonal affairs, with strict agendas and rigid protocols.

The dial tone hummed as I picked up the receiver. Each number clicked and whirred as I turned the dial, muscle memory taking over. One, then another, until the full sequence was complete.

Ring.

Ring.

"This better be important, Black." White's crisp voice cut through the line on the third ring. "You're disrupting my breakfast."

"Good morning to you too." I leant back in my chair, the leather creaking. "I do enjoy your pleasantries."

"If you wanted pleasant conversation, you'd have waited for our scheduled call." A pause. "What's happened?"

The edge of genuine concern in White's voice transported me back to that night she found me—feral, drenched in the blood I'd spilled.

Standing on London Bridge, on the wrong side of the railing. This I remembered with crystal clarity—staring down at the dark river, thinking how cruelly sardonic it was that vampires couldn't drown. That even the Thames denied me the peace I sought.

"Eliza." The name tasted like ash on my tongue. "Fledgling vampire under Marcus Vale. Lived with five others in that house in Brixton. She attacked us last night. By a small marina. Nobody saw—one small mercy."

"Eliza Rosewood?" White's tone sharpened. "What was she doing there?"

"Watching us. Watching me." I trailed my fingers over a knot on my desk, smooth from years of worrying my thumb into it. "Then she went for Flynn Carter. I had to—" The image of her body crumpling flashed behind my eyes. "I eliminated the threat."

"You killed her."

"Yes."

The static hum of the line stretched between us.

"That's concerning, Black. This will only anger the Vale clan further, a second death to their number by your hand."

"I'm aware." I gritted my teeth.

"And the fact she was stalking you…"

"I know." My jaw clenched. "She appeared from nowhere. Could have been following us for who knows how long. And if she was watching—"

"Others might be too." White finished my thought. "How's the boy holding up?"

The boy.

"Flynn is…" I stared at the cinnamon bun, remembering how he'd helped clean that yacht after, his hands steady despite everything. "He's stronger than you might think. Handled it better than most would."

"You sound impressed."

"He's resilient." The words came out soft as silk. "After every-thing—the cambion assaulting him, being marked, Eliza's attack, learning about our world—he's still standing. Still trying to *help*, however he can."

"Interesting." White's tone shifted, almost amused. "You usually describe things with rather more... clinical detachment."

My fingers stilled on the desk. "It's my job to keep him alive."

"Did I suggest otherwise?"

There was an awkward pause.

The cinnamon bun caught my eye again.

Flynn had volunteered to accompany Rory to Fat Cat's thirty minutes ago, taking the long route through the tunnel for their coffee run. It was immensely difficult for me to allow it—to allow him out of my sight, my protection.

As if summoned by my anxiety, my phone vibrated, and a photo of Flynn filled the screen.

I'd asked him to message me when they arrived, not take a picture of him stuffing an entire croissant into his mouth, but I'd happily take it.

Flynn

Rory says I shouldn't waste perfectly good pastries on silly photos but he's just jealous of my model potential LOL

Then, a second later:

(laugh out loud, not lots of love) xxx

I stared at the messages, hypnotised by the Xs. Before I could reply, another message came.

just in case you thought I meant lots of love LOL

btw the xxx was a typo, soz, I'm not flirting!!!

I felt my forehead tug into the frown that surfaced anytime my teammates tormented me with their silly acronyms.

Thank you for clarifying, Flynn.

I hit send before I could add any Xs.

"Black? Are you still there?"

"Yes. I'll have more information by our next call. I just wanted to keep you in the loop, should this develop into anything further."

"Good luck. Continue to show no leniency. If any of Vale's clan fail to demonstrate self-control after fair warnings, we *will* eliminate them."

"Goodbye, White." I placed the handset back into its cradle with perhaps more force than necessary.

The cinnamon bun beckoned. I lifted it, inhaling deeply. Most food tasted like cardboard, but sometimes, if I concentrated hard enough, fragments of flavour broke through.

I ran my tongue along the sticky glaze. A ghost of sweetness, barely there but present enough to remind me of what I'd lost. The cinnamon came through stronger—spice always did. It lingered on my tongue, a whisper of warmth.

Acting of its own accord, my hand unlocked my phone, and swiped back to Flynn's ridiculous photo. His eyes crinkled at the corners, cheeks puffed out like a hamster's. Something twisted in my chest—an echo of an organ that hadn't beaten in centuries.

There were crumbs all over Flynn's face, and my thumb traced the screen, remembering how he'd let me wipe blood from his chin last night. How he hadn't flinched away. How then he'd drawn my hand back to his graze, pushing my thumb against the wound.

The memory of his pulse under my touch, the way his breath had hitched—

I locked the phone.

This was dangerous territory. These thoughts led nowhere good.

But my gaze drifted back to the damned device anyway, to that stupid, wonderful photo of him being absolutely ridiculous in a coffee shop, living and breathing and *human* in all the ways I wasn't.

There was no denying the attraction anymore—not when my thoughts constantly drifted to him, not when every message made my dead heart feel like it might stutter back to life. The first spark of genuine desire I'd felt in twenty years, since James. Yet Flynn was nothing like James had been. Where James was measured and methodical, already settled into his thirties when we'd met, Flynn burned bright with chaotic youth. James had carried himself with the gravitas of an Oxford professor, all tweed jackets and careful words. Flynn wore his heart on his sleeve, spilling crumbs and sending texts with multiple exclamation marks.

What I'd shared with James had been intense, all-consuming—when it ended, my world had shattered so completely that I'd found myself on that bridge, ready for it all to be over. And now here I was, years of careful control later, finding myself lost in sea-blue eyes. Flynn, with his magnetic warmth and that maddening, beautiful ability to make me want to protect him, to shelter him, to lo—

No. I couldn't allow myself to complete that thought. I'd sworn after James that I would never again let myself care for a human.

Their lifespans were cruel enough without having to watch them wither day by day, forced to witness every precious moment slip away like sand through an hourglass while I remained forever unchanged.

Besides, Flynn deserved more than a half-life with someone whose hands were stained with regret. Deserved better than to be bound to a monster who lived in the shadows. He was too full of light.

Though I'd dimmed that light, last night, when I'd crossed the kitchen and made to grab his neck. When I'd detailed how the beast in me would love to rip him apart. I should've been glad to hear his heart rate skyrocket with terror. But I hadn't been. I'd been devastated.

My phone buzzed with another message from Flynn, and I hit the open button lightning fast.

> **Thanks for last night, btw. I don't think I actually thanked you. For saving me at the marina and then everything in the kitchen. For letting me cry all over you, but also for showing me your true self. Even the scary bits. Makes me feel less alone with my own darkness x**

He'd... *thanked me*. Thanked me for terrorising him, for showing him exactly what kind of creature lurked beneath this carefully maintained façade. The wave of emotion that crashed through me was too much—too raw, too honest, too *everything*.

I hurled my phone across the room. It hit the wall with a satisfying crack, before clattering to the floorboards.

"Bloody hell." I pinched the bridge of my nose and forced myself to inhale air.

What was I, a child having a tantrum?

I stalked over to retrieve the phone. The screen had shattered, but the device still functioned—likely a testament to Felix's insistence on military-grade cases.

I'd faced down armies. Survived plagues, countless wars, and the Spanish Inquisition itself. I would not be undone by a few sweet messages from a man who enjoyed taking photos of himself with pastry crumbs all over his face.

This weakness had to end. Now.

The situation with Marcus Vale's clan needed addressing. Their numbers grew weekly and two deaths would indeed spark retaliation—they'd want blood.

I didn't have time for distraction, not with our equally pressing issue of frostbitten bodies cropping up all around London.

Of Flynn marked for icy death.

No!

My fingers curled into fists. I needed to focus. I needed Kit. He would calm me down. He always did, simply with his military precision and tactical mind.

I grabbed my coat from the rack, shrugging it on as I strode towards the door. The brass buttons caught the light as I reached for the handle. Time to be the leader they needed, not the lovesick fool I was becoming.

Kit would be in the weapons room, methodically cleaning each piece of equipment.

First, though, I dialled Felix's number.

"Magpie? I need a new phone screen."

12

Flynn

> **Mum told me you rang her a few days ago. That's good. Hope you're okay. I'm here when you're ready to talk to me.**

My fingers hovered over the keyboard for a moment before I pocketed my phone. This was the first text Katie had sent me where she didn't sound angry, which was good. But I needed to talk to her in person. Not that it was going to be possible anytime soon.

Forget about permission to go to Ireland—I was currently lurking outside room 210, Seb's office, psyching myself up for permission to leave the hotel. I forced myself to knock, feeling like a prisoner begging an officer for their daily exercise hour in the yard.

"Enter." Seb's voice carried through the wood.

I pushed the door open to find him hunched over his laptop, his curls askew as if he'd been running his hands through them. The moment he registered my presence, he quickly hid something in the drawer of his desk as he scrambled to pause whatever was playing, jabbing at random keys until the sound cut off. His fingers slipped on the track pad three times before he managed to close the window.

"I didn't hear you coming over the volume." He tilted the screen down, not quite meeting my eyes.

His usually composed face was so flustered, I couldn't resist asking, "Were you watching porn?"

His head snapped up. "I most certainly was not!" A hint of his Spanish accent slipped through—I must have properly rattled him.

The chair opposite his desk looked inviting, and standing was starting to feel awkward, so I dropped into it. "Suuuure." I couldn't help grinning at the way his eyebrows drew together in indignation.

"It's late. My work has finished for the day. I'm allowed to watch an episode of my television show if I choose to."

I held up my hands. "Alright, alright. Of course you're allowed to watch TV." I was glad he was doing something other than working for once. But the urge to tease him was too strong to resist. "Though I'm not going to believe it's not porn unless you show me what it was."

Seb opened his laptop with an exaggerated sigh. The paused scene showed a blonde girl in dated clothing wielding a wooden stake.

I recognised the show immediately. Katie and I had often watched reruns of it when we were kids, sprawled on the sofa together.

I couldn't help it. I burst into laughter, which only intensified when he scowled at me. "You're sitting in here alone, watching *Buffy the Vampire Slayer*? That's fucking brilliant."

He leaned back in his office chair, the leather creaking beneath him. "Is there something wrong with that?"

"No! I love Buffy. But if you're Team Angel rather than Team Spike we can't be friends anymore."

"Please." He rolled his eyes. "Angel is far too brooding. Though Spike's accent is atrocious, at first."

"It gets better and better."

"Oh, I know. I've watched the whole thing"—he glanced guiltily at the laptop—"too many times to count. It was one of the first things I got Felix to set up for me, actually, when I hired him."

Another laugh slipped out of me. "I bet teaching you how to stream Buffy on your laptop wasn't in his original job description. Or is supernatural TV knowledge part of his pay grade?"

"You jest, but this is important stuff. I need to understand how the general public views vampires." His lips twitched. "For research purposes, of course."

"Of course." I shifted in my seat, the real reason for my visit pressing on my mind. "But look, speaking of social lives, sort of, Emma's invited me around this evening for a small dinner party. And I wondered if I could go. Because I could do with some fun."

Seb's eyes crinkled at the corners, and something in his expression shifted. Had he thought I'd come to his office just to see him?

Because I totally would have, but I wasn't sure if I was even allowed to—if he would want that.

"You should come with me!" The words tumbled out before I could stop them. *Oh shit.* Emma would absolutely murder me.

"That sounds... delightful." Seb's voice went soft. "But she won't want me there." He drummed his fingers on the desk, studying me intently. "I'd rather not take unnecessary risks, but... we're still a way off the dark magic being fully incubated, thankfully. And you're right, you should be allowed a break from the hotel. Have some fun."

"But you could have fun too." My heart started racing at my own boldness. "Emma won't mind. We could walk there together. It's a nice evening for it."

Seb's gaze dropped to my chest for a split second, and I remembered—right. Vampire hearing. He could definitely hear my heart hammering away like an idiot. I willed my face not to flush.

"I should stay here. But I'll have Rory accompany you."

"Umm." I shifted in my seat. "No way is Rory coming into Emma's house. Not after yesterday."

"What happened yesterday?" His brow furrowed.

I squirmed, not wanting to snitch. Rory and I were becoming friends. Maybe. "Well, he was watching me at work. But he spent the whole shift texting Kit about how boring guard duty was, in between trying to chat my ear off. Then he moved on to harassing customers with bread puns. When they didn't laugh, he turned to me and said, 'Hey Flynn, these customers really *knead* to lighten up!' and that's when Emma threatened to kick him out."

Seb rubbed his face with two hands. "I'm so sorry. I'll talk to him. That was incredibly unprofessional."

"He's a professional?" I raised my eyebrows.

Seb's shoulders dropped. "Don't be too quick to judge him. Rory puts up a lot of fronts. He's had a difficult time of it. His pack in the Highlands—they weren't kind to him. Too set in their ways, too traditional." He paused. "Being smaller than most wolves, being different... well. Kit found out that he was sleeping rough in Glasgow."

"Oh." The image of Rory—bouncy Rory, so full of life—alone on the streets hit harder than expected.

"I hired him partially so Kit could keep an eye on him. Though don't tell either of them that." The hard edges of Seb's face softened as his lips curved up into a slight smile. "He drives Kit up the wall, but they're good for each other."

"I like Rory. Even though he's..." I waved my hand, searching for the right word.

"A lot?" Seb chuckled. "True. But he grows on you."

"Like a fungus?"

"Precisely." Seb winked at me. "But don't worry about tonight. He'll drop you there and wait in his car."

"Does he not have plans of his own, though?" The thought of Rory sitting alone in his car all evening... "It's Friday night."

"I pay him generously for these duties."

"Oh yeah?" I leaned forward. "Any positions going, then?"

A smile tugged at the corner of his mouth. "Well, I have been thinking about firing our receptionist, Dolly. She's a tad stiff. She never takes her turn unloading the dishwasher, and between you and me, she's been giving everyone the glass-eyed stare lately."

I blinked at him. "Was that... an actual joke, Sebastián Salazar?"

His lips pursed together in mock anger, then he said, "I'll have you know I'm capable of many jokes. When the occasion arises."

The silence stretched between us, comfortable but charged. His dark eyes held mine, and for a moment I forgot why I'd even come to his office in the first place. The way he was looking at me, with that hint of playfulness, had me melting into a puddle. I found myself wanting to stay right here in this office, watching his face light up as he talked.

Then my phone buzzed in my pocket—probably Emma asking what time I'd be there—and reality crashed back in.

"Well. I'll go get ready then." The words came out quieter than I'd intended. *Or I could forget about the whole thing, and we could stay here and watch some Buffy episodes together.*

Seb nodded. "Have fun," he said, though his lips pressed together afterwards.

I forced myself to my feet, his eyes lingering on me.

"Text Rory when you're ready. Oh, and Flynn? I wanted to let you know how tirelessly the team is working to track down the cambion who marked you. Thank you for your patience, and thank you for agreeing to stay here. I should have said that before."

I almost told him that as bizarre as they all were, Killigrew Street was an upgrade in the housemate department.

At the door, I paused, glancing back. Seb had already reopened his laptop, probably ready to unpause Buffy. The image of him sitting alone in his office all evening made my heart physically hurt.

I pulled the door shut behind me and headed down the corridor, trying not to think about how much I'd rather stay with him.

I shuffled down the dimly lit corridor of the hotel's third floor, munching on crackers I'd nicked from the kitchen.

The last few days had been odd. Since our chat in Seb's office, I'd secretly hoped to spend more time with him.

And I had been—sort of.

Sometimes he'd materialise at my side while I loaded the ancient dishwasher, asking about my sister Katie or what the sea looked like during winter storms in Braymore. If I liked tea more than coffee, if Rising Dough had sold out of bread that day. His questions were precise, calculated, almost like they'd been prepared. He'd smile at my responses—proper smiles that reached his eyes—and stretch past me to grab a tea towel, his sleeve brushing my arm.

But then he'd vanish again. I'd catch glimpses of him striding through the hotel, phone pressed to his ear, that black coat swirling behind him like a shadow. If our paths crossed, he'd give me this tight, strained look before hurrying off to whatever crisis needed his attention.

I knew he was busy—trying to track down Damien, to save my life, or whatever.

But still. The hotel felt colder somehow, when he kept his distance.

I shoved another cracker into my mouth. It was ridiculous to miss someone who was literally in the same building. Especially someone who'd made it very clear that getting attached was a bad idea.

The ice attack on the way home from work earlier probably wasn't helping today's mood. Rory had guided me through it, nattering about his latest dating disasters until my fingers thawed and my breath returned to normal.

I'd put on a brave face, pretending I was peachy fine, but in truth, it had spooked me—it had been the longest lasting and furthest reaching so far, the coldness spreading all the way to my fingertips. It was easier to focus on Rory's chattering than to contemplate how many heartbeats I might have left. Spoiler alert: not as many as I'd like, apparently. I'd received very few updates on my case in recent days, which was not particularly reassuring.

Hours after Rory dropped me back at Killigrew Street, restlessness drove me to explore the hotel's endless maze of corridors.

The hotel's third floor felt like delving into a shipwreck—each empty room a cabin frozen in time, dust motes dancing in shafts of light like underwater debris. Most of the floor remained locked, a layer of dust coating the brass door numbers. My footsteps echoed softly against the worn carpet runner that I was liberally dropping cracker crumbs onto.

A scratching sound caught my attention.

I paused mid-bite, holding my breath. The noise came again—a sort of scrabbling, like claws on wood.

"Hello?" My voice bounced off the walls.

Something small and grey darted out from behind a dead potted plant. Before I could process what I was seeing, the creature leapt straight up—impossibly high—and snatched the half-eaten cracker from my hand.

I stumbled backwards. The thing landed with unnatural grace, its matted fur an odd greenish grey. Its eyes glowed with an eerie yellow light, and patches of... was that bone showing through its skin?

The creature tilted its head, regarding me with those luminous eyes while chomping down on my cracker with sharp, yellowed teeth.

"Bloody hell—"

It shot off around the corner, taking the rest of my snack with it. The patter of its feet faded into silence.

I stood frozen, my hand still raised where the cracker had been.

"What are you doing up here?"

I spun around to find Priya at the end of the corridor, her eyes darting between me and room 303, lips pressed together.

"Just exploring. I got bored." I brushed crumbs off my jumper. "I'll come back down—"

A deep, guttural sound erupted from behind room 303's wooden door. Like the cry of a whale mixed with nails on a chalkboard, it raised every hair on my body.

I stared at the closed door.

"What the fuck is in there?"

Priya rushed forward, grabbing my arm. "We don't talk about room 303." Her grip tightened, and she practically dragged me towards the stairwell, her braid swinging with each hurried step.

I rolled my eyes at her. "Got it. Also, this weird... creature thing just stole my cracker. Greyish green, glowing eyes, bits of *bone* showing—"

"Oh." Priya gave me an odd smile. "That's just Freddy."

"Freddy?"

"Rory's zombie ferret. He died—years ago now—and Rory was so sad, Issac brought him back to life for him, as a bit of a joke." She glanced at me. "You know, Issac, the one we lost? You probably noticed the shrine in the kitchen."

I nodded. "Brought him... back to *life*?"

"Yep," Priya said cheerily, as if this was an everyday occurrence. "Issac was a necromancer. Anyway, as you can imagine, Seb was *fuming* about Freddy. I'm surprised Freddy didn't find his way into a second early grave. I told Issac it was a terrible idea, but does anyone listen to me? No." She shook her head. "Now Freddy roams the halls, stealing snacks and leaving half-eaten mice in our shoes."

"A zombie... ferret." A hysterical laugh bubbled in my throat. A week ago, the strangest thing in my life had been my creepy new roommates leaving me cryptic notes about bin rotas. Now I was being robbed by undead pets in a supernatural hotel. This new reality stretched and warped around me like a funhouse mirror, and I wasn't sure if I was meant to scream or laugh.

"You get used to him. Though I'd recommend not feeding him after midnight. Makes him extra bitey."

Priya guided me into the kitchen and set about making tea.

"So, what's really in room 303?" I asked teasingly.

Slowly, she turned and pierced me with her gaze. "First rule of Killigrew Street, Flynn: we don't talk about room 303."

I arched one skeptical eyebrow. "Yesterday you told me the first rule of Killigrew Street was we never use the haunted elevator. And the day before that, you said we weren't supposed to answer the old telephone in the lobby unless it rings exactly three times."

"All rules are first rules when they keep you alive," Priya replied, refocusing on the kettle. "Now, would you like some chai? I promise it's only slightly medicinal today."

While Priya busied herself with the kettle, my gaze drifted to Issac's small shrine. A necromancer who could bring ferrets back from the dead.

"Am I the only human here?" The question slipped out before I could stop it.

Priya's laugh echoed through the kitchen as she poured steaming water. "Felix is. One hundred percent. Poor guy gets bullied for it. And I'm..." She paused, stirring the chai. "*Gifted*. That's the known term for it. It's a genetic quirk, we think. But sometimes abilities only reveal themselves when triggered by something. Emotional trauma, supernatural exposure, that sort of thing. But my powers are nothing, really. Sensing supernatural energies, a bit of healing."

She brightened suddenly. "Oh, and there's this. My party trick." She pointed at a teaspoon resting on the counter, her face scrunching in concentration. For an awkwardly long moment, I held in a nervous laugh. Then the spoon gave a pathetic little jump before clattering back down. "Ta-da!" She spread her hands with a theatrical flourish. "My grandmother could lift entire tea sets. I got the bargain version of telekinesis, I'm afraid."

She handed me a mug, the spicy scent of cardamom and cinnamon wafting up. "Gran was Gifted also, but she taught me old magic—healing spells, reading cards, protective wards, that sort of thing. Nothing fancy like Seb's eternal life, or raising the dead."

"So you're like... a witch?"

"I prefer 'practitioner.' Less stereotypical, you know?" She perched on the counter, legs swinging. "Though Rory insists on calling me his 'witch doctor' whenever I patch him up."

"I bet he loves that. He's an absolute windup merchant. I don't know how you spend so much time with him. I think I'd punch him."

"He's lucky I love him."

I sipped the chai, letting its warmth spread through me. "So your grandmother taught you everything?"

"Mm." Priya's fingers traced the gold pendant at her neck. "She was quite well known in Manchester's community. People would come from all over for her healing remedies." Her eyes took on a faraway look. "The shop's still there—my parents run it now. To most customers, it's just an alternative medicine place, but..." She smiled. "Let's just say, some of our regulars aren't exactly human. My family wanted me to stay, take over the shop. Escaping to London wasn't what they had in mind for their eldest. But I needed my own path."

"They aren't happy?"

"My phone's full of messages asking when I'm coming home." She took a long sip. "Mum still sends photos of eligible Indian doctors she thinks I should meet. As if I have time for dating with this lot keeping me busy." She gestured downwards, at the basement.

"I understand that—family expectations softly killing you—though in my case..." I traced a pattern in my cooling tea. "I loved the sea, loved the family business. But taking over Seabreeze after Grandad died... the responsibility of it all... knowing I'd never leave Braymore, watching my future shrink down to one single path..." I met Priya's understanding gaze. "Sometimes running away feels easier than disappointing them, doesn't it?"

The bittersweet smile on Priya's face told me she understood me completely, and for the first time since leaving home, the weight of guilt felt just a little lighter to carry.

"It's funny," I said, warming my hands with the last of the mug's heat. "Even though Braymore became home, I always felt like I was playing catch-up with my identity. Spent my childhood in England, and then, even after a decade in Ireland, the locals still called me 'the English lad.' Always with a smile, mind, but..."

Priya nodded knowingly. "That in-between feeling. Not quite belonging anywhere completely."

"Yeah. Grandad being who he was helped—everyone knew Seabreeze Sailing, respected him. But I'd still get comments about my accent being posh, or someone would make a joke about me not knowing some childhood rhyme all the local kids grew up with." I traced the rim of my mug. "Daft little things, really, but they add up. Made me feel like I was always a step out of sync with everyone else."

"Ooh, you've finished!" Priya hopped off the counter, snatching my now-empty mug. "Perfect. I've been dying to do this."

"Do what?"

She tipped the mug sideways, peering inside with intense concentration. "Read your leaves, of course."

"Oh god." I slumped back in my chair. "You're not serious. That's all bollocks, isn't it?"

Priya's head snapped up, eyes narrowing. "I'll have you know my grandmother taught me tasseomancy when I was twelve. Her readings were so accurate, she once predicted the exact day my cousin would give birth *and* that it would be twins."

"Bullshit."

"Honestly." She clicked her tongue. "You've seen a zombie ferret, met two wolves, and you're being protected from demons by a centuries-old vampire. But tea leaf reading is where you draw the line?"

"Fair point." I leaned forward. "Go on then, what do you see?"

Priya rotated the cup, her brow furrowed. "Hmm. There's definitely a bird here—see this shape?" She tilted the cup towards me. "Usually means news is coming. And this curved line... interesting."

"What's interesting?"

"Well..." She fiddled with her long braid. "It could be interpreted two ways. Either you're about to embark on a passionate love affair that will change your life forever..."

I snorted. "Or?"

"Or you're going to be eaten by a large fish."

"*What?*"

"The signs aren't always clear cut!" she defended, gesturing at the tea leaves. "Look, this swooping pattern could be Cupid's arrow *or* a fish's tail. And this cluster here could represent either romantic desire or, you know... teeth."

"Brilliant." I threw my hands up. "So I'm either going to fall madly in love or become fish food. That's really helpful, Priya. Really narrows it down."

"The universe works in mysterious ways." She set the cup down with a satisfied smile. "Though personally, I'm leaning towards the love affair interpretation. These leaves have a distinctly romantic energy."

My traitorous heart couldn't help but cling to her silly game, equal waves of longing and terror shooting through me. The night Tom rejected me, I'd sobbed on the beach and sworn off ever feeling anything for anyone again. Yet here I was, my heart doing backflips over a vampire who'd already friendzoned me so violently it had left emotional bruises.

"You're making this all up."

"I never make things up. The leaves don't lie, Flynn Carter."

I peered back into the cup, remembering how my grandfather used to say you could read the weather in the patterns of waves. These tea leaves swirled like tide pools at low water, promising either romance or a fish attack—though after my years at sea, I knew better than to dismiss either prediction. The ocean had taught me that the most unlikely outcomes often came true.

A shadow fell across the kitchen floor, and I nearly jumped out of my skin as Seb materialised in the doorway. How did a man with so much presence move so silently? Curls damp from a shower, his black coat was draped casually over one arm, but it was his rolled-up shirtsleeves that caught my attention—and held it. There should be laws against exposing forearms like that. I accidentally licked my lips, then dragged my gaze up to his face, where his mouth quirked into an amused smile.

Of course, my heart had decided to perform its usual gymnastics routine at the sight of him. After a full day without seeing him, my body seemed determined to betray just how much I'd missed him.

He leaned against the doorframe, arms crossed. "Are you torturing Flynn with tea leaves?" he asked, with mock scorn. "Go on then Priya, what's it today? Last week, I was apparently destined to be trampled by a herd of ghost cattle."

"That was a perfectly valid interpretation!" Priya brandished my empty cup at him. "And what about the one I did for you the other day? That turned out accurate!"

Seb's dark eyes flicked to me for a fraction of a second.

"Actually," Priya continued, practically bouncing with excitement. "I was just telling Flynn about his *very* interesting leaves. They're showing signs of an incredible romance on the horizon—"

"Or a fish!" I blurted out, my face burning. "She said it could also be a fish. With teeth. That might eat me."

"The fish interpretation was clearly secondary." Priya waved her hand dismissively. "The romantic energy is much stronger. See these swirling patterns here? Classic signs of passion and—"

"Really fascinating stuff about the fish, though," I cut in, desperately avoiding Seb's gaze. "Proper *Jaws* vibes. Very scary. Much more likely than any... other interpretations."

Seb's low chuckle sent a rather delicious shiver down my spine. "Priya's readings do tend to fixate on romance. Last month she told Kit he'd meet a mysterious dark-haired stranger who'd sweep him off his feet."

"And he did!" Priya protested.

"He fell down some stairs and a paramedic with black hair helped him up." Seb's gaze lingered on me, a hint of mischief playing across his features. "Though I suppose we shouldn't dismiss Priya's romantic predictions so quickly. After all..." He stepped closer, and my breath caught. "Her *observations* about new connections have proven rather accurate lately."

My stomach instantly exploded with rabid butterflies. The word choice wasn't accidental—he was definitely referencing our conversation from the other night. But just what was he playing at, flirting once more?

Priya's eyes darted between us, her eyebrows climbing steadily higher.

"Right!" Seb straightened suddenly, breaking the moment. "I need to head out for a few hours. Priya, you're still able to stay until I return?"

"Of course."

"Where are you—" I clamped my lips shut.

"Just a meeting." Seb shrugged on his coat with fluid grace. Tonight's skinny tie was slightly different—a sleek, dark silk that caught the light when he moved.

My heart stuttered. A meeting? *Right.* With who? He'd said he didn't date humans, but what if he had a throng of vampire lovers? Some eternally beautiful creature who shared his darkness, understood his hunger in ways I never could?

The thought of him with someone else—someone supernaturally special and far more sophisticated than me—left me feeling hollow, like someone had scooped out my insides with a rusty spoon.

I was so very mortal and very ordinary. What could I possibly offer someone like him anyway? A boring, average human who'd barely left their tiny fishing village for the past decade.

Not that it mattered. He'd made it clear nothing could happen between us. Even though he kept flirting, the absolute dickhead. Still, watching him straighten his collar, about to leave to meet a mysterious someone... it filled me with nausea.

"Well, I'll be here later!" I cringed at my desperate tone. "You know... because I sort of live here." Until they sorted the demon problem or I died. "For now."

Smooth Flynn. Real smooth. That'll definitely make him forget whatever vampire sex god he's rushing off to meet.

Seb pressed his lips together, clearly fighting a smile. He fussed with the coat on his arm, smoothing the fabric down. "I'll try not to keep you waiting too long."

My heart did a little flip at his words, though his tone remained neutral.

"Good luck with your meeting," I managed, aiming for casual and failing spectacularly.

He turned and strode out without looking back, his footsteps fading down the corridor.

"Well, well, well." Priya's voice dripped with amusement. "Those tea leaves are never wrong."

13

Sebastián

The London streets blurred past as I hurried towards my meeting with Greaves. A week without proper sustenance had left me raw, desperate—a state I despised. It had been torture, rationing what little blood I had, and now hunger clawed at my insides, making me eye every human who passed by.

I'd been avoiding Flynn on and off for days. My gnawing emptiness made it impossible to be near him without imagining biting into that sweet neck of his. His scent permanently lingered in my memory, though some of that could be the fault of keeping my cinnamon bun close to me.

I'd already decided that tomorrow, it was surely my turn again to be with Flynn all day, as long as I obtained at least ten blood bags tonight.

Besides, I needed a replacement bun. Not only had I had several more licks of my current one, it now had a Freddy-sized chunk missing from it.

What a surprise, I chastised myself. Because I was thinking about Flynn *yet again.*

My traitorous thoughts kept drifting against my will to Flynn at any opportunity. His laugh. The way his fingers always seem to find mine when he passed me something. His magnetic energy. The way he'd felt in my arms when he pressed his head against my chest. The trust in his eyes before Eliza's attack shattered it.

It was almost like Flynn kept reaching inside me and playing a discordant note. Each interaction left me off balance, wanting more despite knowing better. Despite what I'd said to him to push him away. Shame burned through me as I remembered that intense conversation. The way

I'd let my guard drop, sharing details about James I'd buried deep. The softness in Flynn's expression as he listened.

My self-loathing deepened as I tormented myself by replaying how I'd acted in the kitchen just now. I was supposed to be *protecting* Flynn—not confusing him, not leading him on. It was like I had no control over myself around him, and for that, I despised myself even more than usual.

I paused at a shop window, studying my reflection. My skin had taken on a greyish tinge, dark circles prominent under my eyes. Good. Perhaps looking like death would remind me what I was—a predator, a monster who survived on blood. Not someone who could offer Flynn anything but pain.

I checked my watch again. Time to meet Greaves. I straightened my coat.

Focus on the task at hand. Get the blood. Feed. Restore control.

I quickened my pace as the underground hospital car park came into view, the stale scent of gasoline and human urine making my nose twitch.

As expected, Greaves's vehicle was parked in the far corner, engine silent and lights off. But something else caught my attention—a massive shape in the harsh fluorescent lighting. I froze. The hyena. That impossible creature, here in the underground car park. It sat perfectly still beside Greaves's car, yellow eyes reflecting the artificial light with an unnatural intensity.

This time, I wouldn't let it escape. I moved forward swiftly, supernatural speed making me nothing but a blur. But as I reached for it, the beast slunk beneath the vehicle, disappearing into shadows. I could have sworn I heard laughter—that distinctive hyena cackle—echoing off the concrete walls.

That's when it hit me. An unmistakable metallic tang permeated the air—the thick, cloying scent of fresh blood. Through the car window, my eyes snapped towards the driver's seat, and I froze.

There sat Greaves, slumped over the steering wheel in a grotesque tableau of carnage. His clothes were shredded, deep gashes crisscrossing his torso like crimson brushstrokes on a macabre canvas. Blood oozed from the wounds, pooling beneath him in a viscous puddle that seemed to breathe with each sluggish drip.

Contorted towards me, Greaves's face was a ruined mask of agony, eyes wide and mouth twisted in a silent scream. His throat... dear Lord, his throat had been torn open, flayed flesh revealing a pale gleam of vertebrae.

I gripped the door handle tighter, knuckles blanching as a guttural growl rumbled in my chest. The scent of fresh blood ignited a primal hunger within me, scorching through my veins like liquid wildfire.

Feed. Feed now.

The call reverberated through my mind, drowning out all other thought. Ancient instincts, older than my conscious memories, clawed their way to the surface. My gaze locked onto Greaves's ravaged form, the gaping wound at his throat like a gruesome beckon. I could already taste the metallic tang on my tongue, my fangs aching to extend and pierce that crimson bounty.

Now now now now now

Part of me recoiled at the feral impulse, disgusted by the depravity it represented. But that voice grew fainter with each splatter of the thick liquid dripping onto the car floor in an agonizing rhythm that hollowed me out until only the hunger remained.

My lips peeled back in a vicious snarl as I yanked open the door. The scent hit me like a tidal wave, crashing over me in dizzying waves that left me reeling. I crawled across the seat towards the still-warm corpse, rationality fraying like a severed thread.

Mine. All mine.

With a low growl, I leaned in closer, fingers digging into the tattered fabric as I inhaled deeply. The coppery musk clung to the back of my throat, urging me to take that final step over the edge into savagery.

My tongue flicked out, brushing against his blood-soaked shoulder, and before I could process what was happening, I was tasting Greaves's essence on my lips.

A tremor of ecstasy shot through me. It had been so long, so very, *very* long since I'd had fresh blood.

I couldn't stop the inevitable.

I pressed my face into the soaked material of his hospital scrubs, dragging my tongue along the fabric in long, greedy strokes.

The rich, salty tang flooded my mouth, and I moaned aloud at the decadent rapture. Every fibre cried out to continue, to bury my fangs in that tempting flesh and gulp down every last drop.

I gathered fistfuls of the blood-drenched scrubs, shoving the fabric between my lips and sucking with desperate, shameful need.

More! More!

My gaze fixed on the ragged tear in Greaves's throat, and before I could stop myself, my mouth was reaching towards that precious fountain of warm blood. Just a moment longer and I'd be—

Through my frenzy, a flicker of humanity sparked within—a memory of a warm smile and tousled, dark blond hair that cut through the crimson haze like a blade. Flynn, at the marina that night, colours dancing in bright blue eyes as he looked at me like he could see into my very soul.

Flynn.

I recoiled as if struck.

What was I doing? This... This was madness. Vile, soulless gluttony that betrayed everything I stood for.

Shame washed over me in waves as clarity gradually returned. I had nearly thrown myself into an orgy of bloodlust over a dead man's corpse, like some ravenous beast without a shred of self-control.

The realization gutted me.

Disgusted, I wiped the back of my hand across my mouth, smearing Greaves's blood in a grim streak. How could I protect Flynn—protect anyone, do my damned *job*—when I still couldn't even protect myself from my own depraved urges?

I squeezed my eyes shut, fighting to regain my tenuous grip on control. When I opened them again, my gaze fell on the name badge still pinned to Greaves's tattered shirt, the white plastic now stained red.

Dr Alistair Greaves. Pathologist.

Like a slap in the face, the reality of the situation materialised. If I hadn't been too busy licking Greaves's blood like a wild animal, I'd have already processed a very important fact—this was no random act of violence.

The open, empty briefcase in the back seat only confirmed it.

This was a personal attack against me.

Against Killigrew Street.

"*Fuck!*" I said aloud, as panic set in. I grabbed my phone, reaching for Kit's SOS button, before changing my mind. There were two people I needed to call first.

Priya answered on the second ring.

"Peacock." My voice came out rougher than intended. "Code Red at the drop site."

"Noctule? What's happened?"

"My supplier won't be making any more deliveries." I glanced at Greaves's corpse. "Ever."

A sharp intake of breath. "Bloody hell. Are you—"

"I need you to lock down the nest. Full security protocol. Check *every* camera feed." My fingers drummed against the car door. "And keep a close eye on our... new friend."

"He's with Magpie in the games room right now, playing air hockey." She paused. "Should I move him?"

"No. Just... watch him." The thought of them all so far away from me, where anything could happen, made my chest tight. "I couldn't secure the supplies. *Any* of them."

"Christ." Her voice dropped lower. "What are you going to—"

"Don't you worry." I cut her off. "Triple-check everything, and keep me updated with messages. I need to know he's—" I caught myself. "That everyone's safe."

"On it. And Noctule?"

"What?"

"Be careful. You're not exactly at your strongest right now."

I ended the call, unable to acknowledge the truth in her words. The hunger gnawed deeper, made worse by my... *lapse.*

I dialled my next number.

"Teddy?" I said, when DI Maxwell picked up, and I couldn't keep my voice from sounding strained. "I need your help. Urgently." My tongue darted out, licking more blood from the corner of my mouth. Shame twisted in my gut as I forced myself to add, "And Detective... I'm afraid I've rather severely compromised a crime scene."

I passed the time waiting for backup by cleaning myself with tissues from the glove compartment. The blood appeared stark against the white, and I fought the urge to taste it. My shirt was ruined beneath my coat, and my black tie was so soaked I stuffed it in my pocket.

I was inspecting under the vehicle for any trace of that damned hyena as Theodore Maxwell's unmarked car pulled up, the small screech of tyres echoing through the quiet underground car park.

"Salazar." His face was grim as he jumped out. "You alright? You look—"

"Like I've had a bath in blood? Yes."

Maxwell stepped towards the car.

"Greaves was already dead when I arrived," I said, repeating exactly what I'd already told him on the phone. I tensed, a part of me prepared for him not to believe me. To suspect this could be a cover-up for a murder I'd committed in bloodlust.

But Maxwell only hummed, rounding the vehicle and using his torch to illuminate the carnage within. "You weren't exaggerating. This is... excessive. And certainly personal, what with the circumstances, I agree. But any idea—"

The roar of a motorcycle cut him off. Kit's massive black bike rolled in with Rory—a surprise addition—clinging to his back. I resisted pinching the bridge of my nose by a hair's breadth. *Perfect. Just perfect.*

Rory yanked off his helmet, golden hair sticking up in all directions. His eyes landed on Maxwell and narrowed. "Oh brilliant. Detective Dickface is here."

"Rory," Kit warned, but Maxwell was already straightening up.

"That's Detective *Inspector* Dickface to you, pup."

"Both of you, shut it," I snapped. "We have a dead body and a potential crisis. Your petty feud can wait."

Kit stepped between them, the perpetual peacekeeper. "What's our next move?"

"There's an unfortunate angle to consider, Kit." I shifted, the blood-soaked tissues heavy in my pocket. "I've... compromised the scene."

Maxwell's torch beam swung towards me, intensifying the moment.

Kit frowned at me. "What?"

"I... licked the blood. From his clothes."

"You *what*?" Kit's face twisted.

"I couldn't help it." The admission tasted bitter. Kit had developed an enormous amount of respect for me over the years, and I couldn't bear to see that faith crumble. "There was so much of it, and I haven't fed properly in—"

"Oh, brilliant." Rory bounced on his heels. "Easy fix then. We torch the car."

"We are not setting fire to evidence." Maxwell scowled at him. "This is a crime scene."

"A crime scene with vampire DNA all over it." Rory rolled his eyes. "Unless you fancy explaining to your forensics team why there's hundreds-year-old Spanish nobleman mixed in with the vic's blood?"

"I'll have to erase Sebastián from the data after we've processed the scene," said Maxwell.

Kit placed a steadying hand on my shoulder. I hadn't realised I was swaying.

"What? Why risk anything?" Rory threw up his hands. "Why don't we drive the car somewhere else? Have a proper look at it all."

Maxwell's voice grew sharper. "That's still tampering with evidence. Which, need I remind you, is also a crime?"

"Everything we do is technically a crime, mate." Rory grinned. "It's kind of our thing."

"I am not your *mate*." Maxwell jabbed a finger at him. "We're following some semblance of procedure here. This dead man has a family."

"Procedure?" Rory's laugh held no humour. "Funny how that's your favourite word—"

"Rory, shut up." Kit's voice carried a hint of a growl. "I mean it."

I pressed my palms against my eyes, trying to focus through the hunger still clawing at my insides. Maxwell's mention of the family Greaves had left behind twisted something dark and familiar in my chest. No, I might not have directly killed Greaves—but he was dead through association.

Another family destroyed. Another set of lives shattered because they'd wandered too close to my orbit. The faces blurred together across the centuries—widows, orphans, parents burying children. Always my fault, my presence that brought destruction. And at the heart of it all, Magdalena's face, eternally young, eternally accusing. Five centuries later, and I was still the same monster who'd condemned his own sister.

It wouldn't matter how many lives Killigrew Street saved, in the end the ledger would always run red. Centuries of blood that could never be washed clean.

"Seb?"

Kit grabbed my arm. "This isn't your fault."

"We need to decide our plan of action, quickly," I said to Maxwell.

An internal struggle played across Maxwell's face as he stared at the car. His shoulders sagged, his torch beam wavering. "I think we'll avoid this going through official channels because of the unique circumstances of the crime. We'll drive the car to a secure location. I'll take some samples, run some tests off the record. See what we can find." He pressed his lips into a grim line. "After a week, we'll find the body in the Thames. I'm not having his family wonder why he's not coming home for any longer than that."

For once, Rory kept his mouth shut. Perhaps even he recognised the weight of Maxwell's compromise.

"We'll work together, Maxwell." I said. "Find who did this, and why." The words felt hollow in my mouth, tasting of copper and guilt.

Kit's hand hadn't left my shoulder. His fingers tightened. "Rory, you go with Maxwell. Take the car to the location. Seb and I will head back to Killigrew Street, run a full assessment."

I knew what he was doing. Kit had seen me like this before, in my darker moments. He wouldn't leave me alone, not with the taste of blood still fresh on my tongue and centuries of ghosts crowding my thoughts.

Maxwell tossed his keys to Rory, who caught them with a surprised blink. "You're driving my car. I'll take this one."

"Seriously?" Rory's face lit up.

"Touch anything except the steering wheel and gear stick, and I'll arrest you myself."

"Aw, handcuffs and all?" Rory twirled the keys around his finger, a wicked grin spreading across his face. "I guessed you'd be into all that."

Maxwell's face darkened, jaw clenching as he stepped into Rory's space. "There's a fucking dead body ten feet away from us. Show some goddamn respect, or I swear to god I'll—"

"Alright!" snapped Kit. "We're moving out! Rory, assist Maxwell with body extraction. You follow his orders to the letter, or there'll be consequences."

Kit pulled on his motorcycle helmet, tossing me the spare one. I slipped onto the back, and as we sped away, I didn't ask him where he was taking us—if I wanted blood immediately, there was only one option remaining.

Kit's bike roared through the empty streets of London, the wind whipping past us. Thirty long minutes later, we pulled up outside Undertone as predicted. My stomach clenched. The last time I'd been here, it hadn't ended well.

We tugged our helmets off, stowing them within the vehicle. "You know this is going to be unpleasant, right?" I said to Kit.

"Do you have any other choice? Unless you fancy another drink from me?"

He said it with a twisted smile. He knew I'd rather not.

The "By Appointment Only" sign glowed dimly in Undertone's window. A bell tinkled as we entered, and the familiar scent of aged vinyl and leather hit my nostrils, barely masking what lay beneath. Jazz music played softly through hidden speakers.

Marlene looked up from behind the counter, their perfect victory rolls and red lipstick unchanged since the 1950s. The vampire's eyes widened. "Sebastián Salazar." They adjusted their cat-eye glasses.

"Marley." I inclined my head.

Their gaze flicked to Kit, then back to me, taking in the blood still staining my clothes. "Are you both... here for a listening appointment?"

"Yes. If possible."

They reached for their rotary phone. "I'll need to check if we have any booths available." Marley's voice remained carefully neutral, but I could sense their curiosity. "I must say, I'm surprised to see you here, Mr. Salazar. I was under the impression you wished never to set foot in here again."

"Circumstances change."

They set down the phone. "I'll take you straight to Dominic."

Marley's boots stomped across the worn floorboards, weaving between towering shelves of vinyl. They led us past countless rare pressings and limited editions that would make any collector weep—the shop's carefully curated façade had fooled many over the decades.

At the back of the shop, three listening booths lined the wall. Marley unlocked booth three, ushering us inside. Kit's shoulders tensed as we squeezed into the tight space, his breathing becoming deliberately measured.

The leather-padded walls still held their original 1960s charm, though the turntable gleamed suspiciously newer. Marley selected a record from a hidden shelf, the needle dropped with practiced precision, and the first notes filled the tiny booth.

The wall behind us slid away with a soft whisper, revealing a steep spiral staircase descending into darkness. LED strips embedded in the steps pulsed in time with the bass from below. The deeper we went, the louder the music became until the staircase opened into a vast underground space.

Kit and I followed Marley straight past the bar constructed from stacked speakers, threading our way through the crowd towards a quieter area.

Dominic's office lay behind a door marked "Master Control Room" in gold lettering. A massive table dominated the space, crafted from hundreds of cassette tapes sealed in resin.

Dominic himself lounged in an elaborate throne-like chair, his platinum hair catching the light.

"Well, well." His long nails drummed against the arm. "He returns. To what do I owe this unexpected pleasure, darling?"

Dominic's lips curled into a smile that made my skin crawl. Despite being nearly three centuries my junior, he'd always acted as though our positions were reversed.

"I require blood," I said, the words scraping my throat. "To purchase."

"The bar's open." He gestured lazily towards the door with one ring-laden hand.

"To take away." The bastard was being deliberately obtuse, as always.

Dominic's smile widened, showing fang. "So, let me get this straight. Four years ago, you barge in here, declare my blood 'unethical,' call me a 'parasitic blood-trafficking degenerate,' and now you're crawling back, begging me for some?" He threw his head back and laughed as if I'd just told the most hilarious joke he'd ever heard.

I kept my expression neutral. "It certainly looks that way."

A soft hissing sound made the hairs on the back of my neck stand up. A massive python slithered out from under Dominic's desk, its scales gleaming in the dim light. Kit and I jumped back instinctively, and his entire body went rigid, his hand closing around my arm. His breathing shifted—shallow and controlled.

I stared at the snake. *This was new.*

"What the hell is this, Dominic?"

He laughed again, softer this time. "Just my pet."

The python wound its way across the floor between us, its tongue flicking out to taste the air. My skin crawled as it circled closer. I tried to ignore it.

"Will you sell me the blood, or not?"

Dominic made a show of considering, tapping one finger against his bottom lip before pulling out his mobile and typing out a message.

We waited in tense silence while the python continued its slow, threatening dance around us.

"Do you have a licence for that animal?" Kit asked.

Dominic's eyes widened with mock innocence. "Does Sebastián have a licence for you?"

A low growl rumbled in Kit's chest.

Thankfully, the door opened and a staff member slipped in, carrying a tray laden with small metal casks—about a dozen of them, each a litre at most. They set the tray down silently, bowed to Dominic, and departed.

"And how many would you like to purchase?"

I eyed the casks, relief flooding through me despite my best efforts to hide it. "I'll take them all."

"That'll be ten thousand per cask. Cash only." His grin turned malicious.

"You have to be joking." Fury rose in my chest.

"Ten thousand for desperate, entitled vampires who've burned all their bridges."

God damn him! I turned to face the door, biting down on my knuckle.

After a moment, I faced him again. "I don't have anywhere near that much cash on me," I explained, voice level. "I have twelve thousand."

Dominic lifted one of the casks, unscrewing the top, drinking deeply, his Adam's apple bobbing with each gulp. The smell hit me—fresh, clean blood. My body shook with need. Kit's grip on my arm tightened.

"Well..." Dominic wiped his mouth delicately with a handkerchief. "Looks like you'll only be able to buy one, then, doesn't it?"

My jaw tight, I retrieved the cash from my bag. I held it out to Dominic, with barely contained fury. Ten thousand would have bought me twenty of Greaves's bags.

Dominic's manicured fingers plucked the notes from my grip. His smile widened as he counted each one with deliberate slowness. He nodded towards the silver casks arranged on the desk.

I reached for the nearest cask, desperate to leave this place and never return.

In a flash of green, the python struck without warning, its massive jaws snapping inches from my outstretched hand. I stumbled, crashing into Kit. He caught me easily enough, but his pulse skyrocketed, and his eyes took on that thousand-yard stare I'd seen before—focused on everything and nothing at once.

There was no time to reassure him—Dominic's laughter bounced off the vinyl-lined walls. "Down, precious." He clicked his tongue, and the snake slithered back to him, coiling around his chair. "Just making sure you weren't thinking of helping yourself to more than you paid for."

I snatched the cask, clutching it to my chest. The metal was cool against my fingers, the contents inside calling to my starved body.

"If you get bored with your little moral crusade," Dominic drawled as I turned to leave, "I can find you work here. Some of our clients would pay handsomely for a taste of Spanish nobility."

I stormed out, through the club and up the stairs. Outside, the rage consumed me before I could stop it, and my fist connected with the brick wall, sending shockwaves of pain up my arm.

Blood roared in my ears. The cask felt like it was burning against my palm, taunting me with its presence. The smug bastard had relished every second of my desperation.

Kit's hand pressed against my back, warm and steady. "Don't let that wanker get under your skin." His voice cut through the fog of fury clouding my mind. "I'll return solo next time. You don't need to see him again."

I pulled my hand back from the wall, flexing my bruised knuckles. "Let's go."

As we travelled back, Kit's hands were steady on the bike's controls—they always were—but I caught how his head tilted at each passing vehicle, how he tracked movement in his mirrors with military precision. Even after we'd left Undertone far behind, his shoulders remained combat ready beneath his leather jacket. Some habits, I knew, were drilled too deep to fade.

Kit dropped me at a tunnel entrance after I promised to ring him if needed. The journey through the network passed in a haze as I clutched the cask to my chest, trying not to calculate how many days it might buy me.

Reaching Killigrew Street's basement felt like a victory. The hotel's familiar musty air wrapped around me, bringing me immense comfort. I checked the kitchen, disappointment flooding through me when it was completely deserted.

Flynn must be upstairs, asleep probably.

I climbed the stairs, body heavy with exhaustion, the silver cask in my hands a reminder of tonight's humiliation at Undertone. At least—

The scent hit me like a battering ram.

Flynn's blood.

My entire body seized both with primal hunger and immense worry. The cask slipped from my grip, clattering against the steps. I scooped it up, then bounded up the remaining stairs, my feet barely touching the ground as I raced down the corridor, following that intoxicating trail.

There, by my bedroom door, two objects were waiting for me. A glistening glass tumbler, partially filled with crimson liquid. A note, reading: "Don't be mad — F".

I stared at the words, something deep within me cracking open.

Foolish, reckless human. I pressed the note to my chest.

There was no doubt in my mind about what I'd do with Flynn's blood. This precious, blessed gift.

With the utmost care, I lifted the glass, my fangs itching to extend with the excitement.

While I unlocked my door, I pulled my phone from my pocket.

I dialled Flynn's number.

14

Sebastián

F lynn answered on the first ring.

"Sebastián," he said on a rushed breath.

"Your blood belongs in your body," I snapped, cradling the glass to my chest as I lowered myself into the armchair in the corner of my room, my limbs heavy after the long evening.

"But I've got so much of it."

The light, teasing quality in Flynn's voice twisted something inside me.

I stared at the glass in my hand, the rich crimson catching the dim light. I *could* tip it down the sink. I *could* march straight to Flynn's door and return it. Both sensible options.

But the scent—Lord help me, the scent. My fingers tightened around the glass as memories of that single taste of his blood flooded back. Every cell in my body screamed for more, my hands trembling as I raised it closer.

Ten sips, I calculated. I could make it last. Draw out each precious drop.

The first taste hit my tongue and my eyes rolled back. That strange electricity I'd noticed before had intensified tenfold, crackling through me like storm clouds ready to burst. Pure ecstasy flooded my senses, a pleasure so intense it bordered on spiritual. This wasn't mere sustenance—this was communion with something sacred.

A moan caught in my throat, and I barely managed to suppress it.

"You know, like eight pints of it or something." Flynn's voice crackled through the phone. "I'm sorry I couldn't get more out for you."

"Flynn, I made myself clear—"

"It was just a little bit!"

The second sip hit harder than the first. My body sang with pleasure, every nerve ending alight. Before I could stop myself, a third mouthful slid down my throat.

My fangs extended with a familiar ache. For once, I didn't fight their appearance. What was the point?

Though the gift was cool, Flynn's blood still warmed every inch of me, sliding down like liquid silk.

"How did you even get it out?" The image of Flynn with a blade to himself turned my stomach. "Do I dare ask?"

"Well, I was just going to slash my arm a bit with a kitchen knife but then Priya helped."

The phone creaked in my grip. *Priya?* What must she have been thinking? "Priya *helped*?"

"Yeah! She did it all properly and everything. Disinfected it all. She only let me give you that tiny bit."

I took a fourth sip. The fury at Priya melted away as Flynn's essence flooded my system. My head fell back against the chair. I couldn't truly be angry, not while I sat there nursing the glass as if it were water in a desert.

A fifth sip. Slower now, savouring.

"Are you drinking it now?" Flynn's voice dropped lower, curious.

I couldn't lie. Not with his blood on my tongue. "Yes."

"Is it... good?"

Divine. Utterly divine. Beyond words.

"Yes."

A breathy little "Oh" escaped Flynn's lips, then his voice dropped to a whisper to ask, "What does it taste like?"

The sixth sip rolled across my tongue. Sweet copper notes mixed with something uniquely *Flynn*—sea salt and citrus and sunshine. But underneath those familiar notes lurked a current buzzing beneath the surface, foreign yet intoxicating.

The seventh mouthful followed close behind. My body hummed with pleasure.

"Why are you using that voice?" I said.

"What voice?"

"That come-hither-and-fuck-me voice."

Flynn broke into a shocked coughing fit. The sound yanked me from my blood-drunk haze, though not enough to stop the eighth sip from passing my lips.

"Look, if that's what you're hearing, that's on you," he said.

The final drops beckoned. I tipped the glass back, letting the sacred liquid pool on my tongue. Flynn's essence filled my mouth—bright and alive and truly the most delicious thing I ever remembered tasting.

I swallowed, once.

It was over. My last ever taste of him.

I mourned its loss as a visceral thing, like watching the last ember of a fire fade to ash. The last hint of him lingered on my tongue. His warmth coursed through my limbs—leaving me feeling strangely strong, considering the tiny amount. Even my fingertips tingled with vitality, as if I could feel every grain in the crystal glass beneath them.

"Show me where Priya cut you. I want to see a photo."

I needed to ensure they hadn't mutilated him. Priya and I clearly had very different definitions of acceptable risk.

"Give me a sec."

The line went quiet. I turned the empty glass in my hands. The remnants of his blood clung to the sides, taunting me.

My phone buzzed.

I swiped—and there he was. Not his arm, but Flynn himself, sprawled across his bed in those ridiculous red-chequered pyjamas. His eyes crinkled with pure joy as he stuck his tongue out at the camera, playful and perfect.

My dead heart tried to beat again.

I almost couldn't believe my luck. I'd looked at the other picture he'd sent me—him stuffing a croissant into his mouth—countless times, and now I had another one to join it.

"That's not what I asked for." I tried to sound stern.

"I know. But you seemed stressed. Thought you could use cheering up."

I stared at the photo again. The warmth in his expression, the way his hair fell across his forehead, slightly messy. The casual intimacy of seeing him in his nightwear. I reached for the metal cask, pouring a measure of blood into the glass. I took a sip. Flat, lifeless—nothing like the symphony of flavours that had danced across my tongue moments ago. Like tap water compared to wine.

I tried not to think about where this blood might have come from, and with how much consent.

"You still there?" Flynn asked.

"Yes." I drained the glass. "Thank you. For both the blood and the photo."

Warning bells erupted in my mind, but I ignored them.

"You know," he said, dropping his voice to a level that bordered on husky, "I was just thinking about photos. It got me wondering about where sexting comes into your vow of celibacy."

"Sexting?"

The photo glowed up at me from my phone screen. Felix had set my lock screen to Monet's water lilies. Would I even be able to work out how to replace it with Flynn's face?

"You know, like sexy messages." He was back to sounding like his usual, slightly awkward self, and my lips tugged into a smile.

"Flynn—"

"This is your fault. You've made me all hot and bothered by accusing me of using a *come-hither* voice."

I let out a long sigh, then a stretch of silence filled the line between us.

My fingers drummed against the arm of the chair as two warring instincts battled within me—the urge to protect Flynn, and the desperate need to allow myself *something*, at least.

I studied his photo again. The playful spark in his eyes. The way his pyjama top had ridden up slightly, exposing a sliver of pale stomach.

"Tell me more about this sexting." The words left my mouth before I could stop them, and I almost couldn't believe what I was saying.

But...

The warmth of his blood still coursed through my veins, dulling the edge of my constant hunger. Flynn wouldn't be staying here for long—once I'd annihilated the evil that dared to harm him, he'd be back to the life he was building for himself in London. Our paths would never cross again. So why shouldn't I indulge in some harmless flirtation, with multiple walls between us and blood in my system to quell my monster?

"Well, how about I show you? It will probably be easier if we hang up. Else I might laugh."

Before I could formulate a response, the line went dead.

I stared at my phone, mouth agape. Had he really just—

A message notification appeared.

My thumb hovered over it, a barrage of second thoughts clouding my mind. This was dangerous territory. I should ignore it, delete the message, turn my phone off and—

I opened it.

The photo loaded.

Christ.

Flynn's pale torso filled my screen. His hand hooked into his pyjama bottoms, tugging them low enough to reveal a band of white cotton beneath. Dark hair trailed down from his navel, disappearing beneath the waistband.

A fierce hunger surged through me—not for blood, but for touch. To trace that trail of hair with my fingertips, to feel the warmth of living flesh beneath my hands. It had been so long since I'd allowed myself to want like this, to imagine the press of skin against skin.

My mouth went dry. The metal cask beckoned—perhaps another measure would steady my nerves. But moving felt impossible. Every muscle in my body had locked into place, transfixed by that strip of exposed skin, that teasing glimpse of what lay beneath.

A flash of desire sparked low in my belly, kindling into flame.

My mind replayed that moment when Flynn had confessed his inexperience, his shoulders tensed as though bracing for mockery or pity. If only he knew how that knowledge had stirred something fierce in me—not simply lust, but an overwhelming need to ensure his first experiences would be nothing short of sacred. Oh, the ways I would worship him, if given the chance. I would take him apart with centuries of practiced patience, piece by precious piece, until he was consumed with pleasure.

Such thoughts were a betrayal of my duty. Flynn was here under my protection, and I shouldn't complicate matters with base desires. It wasn't fair to him.

Still, I found my fingers moving across the keyboard of their own accord.

I hit send before I could think better of it. The message showed as read immediately. I flicked back up to see Flynn again. My trousers grew uncomfortably tight, and I shifted in the armchair, trying to find a more dignified position.

Without thinking, my palm pressed against the fabric, providing a hint of relief. A quiet groan escaped my lips. When was the last time I'd allowed myself this kind of release? Months, at least. Perhaps longer. Time had a way of blending together.

The three dots appeared at the bottom of my screen, and my heart performed a phantom race.

The question paralysed me. Images surged through my mind unbidden—Flynn beneath me, my hands pinning his wrists, my fangs grazing his throat. The monster in me yearned to claim, to possess, to mark. To *feed*. But that path led to darkness. To blood, pain, and loss.

I forced those thoughts down, burying them beneath my practiced, hard-won control. Flynn deserved gentleness. Tenderness. Safety. Everything I wasn't sure I could give him.

> Insist you put your shirt back on because it's cold up here.

> Seb!!!!

His response made me smile, and the ache built between my legs. My fingers hesitated over my belt buckle, toying with the catch.

I could barely contain my excitement as another photo popped onto the screen. *Skin. So much skin.* Flynn's pyjama bottoms were now conspicuously absent, and so was his underwear. Flynn's hand rested on his cock, the base peeking out from beneath his thumb. He was fully erect—though I doubt it was because of my humour. He'd been stroking himself.

I swallowed hard, my own arousal surging. This photo wasn't enough. I needed to see more, all of him. I wanted to see him touch himself, watch as he brought himself to the edge.

My hand moved quickly to my belt buckle, unfastening it. I slid my trousers and underwear down, my hardened length springing free. It was already flushed, slick with a bead of precum which I quickly swiped before rubbing fast circles on the sensitive head.

I closed my eyes, imagining Flynn's cock rubbing against mine. The sounds he'd make. The thought sent dark heat coiling through my veins, and I let out a low groan.

Fuck.

I had been enjoying touching myself so much that I hadn't replied to his last message. One hand kept up its firm strokes while the other typed with manic haste.

> **Well, for one, I'd rip that naughty hand of yours far away from what it shouldn't be touching.**

A stream of those 'emojis' with flushed faces appeared on my screen. I took that as a win. Then:

> **Oh yeah?**

I could practically hear the smirk in his voice, and it made me *want* even more. I continued to stroke myself, my grip tightening as my imagination painted glorious pictures of what was happening in the room a few doors down. Flynn's body, his skin flushed with pleasure, his eyes closed in rapture. I pictured him lying on his back, his legs spread wide, his hand moving in slow, languid strokes over his cock. I imagined the way his lips would curl up into a soft smile as he touched himself, the way his eyelashes would flutter with each ragged breath. His body arching off the bed as he reached the peak of his pleasure, his muscles tensed, his fingers digging into the sheets. And I was there with him, my body pressed against his, my lips tracing the curve of his ear, my fingers intertwined with his as we reached the edge of oblivion together.

It was my turn to reply, and I'd already left it an age. I stared at the screen, fingers hovering over the keys. Five centuries of existence, and here I was, fumbling like a schoolboy over how to compose an erotic message. Poetry would be preferable to this modern dance of digital desire.

What would he want to hear? What would make him writhe between those sheets, make his breath catch? The thought of him waiting for my response, perhaps growing uncertain at my delay, spurred me to action. I had to trust my instincts, let the hunger I felt for him guide my words.

> **Yes. And then I'd worship you properly—on my knees, taking you so deep you'd never think of another's touch again. I'd claim every inch of you.**

Eyes glued to the screen, I waited anxiously for a reply that didn't immediately come. Even more than another message, I'd trade anything for one more picture.

Preferably his face as he came, my name on his lips.

No wait, I wanted—*needed*—to see that cock of his in its entire glory.

My pace increased to frenetic levels, my toes curling.

But Flynn had gone silent, and I felt his absence like a missing tooth.

Just as I was about to message him again, I caught it—a tiny gasp, impossibly faint, muffled by multiple walls. It was as if my hearing had attuned to him and him alone, picking up the tremor in his breath, the subtle catch in his throat.

I reached for my phone.

> Those sweet little sounds you're making? I can hear them. You're performing beautifully for me.

> Want to hear even clearer?

My phone buzzed, and I didn't even hesitate for a fraction of a second.

Obscene sounds burst out of the device, and I jammed speakerphone lightning fast. The wet, rhythmic slapping of skin on skin filled the room, punctuated by Flynn's ragged breaths and desperate moans. It was a symphony of pleasure, and I was the captive audience.

"Fuck!" he said, sounding desperate, needy, *wrecked*. "*Sebastián*."

Lord help me, the way he said my name almost made me break down those walls to get to him.

I brought my palm to my mouth, mustering all the saliva I could, then returned my hand to my rock-hard length.

"Flynn," I rasped, teetering on the precipice of release. "Don't stop. Let me hear every moment." The words reeled out of me. "You're perfection." And then, because desire clouded all reason. "Tell me—would you rather feel me deep inside you, or bury yourself within me?"

"God, *yes*—both." His voice wavered, his breath hitched. "Everything. Anything. Whatever you want."

His words sent a violent shudder through me. Such sweet surrender, such perfect trust—and the promise of claiming and being claimed in return. The depth of want that coursed through me was painful. Dangerous. This beautiful creature would be my undoing, and I found myself welcoming the fall.

Flynn's sounds grew louder, more frantic. The slick slide of his hand over his cock, the hitch in his breath as he neared the edge. I could almost feel the heat of his body, the weight of him in my arms.

If only. If only. If only.

"Yes, just like that," I whispered, my voice cracking with emotion. "I'm right there with you, *mi amor*, holding you close." A strange pang of sadness hit me, and hot tears pricked at the corners of my eyes. This fantasy was the most exquisite torture—being so close to Flynn in my mind while knowing a few mere walls might as well be oceans between us.

"You are?" Flynn's voice was barely audible.

"Of course. My hand is at your hip, drawing you against me," I murmured, my words tumbling out in a rush. "Every inch of you pressed to me. You're burning like sunlight, Flynn. My lips trace the curve of your neck." My throat constricted, and I swallowed hard, trying to clear the lump that had formed. How had Flynn, in such a short time, made me feel more alive than I had in decades? More human. More vulnerable. "Can you feel it?"

"Yes," he whispered with a tremble.

I closed my eyes, letting the fantasy consume me whole. "I'm breathing against your ear, grazing that perfect lobe with my teeth." I could almost taste his pulse there, feel the delicate shell of it beneath my lips, that forbidden spot where I could so easily—

He gasped, a sharp, startled sound, and my body trembled in response, desperate for release.

"I'm pressing my fingers to your lips. First one, then another. And you're taking them into that perfect mouth of yours, your tongue a wicked temptation against them. Such sweet torment." Some deep part of me balked at my bold, explicit words, but I forced myself to continue. My voice dropped to a hoarse whisper. "You're drawing them deeper, and I can feel every detail—the sharp edge of your teeth, the velvet of your lips."

The words had barely left my lips when I was rewarded with the unmistakable sound of Flynn sucking on his own fingers—a soft, slurping noise that made my cock ache impossibly harder.

Holy Lord Almighty.

Spitting once more on my hand, I closed my eyes and imagined my fingers in Flynn's mouth, feeling the wet heat of his tongue as he swirled it around them. Flynn let out a soft moan, and I could almost picture him lying in his bed, his body writhing with pleasure. I wanted so very desperately to be there with him, to feel his skin against mine, to taste him.

As I listened to Flynn's ragged breathing and the sweet sounds of his pleasure, my own body reached its breaking point. I felt the familiar tingle at the base of my spine, and then lightning-hot bliss ricocheted through me, sending me crashing over the edge. My hand moved swiftly, stroking myself to completion, and I felt my cock seize and spasm, releasing a cool, pulsing jet of cum onto my shirt. I let out a low, ragged gasp, panting as the waves of pleasure washed over me, my body trembling with the force of my orgasm. For a moment, everything else was lost, and all that existed was my imagined pounding of my beating heart and the sweet, sweet sound of Flynn's pleasure.

"Flynn," I rasped. "Did you hear what you did to me?"

"Yes." His breathing increased. He was close.

"I'm touching you now," I said. If only it were true. *If only.* "Rubbing my fingers against you. Do you like that?"

"Mmmm," was the only reply.

"I'm inside you, Flynn. Claiming you completely. My fingers are taking you apart piece by piece, pressing just where you need them."

Flynn's scream was sudden and raw, but it was swiftly muffled, as if he'd bitten down on his lip or clamped his hand over his mouth, the sound dying on his lips in a stifled gasp.

"Have you finished?" I asked, voice rough with longing.

He didn't reply.

"Let me taste your pleasure," I breathed. "Every precious drop." My tongue chased phantom sensations, memories that weren't mine to own.

More silence.

A single tear traced down my cheek, catching me entirely off guard. I brushed it away with trembling fingers. After decades of control, how had this single moment managed to crack me open so thoroughly?

"You taste like salvation," I breathed, the words carrying the weight of truth. "Perfect beyond measure. Beyond anything I've known in all my years."

The soft rhythm of Flynn's inhales and exhales whispered through the line, deliberate as a metronome.

"Flynn?" Cold terror swept through me—had I gone too far? "Please, tell me you're well." The silence stretched like a blade between us, and for a moment I was certain I'd ruined everything.

Then finally, the tiniest of tentative voices. "Please come here. I need you. I need to hold you. I promise I won't ask for more than that." Thick emotion coloured his words, and he inhaled sharply. "I need it so badly."

A deafening quiet replaced his plea as my mind raced. The rules I'd made, the boundaries I'd set—they all seemed to crumble in the face of his words. His vulnerability. The promise in his voice of something I'd denied myself for so very long: connection.

I hung up, forcing my body—still trembling with pleasant aftershocks—to its feet.

My rules didn't matter. Nothing else mattered. I had to see him. I had to touch him. I had to have him in my arms.

I knew, as sure as all the stars in the sky, that he'd be safe with me. His blood might sing to me, but his trust meant more. His warmth.

His light. After an eternity of darkness, I'd been caught by his gravity, unable—unwilling—to break free from his orbit.

Though simply to be *entirely* sure of his safety, I swiped the cask off the side and took as large a gulp as I dared, to keep any lingering hunger at bay for a couple more hours.

Energy surged through me, unlike anything before. Usually after feeding, a pleasant lethargy would settle in my limbs, but tonight every nerve ending crackled. My muscles coiled with untapped strength, as if I could run for miles without tiring.

I yanked off my ruined shirt before snatching up a fresh one from a drawer.

The corridor stretched before me, and each step carried the weight of anticipation. The brass numbers on door 208 gleamed in the dim light.

I knocked, and the door opened immediately. Flynn stood there, bare aside from a towel around his waist, skin wet from what must have been a very hasty shower. A small bandage was wrapped above his elbow. Droplets traced paths down a defined torso—his shoulders and arms bore the subtle definition of someone who'd spent countless hours wrestling with sails and fighting tides.

Flynn's ocean-deep eyes widened, filled with a mix of... *hope and disbelief?*

"You came." The words tumbled from his lips, soft and wondering.

The scent of his recent pleasure hung in the air—intoxicating as hell, especially combined with the smell of Flynn's soap.

"You asked me to." I kept my voice steady, though every inch of me sang with awareness of the proximity of his almost naked body.

I stepped into the room, and he shut the door behind me.

"I thought you would say no." His voice dropped to barely above a whisper, raw honesty carving itself onto his face.

The admission stung.

"Come here."

I'd craved another chance to hold him since that night in the kitchen. I opened my arms, and Flynn stepped into my embrace without hesitation. His head tucked perfectly beneath my chin, and I breathed in the citrus scent of his damp hair. My arms encircled him, one hand splaying across his bare back while the other curled around his waist.

His slightly smaller frame fit against mine as if crafted for this purpose, and a deep contentment settled inside me. Like the first moment of silence after the tolling of cathedral bells. Though beneath my palms, I felt tiny tremors running through his body.

"You're shaking," I murmured into his hair.

"I'm fine," he said, muffled against my chest.

I guided him towards the bed, snatching up his pyjama bottoms and a blanket from the nearby chair. "Here." I pressed them into his hands.

"I'm not cold," Flynn protested, though his skin had broken out in gooseflesh.

"I can't join you in that bed unless you're wearing trousers." The words came out firmer than I'd intended.

Boundaries. I still had them. Even if they got murkier by the second.

Flynn's eyes met mine for a long moment before he nodded, stepping back to pull on the pyjamas. He left his chest bare, and my gaze traced the constellation of the few water droplets still clinging to his skin. The thought of touching him, of feeling his lovely warmth beneath my palms, sent a thrill through me.

"You don't want a shirt?" I asked. "I'm afraid I'm not the warmest bed companion." Just one of the many, many ways I was wrong for Flynn, right underneath my intolerance of sunlight, and the fact that my hands had spilled enough blood to fill the Thames.

"Nah. I always run hot. I'll probably sleep way better with you cooling me down." He smiled at me as if it was such a simple thing.

Eyeing his bandage, I beckoned him closer with two fingers. "Show me."

He offered me his arm. "Honestly, this is overkill. It barely needed a plaster."

I unwrapped it carefully, inspecting Priya's handiwork. The cut was small, precise. If I were to lick it, I could speed up the healing process.

But that would be too much temptation.

I rewrapped the bandage, letting my touch linger longer than necessary. "Don't do that again." It almost pained me to say it. "I mean it, Flynn. It was... incredibly kind of you. But not again."

Flynn nodded, then moved towards the queen-sized bed. He slipped under the covers, then patted the empty space beside him. "Come on. You're making me nervous just standing there."

My feet felt like lead as I approached the bed. I lowered myself onto the mattress with all the grace of a statue learning to move, sliding beneath the covers while maintaining a careful distance.

A laugh bubbled up from Flynn's throat. "You look like you're being tortured. Relax." His eyes sparkled with amusement in the dim light. "And take off your shirt."

"I'm not sure that's the best idea." The words came out stiff.

"Please?" His voice softened in a way that made my resolve waver.

I gave a slight nod, my fingers moving to the top button of my shirt. Before I could undo it, Flynn's hand caught mine, stopping the motion. The warmth of his touch made me sharply inhale a breath of air.

He shifted closer, replacing my fingers with his own at my collar. The first button slipped free under his touch. His breath ghosted across my neck as he worked his way down, each movement deliberate, careful. The brush of his knuckles against my chest with each button felt like sparks dancing across my skin.

I remained perfectly still. The air between us grew thick, and I counted his heartbeats instead of the buttons being undone.

When he was finished, he finally looked up, and we shared a look that crackled like lightning trapped in a bottle. That perpetually wayward strand of his hair had broken free again, falling across his forehead. I reached up to smooth it back, my fingers lingering perhaps a moment too long.

His gaze dropped to my mouth, and I mirrored the action, studying the soft curve of his lower lip. The space between us seemed to shrink, charged with possibility. It would be so easy to close that distance, to taste that blessed warmth I could feel radiating from his skin.

Breaking the spell, Flynn reached over and switched off the lamp. The room plunged into near darkness, though my eyes adjusted instantly, allowing me to see his silhouette.

"Turn around," Flynn said.

"What?"

"I want to be the big spoon."

"What?" The word came out again, this time bewildered.

Flynn let out an exasperated sigh. Before I could process what was happening, his hands were on my shoulders, gently but firmly turning me onto my side. He pressed himself against my back, moulding his body to mine until we touched from shoulder to ankle. His arm draped over my waist, pulling me closer.

The sensation overwhelmed me, my brain short-circuiting. *Twenty years.* Twenty years since anyone had held me like this. The simple intimacy of it struck me deeply, and I felt my throat constrict. A hot, sharp ache built behind my eyes as Flynn's warmth seeped into my cold skin. His breath tickled the nape of my neck, steady and reassuring.

My chest tightened with an emotion I couldn't name. Something between grief and joy, between longing and finding. A tear slipped free before I could stop it, trailing silently down my cheek and onto the pillow.

I had forgotten what this felt like. To be held. To be touched with such innocent tenderness. To feel anchored to another, tethered to safety. To feel human.

Like darkness wasn't all I had to offer.

My body betrayed me, trembling beneath Flynn's touch. The shaking started in my hands, spreading through my limbs until I couldn't control it. Panic clawed at my throat at this loss of control.

"Shh." Flynn's voice was barely a whisper as he stroked up and down my arm, his palm leaving trails of warmth.

How strange, to allow myself to be comforted like this. To let someone else take control, even for a moment.

Muscle by muscle, my body began to surrender. The tension in my shoulders melted away first, followed by the rigid set of my spine. The knot in my jaw loosened, then my clenched fists relaxed. Eventually, I became as pliant as clay beneath a sculptor's hands.

Flynn radiated heat like a furnace against my back, his warmth seeping into my perpetually cold flesh. The contrast between us was stark—he was so incredibly, deliciously warm. I was surely stealing all his warmth, like a leech drawn to living flesh.

His hand moved from my arm, circling my shoulders. His fingers trailed down my chest, tentative at first, then bolder. When they brushed across my nipple, pleasant rushes of liquid fire shot through me. The monster within stirred—savage, demanding—flooding my mind with images of how easy it would be to twist, to pin his writhing body beneath mine, to sink my fangs into that perfect throat while he gasped my name.

"Flynn." I caught his wrist.

He made a soft chuckle of disappointment. After a moment's hesitation, his voice came again, small. "Can I... stroke your hair?"

The simple request knocked me senseless. Words seemed beyond me—all I could manage was a jerky nod, my throat too tight to speak.

His fingers soon found their way to my head. He scratched gently at my scalp, threading through my thick curls until my whole body hummed with the attention. The sensation was exquisite torture, and I had to clamp my mouth shut to prevent the shamefully needy sounds building in my throat from escaping.

"Rory rang Priya from that detective's car. He told us what happened. He seemed scared for you. Said you looked shaken. Did you know him well? The guy who sold you blood?"

"No. From what little I saw of him, he wasn't the nicest." Though he still had a family, one that he wouldn't be coming home to.

"How did you meet him?"

"Through another doctor, at the hospital. One who moved out of the area, and thought Greaves could continue to help me in his stead."

"And what will you do now, for blood?"

"That's not for you to worry about," I said softly.

"I can't help it," he whispered, close to my ear. "Worrying about you."

For a moment, I couldn't speak, lying there as Flynn's fingers continued their gentle exploration through my hair. The sensation was both torturous and divine—each stroke causing shivers I fought to suppress.

"If it comes to it, I'll give you some blood. I want to help you. Like you're helping me."

Helping me. The words were a stark reminder of my failure. We'd made pathetically little progress on his case, hitting dead end after dead end. Felix had trawled through hours of CCTV footage, and Kit had exhausted his network of contacts, but Damien remained elusive. We had no idea where he was hiding, or which demon—or other unknown entity—held his leash.

Precious days were slipping by, days we couldn't afford to waste while that mark slowly poisoned Flynn's system.

"It's my job," I said stiffly, and his hand paused its movement. I immediately wanted to kick myself. "That came out wrong. Obviously, I care for you. Quite a bit."

His fingers resumed their hypnotic path through my curls. "Quite a bit, huh? Wow, you do flatter me so."

I gently kicked him with my leg. "Careful with that cheek."

His laugh vibrated against my back as he drew me impossibly close. "Or what?"

A buzzing sound interrupted any retort. Flynn shifted behind me, reaching for his phone on the bedside table.

"Oops, that's the other vampire I was sexting. I forgot to reply to him."

I instinctively tensed for a moment before I processed the joke. "How many vampires do you know, exactly?"

"Just the one grumpy one." He paused. "It's my mother. She's asking when I'm coming home to visit."

It was on the tip of my tongue to suggest he do just that, but I swallowed my words. It would be extremely unsafe for Flynn to travel anywhere—and he'd possibly be endangering those around him.

"She's threatening to come to London if I don't," Flynn continued, tone laden with guilt. "Says she'll organise someone to accompany her. Her carers are amazing, but..."

"Do you miss Braymore terribly?" I asked, dreading the answer.

"God, yes." His voice grew distant, wistful. "Mostly the ocean. There's nothing like being out there alone. Just me and the water, no land in sight. The way sunlight catches the waves just right, turning the whole world into liquid gold, and the salt spray hits your face like a wake-up call. Like the sea's reminding you you're still here, still breathing. And if you're very lucky, dolphins come and say hey. They'll splash you, though. It's their love language."

His description painted such a vivid picture that for a moment I could almost taste the salt air. "I can't imagine it. I haven't been on a boat in living memory."

Flynn propped himself up on one elbow, looking down at me with surprise. "Never?"

"Never."

A slow smile spread across his face, just visible in the darkness. "Well, that settles it. When we can, we'll go together. I'll teach you everything you need to know."

The earnestness in his voice made something in my chest constrict, a painful stab of a knife. How could I shatter this beautiful moment with impossible truths? That even with an umbrella, I could barely tolerate that sunlight he was so fond of? That the ocean he loved could be lethal to me—the deadly mirror of its surface causing my skin to blister and crack?

"We'll go in the evening, obviously," he added quickly. "When the sun's setting. And if we go in Braymore, the weather's always shit there anyway."

He settled back down against me, his chest warm against my back. Reality pressed heavily on my shoulders. Killigrew Street consumed every moment of my existence. The organisation couldn't run itself—between managing supernatural threats, keeping the peace between the wolf packs, maintaining our network of contacts... There was barely time to think, let alone plan holidays to Ireland.

And wasn't that the crux of it? I was supposed to be protecting him, not indulging in romantic fantasies about sunset sailing. Each of Flynn's exhalations tickling my neck should have been a reminder of my failing, rather than this dangerous, delicious respite I couldn't seem to resist.

"Sounds wonderful," I said to placate him. "I'm sure I'll be in safe hands with you at the helm."

I shouldn't have encouraged it. He was twenty-five, a child really, with all the bright-eyed optimism that came with youth—still believing in possibilities where I saw only obstacles. Still viewing the world as an adventure rather than the dangerous game of chess it was.

But logic crumbled to dust with his chest pressed up against my back, his arm wrapped around me, heavy as an anchor.

He'll be gone soon, to become another fading memory. Enjoy his fleeting warmth while you can.

Flynn fell quiet then, his breathing evening out against my neck. For a moment, I thought he might have drifted off to sleep. But then his voice came again, soft and hesitant.

"Do you remember your mother? Your family?"

"No." The word came out oddly sharp. "I know some from my diaries, which I kept sporadically during my human years. I had an older brother who died of disease, and... a younger sister. Magdalena."

When was the last time I'd spoken her name aloud? The sound of it felt foreign on my tongue.

In my office, locked in an ornate chest that had survived hundreds of moves and a dozen wars, lay those early diaries—leather-bound volumes documenting my journey to Inquisitor, then to the monster I became. The time was approaching to read them again. Soon, I would have to unfold those brittle pages and relive it all. Because I didn't deserve the mercy of forgetting.

Flynn's hand stilled in my hair. "I'm sorry, I shouldn't have asked."

I caught his wrist before he could pull away entirely. "It's fine."

He paused before he asked, tentatively, "*One* more question?"

I tried not to sigh. "I can guess what it is." He wanted to know about my turning. Everyone did, eventually. The morbid curiosity of how one becomes a vampire. But the memory of my sire's face flickered through my mind like a shadow, and I couldn't bear to speak of it. Not now, not when Flynn's radiance had finally quieted the darkness inside me. "But it'll be dawn soon. It can wait for another night." I caught myself too late, realising the implication. "I mean, another time."

"The question was just..." Flynn's arm tightened around me. "Are you going to ghost me?"

"What?"

"I'll wake up and you'll be gone?"

"Well, I'm already dead, aren't I? Though I suppose vampires are an upgrade compared to ghosts—all the haunting, none of the walking through walls."

Flynn's answering laugh was barely more than a breath against my neck. His grip remained firm, as if he could physically prevent me from disappearing. Within minutes, his breathing deepened and evened out as sleep claimed him.

As I lay there, surrounded by his warmth, I couldn't keep thoughts of my sire at bay. Of the way he'd corrupted me, isolated me from my family, twisted my faith until I couldn't recognise myself. The way he'd used my position in the Inquisition, my desperate need to prove myself worthy, to manipulate me into killing my own sister.

Some evils should stay buried in the past where they belonged. Flynn didn't need to know about the priest who'd destroyed everything I was, whose obsession with me led him to turn me into this creature of darkness without my consent. Flynn had enough darkness in his life already—he didn't need mine as well.

I twisted carefully, not wanting to wake him as I repositioned us. Now he lay on his back, and I rested my head against his chest, letting the steady thrum of his heartbeat fill my senses. Each beat called to me—but for once, that call wasn't tied to hunger. Instead, it spoke of comfort, of connection.

The little puffs of Flynn's exhales ghosted across my skin like butterfly wings, delicate and precious. I pressed my palm to his chest, to find the skin there slightly cooler than the rest of him. The demon's mark. My jaw clenched.

I should have attempted to sleep—dawn approached, and with it my body's natural inclination to rest—but I couldn't bear to waste these precious hours unconscious. Instead, I committed every detail to memory: the rise and fall of his chest, the softness of his skin, the way his fingers had curled loosely in sleep.

Running the back of my knuckles over his face, I traced the curve of his cheekbone, the slope of his nose, the slight part of his lips. He looked so young in sleep, so defenseless. So *human*.

"My sweet angel," I whispered, the endearment slipping out of me from a hidden corner. "*Mi amor.*"

Morning would come, and too soon. But for now, I would enjoy this stolen pleasure. I would imagine what it would be like to have him in my arms every night, to measure eternity in the rhythm of his breathing.

15

Flynn

Ice crackled beneath my feet as I trudged through the inky blackness, each step more laboured than the last. An impossibly deep chill seeped into my bones, and I shivered violently. The darkness pressed in from all sides, suffocating and oppressive, broken only by eerie flashes of blue light. I clutched my arms tightly, trying to stave off the bitter cold, fear creeping up my spine as something malevolent stirred in the shadows...

I woke with a start to a pitch-black room, my hand flying to my chest. *Another weird dream.* And now, since yesterday's most recent attack, there was a permanent cold spot across my ribs. I hadn't told Seb about the attack. I hadn't wanted to worry him when we'd been rather... occupied with other activities.

Speaking of Seb...

I reached across the mattress, finding empty space where his solid form should have been. I prepared for the punch to the gut that would follow.

"I'm right here." Amusement coloured Seb's voice.

Lamplight flooded the room, and I squinted to find him perched on the arm of the chair that held my pile of clothes, already dressed in a pristine navy waistcoat, curls perfectly styled. How did he look so put together at—I glanced at my phone—6:47 a.m.?

"What are you doing over there?"

"Your pyjama bottoms magically wiggled themselves off in the night." He raised an eyebrow, his gaze sliding meaningfully to where they lay crumpled on the floor.

Heat assaulted my cheeks as I became acutely aware of my nudity. Thank god for the thick bedding—at least it hid my morning predicament, still present despite the nightmare.

"Come back to bed." The words slipped out before I could stop them, rough with sleep and something more. I still couldn't believe he'd actually come to my room, spent the night in my bed. Let me cuddle him like a teddy bear.

Even if I died a virgin—how many people could say they'd had hot-as-fuck phone sex with a devastatingly gorgeous Spanish vampire?

"I need to start work. I was just waiting until you woke up so you couldn't accuse me of 'ghosting' you."

A small smile played across his lips, and I wanted nothing more than to jump up and kiss him. Like that same wild freedom of jumping off the pier. No hesitation, just the breathless rush of taking the plunge.

Seb shot to his feet. His gaze darted between me and the door as if caught in some invisible tug of war. The air crackled with tension, thick enough to choke on. His fingers twitched at his sides.

My heart hammered against my ribs. Was this it? Would he leave and then we'd pretend none of last night had happened?

But then he moved. One step. Two. Three deliberate strides towards the bed.

I forgot how to breathe.

He leaned down, and his lips pressed against my hair—soft, careful, reverent. The touch lasted barely a heartbeat, yet I felt it down to my bones. His breath stirred my messy bed head, and the familiar scent of him wrapped around me like a blanket.

Without a word, without meeting my eyes, he straightened and crossed to the door. His footsteps were silent on the carpet. The door opened, then clicked shut with finality.

I released the breath I'd been holding with a great *whoosh*.

"Holy fucking shit." The words came out as a whisper. I flopped back onto the pillows, pressing my hands to my burning cheeks. "Holy *fucking* shit."

A giddy laugh bubbled up from my chest. Sebastián Salazar—ancient vampire, feared leader of Killigrew Street—had just kissed me.

Okay, on the head. But still.

I couldn't stop myself from grabbing my phone, desperate to tell someone. I automatically scrolled to Katie's number—but the sister I hadn't spoken to didn't know who Sebastián was. And Emma still thought he was a crazy gun-wielding stalker.

So I opened Seb's message thread, my eyes widening at the daring photos I'd taken yesterday before I typed:

> **I just wanted to say thanks for last night. LOL x**

The message became marked as read instantly. He must have had our chat open. Doing what? Looking at the photographs again? The thought left me feeling dizzy.

He began to type, and I held very still as those three little dots tormented me.

Sebastián

> **LOL.**

Even if he was laughing at me, I'd take that as a win.

"Am I going crazy, or does this guy look exactly like me?"

The sofa springs creaked as Rory bounced down next to me, phone thrust into my face. I squinted at the selfie of two blokes grinning at the camera. "What?"

"Look at him—he's literally my clone, right?" Rory's leg jiggled against mine.

"Which one?"

"Oh, very funny." Rory rolled his eyes. "Obviously not the ridiculously gorgeous Indian guy who belongs on a runway."

I studied the pale guy more closely. Blond, but his hair was straighter than Rory's chaotic mess. "I mean... not really? He's blond but—"

"What? Are you actually blind? We're practically identical!"

"Sorry, mate. Also, this guy looks way taller than you."

Rory snatched his phone back with a huff. "I'm a perfectly normal height, thank you very much. But that's not the point—the point is that my ex is clearly dating my actual twin."

"Oh." I blinked at the photo again. "That's your ex?"

"Yeah, Dev." Rory's mouth twisted. "We were together for eight months. He runs with one of the South London packs."

"I didn't know you were gay. Or bi, or...?"

Rory glanced at me. "Gay. And seriously?" He barked out a laugh. "It's literally our running joke that Seb only hires queer people. Well, except maybe Felix—we've got a bet going on that one."

I blinked. I'd been too fixated on Seb's sexuality to give the rest of them any thought. "Everyone? Even Priya?"

"Don't believe me? Next time you're at the bakery, sneak a peek at her sketchbook. It's full of your scary friend with the spiky hair—the one who keeps threatening to ban me."

"Emma?" My stomach clenched. An urge to shield her from all of Killigrew Street's madness surged through me.

"That's the one. She's planning this whole thing with reading her tea leaves next time. Proper smooth, right?"

I shifted on the sofa. "I'm gay too," I said, testing how it felt to just... say it. Back in Braymore, each confession had been a weight in my chest, knowing how the town's Catholic population would react. But Rory's eyes never left his phone.

"Yeah, cool. Now, do you want to see more photos of my ex's replacement me? I swear he went looking for my upgrade."

A flash of grey darted across my vision. Before I could react, that weird ferret from the third floor scaled Rory's leg and arm in one fluid motion.

It crept along Rory's shoulders like some grotesque scarf, its matted fur patchy enough to reveal bone beneath. Despite its supposedly dead state, those eerie yellow eyes tracked my every movement with unnerving intelligence.

"Is that thing actually…"

"Dead?" Rory grinned. "Freddy, are you dead? What do you think, friend?"

I watched as Freddy's head swivelled one hundred and eighty degrees to look behind him. I felt oddly compelled to touch its fur, wondering if it would feel as cold as it looked. Quick as a striking snake, Freddy lunged for my fingers, yellowed teeth snapping viciously where my hand had been a split second before.

"He only likes me." Rory shrugged apologetically. "And food. He likes food."

Loud footsteps thundered down the basement stairs as Kit joined us. Perching on the armrest like some sort of brooding gargoyle, he coughed, then asked, "Is Felix hiding in his cupboard again?" while scowling in that general direction.

"If he wants to do extra work, what's the problem?" Rory said, eyes back on his phone.

Kit turned his scowl on his brother, but before he could respond, Priya bustled in through the bookcase carrying a Fat Cat's Coffee carrier.

"Morning, boys. Got your usual orders." She started distributing cups.

Kit's scowl deepened as he accepted his, eyes sliding to the broken coffee machine. Then he marched off to Felix's lair. Moments later, he returned, dragging a bleary-eyed Felix by his hoodie.

"I was just coming," Felix protested weakly.

"Well, now you're here," Kit answered, depositing him onto an armchair before hovering just behind it.

I checked my phone. 9:02 a.m. Strange. Usually, Seb would have started the briefing by now, pacing around the room, reeling off instructions while the others took notes. Or pretended to.

"Seb's never late," Kit said, frowning at the doorway.

Voices drifted from the basement. The bookcase swung open to reveal Seb with DI Maxwell, the detective from the morgue.

Beside me, Rory tensed. His face hardened as he glared at the man who'd arrested him years ago, coffee cup crumpling in his grip. Mental note: never get on Rory's bad side.

DI Maxwell's gaze swept the room, landing on Rory. Their eyes locked—Maxwell's jaw clenched, muscle twitching beneath his stubbled skin. Was Rory shouting abuse at Maxwell in his head again? Honestly, telepathy seemed like a raw deal.

Seb cleared his throat. "Detective Maxwell will be joining us periodically as we collaborate on several cases." He paused, his expression tightening. "Or rather, *one* case, as it turns out."

Everyone sat up straighter. Priya's coffee cup froze halfway to her mouth.

Seb pulled down a projection screen and connected his laptop. After several failed attempts to get it working, Felix sighed dramatically, shuffled over, and pressed one button. An image appeared—a disturbingly mangled body I didn't recognise.

Maxwell fiddled slightly with his glasses, then held up a hand at Seb—though he hadn't even opened his mouth to talk. He stepped forward, shoulders squared, every inch the authoritative detective addressing his team. "The victim is Dr Alistair Greaves, forty-five, pathologist at St. Etheldreda's Hospital."

"*Was* a pathologist," Seb cut in smoothly. "I found the body at approximately ten oh five last night in the underground car park."

Maxwell cleared his throat. "If I could continue—"

"By all means, Detective." Seb's voice dripped with politeness.

"The cause of death appears to be extreme blood loss." Maxwell gestured to the screen. "Multiple lacerations across the torso and neck—"

"Some inflicted by conventional weapons," Seb interrupted again, clicking to zoom in on particular wounds. The images showed clean, precise cuts—surgical almost—alongside savage, jagged tears where flesh had been ripped away. Dark bruising bloomed around the edges of the deeper gashes. "But others—"

"Show clear evidence of vampire feeding," Maxwell finished, shooting Seb a look. "Including significant trauma to the neck area where tissue was... forcefully removed."

My eyes fixed on the grotesque images. The torn flesh, the ragged edges where teeth had... I swallowed hard, Seb's words echoing in my head: *Would you want to risk that? Risk dying in my bed while I feast on your blood like some rabid animal?*

My hand drifted unconsciously to my own neck. The pain must have been excruciating—being torn into like that, feeling fangs rip through muscle and sinew while still conscious.

A wave of nausea rolled through me. The worst part wasn't even the violence itself, but the terror he must have felt in those final moments.

I felt Seb's gaze on me, watching, assessing my reaction to this display of vampire violence. Did he expect this image to scare me off? I kept my expression carefully neutral, though I couldn't stop my heart hammering against my ribs.

"We've moved the body to a secure location for further examination, off-record," Maxwell continued, clicking to the next slide. "Our DIY search found a strand of hair at the scene—it's being rushed through the lab now. We also lifted several partial fingerprints from the car."

"The blood supply he was meant to deliver to me was missing from his car," Seb added, his voice tight with anger. "Ten bags or so, gone."

Priya leaned forward, her braid sliding over her shoulder. "Could the primary motive have been obtaining the blood bags?"

"More likely it's a vampire who doesn't believe in drinking bagged blood." Seb's words carried a weight that made my skin prickle. "Someone who considers it... beneath them."

"We're done being controlled by you, Black!"

Eliza's words crashed over me like a deadly wave. I could almost feel her nails digging into my throat again, the weight of her pinning me against the concrete. The images of Greaves's mutilated body seemed to blur with my memories of that night, of watching Seb tear the vampire apart to save me.

Maxwell's gaze locked onto mine with an intensity that sent a prickle down my spine. His eyes seemed to widen in surprise before he quickly turned away, clearing his throat. "The violence suggests multiple attackers. The varying types of wounds—"

"Attackers who wanted to send a message," Seb cut in, his dark eyes fixed on the projection.

"Indeed."

Seb remained quite still, and my gaze snagged on his black skinny tie tucked into his waistcoat. I couldn't help but remember how he felt in my bed last night, his body pressed against mine, cool but inviting. My fingers had traced patterns through the light dusting of hair across his chest, marvelling at how soft his skin felt despite its temperature.

"You're perfection," he'd said. *"Tell me—would you rather feel me deep inside you, or bury yourself within me?"*

Fuck, the things those words had done to me.

A hollow ache, so deep I could taste it, threatened to swallow me whole. Last night, Seb's voice alone had led to the most intense orgasm of my life, followed by hours of gentle touches.

Now I wondered if that's all we'd ever be—a collection of moments that would never quite become real.

Here he stood, discussing murder, when just hours ago we'd been a tangled mess of limbs. No wonder he was hesitant to let me close. Every happy moment must feel like borrowed time when you're immortal—each touch a reminder of what you can't keep.

The ghost of his kiss still lingered in my hair, and I softly touched it. How many other kisses had he given that had faded into time like this one would?

The projector cast harsh shadows across his face. In the fluorescent light, he looked otherworldly—beautiful and untouchable. A creature caught between life and death, past and present, loneliness and connection.

Something stirred in my chest, wanting to ease his darkness. Last night, I'd glimpsed a vulnerable Seb, almost human. I wanted to be the one who helped him forget about blood and violence. To show him immortality didn't have to mean solitude.

Our eyes met across the basement. Something soft flickered in his expression before vanishing.

Seb cleared this throat, turning back to the screen. "This morning, we reviewed CCTV of the streets surrounding the hospital." He paused, and the air in the room grew thick with anticipation. "And we saw... this."

His finger tapped the laptop touchpad. Grainy footage filled the screen—three figures walking down a dimly lit street, their backs to the camera.

Seb stared at the footage like it held all the answers to the universe. I glanced between the others, but they seemed clueless. "This is them on their way to attack Greaves."

Another tap. "And this is them on their way back."

The new footage froze, and Seb zoomed in on their faces. My stomach plummeted.

A woman, her chin stained dark with what could only be blood. Next to her, a muscular man with close-cropped hair.

But the third face—I knew those features. That smile I'd thought charming, but now seemed cruel. The same face that had leered at me across the bar at Wilde Card, that had pinned me against the alley wall.

Damien.

My coffee cup slipped from my fingers, hitting the carpet with a dull thud.

Freddy leapt from Rory's shoulders, his bony form diving for the spilled coffee. The zombie ferret's yellow eyes glowed as he lapped at the puddle.

"Ahh fuck, he's not allowed caffeine!" Rory exclaimed. "He goes mental on it!"

"Sorry," I offered meekly, heat rising to my cheeks.

Seb's expression shifted from stern to concerned in an instant. "Are you alright?" His dark eyes searched my face. "I should have warned you about—" He gestured at the frozen image of Damien on screen, frustration evident in the set of his jaw.

"No, really, it's fine." I forced a smile, though my hands still trembled slightly. "Just... surprised. To see his face."

"This was completely inconsiderate of me." Seb took half a step toward me, then seemed to catch himself, aware of our audience. I couldn't help but notice the others exchanging *looks*—Priya's eyebrows raised significantly, then Rory smirked into his coffee cup.

I attempted to pull my face into a neutral, impassive, I'm-not-having-a-breakdown-and-Seb-didn't-spend-the-night-in-my-bed look.

"As I was saying, our two cases appear to be connected," Seb said. "These two are from Marcus Vale's clan. This cambion is evidently working with them."

Kit shifted forward, frowning. "That's unusual. They don't typically submit to vampire control."

"Precisely." Seb's fingers drummed against the laptop. "I'm not convinced we have the full picture here."

"Ooh, is your bat sense tingling again?" Rory shot him a beaming grin.

DI Maxwell made a small, exasperated sound, which made Rory's face fall as fast as a thunderclap.

Seb didn't look at either of them, continuing, "This doesn't add up. Vampires wouldn't send a lesser demon to incubate dark magic within humans—they can't harvest that kind of power themselves. It would be pointless. There must be someone or some*thing* else at play here."

Though it was all beyond my understanding, this revelation seemed to hang in the air, heavy with implications. Even Freddy paused his coffee lapping to stare up at us, whiskers twitching.

Seb's expression hardened as he clicked off the projector. "Given these developments, gathering intelligence becomes our absolute priority. All other cases will be temporarily suspended."

My stomach churned, the air disappearing from the room.

"They knew Greaves's schedule," Seb continued. "They've been watching our movements, our patterns. They knew exactly when to strike." His eyes flickered to me briefly before returning to address the room. "We need to implement additional security measures immediately."

Kit nodded stiffly. "We should rotate patrol schedules, change our routes. Maybe set up false patterns to throw them off. Plant some misinformation."

"We need to act as if they're always watching," Seb said hollowly. "Every move. Every contact." His dark eyes swept the room. "They're waiting for one mistake. One error, one moment of weakness—that's all they need to destroy everything we've built."

The tension was suffocating. Priya shifted uncomfortably, her usual brightness flickering like a struggling candle. "Well," she said, attempting a light tone that didn't quite land. "We could always circle back to using Flynn as demon bait—"

"This is not the time, Priya!" Seb's voice cracked like a whip, making me flinch. His hands clenched into fists at his sides. "Flynn's life is quite literally hanging in the balance. I won't have you making light of—"

"I'm sorry," Priya cut in quietly, her playful demeanour vanishing. She turned to me, genuine remorse in her eyes. "I was just trying to lighten the mood."

"But the mood shouldn't *be* light!" Seb snapped, and even DI Maxwell, who'd shrunk back slightly, nodded. "This is a serious matter, and will be taken as such."

"Of course. Flynn, I apologise."

I wanted to say I wasn't fragile, but couldn't speak. Because I *was* terrified. These vampires had torn someone apart, days after Eliza's attack. They were watching Seb, watching all of us, waiting to strike.

And they were working with the demon who'd marked me?

Kit cleared his throat. "You said Eliza meant to kill Flynn. But that suggests she didn't know about Damien's mark?"

"Didn't know. Didn't care in the moment. It's all unclear." Seb pursed his lips.

"Let's take a brief break," suggested Maxwell. "Any chance of a coffee?"

Kit let out an inelegant snort. "Coffee machine's *permanently broken*, I'm afraid."

"I'll make you a tea!" Priya jumped up from her chair so quickly she nearly knocked it over. Before Maxwell could even respond, she'd disappeared up the stairs, her braid swinging behind her.

The others drifted away too. I pushed myself up, intending to follow Priya to see if she was okay, but Seb stepped smoothly in front of me.

"Don't worry yourself about it." His voice was gentle, at odds with his earlier sharp tone. "She'll be back down in a moment, and it'll all be forgotten."

I glanced toward the stairs. Was this a normal reaction to supernatural horror? Turning it into a joke?

"Sometimes I don't really get it. Get them. I mean, it's just... everyone seems so..." I struggled to find the right words, not wanting to cause offence. "Light-hearted? Especially Rory and Priya. Making constant jokes when you're all discussing murders and dark magic. It feels... strange."

Seb's expression softened even further. "It is rather odd, I suppose. I usually don't mind—they know where to draw the line, most of the time." He ran a hand through his dark curls. "They work incredibly hard, Flynn. What we deal with here... the darkness we face... Sometimes a bit of humour is the only thing that keeps us sane."

"Even zombie ferrets drinking coffee?"

A small smile tugged at the corner of his mouth. There it was again, that rare expression that made him look so human. "I must admit, Freddy has grown on me." He glanced down at the ferret, who was now spinning in dizzy circles, high on caffeine. "Somewhat."

I watched Freddy's manic spinning, a warmth spreading through me despite everything. "You know, when I first came here, I thought this place was completely mental. Still do, actually." I gestured at Freddy, who was now rabidly squeaking. "But there's something... I don't know. Something about it all makes sense, weirdly. Like knowing the world is so much bigger and stranger than you thought, and also so much more dangerous, but at least you're all in the crazy shitshow together."

Seb's eyes gazed into mine, and he took a half step closer. "It certainly helps."

Christ, I was babbling like an idiot. But something about the way he was looking at me, like each fumbling word was somehow precious, made it impossible to stop. "Makes everything before seem a bit... I don't know, grey? Like seeing in colour for the first time."

His low chuckle settled somewhere under my skin. "Yes, I suppose it would." Something flickered across his face. He adjusted one of his brass coat buttons, a habit I'd noticed he had when he was lost in thought. "Though sometimes a little monotony can be a blessing. Especially in our line of work."

"Do you ever miss it? The normal world, I mean?"

Seb's expression tightened. There it was—that familiar wall coming down, blocking out whatever glimpse of vulnerability he'd allowed me to see. "The normal world is a luxury I haven't had in five hundred years. And memory..." He paused, eyes distant. "Memory can be treacherous."

A curl had fallen across my forehead, and Seb's hand moved to tuck it behind my ear. His cool touch sparked memories of last night—my hands in his curls, our bodies pressed together in darkness.

I wanted to lean into him. My body remembered how natural it felt in his embrace. But we weren't alone, and whatever *this* was might not be something he wanted others to know about. Though they probably weren't blind.

I stayed still, skin tingling where he'd touched me. His hand lingered a moment too long, and I caught something in his eyes—hunger? Longing? Before I could be sure, he'd stepped back.

Without thinking, I reached out and caught his wrist. "Don't pull away from me," I whispered, startling myself with my own boldness.

A small crease formed between Seb's eyebrows. "What do you mean?"

My heart thundered out a warning I chose to ignore. Because I wanted to tell him how exhausting it was, this constant dance of coming close then retreating, how every time he pulled away it caused tangible pain. I started to form the words—

"Right, break's over." Maxwell's crisp voice cut through the moment.

Seb straightened, shoulders squaring as he shifted seamlessly into leadership mode. "Of course." His wrist slipped from my grasp. "Everyone back to their seats."

I tried to catch Seb's eye, wanting him to understand this conversation wasn't finished. When he finally glanced my way, I held his gaze, trying to convey without words that we needed to talk about this—about *us*—properly.

Back home, my grandad used to say I was like a tide against a cliff face—wearing away at any obstacle through sheer bloody-minded persistence. Katie had called it my most infuriating trait. Tom had called it almost endearing, once.

But they'd all agreed on one thing: when Flynn Carter set his course, not even a storm could throw him off it.

And right now? My compass pointed straight at Sebastián Salazar.

16

Flynn

The morning rush at Rising Dough filled the bakery with fresh bread and coffee scents. After days of supernatural chaos, the normalcy of arranging the display case was a relief.

Emma cursed at the sink's spray nozzle.

"This bloody thing's been attacking me all morning," she grumbled, holding up her soaked apron. "Your turn to deal with it."

I took over the washing up, but the spray behaved perfectly—almost seemed to curve away from my hands. Emma stopped mid-pastry-fold to stare.

"How are you—? It was literally trying to drown me a minute ago."

I shrugged. "Must be your technique."

She muttered something unflattering and turned back to the pastries. I lost myself watching the water flow, oddly mesmerised by its movement until Emma's voice snapped me back.

"Oi." She poked me. "You've got that faraway look again." She dabbed flour on my nose. "The cinnamon buns need checking."

At a corner table, one of Maxwell's officers sat reading, watching me discreetly. The arrangement had taken some arguing—Seb hadn't wanted me working at all, but I'd refused to hide in that dusty hotel.

"They wouldn't attack in broad daylight," I'd insisted. He'd agreed reluctantly, his clenched jaw speaking volumes.

I felt guilty about the extra security, knowing the team had Damien to hunt for, and Greaves's murder to investigate. At least Maxwell's solution had worked out—his officer looked like any other suited professional enjoying coffee.

As sunset approached, Seb arrived in his signature black coat. The officer left without acknowledging him, just smiled at Emma and me before departing.

"Ah, one cinnamon bun left. I'll take it, please." Seb's eyes sparkled.

I wrapped the pastry, though I wasn't sure why he wanted it. "You don't have to pay. It'll only go to waste otherwise."

"How generous." His fingers brushed mine as he accepted the bag.

Emma's broom scratched against the floor as she swept, her movements deliberately slow.

"I can finish locking up," I told her. "You should head home early."

She paused mid-sweep, eyes darting between Seb and me. "Are you sure?"

"Course." I forced a casual tone. "Go on, you've been here since five."

Emma's frown deepened as she untied her apron. "Text me when you get home, yeah?"

After she left, silence settled over the bakery, thick as dough, as I caught Seb's eye and held it.

"We should get going," he said.

Blood rushed in my ears as every muscle in my body coiled tight. "Not yet."

Seb's expression shifted, subtle changes flickering across his features like shadows on water. He remained silent, waiting.

"Look." I gripped the edge of the counter, steadying myself. "I need to say something, and I need you to just... listen."

The paper bag crinkled as he set the cinnamon bun down.

"Whatever this is between us—" My voice failed me, and I cleared my throat. "I'm developing... feelings for you. And believe me, I've tried not to. But they're there, whether I like it or not. Whether you like it or not."

The silence stretched between us, heavy with unspoken words.

"It's all well and good to joke that you're just *making observations* when you look at me that way, or when you touch my hair, or send me those messages. But we both know it's more than that." I forced myself to meet his dark eyes. "The other night proved that. I haven't been able to get it out of my head. I saw the way you looked at me then. The way you're looking at me now."

It was true. Though his posture remained perfect, the line of his mouth had softened, and those liquid-dark eyes burned with the same heat I remembered—equal parts wanting and warning.

"And before you remind me, I know we can't... have full-on sex or whatever." Heat flooded my cheeks, and I tugged at my jumper sleeve, suddenly fascinated by a loose thread. Christ, I sounded so awkward to my own ears. "But that's okay. I don't need it. I promise."

The words caught slightly in my throat, but they were honest enough. That night—just lying there with him in my arms, breathing in the faint scent of him, feeling his cool, solid weight—it *had* been more than enough. Just having someone *there*, someone who saw me, really saw me, made the lonely ache in my chest finally quiet down. It was more than I'd dared hope for back in Braymore Bay, crying on the beach and dreaming of a different life. If that's all we could have, if that's all he could give... I'd take it. I just wanted to coax out more of those rare smiles of his, learn the stories behind each tiny crease around his eyes, maybe even drag him away from his paperwork and his cases long enough to remember what living felt like.

I tried to smile at him, to lighten the mood, but my lips wouldn't obey.

"But I can't keep dancing around this. I had enough hurt back in Braymore, and I ran away from that, all the way to London. So I need you to decide what this is."

My fingers trembled, and I clasped my hands together. "Because if you're just... passing time, or if I'm just interesting because I'm new and convenient, or if this is some vampire thing I don't understand—I need to know. Now. Before I fall any deeper."

The words hung in the dimming bakery, raw and honest between us. Seb's face remained unreadable, but something stirred in those burnt caramel eyes that I first fell into in this very building, a lifetime ago now.

"I can see how lonely you are," I said. "Even if you do your best to hide it. And I know you got hurt last time. But twenty years is a long time to keep your heart locked away. And maybe... some chances are worth taking again."

The pain hit like a bolt of lightning. One moment I stood waiting for Seb's response, the next my chest exploded in agony. A scream tore from my throat—distant, as if someone else were making the sound. My legs buckled, and the world tilted. The back of my head cracked against the bakery tiles.

White spots danced across my vision. Every breath burned like shards of glass in my lungs. "It hurts! *Fuck*, it hurts—"

"Flynn!" Seb's face swam into view above me. His cool hands pressed against my shoulders. "Try to stay still."

I clutched at my chest, fingers scrabbling against my jumper. The pain radiated outward from my heart in icy waves. My teeth chattered. "It's never been this bad!"

Seb pushed my hands aside and yanked up my shirt. The sharp intake of his breath sent fresh panic coursing through me.

"What? What is it?" My voice came out thin and reedy. When he didn't answer, I pushed myself up on trembling arms to look.

Delicate patterns of frost spread across my skin like spider webs, emanating from just above my heart. The marks shimmered faintly in the dim light, beautiful and terrifying.

A moan escaped me as another wave of pain hit. I slumped back against the cold tiles. My hands felt clammy, skin breaking out in a cold sweat. "This is it, then. I'm really dying."

"No, Flynn." But the tremor in Seb's voice betrayed his fear.

My thoughts scattered like leaves in a storm. Panic clawed up my throat as another wave of pain ripped through me. "Hospital. Take me to the hospital." I pushed against the tiles, trying to stand.

Seb's hands pressed me back down, his grip firm but gentle. "It won't help. I'm sorry, Flynn."

"I need to try at least!" The words came out as a desperate sob. "For my mum! And Katie!"

My chest tightened with more than just pain. Mum and Katie would never know what happened to me. The image of Mum staring out the window like she used to after Dad died, waiting for someone who'd never return, made me want to scream. And Katie... I'd never get to talk to her, tell her what happened with Connor. I should have tried—even if she didn't believe me, I'd have done what was right.

The guilt I'd carried since leaving crashed over me like a rogue wave, threatening to pull me under. Now they'd never know the truth. They'd just be left with another empty chair at Christmas, and a lifetime of unanswered questions.

Seb reached out to stroke my hair, but I batted his hand away. The frost inside me pulsed with each thundering heartbeat, spreading further across my chest.

"I'm going back to Ireland!" I declared, voice cracking. I glanced outside at the cold, dark street, illuminated by a single lamppost. "This evening. I need to see my family. I can't die without saying goodbye!"

"That's not safe, for you or them!"

An exasperated scream tore from my throat. My head thumped against the tiles, each pulse sending shockwaves of agony through my skull. This was different from the previous attacks—so much worse. Like someone had replaced my blood with buckets of ice water, freezing me from the inside out.

I curled into myself, shivering violently. The cold radiated outwards from my chest, stealing my breath. Through chattering teeth, I managed to gasp, "Please... please..."

But I didn't even know what I was begging for anymore.

"Let's get you back to Killigrew Street. Priya will be able to do something for the pain."

"I can't—" Another violent shiver racked my body, and I tried again to force my legs into action. "My muscles won't work. They're seizing up. The cold. It's like... ice in my veins." My teeth chattered so hard I could barely form words. "I can't stand."

Seb's jaw tightened. He rose to his feet, grasping both my hands in his. "Let me help."

He pulled, and for a moment I started to rise—then his grip faltered. I crashed back to the floor with a yelp as Seb stumbled sideways, catching himself against the counter.

"What's wrong?" Through the haze of pain, I noticed how he swayed, his usual grace absent.

He pressed a hand to his forehead. "I haven't... had any blood in far too long. I'm sorry, I didn't realise how weakened I'd become. Kit's currently out buying more for me." His voice came out rough. "Give me just a second."

"Come back," I mumbled, fingers catching the fabric of his trousers. I tugged weakly.

Seb resisted for a moment, then his knees buckled. He looked awful—skin ashen, dark circles under his eyes that I hadn't noticed before.

I pulled again, and he finally gave in, collapsing to his knees beside me. With the last of my strength, I drew him into my arms. He made a soft sound—surprise or protest, I couldn't tell—but didn't pull away.

We lay there on the bakery floor, my body racked with painful shivers, his unnaturally still. Moonlight spilled onto the tiles, and I tried to focus on the patterns in the stone, and Seb's weight anchoring me, to make the pain a fraction more bearable.

"I'll ring someone to come fetch us," Seb said, and I just moaned in response.

Through the fog of pain, I watched Seb reach for his phone. His arm stopped mid-motion, muscles tensing.

"What?"

Then it hit me. The familiar ambient sounds of London—traffic, distant sirens, the hum of street lights—had vanished.

"The street has gone quiet. Too quiet." His voice dropped to barely a whisper.

The silence pressed against my ears like cotton wool. Even the usual creaks and groans of the old building had ceased. The world felt frozen, holding its breath.

CRASH!

The bakery windows exploded inward. A symphony of shattering glass filled the air as shards rained down, glittering like deadly diamonds in the moonlight. The display case splintered, sending fragments skittering across the floor tiles. The force of it sent the little tables near the windows toppling, their metal legs scraping against the floor.

I tried to scramble away from the destruction, but my frozen muscles refused to cooperate. All I could do was cling to Seb, fingers digging into his coat. "What's happen—"

The world plunged into darkness.

Not like someone had flipped a switch—more like the light itself had been devoured, leaving nothing but a void so complete my eyes couldn't adjust.

"Seb?" My voice came out small, frightened.

A rush of movement. Strong hands seized my ankles and *pulled*.

I slid across the floor, ripped away from Seb. The tiles scraped against my back as whatever had me dragged me through the darkness. Pain blazed through my frozen muscles.

"Flynn!" Seb's voice cut through the darkness, desperate and raw. "Let him go—"

More sounds—crashes, thuds, the distinctive crack of breaking wood. Seb shouting words I couldn't make out, his voice growing more distant.

Something hard struck the back of my head. Stars exploded behind my eyes, and a scream tore itself from my throat—only to be cut off by a cold hand clamping over my mouth. The pressure against my face was crushing, making it impossible to breathe.

The blackness pressed in, absolute and suffocating. My lungs burned for air. Through the crushing dark, Sebastián's anguished cry of my name pierced the void, then faded into oblivion.

17

Sebastián

I knelt in the wreckage of Rising Dough, blood dripping from my forearm onto shattered tiles. Glass crunched beneath my knees. The stench of decay still clung to my nostrils—rotting flesh animated by dark magic. *Deadwalkers.* Four of them. The last one's head lay three feet from its body, mouth frozen in a rictus grin.

Flynn was gone.

Taken. Taken from me.

Mine. They'd taken what was mine.

The gash in my arm refused to heal at its usual pace, carved by no ordinary blade. My skull throbbed where they'd smashed it against the floor. Black spots danced at the edges of my vision. Hunger gnawed at my gut, a savage beast demanding to be fed.

None of it mattered.

Flynn's scent still lingered in the air—*him*, blended with fear and pain. The echo of his scream as they dragged him away tore through my chest like barbed wire.

I hadn't been strong enough. Fast enough. The deadwalkers had delayed me, keeping me occupied by having to slaughter them while their companions spirited Flynn away through the darkness they'd conjured.

Five hundred years of existence, and I'd never felt rage like this. It burned through my veins like holy fire, consuming everything but the need to hunt. To destroy. To reclaim.

Whoever did this would soon feel the full wrath of my fury. And it wouldn't be pretty.

I pushed myself to my feet, ignoring the way the world tilted. Blood and pain were temporary inconveniences. Nothing would stop me from getting Flynn back.

Even if it killed me.

18

Flynn

Consciousness returned in fits and starts, like a tide lazily lapping at the shore. First came the darkness, then disjointed sensations washing over me in waves: the metallic taste in my mouth, the throbbing at the base of my skull, the nauseating sway of movement.

Metal dug into my shoulder, then my hip, then back again as I rolled across the floor of what had to be a van. Zip ties bit into my wrists, twisted behind my back.

Bang. My forehead smacked against something solid. More rolling. The vehicle swerved, and I slammed into the wheel well. Everything ached.

How long had I been out? The van's interior was pitch black, offering no clues. Each bump sent me tumbling, unable to brace myself.

At least the bone-deep cold had receded. Small mercies. Was the dark magic ready to harvest? Were they about to cut it out of me?

Another sharp turn sent me crashing into the opposite wall. Pain bloomed across my ribs, but it felt distant, disconnected. Everything felt distant. The terror that should have been overwhelming me just... wasn't there. Instead, a heavy numbness had settled in my chest as I bounced from side to side like a forgotten parcel.

What a rubbish way to go. All those dreams I'd had about seeing the world, gone. Completing my solo sail across the Atlantic. Falling in love.

Mum would never know what happened to me. She'd be devastated. First Dad, then me. And Katie... God, Katie. She'd blame herself for not trying harder to get me to come home. Tom too. *Fuck,* he'd feel awful.

And Seb. He'd tear himself apart, convince himself it was his fault. He'd carry that weight forever—however long forever was for a vampire.

Now I'd never know what he might have said back, after everything at the bakery.

The van hit another pothole, and my head cracked against the floor. Deep-rooted pain bled across my skull. All I could do was hold on to an image of Seb's face—that rare, genuine smile that felt like it belonged to me.

19

Sebastián

Cold blood trickled down my arm as I paced outside Rising Dough, feet crunching in the scattered glass from the bakery's shattered windows, which leaked out the putrid stench of deadwalkers.

On my phone, I jabbed Kit's button again. Straight to voicemail. *Damn it.* He'd gone to Undertone to get blood for me. Was there trouble there? I pushed the thought away.

My fingers found Felix's contact. "Magpie! I need a car."

"Like... an Uber?"

I clenched my jaw, fighting to keep my voice steady. "No! I need a car to drive. Flynn's been taken. We were attacked by deadwalkers. I heard some sort of vehicle speed away. I need to follow, *now*."

A sharp intake of breath crackled through the line. Then Felix's voice, distant but urgent: "Peacock! Get over here!"

Her footsteps approached, followed by rapid-fire questions that grew louder as she reached the phone. "What's happened? Where's Flynn? I'll call Terrier—he's on a date in Shoreditch—"

"Poodle isn't picking up," I cut in, addressing Felix again. "Can you get me a car?"

"Like... delivered to your location?" Felix's keyboard clattered in the background. "Not... anytime soon!"

My gaze locked onto a Volkswagen Golf parked across the street, its paint peeling around the wheel arches. Perfect.

"Magpie. I need you to talk me through hot-wiring a car. Pull up a video tutorial if you must."

"*What*? I have no idea about any of that. We'll be here all night!"

"How hard can it be?" I practically snarled down the phone.

"Hold on!" Felix's voice brightened. "I've got an idea. Let me scan the street you're on."

The line went quiet except for rapid typing. Blood dripped steadily from my arm onto the pavement, each drop a reminder of my failure to protect Flynn.

"Peacock," I called to Priya. "Call Teddy and tell him he needs to get a cleanup crew to Rising Dough ASAP. Two demobilised deadwalkers."

She gasped. "Deadwalkers? That's—"

"Just make the call."

More silence from Felix, though he was muttering numbers under his breath, a habit he had when he was checking and rechecking his work.

But every second felt like an eternity, another moment of Flynn slipping further from my reach. The image of his face, twisted in pain as he collapsed, burned behind my eyes. He could be dead already. The thought sent a wave of nausea through me that had nothing to do with my gnawing hunger.

A muffled whoop of triumph burst through my phone speaker. "Right, walk south. Two hundred metres down the road," Felix directed.

I darted forward. Blood continued to drip from my arm, though the wound was knitting itself closed, albeit slowly.

"You're looking for Mercedes-Benz EQS. Midnight blue. Chrome trim. Latest model with the enhanced autopilot and quantum encryption. Enough computing power to launch a space mission."

I spotted it gleaming under a streetlight—a sleek predator of a machine, the sort that people with more money than sense buy.

"I've unlocked it for you." Felix's voice carried a distinct note of pride. "The owner's some tech CEO who really should've updated his car's firmware. Left himself wide open to a remote override through the entertainment system. I redirected the authentication protocols through a ghost network I set up—"

"English, please."

"Right. Sorry. Car's yours. Keys are virtual. Just get in and press the start button."

I slid into the sleek leather driver's seat. The dashboard lit up with a soft blue glow.

"The GPS is already programmed to track your phone's location," Felix continued. "And I've looped the CCTV feeds along every possible route for a mile radius so far. No one can see you."

"Good work." I pressed the start button, and the engine purred to life.

"I'm sure this is *exactly* what my mother had in mind when she paid for my masters in cybersecurity and digital forensics," Felix muttered.

The steering wheel creaked under my grip as I fought to keep my hands steady. Every inch of me screamed to move faster, to tear through the streets until I found Flynn. The wound in my arm had closed, but the memory of his pain-filled face haunted me.

"Boss!" Priya's voice crackled through the car's speakers. "I've got footage from outside the bakery. Two deadwalkers loaded Flynn into a white Transit van. They're heading south."

"Scan the numberplate. Now!" I slammed my foot on the accelerator, the Mercedes's electric engine whining as we shot forward.

"On it," Felix replied. Then, "Got it! Cloned plates. Running them through the system." More typing. "Right, follow the A23. Peacock and I are tracking them through the CCTV network. I've triple-checked the feeds."

"Turn left onto Whitecross Road," Priya directed.

I yanked the wheel, tyres squealing. A notification flashed on the dashboard as Felix tried to engage the autopilot.

"Stop that," I growled, swerving around a taxi. "I'm driving."

"The AI would be safer—"

"No."

There was no way in hell I was obeying the highway code right now. The speedometer crept past ninety as I weaved through traffic, ignoring red lights and blaring horns. South London blurred past in streaks of neon and shadow.

"Right at the next junction," Felix called. "They passed through here nine minutes ago."

I cut across three lanes, barely missing a bus. The car's suspension groaned as we bounced over a speed bump at full throttle.

"Noctule, the van's heading out of the city," Priya announced. "Last sighting shows them taking the A23 towards Brighton."

The buildings thinned out as we reached the edges of London, streetlights giving way to darkness. My fingers tightened on the wheel as we hit open road, the countryside swallowing us in black.

"Still tracking them," Felix assured me. "They're keeping to the main road."

"Yes. We're going to get him back. Don't worry." Priya's soothing voice did nothing to calm me.

The engine whined as I pushed it harder. As soon as I reached the dual carriageway, the digital speedometer climbed past a hundred and twenty. Every second felt like an eternity, another chance for them to hurt Flynn.

"Slow down!" Felix shouted. "The last thing we need is a police chase right now!"

I eased off, my speed dropping to a more reasonable hundred, though every instinct screamed at me to push harder, faster.

"They've left the main road." Priya said. "Tracking them onto... some kind of side route. Few minutes ahead of you." A pause. "It's a small track. Nothing but disused buildings for miles."

Tyres crunched onto gravel as I followed their path. Shadows stretched across the narrow track, branches scraping against the pristine paintwork.

"Noctule." Priya's voice cut through the darkness, stern and commanding. "You *need* to slow down now, else you'll kill yourself and you'll be no help to him at all."

I barely registered her warning, my focus narrowing on the path ahead. "Am I close? Where is he?!"

"There's no CCTV here." Felix's typing grew more frantic. "We're off grid. But there's only one road. Keep going."

My headlights carved through the darkness, illuminating patches of overgrown track. Then—something massive lurched into the beam of light. That impossible creature again. The hyena stood in the middle of the road, its muscled shoulders hunched, yellow eyes blazing in my headlights. I slammed on the brakes instinctively, the car fishtailing slightly before I regained control.

"Seb?" Priya's voice crackled with concern. "What happened?"

That same creature I'd seen before—a hyena in London, of all things. Each appearance heralding disaster. Was it... warning me? Following me? But there wasn't time to dwell on such impossibilities now.

My hands clenched the wheel as we bounced over potholes and debris. Then—*there*—a flash of white metal in the distance.

The van.

I zoomed towards it, closing the distance between us. The van's taillights burned like prey in my vision, growing larger with each passing second.

Twenty metres. Ten. Five.

The distance between us shrank, my entire world narrowing to that white van. I barely registered Felix's voice in my ear, or Priya's continued warnings. Nothing mattered except closing those final metres.

Then my foot hovered over the accelerator as I calculated distances, angles, risks. Flynn was in there. I couldn't simply charge up and ram it from behind.

"Boss? What's the plan?"

I fumbled with the sleek dashboard, my fingers sliding uselessly across the glossy touchscreen. Black glass until touched, and even then, the icons made no sense. *Bloody modern cars.*

"Felix," I growled, "where are the damn lights?"

"Left panel, boss. Swipe down, then right. The little sun icon—no, not that one. The other one. There you go."

Finally, the Mercedes-Benz's LED array blazed to life. State-of-the-art. It could probably illuminate half a football field.

"Peacock." My voice was tight. "I was thinking... The deadwalkers. Their eyes... How sensitive are they?"

"Possibly extremely. Their retinas are likely partially decomposed, leaving the optic nerves exposed. Why— Oh! Do it!"

I slammed the high beams on full. The LED array blazed like artificial daylight, flooding the narrow track with searing white brilliance.

The van swerved violently. Its wheels caught the muddy verge where the track dropped away sharply. For a stretched moment, it teetered—

Momentum took over.

Metal screamed as the van tipped.

I slammed on the brakes, tyres fighting for purchase on the uneven surface.

The world slowed to a crawl as the van rolled, once, twice, sliding sideways across the soggy track in a shower of mud and gravel.

"Flynn!" The name tore from my throat.

"Noctule!" Priya's voice cut through my panic. "Wait—"

I barely heard her. The car hadn't even stopped moving before I reached for the door handle.

I sprinted towards the overturned van, slipping slightly in the mud. The passenger door had crumpled on impact, metal twisted like origami gone wrong.

Two figures crawled from the driver's side window. Their movements were disturbing—joints bending at impossible angles, heads lolling on broken necks that should have killed them. The first one's jaw hung loose, connected by strips of grey flesh, while maggots writhed in the cavities where its eyes should have been. The second's ribcage was exposed, yellowed bone gleaming wet in the Mercedes's harsh lights. Their smiles stretched impossibly wide, lips peeled back to reveal blackened teeth. The stench of decay rolled off them in waves—sweet rot and grave soil.

I forced down my revulsion. No matter how many times I'd encountered the risen dead, that first moment of wrongness never quite faded.

They charged at me with that unnatural, jerky gait. I ducked the first one's swinging arm, feeling the wind of its passing. The second grabbed my jacket with fingers like steel cables. I twisted free, fabric tearing, and drove my elbow into its face. Bone crunched, but it didn't slow—these things felt no pain.

My vision blurred from hunger as I fought. Every movement drained what little strength I had left. I managed to snap the first one's neck completely, but it kept coming, head flopping grotesquely. Who was controlling these puppets? Necromancers were a rare breed, and only the most powerful could animate corpses with such precision.

The second deadwalker slammed me into the van's side, light exploding behind my eyes. Its hands found my throat, squeezing. I clawed at rotting flesh, but my weakened muscles betrayed me. The weight of my ancient dagger at my hip burned, begging to be used, but my arms were pinned. Darkness flickered at the edges of my vision. Something sharp—a broken rib from its exposed cage—tore through my side. White-hot agony ripped through me as the jagged bone carved deep into my flesh. When was the last time I'd felt this level of pain? Too long ago to remember.

A muffled cry came from inside the van. "Help!"

Flynn's voice shot through me like lightning. With the last dregs of my energy, I ripped my right arm free, fingers finding the familiar carved handle of my dagger. I wrenched the deadwalker's head back while drawing my blade across its throat—the ancient silver parting flesh and sinew until vertebrae cracked like wet chalk.

It dropped, twitching. I spun to face the other one, letting instinct take over. Dropping my blade, my hands plunged into its chest cavity, ripping through bone and gristle until I found what remained of its heart. Putrid blood coated my fingers as I crushed the organ to pulp—viscous and jellied, squishing between my fingers like rotting fruit—and the creature collapsed, finally still.

Cool blood—my own—soaked through my shirt, the wound in my side burning like holy water.

I wiped my gore-covered hands on my coat. Fourth time this month I'd ruined it. The brass buttons were tarnished with blood, the wool matted with fluids.

Flynn.

I stumbled towards the van, my side screaming in protest. The back doors had buckled inward from the impact, metal twisted and warped. Gritting my teeth against the pain, I hauled myself up onto the vehicle's side, fingers finding purchase in the dented panels.

The interior was pitch black. "Flynn?"

"Here!" His voice was shaky but strong.

I crawled through the wreckage, feeling my way forward. The van's cargo space was empty except for a huddled shape against the far wall—now the floor. My hands found Flynn's shoulders, and relief flooded through me so intensely I nearly collapsed.

"Are you hurt?" I ran my fingers over his arms, his face, checking for injuries. "Did they—"

"I'm okay." Flynn's breath was warm against my palm. "Just slightly bruised. What happened? *Fuck*, I thought that was the end." He shuddered out a sigh.

"I'm sorry." The words felt hollow, inadequate. My hands trembled against his skin. "Flynn, I'm so sorry. I should have known, should have protected—"

"Don't." Flynn's pulse thrummed against my fingertips, alive, *here*. "This wasn't your fault."

"But I—"

"No." His grip tightened. "Stop. Not everything bad that happens is because of you, Seb. I'm the one who insisted I go to work, remember?" He tipped his head back, resting it on the metal. "Who even were they? Vampires?"

I shook my head. "We call them deadwalkers. They're products of necromancy. Thralls under the control of another. They tend to be pretty mindless, but these two managed to drive this van well enough.

They were also surprisingly well coordinated." I had the wound to prove it.

He shuffled about. "These zip ties are cutting off my circulation. Can you get them off?"

My hands found his wrists, bound tight with plastic restraints. Without thinking, I extended my fangs and bent down. The sharp points sliced through easily.

Flynn flexed his freed hands. "That's... actually quite useful."

"First time anyone's called them useful." I cut through the ties around his ankles. "Usually it's more along the lines of 'horrifying.'"

"Well, I'm grateful for them." His fingers brushed my cheek, coming dangerously close to my fangs.

I froze, caught between wanting to pull away and lean into his touch. No one had touched me like this since James.

"Can I..." His hand hovered, uncertain. "Can I see them properly? Please?"

Slowly, I parted my lips. My fangs extended fully—sharp, deadly things designed for tearing flesh. I waited for the horror to cross his face, for him to recoil like any sane person would.

Instead, his fingertip traced the curve of one fang with careful precision. The touch sent electricity down my spine.

"There we are," he whispered, wonder in his voice.

My hands trembled. I wanted to tell him this wasn't *me*, that I was more than just teeth and hunger, but the gentle acceptance in his eyes stole my words.

His finger followed the line of the other fang. "They're beautiful."

I made a choked sound. Beautiful? These weapons that had torn so many throats, spilled so much innocent blood?

"They are," Flynn insisted. "Like every piece of you." Then his gaze dropped—he'd caught sight of my shirt, soaked through. I should have buttoned up my coat.

"You're bleeding."

"One of them managed to take a chunk out of me. But it's nothing." The wound in my side throbbed, reminding me it was very much something. "Can you stand?"

I pushed myself up, ready to help Flynn to his feet. The world tilted sharply, and my legs gave out. I collapsed onto the van's metal floor with a dull thud, clutching my side.

"*¡Joder!*" The curse echoed in the confined space. Blood seeped between my fingers, chilled and sticky. How dare my body betray me like this? Not here, not now, not when I just got him back, safe again.

Flynn scrambled towards me. "Seb?"

"I'll heal." The words caught in my throat. Would I, though? The bone had torn deep—I could feel air assaulting the ragged edges of the wound, the way it gaped wider with each breath. And the hunger... *Lord,* the hunger. I felt my grip on reality slipping through my fingertips.

"You're lying." Flynn's voice shook.

I didn't answer. What could I say? The truth was written in every drop of blood pooling beneath me, in the way my limbs felt heavier with each passing second.

"You're safe now," I managed to croak. "And even if I go, one of the others will be here soon."

"*Go?* What do you mean, *go? Die?!*"

In the cramped space, Flynn shuffled closer. His hands found my shoulders, and he pulled me onto his lap with surprising gentleness. The movement sent fresh agony through my side, but I bit back another curse. His warmth seeped into me, a stark contrast to my own skin, now even cooler than usual.

I tried to offer Flynn a smile. "Don't be sad. I've had over five hundred years of life." *Most of them spent in shadows, watching the world pass by me. Strange, how a few weeks with you made me feel more alive than I could have imagined. So many sunrises wasted...*

"That's not funny." His hands trembled against my shoulders.

"Listen to me. Earlier, in the bakery..." I drew in a shaky breath, needing to get the words out. "You asked what I wanted from you."

Flynn stilled, his heartbeat quickening. The sound called to me, whispering dark promises.

"The truth is, I want everything." The confession scraped raw in my throat. "*Everything*. And that terrifies me."

His fingers tightened in my ruined shirt.

"And you're not *convenient*." I reached up, cupping both cheeks with trembling fingers. "God help me, Flynn, you're the most inconvenient thing that's happened to me in two decades. And I still can't stay away."

The van's metal walls seemed to close in around us, the darkness pressing closer. Or perhaps that was just my fading consciousness. I fought to keep my eyes open, to memorise every detail of his face above me.

"You deserve someone whole, someone unmarked by centuries of darkness. But I'm selfish enough to want you anyway."

I could picture him finding someone steady as the shore, someone who'd give him roots instead of a storm-tossed existence. They'd build a life together, far from the darkness of my corner of the world, and Flynn's smile would shine as bright as sunlight. He deserved that peace, that certainty—not the tumultuous depths I offered.

Flynn's arms encircled me, pulling me closer into his lap, clinging tightly. *If I die here, at least it'll be while being held like something precious. Something worthy.*

One of his hands loosened. The zipper of his hoodie tingled as he tugged it down. His head tipped back against the van's metal wall, exposing the pale column of his throat.

The realisation hit me like the toll of cathedral bells. He was offering himself to me with devastating simplicity, with complete trust.

Yes! Yes! Take what he offers.

"No!" The word tore from my throat. "I'll drain you dry." His blood was the sweetest drug, and I'd tasted enough to know one hit would never be enough. I was an addict staring at his poison of choice, knowing it would destroy us both.

"No you won't." Flynn's fingers threaded through my hair, gentle yet firm. "And if you don't behave, I'll pin you down and force feed you."

I shook my head, fighting against the overwhelming urge to sink my fangs into his flesh. "I can't. You know that." Why was he doing this to me?

"Shhh." His hand stroked through my curls, each soft touch weakening my resolve like water wearing away stone. "It's okay, Sebastián. Let me help you."

Feed. Feed. Feed.

My fangs fully extended, drawn to his pulse point like a compass finding true north. Retracting them was futile. The steady thrum of his heartbeat called to me, begging me to claim him.

Delicious, delicious Flynn. Lovely Flynn.

My Flynn.

"No," I tried again, the word a whisper.

"Yes," he said simply.

My world narrowed to the blood coursing through his veins, to the sweet scent of his skin, to the gentle strength in his touch as Flynn's hand cupped the back of my head, guiding me to the crook of his neck.

Finally mine.

20

Flynn

In all my dreams of Sebastián's mouth on my neck, none had prepared me for the reality of his fangs.

The initial shock of those razor-sharp teeth piercing my neck sent lightning through every nerve—sharp, white-hot agony that made me gasp and clutch at his shoulders. My fingers dug into the fabric of his coat as my body went rigid.

"Breathe, Flynn," he rasped against my skin, having pulled back. "You must breathe."

The second pierce went even deeper. Hot tears burst into my eyes. My body trembled, and I clung to Seb, squeezing him tightly instead of hissing out my pain. *Don't show him how much it hurts.*

The metallic tang of blood filled the air. *My blood.* Seb was drinking *my blood.* My heart hammered wildly, rabbit-fast, pumping harder, faster. How much was he taking? And would he actually be able to stop? Oh god, why hadn't I expected it to hurt quite this much?

But then his tongue—warm, gentle, almost languid—lapped at the wounds in between his little sucks. The pain began to ebb away, replaced by waves of dizzying sensation, and each draw of blood sent sparks dancing behind my closed eyelids. My chest felt tight—another ice attack? *No.* Instead, a radiating heat bloomed within me that made me arch closer to him with a quiet gasp. His arm tightened around my waist in response.

A soft sigh escaped my lips as the glorious warmth spread through my limbs, and my grip on his shoulders loosened. One hand continued to cradle the back of his head, fingers threading through those dark curls. The steady rhythm of his drinking became hypnotic. The world narrowed to just this—his mouth latched onto my neck, the light scrape of his stubble against my skin, the gentle press of his body against mine, keeping me anchored.

Time lost all meaning. There was only the soft wet sounds of his feeding, my uneven breaths, the thundering of my pulse. My head fell back further, offering even more of my throat. His appreciative growl vibrated through me as he nuzzled deeper against my skin.

Tongue swirling patterns between draws, Seb soothed any lingering burn. Pleasure coursed through my veins like liquid gold, making me tremble for entirely different reasons now. My fingers flexed in his hair as another moan slipped past my lips.

"Seb," I breathed, barely recognizing my voice.

He made a sound deep in his throat that rippled through me like a wave breaking against rocks. His free hand slid up my body to find the back of my head, his thumb rubbing concentric circles into my scalp.

Then I was drowning. Drowning in sensation.

The van's metal floor was cold beneath me, but everything else burned hot. So hot. The first curl of arousal caught me by surprise—a warm flutter low in my belly that quickly intensified with each pull of his mouth. A loud moan filled the dark van, and it took a moment to realise it was my own. The pleasure coursing through me was soon overwhelming, threatening to sweep me away entirely. I needed—god, I needed to hold on to something. Someone. Him. My arm flailed out, desperate to find purchase.

"S-Seb," I gasped, my fingers scrabbling down the rough fabric of his coat.

Finally, *finally*, I found his free hand. I threaded my fingers through his, clutching tight enough that it should have hurt. His fingers clamped around mine in return, their grip like iron bands. The pressure grounded me, gave me something to focus on beyond the dizzying waves of sensation.

A particularly deep draw had me arching up with a broken sound. The pleasure intensified, spreading like wildfire through my veins. My toes curled in my shoes. Every nerve ending sparked and fizzed.

My hips shifted restlessly as the feeling grew, heat pooling deeper, transforming into an overwhelming tide of need. Each wave of pleasure crashed higher than the last until I was lost at sea, anchored only by Seb's steady grip on my hand and the sweet, burning pressure of his mouth against my throat.

"I need—" My cry stopped me from finishing my sentence... *your hand on me.*

Seb's lips continued to move against my throat, his tongue never leaving my skin. The brush of his curls against my neck sparked electric shivers that shot straight to my straining cock. My hips snapped up of their own accord, desperate for release. The drag of denim from my jeans, combined with Seb's soft, throaty sigh of contentment, was my undoing.

My mind emptied, leaving only raw sensation behind. Sparks exploded behind my eyelids as pleasure built inside me, coiling tighter and tighter until it burst. I screamed with euphoria, the sound lost in the darkness of the van, as I came hard, untouched.

Hot cum spilled into my underwear, soaking through the fabric and leaving me gasping for air. My body shook with the intensity of the orgasm, every muscle clenching and unclenching in a frenzied dance of bliss.

His mouth never leaving my neck, Seb held me close as I thrashed about, coming apart in his arms. His grip on my hand tightened, grounding me even as everything around me seemed to blur and fade away.

A glorious heat bloomed and spread through my limbs, making me feel boneless and utterly spent. The waves slowed, my shudders lessening until I was left panting for breath, completely wrecked. I tried to open my eyes but found I lacked the energy.

The darkness spun lazily around me, everything wrapped in a sweet, hazy glow. Everything felt... perfect. Light. As if I were floating just beneath the surface of a sun-warmed sea, the water holding me suspended in this moment of pure bliss. I never wanted it to end. My thoughts drifted like leaves on a gentle current, too scattered to grasp. Nothing existed beyond the warm cocoon of sensation enveloping me, beyond Seb's solid presence anchoring me to reality.

His fingers were still threaded through mine, our palms pressed together. I couldn't have moved if I tried—my muscles had dissolved into *honey*, thick and golden. Even breathing felt like too much effort.

The euphoria began to fade, though the heaviness in my limbs did not. My thoughts turned almost sluggish, like trying to wade through deep water. The van's metal floor seemed to tilt beneath me, though I knew we weren't moving.

He was taking too much.

"Seb," I whispered, giving his shoulder the gentlest nudge. My arm felt like it weighed a thousand pounds.

He didn't respond. Was he lost in his feeding? The steady pull of blood continued, each draw making my head spin faster.

"Seb, you need to stop now." My voice came out barely above a whisper. "Please."

His only answer was another deep draw that made the world darken. My heart fluttered like a trapped bird, struggling to keep up.

"Sebastián!" I shoved against his chest with every ounce of strength I could muster, but I had all the impact of butterfly wings. The effort left me even more lightheaded.

As my arm flopped uselessly back to my side, I sank deeper into the strange floating sensation. Somewhere in the back of my mind, a voice whispered that I should be terrified. He wasn't going to stop. I was going to die here, drained dry in the back of a van.

But panic felt too far away, like watching storm clouds gather on a very distant horizon. Instead I felt... peaceful. As if I were drifting off to sleep in a warm bath, letting the water carry all my worries away.

"You remind me of the ocean," I murmured into the darkness. "Wild and endless and home."

The world swayed gently. My thoughts foamed, dissolved, scattered.

"The sea's too big without you." The words slipped out, barely a breath, as darkness crept in at the edges. "Don't want to be alone again."

Then, he was gone.

His mouth tore away from my throat with a deafening snarl that shook the van. The sudden absence left me reeling, adrift without my anchor. Through blurry vision, I caught a glimpse of him—horror, clear as day on his bloodstained face. His hands trembled as they cupped my face, thumbs brushing my cheeks, tender yet desperate.

"Flynn?" Seb's voice came from very far away, laced with fear and concern. His hands moved to my chest, my thigh. He rubbed soothing patterns on my hipbone. "Say something."

I managed a small hum in response, forcing myself to take steady breaths.

"I'm... I'm so sorry, Flynn." Seb's voice wavered. "I took too much." His hands violently shook against my skin. "Good god, I couldn't stop. I completely lost myself. I should never have let myself drink from you."

Even through my blood-loss haze, the self-loathing in his voice hurt my soul. I wanted to reach for him, to tell him it was worth it—that *he* was worth it—but my tongue felt too heavy to form the words.

The van tilted and swayed around me like a ship in rough seas. My head felt stuffed with cotton wool, thoughts drifting lazily through a fog. Seb was right—he'd taken far too much.

But all I felt was a surge of warmth blooming in my chest as I looked at him. Even through my hazy vision, the raw anguish on his face tugged at something deep inside me. He looked so lost, so broken. *My vampire.*

With monumental effort, I pushed myself up to a sitting position. The world spun violently, and I had to pause, waiting for the dizziness to subside. When my vision cleared enough, I took in the sight of him—slumped against the van's side, eyes fixed on the floor, shoulders hunched in defeat. His white shirt was torn and soaked dark crimson, though the wound that had been pouring blood earlier was no longer bleeding.

Moving with the careful deliberation of someone deeply drunk, I shifted forward. My knees found purchase on either side of his thighs as I settled onto his lap. His skinny black tie had somehow survived the chaos relatively intact. My fingers closed around the silk, using it to steady myself.

"What are you—"

I pressed my finger against Seb's lips, silencing any further spiral of self-recrimination. His eyes widened as they fixed on mine.

"Putting this stupidly pretentious tie to good use."

I yanked the silk, pulling him towards me, and smashed our mouths together.

There was no preamble, no gentle slide of lips, no tongues easing their way in. The kiss was hard and deep and messy, pulling us both under. Our lips crashed together like waves against rocks, desperate and wild. His tongue swept into my mouth, claiming every inch of it. I met him stroke for stroke, both of us frantic, as if we had mere moments left to live and needed to say everything all at once.

My feverish skin burned wherever it met his cool touch. The weight of darkness pressed around us, making every brush of fingers electric.

And I couldn't get enough of him.

There was an ocean's worth of starlight breaking against my ribs. Like high tide rushing in, warmth flooded every hollow space inside me. My heart swelled like a wave before it crashes, and the undertow of desire pulled me deeper.

Seb's mouth moved against mine with a steady rhythm. Our kisses ebbed and flowed, deep then shallow, urgent then leisurely. I chased the metallic tang of my own blood across his tongue, the taste foreign and thrilling. His cool lips warmed beneath my own, as each kiss felt like falling through velvet darkness.

"Sebastián," I breathed like a prayer.

"This is what it feels like," he murmured against my cheek, between kisses.

"What?"

"This is what it feels like to be alive."

My breath hitched as his hands gripped my hips, anchoring me. I pressed one hand against his chest, over the place where his beating heart once lay.

"Then I've been dead until now too."

A broken noise fell from his lips, and I rocked against him, turning the sound into a deep rumble of a groan. The fog in my head abruptly cleared, like morning mist burning away under the sun. My limbs still felt heavy, but the worst of the dizziness had subsided.

Seb captured my chin. "Are you okay?"

"Very okay."

Capturing his mouth again, I whimpered around his tongue, desperate for more as I ground my hips down on him, my cock happily hardening again. My fingers itched to tear the clothes from both our bodies—if only we weren't blood-soaked in the wreckage of a van.

I pulled back, breathing heavily. "When you bit me, you made me..." I half nodded towards my groin, heat rising in my cheeks.

Seb's eyes widened as understanding dawned. His fingers traced up my inner thigh, stopping at the damp patch on my jeans. Something shifted in his expression—a flash of hunger very different from before.

In one fluid motion, he flipped our positions. My back pressed against the cold metal floor of the van as he loomed over me, his curls falling forward to frame his face. The grace of the movement left me breathless.

His fingers brushed my belt buckle. "May I?"

Well then. Apparently Seb had no qualms about our situation in this wreck of a van. I nodded, not trusting my voice.

With nimble fingers, he undid my belt, and carefully worked my jeans and briefs down just enough. I sprang free, a sticky mess, and Seb's gaze raked over me appreciatively before meeting my eyes again.

"Nice to finally see the other half," he murmured. "The preview didn't do you justice."

Anticipation buzzed through every nerve ending as his cool fingers ghosted closer.

Seb kissed the soft part of my flesh just above my hip bone, and I shivered at the contact. He pressed his cool, flat tongue against my skin. Taking his time, he cleaned me everywhere but my dick. With every lick, I writhed beneath him, until he pinned my thigh with a hand to still me. My cock thickened under the attention, until the poor swollen sod was twitching, begging for Seb's wet mouth.

He looked up at me, his eyes locked on mine. "I should have guessed that every part of you would be equally delicious."

Finally, he took mercy on me—his mouth closed around the head of my cock, and I cried out in pleasure. His tongue swirled around the sensitive tip, teasing and tasting me.

As his mouth worked over me, my fingers traced his face reverently, mapping every perfect feature. Watching his lips stretch around my cock had my head spinning. The way he fluttered his tongue around the head, then licked up the length with little whimpers that vibrated through me—oh my *fucking hell* was Seb good at this. No, not *good*... amazing beyond belief.

I couldn't help myself—my fingers twisted into his hair as I thrust up into the wet coolness of his mouth. My whole body was drawn bowstring-tight, every nerve ending singing with pleasure as he *devoured* me. His rough tongue, the way he gripped my shaft and pumped in time with his sucking—it was overwhelming, in the best way.

Then, in one earth-shattering moment, he took me impossibly deep into his throat.

Then swallowed.

My whole body jerked as pleasure crashed through me. I came for the second time, just as hard, just as intense. Seb fisted the base of my cock and sucked the head, swallowing every drop as I came apart beneath him. Tremors racked through me, and when the last aftershocks faded, a deep, sated laugh bubbled up from my chest.

He took his time cleaning me with gentle licks, making sure not a drop remained, before pulling back with a satisfied hum.

"You'll have to forgive me," he murmured, running a hand through his dishevelled curls. "I'm a few decades out of practice."

"Shut up," I managed, still breathless. My head spun as I pushed myself up to sitting, tucking myself away with trembling fingers.

But I needed more. Needed *him*. I grabbed his tie again, pushing him back to reclaim my seat on his lap, and yanked him into a desperate kiss, tasting my saltiness on his tongue and not caring one bit.

Seb pulled away, and a whisper-soft keen trembled in the air between us. His voice, rough as burnt sugar, broke through my haze. "I can hear a car coming. Probably one of the team."

"I don't care."

My hands found his hair, and I kissed him again.

After all the empty kisses with faceless tourists, after Tom's gentle rejection, after Connor's drunken advance that left me feeling hollow, this felt like coming home to a place I'd never known existed. This was magic spilling from Seb's lips into mine, turning all those painful memories to dust.

So I slid my lips against his, desperate to memorise everything—the perfect bow of his upper lip, the way his tongue moved against mine. Curiosity made me bold, and I traced his teeth with my tongue, lingering over his canines—deadly sharp even when retracted. I tried to burn every detail into my mind: the quiet sounds he made when I pressed closer, the way his fingers dug into my hips hard enough to bruise. If only I could see his face properly, watch those dark eyes go soft and hungry at once, count every one of his wild curls.

"More," he whispered against my lips. His hands slid up my back, pulling me impossibly close. "Just a moment more."

I melted into him, my body fitting against his like we'd been carved from the same stone. His mouth moved to my jaw, trailing kisses down to my throat—careful to avoid the tender spots where he'd bitten me. Shivers trilled through me as his cool lips ghosted over my skin.

Then I heard it myself—the sound of a vehicle—and reality crashed back in like a bucket of cold water. What would the others think, finding their boss tangled up with me in the back of a van, with bite marks on my neck?

I pulled back slightly, though my hands remained buried in his curls. "We should pick this up later."

Tensing, I waited for him to challenge me—to say there would be no *later*. But he didn't. And that unspoken promise steadied something inside me that had been adrift for weeks.

His fingers traced the spot where he'd bitten me, his touch feather-light. "I hurt you."

"It only hurt for a second. I didn't know… I didn't know it would be like that." So intense, so all-consuming. It was easily the most overwhelming yet extraordinary experience of my life.

And I'd do it all again, in a heartbeat.

"I've never felt anything like that before. It was like I was high. Impossibly high. It was…" I flailed an arm around, words failing me. "Fucking amazing."

"When we feed, there's this compound that releases into our saliva," Seb explained, his thumb still stroking gentle circles on my neck. "It releases endorphins, makes the feeding pleasurable for our prey. Historically, it helped us feed without drawing attention. That, and our ability to compel human minds. But a willing victim is far less likely to scream."

"So you're saying I'm not special?" I tried to sound offended, but couldn't keep the smile from my voice.

"Actually…" Seb caught my wrist, his touch impossibly gentle. His expression shifted, becoming more serious. "There's something I need to tell you. I should have realised it when I drank your blood from the glass."

"What?"

"Your blood. It *is* special." His eyes fixed on mine. "Each time I've tasted it, it's been different. More potent. More… powerful. Like the dark magic incubating inside you is growing stronger, seeping into your blood."

"Really? But I feel the same, though, apart from the ice attacks and the weird dreams."

Seb nodded. "I'm certain. Most humans would still be barely conscious after losing that much blood. The fact that you've recovered so quickly—"

"I'm absolutely fine," I interjected.

"And it's way more energising than normal blood, even fresh blood. My senses are sharper. Your blood is getting stronger and stronger. The effect it had on me tonight—healing my wound so quickly..."

He guided my hand to his ribs, pressing my palm flat against the spot where the deadwalker had torn through his flesh. Instead of the ragged wound I expected, my fingers met smooth, unbroken skin through the torn fabric of his shirt.

"That's not possible."

"I heal quickly, but this... This is impressive."

"Fantastic. Demon-enhanced blood donor, at your service. I'll be sure to leave every pint of it to you when I die."

The joke died in the air between us. Seb's eyebrows drew tight, lips pursing. Before he could respond, tyres screeched outside the van, followed by the sound of car doors slamming and boots pounding against concrete.

"Seb?" Kit's voice rang out. "Fucking hell!"

Metal screamed as Kit wrenched open the only functioning back door. His silhouette appeared in the narrow opening, broad shoulders blocking out some of the stark light from the vehicle's headlights. I squinted at him. For some stupid reason, I hadn't yet moved from straddling Seb's lap, with both of us covered in blood, my neck sporting fresh bite marks.

Mortifying.

"We're both alright, Kit," Seb said, his voice steady despite our awkward situation. "Don't worry."

Kit's eyes narrowed as he looked between us, taking in the scene. His expression shifted from concern to something more calculating. It was painfully obvious what had happened, but surely he wouldn't embarrass us by saying anything.

"Well, well." Rory leaned around Kit's shoulder with a grin. "Looks like someone's been having a *bloody* good time."

21

Sebastián

It felt like hours before we all poured into Killigrew Street's basement through the bookcase entrance. My body thrummed with a peculiar energy—Flynn's blood had done more than sate my hunger. Every nerve ending sparked with vitality.

Combined with Flynn's worst attack yet at Rising Dough, it was safe to say the dark magic within him was maturing far quicker than we'd like. My gaze drifted to his chest. What marks currently decorated his skin?

Despite the late hour—nearly eleven—the team gathered in the basement. I deliberately chose the armchair opposite Flynn's position, maintaining a careful distance. He'd zipped his hoodie up to his chin, the fabric dark with grime, hiding any evidence of my... *indiscretion*.

The phantom taste of his blood still lingered—sweet and electric—a haunting reminder of how close I'd come to draining him completely. My fingernails bit into my palm at the memory—his writhing form beneath me, those breathy moans of pleasure that had only encouraged my bloodlust.

The recollection of Flynn's voice pierced through my shame—how he'd reached me even in those depths, with his promises of home.

In that moment, even covered in blood and gore, Flynn had seen past the monster to whatever fragment of humanity still existed within me. He'd offered not just his blood, but his heart. His trust.

And I'd nearly destroyed both.

Rory broke my thoughts by collapsing onto the sofa beside Flynn, his usual bounce conspicuously absent. I watched Flynn blink at him, his gaze tracing the precise lines of Rory's eye makeup with obvious curiosity.

"Thanks for ruining my date." Rory's head lolled against the back of the sofa. "Spent a good thirty minutes on this makeup, you know. Got us VIP seats at my friend's drag show and everything."

Flynn gave an exaggerated grimace.

"And let me tell you," Rory continued, crossing his arms, slumping further into the cushions. "They did *not* believe my story about my pet ferret being sick."

Kit's exasperated sigh cut through the room. "I've told you before about this. A sick ferret is not a reasonable excuse for cancelling plans!"

"But poor Freddy *is* sick! He's literally dead!"

"Next time, just say you've got food poisoning like a normal person, and they might let you reschedule."

Before the brothers could continue bickering, Felix appeared with a tray of steaming hot chocolate, its rich aroma filling the air as he set it on the table.

Then Priya bounded down the stairs, beelining straight for Flynn to launch herself at him. Her arms wrapped around him in a fierce embrace that made him stiffen momentarily. "We were so worried," she mumbled into his hoodie.

Flynn's hand came up to pat her back awkwardly. "I'm okay. Really."

My jaw clenched at the lie. He was far from okay—the dark magic consuming him, my loss of control with his blood, being attacked and kidnapped. But watching Priya fuss over him stirred something warm in my chest. Flynn needed this—needed to know people cared about his well-being.

Felix hovered nearby, fingers twisting his hoodie hem. His gaze darted between Priya and Flynn, longing flashing across his face before he looked away.

Priya settled between Flynn and Rory, distributing mugs. Silence fell as five pairs of eyes turned to me, waiting. They expected analysis, tasks, security protocols...

But exhaustion lined every face. Dark circles under Felix's eyes, Rory's energy dimmed, Flynn nearly collapsing into his mug—an inevitable effect of serving as an impromptu blood bank.

I cleared my throat. "You're all tired. We'll pick this up first thing tomorrow morning."

A collective sigh of relief rippled through the room. Bodies sank deeper into cushions, tension bleeding from shoulders.

My gaze drifted to Flynn, who'd buried his nose in his hot chocolate. A dollop of whipped cream clung to his upper lip, and my throat tightened. Our kiss had been everything I'd denied myself—passionate yet tender, igniting a fire that had smouldered for decades. In that moment, I'd felt truly alive, buzzing with want and need.

The urge to lean across and lick the whipped cream from his lip crashed through me with startling intensity. Before I could stop myself, I reached out, wiping it away with my thumb.

Flynn's breath hitched. Our eyes locked, and the basement air grew thick. My thumb remained glued to his cheek. So easy to bring it to his mouth, for him to—

Rory's loud, deliberate cough shattered the moment.

I jerked away, dropping my hand as if burned, then tried not to catch anyone's eye as they drained their drinks. Thankfully, Priya, Felix and Rory soon said their goodbyes and headed for the bookcase.

Kit lingered in his seat, knowing I'd want to talk to him. When I took a step towards him, Flynn blocked me.

"Come sleep in my room." Flynn's eyes sparkled with a light I was about to dim.

I shifted my weight, guilt coiling in my gut. "I really don't ever *sleep* much, especially at this hour. Perhaps a few hours before dawn, but..." The words caught. How to explain that while nothing would please me more than to lie beside him all night, duty called? "I have work that requires my attention."

No, Sebastián. Those were certainly not the right words.

His face fell, the sparkle extinguishing. The sight struck deeper than a wooden stake.

"However..." I stepped closer, dropping my volume. "I could come to your chambers later. You'll wake to find me there."

Flynn eyed me, a mix of hope and wariness crossing his features. "Promise?"

Promises were not something I made lightly—not after centuries of watching them shatter. "I promise I'll try, Flynn."

"Sorry." He ducked his head, cheeks flushing. "I'm being—"

"No." I caught his chin with my fingers, tilting his face up. "Don't apologise. The fact you desire my presence in your bed at all..." I paused, searching for the right words. "It honours me more than you know."

My gaze followed Flynn as he left the basement, watching until his silhouette disappeared up the stairs. Even then, my eyes lingered on the empty doorway, tracking the echo of his footsteps.

"So..." Kit settled into the armchair opposite me. "Do we... need to talk about this?"

I sighed. "Go ahead."

Kit's fingers drummed against the arm of his chair, his expression unreadable. "I see you've gotten rather *attached* to our guest. And I don't just mean your fangs attaching to his neck."

"Just a bit." I grimaced. "I think... I may have gotten attached from the moment I saw him at Wilde Card. So bright. So trusting. Showering attention on that foul demon. Looking at him like he'd never seen true darkness in this world."

"He's got an adventurous spirit." Kit leaned forward. "Lad's young, Seb. Got wanderlust in his blood. He was telling Rory he means to sail the Atlantic one day. All I'm saying is, he might not stay in London forever."

The words struck like ice through my chest. I knew all this—I wasn't stupid, or in denial.

Just a bit lovesick.

Kit's words about Flynn's wanderlust echoed in my mind, stirring uncomfortable truths I'd been avoiding. A relationship with Flynn could only end in two ways—his departure or his death.

Humans were ephemeral creatures. Their lives blazed bright and brief, like shooting stars across the night sky. Even if Flynn chose to stay, time would claim him eventually. His golden hair would silver, while I would remain unchanged, forced to watch him fade.

I'd sworn after James never to entangle myself with mortals again. The pain of our separation had nearly broken me. Yet here I was falling into the same trap with a boy who dreamed of sailing across oceans.

A phantom tingle spread across my tongue—Flynn's blood, tasting of salt and freedom. Perhaps that's what drew me to him—that wild spirit that refused to be caged.

Time. Such a peculiar master to serve when you'd lived as long as me. I'd watched horse-drawn carriages give way to motorcars, witnessed the birth of electric light. Yet somehow, these grand sweeps of history felt less real to me than the simple movement of Flynn's hands as he gestured while speaking, the way his eyes crinkled when he smiled.

The curse of immortality wasn't in watching the world change—it was in watching it remain achingly, beautifully the same. The way lovers still met on rain-soaked streets, the way mothers still cradled their children. Time had stolen so many of my memories, turned five centuries into a fog of half-remembered faces and places, but it had never dulled the sharp edge of loss. James had taught me that.

And now Flynn threatened to make time matter again, to make each second precious and terrifying. To make me count the hours between messages, the minutes between touches, the moments until I might see him again.

"But that's no reason you shouldn't *try*, Seb," Kit continued, tone softening. "Seven years I've known you, and you've never let anyone close. You deserve a bit of happiness, aye? Something normal?"

I barked out a laugh. "Normal? There's nothing normal about this situation. And what if it doesn't work out?" The words tumbled out, questions that had been circling through my mind for days. "What if it ends just like it did with James?" The memory of that heartbreak crashed through me—the worst pain imaginable, the rage that followed. "I've told you what it did to me. How my mind broke, the weight of eternity alone too much. The senseless slaughter of all those innocent lives."

"But it's different now, Seb." Kit's certainty caught me off guard. "You've got your feet on solid ground. You've got Killigrew Street. The way you told it to me, back then you were adrift, nothing to anchor you. James became your whole world. No wonder it destroyed you when it ended. But now?" He gestured around the basement, then leaned forward, grabbing my wrist. "Look what you've built here. You've made yourself a family. That changes everything."

"Thank you." I held his gaze. "Your friendship means a lot to me, Kit."

"Ach, you're going soft on me." He barked a laugh, rolling his eyes. "Course I love you. Wouldn't have faced that tosser Thrift alone otherwise."

"How did it go?"

"Got you five casks." Kit's lip curled. "Right piece of work, he was. Glad you weren't there to deal with him."

"Thanks. I should be able to make them last. I have a feeling the blood I drank from Flynn should keep me going for a while."

"About that." Kit leaned forward, elbows on his knees. "You mentioned something about the demon's mark affecting it?"

"Yes." I closed my eyes, remembering the surge of power. "It was... extraordinary. Like drinking liquid lightning. Every cell in my body felt charged, alive. The demon magic in his blood—it amplified everything. My healing, my strength, even my senses. I could hear heartbeats from sheep three fields away. I'm still feeling some of the effects now."

"Bloody hell."

"Indeed." I opened my eyes to find Kit studying me intently. "The power of it... I don't think I've experienced anything like it. But it only goes to prove that we're out of time."

One grim nod from Kit. "If he's following a similar timeline to some of the cases we've got more data on, he has about—"

"Seven days left."

"If we're lucky."

Kit and I looked at each other, the weight of it hanging between us.

I pushed myself up from the armchair to pull over our corkboard, the squeak against the floor harsh in the basement's silence.

Papers and photographs cluttered the surface, connected by a web of red string. My fingers traced the string connecting Flynn's name to the other victims. Was there a pattern here, just beyond my grasp?

Kit cleared his throat. "You've got that look."

"What look?"

"The one where you're about to go full conspiracy theorist with the strings."

I narrowed my eyes, dropping my hand from the board. At least I hadn't told him about my suspected hyena stalker.

"Vampires and demons don't mix. The last time I saw them work together was Paris, eighteen thirty-two. My diaries imply that half the supernatural population died. The Seine ran red for days."

"Cheerful as always, boss." Kit said. "You think this is similar?"

"I don't know." I studied the photograph of "Damien." The sight of his sneering face made me want to punch something. Preferably him. We'd shown his picture to over fifty supernaturals, with little success. Cambions were essentially foot soldiers, with a higher power often directing them. We were keeping tabs on over thirty of them, but Damien had appeared from nowhere. He came onto our radar after a contact reported overhearing him talking to another lesser demon in an ancient dialect, one typically reserved for those in positions of power.

"Someone with considerable influence must be pulling the strings."

Kit stretched, his joints popping. "Could be that demon you mentioned? The one from the East End who's getting a bit too big for his boots?"

I shook my head. "*Lord Vasquez,* as he calls himself, controls his territory too carefully to risk such a mess. Besides, he despises vampires. Claims we smell of death."

"That's rich." Kit snorted. "So what about the Brixton clan? That Marcus Vale fancies himself in charge of?"

"That's what worries me." I leaned forward. "The Brixton vampires have been a massive problem ever since Vale started building his little cult. Those vampires have always despised my interference. I can only imagine their anger towards me now I've killed two of them." When I finally met Vale face to face, he'd likely have some choice words for me. "But Vale's clan have never been particularly organised. Never seemed to have an agenda, beyond their bloodlust. But obviously..."

I stood, pacing to dispel my nervous energy, staring at the photographs on the board, the twelve victims of the dark demon magic. I refused to let Flynn become number thirteen.

"There's something more at play here. We need to speak with White again." Twenty years of loyalty, and I still wasn't convinced she was always as forthcoming with her help as she could be.

"When's your next scheduled check-in?"

"Given recent events, I'm going to have to bring our meeting forward."

Kit's eyes gleamed with familiar mischief. "Try to sound less enthusiastic about it. You know, some people actually enjoy their weekly therapy."

I shot him a look that would have withered a lesser man. Kit just grinned, as immune to my glares as he'd been since we'd met seven years ago.

"Go home, Kit." I waved him away. "Get some rest. I'll see you in the morning."

Kit rose, but paused at the bookcase. "You should get some rest too. And by rest, I don't mean brooding in your office all night."

"I already made such a promise."

"Spending the night in Flynn's room, then?" Kit's grin turned wolfish. "How domestic of you."

I refused to dignify that with a response.

Upstairs, the hotel's corridors stretched dark and silent before me. As I passed Flynn's door, his steady heartbeat called to me, tempting me inside. But work demanded my attention first. I had promises to keep, yes—but also a lesser demon to hunt.

Dawn would arrive soon enough. Perhaps then I'd allow myself the luxury of lying beside Flynn, watching his face in sleep, memorising the precise rhythm of his breathing.

As I slipped into my office, Flynn's blood still sang through my veins, a reminder of both pleasure and peril. Of darkness and dawn.

Of promises made, and promises yet to keep.

22

Flynn

The mattress springs creaked as I shifted position for the hundredth time. My temporary room at Killigrew Street was as homely as I could make it—with my clothes creating an impromptu textile installation across every available surface—but it was safe to say I was absolutely sick of it.

19:47. My phone screen glared back at me. No new messages.

I'd spent the day wandering between Felix's lair and the kitchen like a lost puppy, desperate for any scrap of attention. The others rushed past with tight smiles, too caught up in their work to stop to chat. Even Freddy had better things to do than entertain me, despite my wandering the corridors with crackers.

This morning, Seb had kept his promise to be there when I awoke—his cool fingers threading through my hair, warm chestnut eyes fixed on mine. But then, just a brush of lips against my forehead and he was gone, muttering an extremely vague suggestion about seeing me "later" before disappearing in a swirl of coat.

Later. *Right.*

My thumb hovered over the camera icon. I was already in my pyjamas, ready for bed. Maybe if I sent him a photo... Nothing provocative, just... something to remind him I existed?

God, this was now getting pathetic beyond belief.

He was out there protecting the world from supernatural evil—and trying to save my life—and I was here moping around pining for him because I hadn't seen him in over twelve hours?

There was something *seriously* wrong with me.

I scrolled through social media instead, trying to distract myself. Images of some of my friends out on the water made me feel so homesick it hurt. When I saw Tom's name, I quickly swiped past it.

Then a photo of Katie popped up—she was grinning at the camera, birthday cake in front of her, candles casting a warm glow across her face. *Shit*. Her birthday. I'd been so wrapped up in all the crazy drama I'd completely forgotten to message her.

The realisation hit like a punch to the gut. What was I doing? Sulking about the affections of a vampire I'd met only weeks ago, while my sister celebrated without me. For all I knew, I could die tomorrow.

Before I could talk myself out of it, I hit the call button. The phone rang once, twice.

"*Flynn*?!" The emotion in that *one* word.

"Happy birthday," I said weakly.

"Fuck you." It was more sarcasm than anger, but it still hurt. "Seriously? Are you going to pretend everything is normal?"

"I miss you," I all but whispered, hot prickles building behind my eyes. "I miss everyone so much."

Katie's tone softened. "Hey. I miss you too. Is everything okay in London? You haven't been squashed by a bus yet?"

I gripped the phone tighter, throat constricting. "I need to talk to you. In person. But I can't come home to Ireland."

She was silent for a moment. "Well, I can't just leave Mum here all alone, can I?"

"Don't say it like that." The words burst out sharper than intended. "You sometimes go a whole week without seeing her!"

The unspoken accusation hung between us—unlike me, who'd tried to visit every other day before... everything. Another wave of homesickness crashed over me.

"I can't just abandon my shop, Flynn. At least tell me what this is about."

I opened my mouth, but nothing came out. In the background, Connor's laugh reverberated through the phone, followed by another voice.

My stomach turned at the sound. The last time I'd tried telling Katie about Connor's behaviour—years ago now—she hadn't believed me. He'd slapped my ass in the kitchen, made some crude comment about my jeans. When I told Katie, she'd laughed it off.

"Is Mum there? Are you all having a party?" *Without me?*

"Mum just left, actually. She brought my birthday cake round."

"Was it her chocolate fudge one?" I traced patterns on the duvet with my finger.

"Flynn." Her tone dropped to deadly serious, and my stomach clenched. "What is going on? Please, this is getting ridiculous. And look, don't be mad, but Tom spoke to me. Only because he's so worried he hurt you—"

"Stop." I closed my eyes, falling back onto the bed. "Yes, that whole thing was awful, and I still need to properly fix it. But this is nothing to do with him."

A soft knock at the door made me jump. The handle turned slowly, and Seb's dark curls appeared around the frame. His eyes met mine, questioning. *Shall I come back later?*

"*No!*" The word burst out before I could stop it.

"Flynn?" Katie's voice crackled through the speaker. "What's wrong?"

"We need to talk, ASAP. There are things I need to say, and I might not have that much time left to say them."

Closing the door behind him, Seb gave me a look that said, *"Are you sure that's a sensible thing to say to a family member over the phone?"*

And he was right.

Katie exploded.

"*What*?! Are you in serious trouble or something? Do you need money?"

Oops.

"No, no. Nothing like that. Sorry, forget what I just said. Everything's fine, I promise. I'll talk to you soon. Enjoy the rest of your birthday." After all, there was no point ruining her party.

Katie made a noise of pure exasperation down the phone. "Just... be careful, okay?"

"I love you." The words came out choked.

"I love you too, you absolute idiot."

The line went dead. The room fell into silence, broken only by the very distant hum of London traffic outside.

Seb crossed the room in that graceful way of his, each movement deliberate and controlled. His mouth opened, probably to ask if I was alright, but before he could get a word out, I launched myself at him. My arms wrapped around his middle, face pressed into the soft material of his shirt and silky tie. His fancy cologne—all dark spices and sexiness—washed over me.

"This is what happens when you lock me up all day." My voice came out muffled against his chest.

"You can't trick me into feeling guilty about keeping you safe." His tone was stern, but his hands came up to rest against my back. "What happened with your phone call? Your sister? Is everything okay?"

"No," I said honestly. "Not even remotely. She's dead worried. I told her I need to talk to her in person, but I obviously can't go back to Ireland right now, and she doesn't understand why."

Seb pulled back, gripping my shoulders. "Talk to her in person because... you miss her so much?"

"Well, yes, there's the whole needing to say goodbye before I die thing"—he grimaced—"but I actually need to tell her the reason I left Braymore." I stared at a worn spot on the rug. "I should have gone straight to her that night, rather than run away. I've made it all so much worse. But..."

Seb captured my face. "Will you explain to me what happened? I promise you'll receive no judgement."

I pulled away from his touch, needing space to get the words out. I crossed the room to retrieve the worn photo frame on my bedside table—Mum, Katie, and me at Giant's Causeway, all windswept smiles.

"It was her husband, Connor." The name tasted bitter on my tongue. "The night I left... I was on the beach. Crying about Tom. About everything, really." I swallowed hard. "Connor found me there. He... He kissed me."

Eyes widening, Seb fell very still.

"Katie and I were so close growing up. After Dad died, she basically helped raise me. But years ago, at a party, Connor... He touched me. Inappropriately. When I told Katie, she laughed it off. Said I was confused." A hollow laugh escaped me. "So this time, I couldn't face her not believing me again. Or worse—thinking I'd somehow encouraged him. Or even that I was so heartbroken about Tom, I threw myself at him."

"Flynn—"

"She's my *sister*." The words came out raw. "She deserves to know why I left. But how do I tell her that her husband..." I pressed the heels of my hands against my eyes. "That the reason I abandoned her, abandoned Mum, was because her husband cornered me on a beach when I was at my lowest?"

Silence fell heavily in the room as Seb's lips pressed together in a firm line.

"Katie's always been the strong one. After Dad died, she held us all together. Made everything beautiful again, like she does with her flowers. But this? This would destroy her. And I can't—" I faltered. "I can't be the one who does that to her."

Seb's eyes blazed with a new intensity. "Listen to me very carefully," he said, low, dangerous. "That man is a predator. What he did was not your fault. And your sister deserves to know exactly what kind of monster she married."

I blinked rapidly, trying to process the vehemence in his tone.

"I'd like to think she's going to surprise you, when you get to talk to her." He gentled his voice. "Just... wait until we've dealt with the immediate threat to your life." In three long strides, Seb was in front of me again, his fingers brushing my cheek, feather-light. "And then... if you wanted... Know that you wouldn't have to do it alone."

The tenderness in that touch undid me completely. I leaned into his hand, letting out a shaky breath.

"*Flynn.*" Just my name, but filled with such meaning. "You deserve far better than what life has dealt you so far. And I will do everything in my power to ensure you survive to have that conversation with your sister."

My throat tightened. I couldn't think about Katie anymore, not tonight. "How's the investigation?" I asked.

Seb's shoulders dropped as he let out a long sigh. "We've been searching Brixton all day. Not a single trace of the vampires." His fingers traced patterns absently on my back. "Kit and Rory are continuing the search through the night, but they forced me back here. They said I'd been at it too long. Apparently, it was affecting my mood."

I pulled back just enough to look up at him. The shadows under his eyes seemed darker than usual.

"How long?"

"Fourteen hours, give or take." His mouth twisted.

My hands slid up his chest, coming to rest around his neck. The silk of his tie brushed against my fingers as I played with the short tufts of hair at his nape. "Well, I'm more than happy to help you relax."

Seb hummed as he ran his thumb over the collar of my flannel shirt. "These pyjamas again. You're like a walking picnic blanket."

"Lucky for you..." I tilted my head with a nervous smile. "I've been told I make a pretty tasty snack."

Previously, high on adrenaline and blood loss, I'd been bold enough to throw myself at him. Today, with a clearer head, I searched his eyes for permission before moving closer. His gaze dropped to my mouth, pupils dilating slightly.

The tension in the air thickened, crackling around us.

Yesterday, our kiss had been phenomenal. Electric. Beyond words.

Everything I'd ever dreamed kissing someone could be.

Let's see if it was a fluke.

I leaned in, brushing my lips against his. The first touch was gentle, tentative, until Seb's hand slid up my back to cradle my neck, drawing me closer. His mouth moved against mine, soft yet certain, and I melted into him with a quiet sigh.

The kiss deepened naturally, his tongue sliding against the seam of my lips. I opened to him eagerly, and that spark from yesterday blazed to life once more. His other hand gripped my waist, pulling me flush against him as our tongues met, sliding together as if coming home to one another.

Definitely not a fluke.

My fingers tangled in his hair as the kiss grew more heated. Seb made a low sound in his throat—something between a growl and a groan—that resonated through my entire body. His cool lips warmed from our contact, the sensation intoxicating.

My breath hitched when he suddenly took control, backing me against the nearest wall. His movements were fluid, graceful, yet tinged with a hint of desperation. My head tipped back as his mouth traced a path along my jaw, each press of his lips sending jolts of electricity through my body.

"*Definitely* not a fluke," I managed to breathe out, my voice embarrassingly shaky.

Seb pulled back just enough to meet my gaze, his eyes dark and intense. Swollen lips. Hair thoroughly mussed from my fingers. The sight of him like this—dishevelled and wanting—sent desire coursing through me like wildfire, and my cock instantly hardened, straining against my briefs.

"No," he agreed, voice rough. "Not even close."

Then his mouth was on mine again, and coherent thought became impossible.

The kiss deepened further, becoming almost desperate. My fingers dug into Seb's curls as his tongue swept against mine. The wall behind me was the only thing keeping me upright as my knees threatened to give way.

My lungs burned for air, but I couldn't bring myself to pull away. Seb's mouth was addictive—cool and sweet and perfect. The need for oxygen became secondary to the feeling of his lips moving against mine, his hands gripping my waist. He didn't need to breathe, could kiss forever if he wanted to, and part of me wanted to test that theory until I passed out from lack of air.

Just when black spots started dancing at the edges of my vision, Seb broke away. But before I could protest the loss, his lips found my jaw again, raining butterfly kisses along the sensitive skin there. My head hit the wall with a soft thud, eyes rolling skyward at the sensation.

My hands moved to his shoulders, gripping the expensive fabric of his shirt as the room started to spin. His kisses grew more intense, and I held on tighter, certain I'd collapse without his solid frame anchoring me in place.

"I need you," I found myself saying, pushing my aching cock against his thigh in case my words weren't clear enough.

Before my bravery faded, I reached for Seb's tie, fingers trembling despite my best efforts. His eyes watched my every movement, intense and unblinking, as I worked at the knot. The tie slid free with a soft whisper of fabric, and I let it drop to the floor.

"I want you." The words came out barely above a whisper. "Please."

Seb caught my hands in his, bringing them to his lips. He pressed a gentle kiss to my knuckles, the touch achingly tender. "I want that too. God, I can't even tell you how much I want that." His voice was turbulent, raw. "But it's too dangerous. We can't risk it."

My heart clenched painfully in my chest. The mark over my heart seemed to pulse with a dull ache, a constant reminder of my doom. "I might only have a few days left."

The moment the words left my mouth, I wanted to snatch them back. It was a low blow, using my possible death as emotional leverage. *Despicable.* Guilt twisted in my stomach as I watched pain flash across Seb's features.

His expression turned serious, almost sombre. "Well, if you really want that, there are others who will help you, I'm sure."

I flinched away as if he'd struck me, his words cutting deeper than any blade.

"You'd be okay with that?" I asked flatly.

"No, of course not!" he snapped. "But if it's what you want…"

"It's not." I swallowed hard against the lump in my throat. "I don't want anyone else. I don't want some meaningless fuck with a random man." My fingers curled into the fabric of his shirt, holding on tight. "I want it to be with someone I trust completely." *I want to make love to you.* The thought reverberated in my head, but I couldn't bring myself to say those words aloud. He'd probably run an absolute mile. "I only want you. But I'm sorry. I'm not thinking straight." Pressing closer, I wrapped my arm around his waist, terrified I'd pushed him too far. "I genuinely meant what I said in the bakery. I'll take whatever you can give me, for however long that might be. That's enough, I promise."

Seb's hand moved to cup my chin, his thumb stroking gently across my cheek. The grip was strong, and I found myself falling deeper into those burnt caramel eyes, drowning in their depths. This closeness, this intimacy—it really was more than enough.

Something shifted in his expression. His pupils dilated as they fixed on mine with an almost predatory focus. Then he muttered, "*Serás mi perdición,*" and squeezed his eyes shut. "Stay here."

"What?" I blinked, trying to focus. "Where are you going?"

"To get supplies."

"What sort of supplies?"

Seb raised one perfect eyebrow, and my stomach did a backflip.

"Oh…" My heart thundered against my ribs as realisation dawned. "What?" I managed to squeak out as heat rushed to my face. "Okay, well, I got tested at the end of the summer, and if it's really been twenty years since you last slept with someone, we're probably fine without a condom unless you want one, and I already have lube, so…" My embarrassed mumbling dwindled to a stop.

"I didn't mean lube." His lips twitched with amusement. "Hold on. I'll be right back."

He slipped out of the room with that uncanny grace of his, leaving me alone with my rapidly spiralling thoughts. Was this actually happening?

After weeks of tension and wanting and stolen glances, were we really about to...?

The nervous energy coursing through my body made it impossible to stand still. I paced the length of the room, trying to calm my racing heart.

What if I wasn't any good? What if I came straight away? What if—

I caught sight of myself in the mirror and grimaced. My hair was a proper mess now, cheeks flushed pink, lips still swollen from our kisses. I looked exactly like what I was—a complete disaster who had no idea what he was doing.

This was Sebastián Salazar. Actual centuries-old vampire. Probably had countless lovers over the years. And here I was, a tragically inexperienced virgin, who was already having a panic attack over doing something I'd practically begged him for.

My stomach twisted with nerves as I waited, each second stretching into eternity. The marks over my heart gave a dull cold throb, as if sensing my anxiety. I pressed my palm against it, trying to steady my breathing.

The door opened, and Seb slipped back inside. He took one look at my face and sighed.

"You've been in here catastrophizing this whole time, haven't you?"

"No," I insisted, but my voice came out higher than usual.

Seb placed an assortment of objects carefully on the dresser before crossing the room. His cool hands gripped my upper arms, steadying me. "Flynn." The way he said my name made my knees weak. "Look at me."

I lifted my gaze to meet his, and once again, I was drowning.

"Do you have any idea how attracted I am to you?" His thumb traced circles on my biceps. "How incredible I think you are?" He pressed a soft kiss to my jaw, making me shiver. "How honoured beyond words I am that you want me to be your first?"

Another kiss, this time to the corner of my mouth. My eyes fluttered closed as his lips brushed against mine, gentle and sweet.

First.

Kiss.

Last.

Kiss.

Everything.

Warmth bloomed through my chest, chasing away the cold pangs of anxiety. I melted into him, all my earlier fears dissolving under the tender press of his mouth against mine.

"I can't wait to hear those gorgeous sounds of yours again," he all but whispered into my ear, before taking my lobe between his sharp teeth.

I couldn't help it. A tiny moan escaped me, and he chuckled.

"Are you... Are you going to bite me again?" I said, on a rushed breath. The prospect had me dizzy with excitement.

He pulled back, frowning. "No. Definitely not. In fact..." He grabbed one of the items from the dresser—a small metal cask. He wiggled it, and liquid sloshed. "I'm going to sate myself as much as possible, on this extraordinarily overpriced blood."

"Was it terribly expensive?"

"Yes." Seb's lips curved into a smile. "But don't you worry about that." He pressed a soft kiss to my forehead, making my heart flutter. "Having that sweet cock of yours inside of me will be worth every penny."

My breath caught in my throat. *Oh.*

I wasn't sure if I was disappointed or relieved. The pressure of being more in control hadn't even occurred to me until this moment. I'd watched a fair bit—okay, a *lot*—of porn, but I suddenly felt woefully unprepared. How badly could I mess this up?

But then again, the thought of Seb wanting me like that, of him trusting me enough... My dick gave a hearty throb, as if telling me to shut up, that it was up for the challenge.

"Is that how... you want to do it?" I managed to get out, my voice embarrassingly shaky.

Seb considered me. "You told me..."

"I know," I said quickly. "That's fine. I mean, that's great."

Seb's hands slid lower. "Though I'd love nothing more than to plunge myself into your tight heat..." His voice was rough against my ear as his fingers pressed more firmly, drawing a whimper from my throat. "That pleasure will have to be yours to take. Because..."

He reached for the other items on the dresser, and my jaw dropped as I took in what he held. A length of thin rope, deep burgundy in colour, and something black. Black and leather.

"No." I pressed my hand to my mouth, unable to stop the nervous laugh that bubbled up. "You want to be tied up? And wear a muzzle?" The question came out high-pitched. *Why the fuck does he even have that?* "Where did you get that from?"

"It's not personally mine." Seb's lips quirked. "But you'd be amazed what we've got stored in these rooms."

His thumb traced circles on my hip, but I couldn't move past the muzzle gleaming dully in the low light.

"Is this... what you're into? *Bondage?*" I felt like I'd just skipped easy mode and gone straight to level one hundred.

His soft laugh rumbled in his chest. "It's a safety precaution. But if this all makes you uncomfortable..."

"I guess..." I shifted my weight, trying to find the right words. "I just... I wanted our first time to be more... I don't know. Natural? Normal?" My throat tightened. "With two equally active parties? And less like you're some kind of dangerous animal that needs restraining."

Seb's expression softened. "Flynn." He set the items down and cupped my face in his hands. "This is only about keeping you safe. If I lose control, even for a moment..." His thumb traced my bottom lip. "I could tear your throat out without meaning to. The bloodlust, combined with how good it's going to feel... it's too risky."

"But when you bit me before—"

"That was different. With the amount I want you, this is going to be far more intense." His eyes held mine, serious. "Either we do this with precautions, or we don't do it at all. I won't risk your life just for pleasure."

I glanced at the rope and muzzle again.

"Okay," I whispered. "If that's what you need to feel safe."

I was still processing the whole bondage situation when Seb's expression shifted to something more playful, eyes glinting.

"You know," he purred, stepping closer. "We could make this fun. Add a dash of roleplay to ease the tension."

"What?" *Roleplay* now?!

His hand slid down my chest, coming to rest at my hip before brushing against the front of my pyjamas. Though light, the pressure had me quivering.

"Mmm. Perhaps you could be a vampire hunter." His voice dropped lower, the sound like dark velvet against my skin. "One who's finally caught the big bad vampire he's been chasing." His fingers traced the outline of my bulge, and I hissed softly. "And now you get to do whatever you want with your captive."

I almost laughed at the absurdity of it—me, playing at being some kind of badass vampire hunter. But before I could tease him for watching too much Buffy, Seb had dropped gracefully to his knees in front of me. My brain short-circuited at the sight.

His mouth pressed against me through the chequered fabric, tongue tracing the length of my cock. Even with the barrier, the sensation was glorious. My head fell back against the wall with a thud as a moan escaped my lips.

Seb pulled away from me, and a disgruntled noise slipped out of me.

"Hold on. I'll quickly drink."

"Oh. Right. The very expensive blood."

He crossed to the dresser in fluid movements, grabbing the cask. The scent hit me—metallic and rich. My stomach twisted slightly, but I couldn't look away as Seb lifted it to his lips.

He drank deeply, his throat working as he swallowed. His eyes never left mine, burning with an intensity that made my breath catch. A drop of crimson escaped the corner of his mouth, trailing down his chin.

My hand drifted to my thigh, then my groin, fingers pressing against the growing ache there. Seb's gaze tracked the movement, and he took another long pull from the cask. His predatory stare as he drank set every nerve ending ablaze, molten desire spreading through my body.

I shifted, trying to find some relief from the building pressure. My palm rubbed slow circles over my dick as I watched him feed. There was something mesmerizing about it—dangerous and beautiful all at once.

Seb kept drinking, swallow after swallow. To keep himself under control. For me.

Something wild fluttered in my chest at the thought.

"Does it taste nice?" I asked innocently, though I knew he'd understand what I wanted to hear.

The empty cask clattered against the floor, rolling away into a corner. Seb's mouth glistened crimson as he swiped the back of his hand across it in one feral motion.

In a blink, he crossed the space between us. His hands gripped my waist, pulling me flush against him. The coolness of his body seeped through my clothes, making me gasp.

"Like dirt compared to how you taste, sweet angel. You were absolute *perfection*."

Fucking hell. My legs turned to jelly, and I started to slip from his grasp. His grip tightened instantly, keeping me upright. My hands found purchase on his shoulders, steadying myself.

"Are you ready?"

"Yes." I bit into my lip. "But sorry in advance if it's not the best."

Seb's cool fingers caught my chin, his thumb gently tugging my lip free. "It's already the best," he murmured, eyes so, so soft. "Whatever happens—it's already perfect because it's you."

Heat bloomed across my cheeks at his words. How did he know exactly what to say to make my heart feel like it might burst?

"Besides." His lips quirked into that devastating half-smile. "I haven't had sex in twenty years." He winked. "So I'm practically as virginal as you are."

I rolled my eyes, but the tension in my shoulders eased slightly.

"Let me have one quick taste first," he said silkily, dropping to his knees again, tugging on the elastic of my pyjama bottoms.

My breath caught in my throat at the sight of him looking up at me through those dark lashes. But...

"Not if you want me to fuck you," I said, face aflame. "At this point, I'll literally explode straight into your mouth."

A rich chuckle rumbled through Seb's chest as he rose to his feet. He reached for the light switch. Darkness fell, save for a silvery shaft of moonlight streaming through the window.

He positioned himself deliberately in that ethereal glow, and my breath caught. The chiaroscuro effect of moonlight against shadow transformed him into something otherworldly—a painting come to life—all dramatic shadows and luminous skin, beauty tinged with danger.

His fingers moved to the buttons of his fitted waistcoat, undoing each one with careful precision. The garment slid from his shoulders, joining his discarded tie on the floor with a whisper of fabric.

Next came his crisp white shirt. He took his time with those buttons too, revealing inch after inch of golden skin. The shirt fell away, and I couldn't help but stare at the lean muscles of his chest and abdomen, carved like marble beneath a light dusting of dark hair. It trailed enticingly down his stomach, disappearing beneath his waistband.

His hands moved to his belt, and the soft hiss of leather through belt loops made my pulse quicken.

When his fingers found the button of his tailored trousers, I gripped the edge of the dresser behind me. They joined the growing pile of clothes, leaving him in nothing but black briefs that clung to his thighs.

He hooked his thumbs into the waistband of his underwear, pausing for just a moment—teasing—before sliding them down and stepping free.

My mouth went dry. Within a dark nest, his cock hung thick and heavy between his thighs, already half hard and impossibly splendid. He stood before me like some ancient statue of Adonis, all perfect proportions and classical beauty, but with an underlying current of power that no marble could capture.

He shifted, and the moonlight turned his skin to alabaster, catching in the strands of his dark hair and making shadows dance across the planes of his face. His eyes, when they met mine, gleamed with hunger.

I fumbled for the burgundy rope. "I'll tie you up."

Maybe this whole thing *would* be easier in the role of a vampire hunter.

Seb moved to the queen-sized bed with feline grace, stretching out. He lifted his arms above his head, crossing his wrists against the ornate metal headboard.

My hands shook slightly as I picked up the rope, then muscle memory took over as I quickly formed a Highwayman's Hitch, looping the loop around his wrists and the wooden frame of the headboard. The motions were familiar—*around, through, over, under*—the same pattern I used to secure boats at the harbour.

"My grandfather taught me this one." I tested the tension with a gentle tug. "Though I doubt this is *quite* what he had in mind for its application."

"Is he the type to roll in his grave?"

"Oh, definitely spinning as we speak." I couldn't help but smile as I completed the final loop before shuffling awkwardly back from the bed. The contrast was comical—Seb completely naked and bound, while I stood fully clothed.

"Well then, hunter." Seb's low voice teased. "What are you waiting for? Don't you want to claim your prize?"

God, he was going to kill me before we even started.

"Only if you're comfortable with that," he added. "I'll do whatever you want me to do." He pulled at his binds. "This is all to keep you safe, Flynn."

"No... it's— I just need a minute," I managed. "To... get into character."

I practically fled the room, closing the door behind me. In the hallway, I pressed my forehead against the cool wall, trying to steady my breathing.

What the fuck am I doing?

This was mad. All of it. The bondage, the roleplay, the fact that I was about to have sex with a centuries-old vampire who was currently tied naked to a bed.

A really hot, really quite nice vampire, my brain helpfully supplied.

I squeezed my eyes shut, feeling myself spiral into oblivion.

No. Stop.

I straightened up, squaring my shoulders. Seb wanted this. Wanted *me*. He'd made that abundantly clear.

You are a vampire hunter, I told myself. *Confident. In control. Ready to make that vampire yours.*

Taking a deep breath, I pushed open the door.

Moonlight spilled across Seb's bound form, creating shadows that emphasised every perfect line of his body. His eyes found mine, challenging.

I leaned against the doorframe, letting my fingers trail over the fading marks on my neck. "You've been a naughty, naughty vampire," I said, injecting my voice with a playful authority that surprised me. "Having little sips of my blood while I was sleeping. Did you think I wouldn't notice?" I tapped the bite marks meaningfully.

A smirk played at Seb's lips as he tested the ropes binding his wrists. "I can't help it that you taste so good," he crooned, defiant. "And by the way you writhed in your sleep, shouting and begging me to take it... I'd bet you didn't mind."

I pushed off from the doorframe, slammed the door shut, stalked closer to the bed. "You're going to pay for this, vampire."

"Foolish mortal," Seb drawled, somehow looking regal despite being tied to my bed. "You dare challenge one who has walked these lands for centuries?"

I swiped a neglected wooden coat hanger off the floor. At least the hook bit was sort of pointy.

"Your reign of terror ends here, creature of the night!" I brandished my prop stake.

"A coat hanger?" Seb tugged at his bonds, all coiled grace despite his restraints. "How *pedestrian*. Though I suppose I shouldn't expect more from a hunter who wears red-chequered pyjamas."

I jabbed the hanger towards him. "They'll be the last thing you ever see, beast!"

His rich laugh boomed across the room. "Come closer then, fearsome hunter. Let's see how steady your hand is when faced with true evil."

I traced the hook down his chest, tantalisingly slowly. "Are you scared?"

"Oh no," he breathed, smirking. "Whatever shall I do against such... exquisite torture?"

My gaze dropped to where his cock had hardened considerably, standing proudly in the center of the bed.

"Don't you dare enjoy this, vampire!" I gasped sharply, slapping the wood against his chest as hard as I dared.

"Mmm," he moaned, shameless and deliberate. "Is that the best you can do, *hunter*?"

"Enough!" I straddled him in one fluid movement, pinning him with my weight. His thick cock pressed up against my own, the flimsy material a poor barrier, and my aching dick throbbed impatiently. "I think it's time to silence that smart mouth of yours."

The muzzle was waiting for me on the bedside table.

My hands shook as I brought it towards Seb's face.

Viper-quick, he snapped at my fingers, teeth clicking together inches from my skin. I jerked back with a startled yelp.

"Careful, lovely hunter," he taunted, eyes glinting. "I bite."

Steadying myself, I grabbed a fistful of his hair, yanking his head back. The motion exposed the elegant line of his throat.

"That's the last time you'll try that, creature." I tightened my grip on his hair, satisfaction coursing through me at his sharp intake of breath. "You're going to be punished for your disobedience."

His lips curved into a wicked smile. "Promise?"

I secured the muzzle around his head, tightening it enough to stay in place. The metal and leather contraption transformed him into something even more dangerously beautiful.

"Now then." I traced a finger down his chest, feeling the muscles tense beneath my touch. "I think I deserve to have some fun with my prey before I end your miserable existence."

Seb's eyes blazed with challenge above the muzzle, and he arched up against me in silent defiance.

"Oh yes," I breathed, maintaining my grip on his hair. "I'm going to enjoy making you submit, vampire."

He made a muffled sound of protest, testing his bonds. I dragged my nails down his chest, watching him shiver.

My hand froze as reality crashed over me like an icy wave. What was I *doing*?

This wasn't me—this confident, dominating person. I was Flynn Carter, the guy who'd run away from his hometown because he couldn't even handle kissing his best friend.

A muffled sound from behind the muzzle drew my attention back to Seb. He cleared his throat, the noise distorted by metal and leather, and made an encouraging "mm-hmm" sound.

I met his eyes. Gone was the playful defiance from our roleplay. Instead, his gaze held nothing but warmth and understanding. He nodded slightly, a gentle motion that seemed to say, *"It's okay, I've got you."*

Those dark eyes pleaded with me to continue, to trust in this moment between us. There was no judgment there, no expectation—just acceptance and desire.

My racing heart steadied. This wasn't Braymore Bay. This wasn't about my past or my fears.

This was just me and Seb, finding our way together.

I reached for his hair again, fingers threading through those soft curls. "Now then, vampire. Where were we?" My voice grew more confident. "Ahh yes, you're all tied up and muzzled. At the mercy of a mere mortal."

Another defiant arch of his body.

"Ah-ah." Pushing him down, I caught his chin, forcing him to meet my gaze. "I decide what happens now. When you move. When you moan." I shifted my weight deliberately against his growing hardness. "When you come."

The sound he made then was decidedly undefiant.

"And if you're a very good vampire for me, then I *might* grant you the privilege of having your cock sucked."

His whole body went taut beneath me, a shudder running through his muscles. Above the leather muzzle, his eyes blazed with a mix of desire and challenge, as if daring me to follow through on my threat.

I ripped my shirt off, then rocked back on my heels, quickly shimmying out of my pyjama bottoms without leaving my position above him. My cock sprang free, desperate for his. I rubbed myself against him, the friction fucking incredible.

A strangled sound escaped him then—not of pleasure, but something raw and wounded. His eyes fixed on my chest, where faint frost marks traced their ghostly patterns across my skin.

"Hey," I murmured, catching his chin with my fingers, pressing a kiss to his forehead. "Not now. Just be here with me."

Seb made a low sound in the back of his throat, not sounding convinced. I traced my fingers down his chest, determined to draw him back into the moment, to chase that haunted look from his eyes. "Let me take care of you," I whispered against his skin. When his body finally relaxed beneath my touch, I smiled.

Reaching for the top drawer of the nightstand, I pulled out the bottle of lube I'd stashed there. It was strawberry flavoured, the only kind they'd had at the shop. Luckily, Seb couldn't mock me for it. Not presently anyway.

As I squirted some onto my fingers before teasingly tracing it around my groin, Seb's gaze followed the movement. Then, with a wicked grin, I dolloped a generous amount onto his cock.

His hips bucked involuntarily at the contact, and I couldn't help but laugh. "Easy there, vampire. We're just getting started."

My fingers trembled slightly as I reached for his dick. It was beautifully thick, heavy in my palm, and my mouth watered as I stroked up and down its smooth, silken length. Seb's hips jerked, a muffled groan escaping past the leather.

I paused, and for a moment, the only sound in the room was my shaky exhale of breath. I pressed myself into him, then taking both our cocks in one hand, I began to stroke us together. My fingers strained, stretching so wide around us both. But the feel of Seb's pulsing dick against mine was worth it—the silky smoothness of his skin, the delicious friction. I could feel every ridge and vein of his, and the coolness of his length against my burning heat shot a tremor straight through me.

My breathing grew ragged as I continued to stroke us, fiery pleasure building higher and higher. Seb's eyes never left mine.

With a Herculean effort, I dropped my grip on us. From my position seated on him, I could feel the tension in his body, the way he strained against his bonds.

"Not yet, vampire," I whispered, voice hoarse. "We're not done playing yet."

I leaned down, pressing a kiss to his leathery, muzzled mouth.

"You're mine now," I murmured against his sharp cheekbone. "And I'm going to make you scream my name before this is over."

Bound and at my mercy, the body of Sebastián Salazar was mine for my mouth to explore.

Starting with his chest, I traced my fingers over the defined lines of his pectorals. His nipples were small and hard, and I pressed my mouth against one, to roll it between my teeth. My tongue flicked out against the hardened bud, and Seb writhed beneath me.

I leaned forward, running my tongue along his bound forearms, just like I'd fantasised about the day we properly met. When I reached his hands, I linked our fingers together, and his gentle squeeze gave me the courage to continue. Moving back, I nuzzled my cheek against his chest hair, working my way down his stomach, past tight, ridged abs. I tongued across his V, and when I reached his groin, I couldn't help but press gentle kisses to the crease of his hips. I burned all over with anticipation, and so I pressed his cool, rigid cock against my cheek, chilling my flushed skin.

Any nerves about not performing well enough for him were long gone. This powerful vampire wanted me—as evidenced from the sounds he was making, and the bead of precum on his throbbing cock.

I sucked along one side of it, moaning against it like it was a strawberry ice-lolly I was dying to lick. A suck of his cockhead later, his firm heaviness lay on my tongue. My lips stretched around his impressive girth, and I swirled my tongue around his glans, nipping, sliding.

With my palm pressed against his hip, I could feel the tension coiled tight in Seb's every muscle—he was restraining himself from thrusting. I rewarded my captive's valiant efforts by taking him as deep into my throat as I could manage.

That was all it took.

He unleashed a muffled cry of warning—then his hips snapped up, his cock tearing deep into my throat, and he came, drowning me. I half choked on his cum, coughing it back up into my mouth. The taste was unique—metallic and cold, like ice water on a hot day.

I replaced my mouth with my fist, milking Seb through the last of his orgasm. Tremors rippled through the firm muscles of his stomach. *So fucking hot. So fucking hot and he was mine.* Sent half delusional with need and lust, I spat some of his cum into my palm, then used a finger to mark a cross over his cool chest.

"This is where I shall stake you later, fiend."

Above the muzzle, his eyes flashed with dark amusement, and he arched his back in clear invitation. A muffled laugh escaped through the leather.

"But first," I traced my finger lower, following the trail of dark hair down his stomach, "I think there are other places that need conquering."

Reaching for the bottle on the nightstand, I added more slick to my already wet fingers. Seb's eyes followed my every movement as I traced patterns on his inner thigh.

"I do wonder," I murmured, circling closer to my goal. "If you'll beg for me once I remove that muzzle."

As I breached him with one finger, his body arched off the bed again, higher now, unleashing a cacophony of muffled, desperate sounds as I inched inside him with careful dedication.

The tight coolness of him gripped my finger as I took my time stretching him, mesmerised by the way his body yielded to my touch, drinking in his every reaction.

When I crooked my finger *just so* against his prostate, his whole body went taut. "You know, vampire. If you keep responding like this, I might have to keep you around a little bit longer."

I weaved a second finger inside, sinking them deeper. My tongue followed, circling his rim, tasting the salt of his skin. The proud vampire lost all pretense of control then, his hips working in desperate circles as he fucked himself on my fingers.

My heart hammered a frantic rhythm, blood rushing in my ears like waves crashing. I withdrew from him and reached for the lube. The click of the cap seemed impossibly loud in the heated silence. I stroked myself, coating my length, fighting to keep my hand steady.

"Last chance to beg for mercy, vampire." He lifted his legs, placing them heavily on my shoulders. I lined myself up, the head of my firm cock pressing against him. "Or would you be begging for me to be inside you?

Through the muzzle came what might have been a laugh, cut short as I pushed forward.

The resistance I expected never came—Seb's body welcomed me in like he was made for me, drawing me deeper until I was fully seated inside him. I whimpered at the sensation of cool silk around my cock, so different from anything I'd imagined. My hips trembled with the effort of staying still, letting us both adjust.

"*Fuck,*" I breathed, my composure slipping. This ancient creature—this lovely, *lovely* man—was letting me claim him, take him, *possess* him, and the thought made my head spin.

When I finally began to move, setting a slow, deep rhythm, Seb's cock filled again against his stomach. I wrapped my fingers around him, and he twitched delightfully in my grip.

"Already?" I managed through ragged breaths. "Insatiable creature."

I lost myself in the rhythm, each thrust sending sparks of pleasure up my spine. The cool grip of his body was like diving into deep water, pulling me under until I could barely breathe. My world narrowed to the push and pull, like the tide against shore, each wave building higher than the last.

Wherever Seb's heated gaze landed, phantom touches followed—trailing fire down my spine when his eyes traced the length of my body, teasing across my nipples when his stare fixed there, caressing my thighs as his gaze roamed lower. Even when his eyes locked onto my mouth, I felt the ghost of a touch brush against my lips. The sensation made me shudder. A vampire trick? My imagination running wild?

Something shifted then, like a current changing direction. The playful hunter and prey dynamic crumbled as I stared down at him—at the way his dark curls clung to his forehead, how his eyes burned with an intensity that made my chest ache. Every thrust felt more intimate, more real, until that damned muzzle between us became unbearable.

I needed to taste him. Needed to feel his mouth against mine more than I needed my next breath. His eyes traced the path of my hand as I leaned forward, fingers fumbling with the buckles of the muzzle, hands shaking as I worked it free. It fell and I finally saw his full face—lips parted, expression raw with a vulnerability I'd never seen before.

He croaked out, "Flynn—"

"I need to kiss you," I whispered, my movements stilling completely. Gone was the confident hunter, the playful captor. In that moment, I was just Flynn Carter, terrified and wanting.

Time froze.

"Kiss me." Seb's eyes flickered to my lips. "Please."

That single word undid me. I crashed down to meet his mouth, swallowing his groan as our lips finally met. The kiss was desperate, messy, all teeth and tongue and need. I started moving again, my hips finding a new rhythm that matched the way our mouths moved together. The cool slide of his tongue against mine made me moan—like diving into the deepest part of the ocean.

As if dancing to its own tune, my tongue explored his mouth, seeking out and finding the sharp points of his fangs. They weren't extended, but as I traced their edges with my tongue, they lengthened. A fierce growl rumbled deep in Seb's chest, the sound vibrating between us.

These lovely fangs were as much a part of him as his curls, his careful words, his hidden smiles. I wanted—*needed*—to show him I accepted every piece of him, even the parts he tried to suppress. And so my tongue traced their shape reverently, and when the sharp point caught my flesh, sending that bright spark of pain and metallic taste through my mouth, I didn't pull away.

Seb went rigid beneath me, a broken sound escaping his throat.

Then he thrashed—the bed creaking as he strained against the rope. His mouth was desperate against mine, sucking at my tongue with a hunger that made my whole body shudder. Each pull of his lips matched the rhythm of my thrusts, a feedback loop of pleasure that had me seeing stars. The small wound on my tongue throbbed in time with my racing pulse, and it was as if every drop he took forged a deeper connection between us.

He moaned obscenely into my mouth—a sound of pure desperation, of need barely contained. His body clenched around me, cool and perfect, as if trying to draw me even deeper. The phantom touches from before returned tenfold, like he was trying to touch every inch of me at once, claiming me just as thoroughly as I was claiming him.

Every draw of his mouth sent euphoric waves of pleasure dancing through me, and I wanted nothing more than to let him continue, let him take as much as he wanted. But the memory of how upset he'd been with himself after last time...

I pulled back just enough to break the connection, my breath coming in harsh pants. "That's enough."

Seb whined—a desperate, inhuman sound that shot straight through me—but he didn't chase my mouth. His eyes were wild with black hunger, those deadly fangs fully extended, every inch of him screaming need, but he submitted, ducking his chin.

He held himself perfectly still beneath me. Waiting. Obeying.

"There's my lovely vampire," I whispered, carding my fingers through his hair. He pressed into my palm like a pleased cat, the gesture so trusting it made my throat tighten. "So perfectly behaved for me."

I was so close, teetering on the edge. The phantom touches were everywhere and nowhere at once, and suddenly I couldn't bear it—couldn't bear the distance between us.

"I need you to hold me," I gasped, my rhythm faltering as I reached for the knot. When I saw the flash of concern in his eyes, I pressed my forehead to his. "It's okay, Seb. I trust you. More than I've ever trusted anyone. Let me feel you properly."

I pressed my lips to his mouth as I tugged the rope free. The soft sigh of relief that escaped him was echoed by my own as his hands found me instantly—everywhere at once, real and solid and everything I needed. Cool fingers traced my arms, tangled in my hair, cradled my face like I was something precious.

In one fluid motion, he lifted his legs from my shoulders, wrapping them around my waist instead. The change in angle had me moaning, pleasure coiling tighter in my gut. My thrusts were growing erratic, muscles trembling with fatigue, but Seb's hands found my hips, guiding me, supporting me, keeping the rhythm steady and deep.

"Flynn," he moaned, one hand cupping my face, making me look at him. "My Flynn." The possession in his voice, the way his eyes burned into mine—it was too much, too perfect.

"*Yours,*" I managed, the word breaking on a sob. "God, Seb, I'm all yours."

"I've got you," Seb breathed, his hands tightening on my hips. "Let go for me, *mi amor.*"

The pleasure crested like a wave, dragging me under. I spilled deep inside him, crying out his name again and again as my vision went white at the edges. Then he was gasping against my mouth, his own release spurting coolly between us as his body clenched around mine, drawing out every last drop.

His hands stroked soothingly down my back as aftershocks rippled through me, keeping me anchored when I felt like I might float away entirely.

"Don't move," I said.

Something in my voice must have concerned him, because he made a soft cooing sound, drawing me closer to him. Shuffling slightly, I slid out of him before collapsing on top, my softening cock still twitching against him.

"Thank you," I whispered thickly against his throat. "That was..."
Perfect.
Beautiful.
More than I ever hoped for.
"Flynn," he breathed, and my name held so much longing in that one syllable. His cool fingers traced patterns on my back. "You gave me something precious beyond words."

"I..." I started, struggling to keep my eyes open, to put into words everything bubbling up inside me. There was so much more to say, so much I needed him to know.

"Hush, my sweet angel," Seb murmured, still sending blissful strokes across my back. "Rest for a while, then I wish to wash you in the shower."

He pressed a kiss to my temple. "It's definitely my turn to be your big spoon."

With gentle hands, he shifted us onto our sides, pulling me back against his chest. His arm draped over my waist, cool and secure, like an anchor holding me safe in harbour. For the first time since leaving Ireland, since leaving everything I knew behind, I felt like I'd finally found home.

23

Sebastián

As Flynn slept, I traced my fingers over his chest. *Cold.* So damned cold. And I was sure being wrapped around me all night hadn't helped. The first rays of sunlight crept through the gap in the curtains, casting a soft glow across his face.

Flynn's peaceful expression shattered. His brow furrowed, lips twisting into a grimace of pain. A whimper escaped his throat as his head thrashed against the pillow.

My hand froze above his ribs, above the darkness I couldn't chase away. His legs tangled in the sheets as he fought whatever horror played behind his closed eyes.

"Flynn." I gripped his shoulder, giving him a gentle shake. "Wake up."

His eyes snapped open, wild and unfocused. His hand clutched at his chest, right over the spot where that damned mark festered.

"It was all…" Flynn's voice rasped. "Dark. Dark and cold."

I brushed his hair from his forehead. "The magic can cause strange dreams. But you're okay now." I pressed my lips to his temple, lingering there.

His breathing slowly steadied, though his fingers remained splayed across his heart. "Are you angry at me?"

I frowned at him.

"For last night? Untying you. It felt right in the moment, but I know you said…"

"No, I'm not angry." As if I could harbour any amount of annoyance after sharing something so special.

"And you stopped right away. I asked you to stop, and you did immediately. But—"

I silenced him with a kiss, recalling how I'd sucked the blood from his tongue after he'd cut himself on my fang. Those blood-drenched kisses... I could have happily lapped at the wound for hours, but Flynn had asked me to stop, and I had. I'd controlled myself. For him.

My dead heart stirred like winter ice breaking in spring, a cascade of emotion flooding through the cracks—relief, pride, gratitude. *Devotion*.

Our kiss deepened—his lips parting sweetly beneath mine—but I couldn't allow myself to indulge in him again, not now. If we started that, I may never leave his bed.

Pulling away, I traced my fingers along his jaw. "If anything, I'm in awe of your trust. Your bravery. You've trusted me with your life. Your body. And also your heart, by telling me everything that happened with Connor."

He'd given me so many pieces of himself now, so it was surely my turn. My fingers stilled in his hair as the weight of what I was about to share pressed down on my chest. Even here with him, the looming date cast its shadow. "Six days until the thirty-first of October."

Flynn shifted beside me, propping himself up on one elbow. "You don't like Halloween?"

A hollow laugh escaped my throat. "It's the date I have to read a certain collection of diaries." I settled back against the pillow and stared at the ceiling, counting the cracks in the plaster. "My oldest diaries. From my human years."

"You *have* to read them?"

"I force myself to read them every ten years. On the anniversary of her death." The words came out clipped, mechanical. "To make sure I never forget what I did to her."

Flynn fell very still. "*Her*?"

"My sister. Magdalena." The name summoned a hazy fragment of her—thick brown hair dancing in a warm breeze, dappled sunlight through leaves, a moment frozen in time before I destroyed everything.

Flynn's hand found mine under the covers, but I barely registered his touch. Every decade, October always felt like this—a noose gradually tightening around my neck, each day bringing me closer to those blood-stained pages.

"I spend the whole month dreading it." My voice was a whisper. "Like a ticking time bomb, counting down the days until I have to face myself again."

Flynn's face crumpled as he absorbed my words. The sheet slipped down his chest as he sat up abruptly, revealing the faint delicate frost patterns that now adorned his skin. They looked almost beautiful, like intricate mantilla lace. A stark contrast to their true meaning—death's fingers slowly claiming him.

He shifted, expression gentle yet determined. "Hey... Why do we have to wait until Halloween? If this is hurting you this much..." He reached for my hand. "Maybe we could face it together. Today."

"Flynn—" The protest died in my throat. How could I explain that these memories were like a poison so potent they had to be contained to a single day every ten years?

"I know it's your private ritual, and I'm not trying to dismiss that." He squeezed my fingers. "But watching you torture yourself with dread for the next six days..." He shook his head and started to pull on his clothes. "You don't have to do this alone anymore."

My teeth ground themselves together. The weight of his earnest gaze was almost unbearable. "You won't like what you find."

"I don't care. I want to know every piece of you, Seb. Even the bad parts. *Especially* the bad parts."

Self-disgust coated my tongue like ash. Memories threatened to surface—flames licking at wooden stakes, screams echoing through stone corridors. "The things I did... The person I was..." My voice roughened. "Once you know what I am—what I've done—you'll see me differently. You'll look at me and see a monster."

"I already know exactly what you are," Flynn insisted. "I've seen you kill. I've felt your fangs against my neck. I've watched you struggle against your own nature, to keep me safe. And I'm still here, wanting more of you, not less."

I shook my head, chest tightening with a familiar panic. These were methodical acts of cruelty, performed in the name of God. "This is different. This is…" The words stuck in my throat. How could I explain the magnitude of my sins? The weight of centuries of guilt?

"This is something you did five hundred years ago? Yeah, I think I'll get over it. Come on."

I stared at Flynn until the reality of his determination sank in. Bloody hell. He wasn't going to let this go. That stubborn streak of his was now fixed firmly on me. With a groan that could have woken the dead—and I would know—I dragged myself from the warmth of the bed.

My clothes from last night lay scattered across the floor. As I retrieved each item, I felt Flynn's gaze burning into my back. When I glanced up, he quickly averted his eyes, a delicious blush creeping across his cheeks.

"Do you want to take a photograph?" I couldn't resist teasing.

"Just making sure you're actually getting dressed and not trying to distract me."

"Distract you? Me?" I buttoned up my shirt with deliberate slowness. "I would never."

"You absolutely would." Flynn grabbed my hand, tugging me toward the door. "Come on. Your office. Now."

I dug my heels in, though not enough to actually stop him. "I have work to do, you know. Important vampire business. Very pressing matters."

"More pressing than this?"

"There's a list of sightings I need—"

"They'll wait."

"And Kit needs me to—"

"He'll survive."

I let him pull me down the corridor toward my office, grumbling under my breath about pushy humans who didn't understand the complex responsibilities of leading a supernatural crime task force.

We reached my office door, and I made one last attempt. "You know, I could make you breakfast instead... I'm sure a bowl of cereal is within my skill set."

"Nice try." Flynn pushed open the door. "In."

I went straight to leaning against my desk, eyeing Flynn's determined stance. "My, my. Your vampire hunter persona from last night has really gotten to your head, hasn't it? Should I be worried about coat hangers appearing from hidden pockets?"

"Shut up." Flynn's lips twitched. "If I remember correctly, you rather enjoyed being at my mercy."

I lunged forward, catching his waist, lifting him effortlessly and spinning us both around. His surprised gasp turned into a laugh as I deposited him on the edge of my desk, stepping between his knees. Papers scattered, a pen clattered to the floor.

My fingers tangled in his hair, tilting his head back to expose the line of his throat. The marks from the other night had already faded—a fact that both pleased and disappointed me.

"I think my fearsome vampire hunter needs a punishment. Or three." I let my voice drip with promise.

Flynn laughed and planted his palm firmly against my chest, pushing me back. "Stop it. No deflecting."

His eyes sparkled with his stubborn defiance, and my heart attempted to stutter.

"You're infuriating."

Flynn gently weaved out of my grip, heading to my bookcases, which were stuffed beyond logic. "Where do we need to start?"

Tension coiled within me as my gaze shot straight to the chest tucked away in the corner. Ancient wood, reinforced with iron bands that had rusted over centuries. The lock—newer than the rest—gleamed dully.

"In there?"

I nodded, unable to speak. The chest seemed to pulse with malignant energy, though that was only my imagination.

Flynn's hand found mine, squeezing gently. The playful atmosphere firmly evaporated.

We crossed the room together, retrieving the key from my desk drawer. I knelt before the chest, and Flynn settled beside me, his shoulder pressed warm against mine.

"It's rare that a vampire as old as I am would have perfect recollection of their entire life, but my memory has always been rather awful. I think it's because of what happened within these diaries. I wanted so badly to escape from it all. To forget."

The key slid into the lock with a click that echoed through my bones. "I translated every single one of my documents about a century ago. Laid tracing paper over each page. The original Spanish underneath, English on top." The lid creaked as I lifted it. "I was afraid I might... forget. That the Spanish might slip away like so many other memories have."

"But you can still speak it?"

"*Sí.*" I managed a weak smile. "Though... it's as if the vocabulary remains, but the soul of it has faded. If that makes sense..."

"It does."

"Regardless, my accent's probably atrocious by modern standards."

Inside the chest, leather-bound volumes lay stacked in neat rows, their spines cracked and faded with age. I forced my hands not to tremble as I lifted them out, arranging them chronologically across the floor. Each one represented a piece of my human life—fragments of memories I could no longer fully trust.

The sight of them, laid out like corpses at a wake, made my throat constrict. These weren't just books. They were evidence. Testimony. A record of my sins written in my own hand.

"These..." I had to clear my throat and start again. "These detail everything leading up to Magdalena's death. And... *him.*"

Flynn shifted closer. "Him?"

"*Rodrigo de Valencia.*" The name tasted like poison. "Though I knew him as Padre Rodrigo back then. Father Rodrigo. He was the one who..." I couldn't finish. It had been so long since I'd spoken his name aloud.

"The one who what?"

I forced the words out. "The vampire who turned me."

Flynn's sharp intake of breath cut through the silence. His hand found mine, squeezing tight.

"He was a priest?"

I stared at the diaries. "He took everything from me. My life. My soul." Something ancient and dark twisted in my chest, rearing a hideous head. "My sister."

24

Flynn

March 15th, 1520

Today, after High Mass at Santa María la Mayor, I was approached by Padre Rodrigo de Valencia himself. My hands still tremble at the honour. He spoke of having observed me these past months—my dedication to prayer, my earnest study of the Holy Scripture.

"God has shown me your destiny," he said, with certainty. "You, Sebastián Salazar, are meant for His greater purpose."

That a man of such standing—personal confessor to the Duke of Medina—should take notice of me! Though Father says our family's position demands such attention, I cannot help but feel blessed. Padre Rodrigo has offered to guide my theological studies personally, speaking of how Spain needs strong, educated men of faith in these troubled times.

If only Magdalena shared such divine inspiration. Again, she refused Mass, claiming illness. Mother believes her, but I heard her in the gardens, singing those peculiar songs. I pray she will soon see sense—her soul depends upon it.

Padre Rodrigo says I have the makings of an Inquisitor. The very thought makes my heart soar. To serve God and Crown, to protect Spain from the poison of heresy... What greater calling could there be?

He wishes to meet again tomorrow, to discuss my future path. I must prepare myself to be worthy of such attention.

- *Sebastián Salazar*

December 24th, 1520

The eve of Our Lord's birth, and my heart is full of His purpose. These past months under Padre Rodrigo's tutelage have opened my eyes to depths of theological understanding I never dreamed possible. Today we discussed Aquinas's treatise on divine law—Padre Rodrigo says my grasp of Latin surpasses many seminary students twice my age.

Mother is pleased with my studies, though she frets I spend too many hours in Padre Rodrigo's library. But how can I refuse when he shares such rare manuscripts? Yesterday, he showed me documents from the Holy Office itself—actual transcripts of interrogations! He says such knowledge will serve me well when I take my place among the defenders of the faith.

But my joy is tempered by growing concern. Magdalena was caught with a strange book today—symbols and foreign script. When Father threatened to burn it, she became hysterical.

Padre Rodrigo, who was taking Christmas confession with us, suggested I keep the book to study its heretical nature with him. It contained a crude drawing that still disturbs me. A woman with serpentine features, surrounded by beasts that looked like wolves or hyenas, rising from water. "The oldest evil," Rodrigo whispered, crossing himself. "She who refused to submit to Adam."

He grows increasingly troubled by my sister's behaviour. "Your own household," he warned me, "is where vigilance must begin."

I shall pray extra hard tonight for Magdalena's soul. Padre Rodrigo says God has chosen me to guide her back to His light.

- Sebastián Salazar

I flicked through the pages of 1521 and 1522, scanning entries that charted Seb's descent into religious fanaticism. The handwriting became neater, more controlled—like watching someone grow up through their penmanship. Most entries mentioned Padre Rodrigo: dinners at his private quarters, late-night theological debates, gifts of rare books. Christ, the manipulation was obvious, but younger Seb had written about him like he hung the moon. Between the lines of formal language and religious devotion, I could see Rodrigo slowly isolating him, turning him against his sister while positioning himself as Seb's only true guide. It made my stomach turn. I skipped to summer 1523, where the handwriting underneath the English translation looked oddly messy.

June 18th, 1523

I witnessed my first trial two days ago. Even now, my hand shakes as I commit these words to paper.

Padre Rodrigo arranged everything. A special dispensation from the Holy Office allowed me to observe from the gallery as they brought forth the accused—a woman barely older than Magdalena, charged with Jewish practices. The evidence was irrefutable; witnesses testified to seeing her light candles on Friday evenings, and salt was discovered beneath her floorboards.

I confess, when they applied the instruments, I nearly fled. But Padre Rodrigo's hand on my shoulder anchored me. "Watch," he whispered, his breath warm against my ear. "This is God's mercy in action. Through pain, we save their immortal souls."

The woman confessed within the hour.

Afterwards, Padre Rodrigo insisted I join him in his study to discuss what we had witnessed. Though the hour grew late, he would not let me leave until I had understood every detail of the proceedings. His knowledge of interrogation techniques is remarkable—he speaks of them with such passion, such intensity. When I mentioned the lateness of the hour, he grew agitated. "Your soul's education cannot be bound by mundane concerns of time," he said, his eyes so bright in the candlelight.

Padre Rodrigo presented me with a silver crucifix today, claiming it was blessed by the Archbishop himself. "A symbol of your dedication," he said, pressing it into my hands. I shall treasure it always.

But I write now of graver concerns. Upon returning home that eve, I found Magdalena's room empty. The servants discovered her in the olive grove, dancing. There were markings in the dirt, symbols that made

Padre Rodrigo cross himself when I described them to him today. He insists I bring him anything else I discover about her activities.

My sister's soul weighs heavy on my conscience. I know the price of heresy, and I cannot bear to think of her facing such consequences. I must save her, whatever the cost.

- *Sebastián Salazar*

April 3rd, 1524

Another three condemned today. The weight of such judgements should grow lighter with practice—how many has it been now? Twenty? Thirty? I've lost count.

Sometimes, in the dark hours before dawn, their faces haunt me. The merchant's wife who wept for her children. The old man who quoted Scripture even as they led him away. But Padre Rodrigo reminds me of our holy purpose. "Through us," he whispers. "God cleanses Spain."

My position on the Tribunal grows more secure with each passing month. Father speaks of family pride, but if he knew the true honour... To serve God and Crown in such a manner! My signature carries the weight of divine justice now. The other Inquisitors seek my counsel, praise my dedication to rooting out heresy. Padre Rodrigo says I've exceeded even his expectations.

Yet my joy is tainted. Magdalena's behaviour worsens with each passing moon. Yesterday, I discovered dried herbs beneath her pillow, tied with red thread—a clear sign of folk magic. When confronted, she spoke of "older ways" and "natural healing." I confiscated the items immediately.

Today, Magdalena asked to see my crucifix. Something in her eyes troubled me—a hunger I did not recognise. When I refused, she grew angry. "You trust his gifts more than your own blood?"

Padre Rodrigo visits our house almost daily now, taking an unsettling interest in these discoveries. "Your sister's soul weighs in the balance," he reminded me over dinner last evening, his fourth visit this week. He stayed until well past midnight, pressing me for every detail of Magdalena's movements. When I suggested some matters might remain private within the family, his demeanour turned cold. "There can be no privacy," he said, "in matters of faith."

This morning, a messenger arrived with a note demanding my presence in his private quarters. When I explained I had duties at the Tribunal, another message came within the hour. And another. Each more insistent than the last.

I find myself thinking of the accused woman from last summer's trial. Her eyes, when they brought in the instruments...

God forgive me these doubts. Padre Rodrigo has only ever guided me towards His light. Without his mentorship, where would I be? I owe him everything.

But Magdalena... Sweet Christ, guide me.

- Sebastián Salazar

I lowered the diary, my throat tight. Beside me on the wooden floor, Seb sat rigidly, his dark eyes fixed on nothing. Reading these words had painted something horribly raw across his face.

I reached for his hand. His skin was cool against mine, but his fingers curled into my grip.

"We can stop," I whispered.

He shook his head. "No. I need..." His accent thickened with emotion. "I need to remember. Remember it all. *Properly.*"

Something told me he remembered everything these diaries recounted crystal-clear already.

I leaned over and pressed my lips to his temple, lingering there. His curls brushed against my cheek, and I caught the faintest tremor running through him.

"Right, then," I said, keeping hold of his hand as I picked up the diary again. "Let's remember together."

October 22nd, 1525

My hands shake as I write. Tonight has destroyed everything.

I followed Magdalena. God help me, I followed my own sister into the woods beyond the city walls. Padre Rodrigo's whispers proved true—she was not alone. A gathering of women, dancing beneath the winter moon, speaking in tongues that made my blood run cold. Magdalena led their chants, her hair wild, her feet bare despite the frost.

Their voices carried fragments I recognised from my studies of Hebrew—"mother of night, first woman, she who rules the waters." But worse was their altar: a clay bowl filled with water, and within it, a horrifying figure shaped from wax—a woman with a crown of serpents, surrounded by prowling beasts. The same unholy image from that book she had years ago.

And there, gleaming in the moonlight upon their unholy altar, my silver crucifix—stolen from my chambers. She held it high as she danced, defiling its blessed purpose.

I fled before they saw me, but when I returned home, Padre Rodrigo was waiting in my chamber. How did he know? He pressed me for every detail, his eyes alight, his hands gripping my shoulders until they bruised. "You owe me the truth. You owe me everything," he hissed. When I confessed about the crucifix, his rage was terrifying. "She must be stopped."

He's right that I owe him. Without his guidance, his teachings, his faith in me, I would be nothing. And yet...

He speaks of using my position in the Tribunal. He says I must be the one to bring the charges. "God has placed you here," he insisted, "for this holy purpose." When I begged for time to speak with her, to save her, he struck me across the face. I can still feel the sting of his hand, even now.

He's sent three messages since returning to his chapel. A brother of the order waits below my window even now, watching. Another stands at our gate.

Mother weeps behind locked doors. Father has not emerged from his study. And Magdalena sleeps, unaware that by dawn, everything will change.

Padre Rodrigo is right. He's right. He must be right.

Sweet Christ, let him be right.

- Sebastián Salazar

31st October, 1525

It is done. My sister is dead.

A week ago, Padre Rodrigo brought the warrant himself after Vespers. "Your signature," he said, "will save her soul." When I hesitated, he reminded me of all we had discussed—how a quick trial now would spare her the torture chamber, how my influence could ensure a merciful end.

"Sign," he whispered, standing so close I could smell the incense on his robes. "Sign, my Sebastián, and prove your devotion—to God, to Spain, to *me*."

The ink was still wet when they took her.

Magdalena did not cry out when the guards came. She looked at me only once, but I will carry that look until my dying day. My crucifix—the one she had stolen for her ritual—hung from the guard's belt. When Padre Rodrigo saw it, his eyes gleamed strangely in the torchlight. "She must hold it," he announced. "Let her clutch it as the flames rise. Perhaps its blessed silver will grant her final salvation."

I did not watch her burn today. Neither did Mother, or Father. Cowards, all three of us.

Though even now, I smell the smoke. The crucifix lies before me, stained dark with her blood. Padre Rodrigo placed it in my hands himself, a phantom warmth from the pyre. "Keep it always," he whispered, his fingers lingering over mine. "A reminder of your dedication to our holy purpose."

Padre Rodrigo stays with me now, has not left my side since it was done. He speaks of pride, of divine purpose, of my great destiny. His hands never leave me—my shoulder, my arm, my face. He says we will be bound together, forever. That none will understand me as he does.

I feel ill. The room spins. He brings me wine, insists I drink.

God forgive—

The entry ended abruptly there, the pen having scored a line across the page.

I flicked to the next page to find it empty, and the next, for the rest of this volume. "What happened after?" I asked, though the violent slash of ink across the page told its own story.

Seb's hand was still in mine. When I looked up, his face had that distant quality it got sometimes, like he was staring through time itself.

"That was my last entry as a living human," he said quietly. "The memories after... They're like trying to catch smoke. Impressions. Feelings. Terror, mainly."

I waited, barely breathing.

"I believe Rodrigo said God had shown him the way for us to be together forever. That he would make me eternal, make me his. I remember his hands on my face, so cold. I didn't understand why they were so cold." He swallowed hard. "Then, he bit me." His free hand drifted to the junction of his neck and shoulder.

I couldn't help but picture it: a younger Seb, drunk on doctored wine, confused and afraid, with that monster's teeth at his throat.

"I remember fighting when he tried to make me drink his blood," Seb continued, voice hollow. "I think I might have vomited. He grew angry. Held my jaw, forced more down my throat. Said I was being ungrateful. That this was God's will."

"Fucking hell, Seb." I pulled him closer, pressing my forehead to his temple. Every muscle in his body seemed to tremble.

"I don't remember dying," he whispered. "Just the terror. The confusion. Wanting my mother."

I held him tighter, wishing I could reach back through time and save that scared man who'd written these entries. Who'd trusted the wrong person. Who'd lost everything.

He turned his face into my neck and stayed there, silent, letting me hold him together. "I hate him," I said. "He's the worst sort of evil." After a pause, I asked, "Do you remember those early days? As a vampire?"

"Not much. An eternal hunger. Rodrigo stroking my hair, calling me his perfect creation—"

I must have made a sound of disgust because Seb stopped. His cool thumb brushed my cheek, catching a tear I hadn't realised I'd shed.

"Don't cry for me, Flynn. I escaped him, eventually. Had to sacrifice ever seeing my family again, but..." He shrugged. "I lived in shadows for years, but I found others. Good people who taught me how to survive. How to feed without taking too much. How to find willing donors."

He gestured to the bookcase. "These all document much happier times. My European travels through the Renaissance. Dancing in the courts of France. Learning to paint in Florence. Great love affairs—"

"Love affairs?" I pulled back, hating how my voice pitched up.

A smile tugged at his mouth. "Don't be jealous."

"I'm not!" But my face heated, and his knowing look didn't help.

His smile grew wider. "You know," he said, lifting our still-joined hands to press a theatrical kiss to my knuckles. "All those centuries of experience just led me here. To this moment. To you. My favourite vampire hunter."

"Oh my god." I tried to pull my hand away, laughing despite myself. "That was terrible. You're terrible."

"Was it?" He kept hold of my hand, eyes sparkling now. "I thought it was rather romantic. I could try again. Perhaps compare thee to a summer's day? I did meet Shakespeare, you know. Or at least, someone pretending to be. It isn't entirely clear..."

"You're such a prat." But I was grinning, my chest warm, not even a hint of chill in that moment.

I stacked the diaries carefully. "Thank you," I said. "For sharing this with me. And Seb... you shouldn't feel guilty about your sister."

Seb's face twisted. "I absolutely should. What kind of man condemns his own sister to death?" His voice cracked. "A monster, that's who."

"But you were groomed!" The words burst from me. "Christ, Seb, I just read it. He isolated you, manipulated you, used your faith against you—"

"I was weak!" Seb slammed his fist against the floor, making me jump. "I should never have listened to him! Should have seen through his lies, should have protected her..." His accent thickened with each word until he was practically spitting them out.

I crawled closer, wrapping my arms around him from behind. He tried to pull away, but I held on. "You were young," I whispered against his neck. "Sheltered. Impressionable. You trusted someone who was supposed to guide you. To protect you. He was the monster, Seb. Not you."

His whole body shuddered. "You don't understand. I signed the warrant. My hand. My signature. I killed her as surely as if I'd—"

"No." I tightened my grip. "He killed her. He murdered you both that night. You were just as much his victim as Magdalena."

Seb's hands came up to grip my arms, his fingers digging in almost painfully. But I didn't let go. I pressed my face between his shoulder blades and held on while he shook.

"I still see her face," he whispered. "It's like the diary entry says. I'll forever remember it. When they took her. She just... looked at me. Didn't even cry out. Just looked at me like..."

I stroked my thumb across his chest, right over his heart. "Like she knew it wasn't really you doing it. Like she knew her brother was trapped too."

A sound escaped him then—something between a sob and a growl. He turned in my arms, burying his face in my neck, and I held him while five centuries of guilt poured out of him.

We stayed like that for a long time, until the tension slowly leaked from his shoulders. When he finally pulled back, his eyes were rimmed with red, but there was something lighter about him. Perhaps I'd helped, in some small way.

Picking up the diaries, I leaned over to place them back in the chest. Something inside it caught my eye—a glint of silver that compelled me to touch it.

"Is this... the crucifix?" I reached down, fingers closing around the metal.

White-hot agony exploded across my right palm. I screamed, the silver cross clattering to the floor as I yanked my hand back. Seb was there instantly, twisting my hand to examine it. Angry blisters were already forming, the skin an ugly red.

"What the fuck?" I hissed through clenched teeth. The pain radiated from my palm in waves of searing heat, like I'd grabbed a hot coal from the fire. Each throb sent fresh sparks of agony shooting up my arm.

Seb unleashed a low stream of curses in what sounded like three different languages. "Does it hurt terribly?"

"*Yes*! It feels like it's still burning!" I cradled my hand against my chest, but even the light brush of my shirt against the blisters made me wince. The skin had gone a horrible scarlet, puckering around the cross-shaped burn mark. The pain wasn't fading—if anything, it was intensifying, spreading deeper into the flesh like acid eating through layers.

Seb grabbed his phone, jabbing at the screen. "Peacock? Are you in the building yet?" A pause. "My office. Now. Flynn's hurt. *Run*."

To Priya's credit, she followed Seb's instruction very literally—I heard the thundering of footsteps before she burst through the door, hair escaping her usually neat braid, Rory hot on her heels. Freddy sat perched on his shoulder like a parrot.

"What happened?" Priya's eyes darted between us, seeming to zero in on my neck. "Sebastián?"

"It wasn't that," I managed through gritted teeth. The burn pulsed with each heartbeat. "The crucifix—"

"He touched this." Seb gestured to the silver cross on the floor.

"Don't!" I shouted as Rory bent to pick it up, expecting his skin to sizzle like mine had. But nothing happened. He turned it over in his hands, frowning.

"Why'd it burn you and not me?"

"Don't move," Priya muttered, already rushing back out.

She returned moments later, dumping an armful of supplies onto the floor—bandages, bottles, dried herbs.

"This will hurt," she warned, examining my blistered palm with gentle fingers. "But it'll help with the burning sensation."

"Here, mate." Rory dug in his pocket and offered me a small white pill. "This might take the edge off."

"What is it?"

Rory shrugged. "Could be a painkiller. Could be my ADHD meds. Could be—"

"I think I'll pass."

He went back to examining the crucifix. "This isn't Flynn's blood, is it?"

Staring at the cross—though the pain made it hard to think—I noticed a small splattering of dark crimson.

"No," Seb replied. "It's a relic from my human years." His face darkened. "The blood... It's my sister's. Magdalena's. Padre Rodrigo—my sire—he gave me the crucifix first as a gift. Then Magdalena stole it for some ritual in the woods. When they caught her..." He trailed off, staring at the cross in Rory's hands as if seeing it anew. "They made her clutch it as she burned. Rodrigo returned it to me afterwards."

"Hold up," Rory said, turning the crucifix over in his hands. "If she was holding this when they... Shouldn't it have melted? Or at least got a bit mangled? It looks mint apart from the blood."

Seb went very still. "I'm... not sure."

Priya continued her ministrations, spreading a cooling paste across my palm that provided blessed relief for about three seconds before stinging like hell. I tried to hold in my grunts of pain, but a few escaped. Seb's hand remained steady on my shoulder, thumb rubbing circles through my shirt.

"Almost done," Priya murmured, wrapping gauze around my hand.

"So silver doesn't burn vampires?" I asked Seb, though why he'd keep that damned crucifix if it did was beyond me.

"No," he said quietly. "Though it's very harmful to shifted wolves, various other entities. Including demons."

Priya's head snapped to Seb's. "Ah."

"Ah."

Looking between them, I waited for them to explain.

"It's possibly... *probably*... something to do with your demon mark." Priya's brow furrowed as she examined my bandaged hand. "But this level of burn? Considering you're not actually a demon?"

My throat tightened. *Fucking hell.* First Seb tells me my blood is demon-ing, and next I'm getting burned by a silver ornament? When was this nightmare going to end? It took all my patience each day not to question Seb, not to ask him if he was finally close to saving me.

With a large sigh, Seb took back the crucifix, holding it up to catch the light. "Something has compelled me to keep this, all these years," he said quietly.

"It's... lovely," Rory said, his mouth twitching. "Really brings out the whole 'centuries of guilt and trauma' vibe you've got going on."

"Rory!" Priya smacked his arm.

He dodged away, grinning. "What? I'm just saying—"

The door burst open, making us all jump. Kit strode in, his face grim. "We've got something. A lead on the Brixton vampire clan."

Seb was on his feet instantly. "What is it?"

"Source spotted their leader, Marcus Vale, meeting with your friend Damien last night at that underground club near the market. Reliable intel—came through an old military contact."

My stomach lurched at Damien's name. The memory of his cold hands, that smile...

Seb's entire demeanor shifted, a dangerous energy crackling around him. "Finally, something solid to work with. Let's go."

25

Flynn

I slumped further into the spare office chair Felix had dragged out for me. The hum of multiple computer fans created a white noise that made my eyelids heavy. If my right hand wasn't still in agony from the burning incident, I could have fallen asleep.

Felix's workspace was impossibly tidy—every cable zip-tied and labelled, monitors positioned at perfect right angles. The rest of the basement might be chaos, but Felix's domain was a temple to organisation.

The door banged open, making me jump. Felix stormed in, clutching a metal lunchbox decorated with stickers.

"He's done it *again*."

"What?"

"Rory's eaten half my kimbap, the absolute prick. I spent hours making them last night. They were all... They were perfect."

He thrust the box at me. Inside lay neat rolls of rice and vegetables wrapped in seaweed, arranged in precise rows, though several spaces were conspicuously empty.

"Here, you might as well have some. Then I'm building a wall of oat milk cartons in the fridge to hide it."

I picked up a piece with my good hand. "Sounds like a productive afternoon."

Felix dropped into his chair with a huff, pausing to adjust his keyboard, even though it seemed perfectly aligned to me. His fingers hovered over the keys, tapped once, then pulled back. He shook his head slightly and started again, this time seeming satisfied with whatever internal criteria had been met.

"Do you ever get jealous?" I asked, spinning the chair slightly. "Having to stay here while they go out and have fun?"

Felix's fingers paused over the keyboard. He turned to me, eyebrows shooting up behind his messy fringe.

"Have... *fun*? You mean get stabbed, shot at, and covered in various bodily fluids while fighting the forces of evil?"

"Well, when you put it that way..."

"Trust me." He pushed his giant headphones back from one ear. "I've seen the state they come back in. Once, Rory returned with half his intestines hanging out. And before that, Kit had to get thirty-seven stitches. And Seb..." He shuddered. "The things I've had to watch him heal from? No thanks. I'll stay here with my nice clean keyboards and zero percent chance of dismemberment."

"So you don't feel left out?"

"Left out of what? Getting thrown through windows? Having bits of you catch fire?" He gestured at his screens. "I see everything anyway. Multiple angles, usually in HD. Sometimes I even add dramatic background music."

I snorted so hard I choked on my own spit.

Felix continued tapping away, and I stood up to stretch. Something snagged my attention—a wad of paper fresh from Felix's printer that looked like... *someone's social media feed?*

My uninjured hand snatched it up. The top photo was a distinguished-looking man in his late fifties, grey peppered through his dark hair. He was crouched in a park, attempting to wrestle a miniature dachshund into a tweed jacket while wearing an expression of utmost academic seriousness. The caption read: *Can tweed protect against squirrel attacks? Early results inconclusive. Poor Aristotle remains traumatised.*

"Felix, what on earth is—"

There was a name above the photo: James Stott.

"Hmm?" Felix spun around. "Oh. That. Put that back, please. I need to give it to Seb later. He makes me print stuff because he just can't with email attachments." He rolled his eyes, turning back to his screen.

"But… what is it?" I whispered.

Felix threw me a glance. "It's quite sad, actually. It's his ex-boyfriend from like, decades ago. Seb likes to know how he's doing. I offered to make him his own profile, but he didn't want one. James Stott is an Oxford professor, so I made a fake account looking like someone in academia, and he accepted me straight away."

"An… Oxford professor? You're joking!"

"Nope."

"So *this* is his type?" I waved the paper at Felix like it had personally offended me, which only served to deepen the poor guy's confusion. I was surprised Rory or Priya hadn't told him about our… whatever it was.

I stared at the photo, my stomach churning more violently than a stormy sea. *Of course* Seb's ex was an Oxford professor. Of course he had a cute dog, was distinguished and successful and funny, and probably knew which wine to order at fancy restaurants. And here I was, a failed boating tour guide who'd run away from a tourist village with nothing but a backpack and mounting guilt. The gap between who I was and who James was yawned wider than the Atlantic. What could Seb possibly see in someone like me when *this* was his type?

"Umm… I guess so?"

"When did Seb ask you for this?"

Felix stared at me. Some level of understanding was starting to dawn on his expression.

"Felix! When?"

"Umm… it's sort of a rolling monthly thing…" Felix bit into his lip, as if he knew he should stop talking.

His eyes kept darting to the paper in my hand, his fingers twitching against his keyboard. When I finally set it back in the printer tray, he leaned over and carefully adjusted its position, aligning it precisely with the edges.

"But really, *monthly*?! Well he's not over him, then, is he?" I wanted to snatch the paper back and crumple it with my fist. I desperately tried to ignore how my heart was pounding. *Twenty years.* Twenty years, and Seb still needed monthly updates.

With a groan, Felix jumped up from his chair, his headphones clattering to the desk. "No, no. I didn't mean to—" He tore his hands through his hair. "Look, I don't even know if Seb actually even looks at the printouts I give him."

I crossed my arms. "Right."

"And anyway, James is... Well, he's boring. Really boring. All his posts are about his kids passing their driving tests, medieval literature, or his dog's anxiety issues." Felix moved closer, lowering his voice. "He's married to some historian. They collect antique maps together." He made a face. "Trust me, it's as thrilling as it sounds."

"But Seb still wants to know about him."

"It's... complicated, though, don't you think? When you live as long as Seb has, I think you need to know the people you cared about are okay. That they're happy. Even if you're not part of their lives anymore."

Felix earned a glare for his logical wisdom. The idea of watching someone you loved grow old without you, knowing you'd stay frozen in time while they moved forward—it must be torture.

Felix leaned back against his desk, fiddling with a USB stick. "You know, Seb *has* been acting strange of late." His tone held a teasing lilt.

"Oh yeah?"

"He keeps smiling way more. It's weird." He shuddered dramatically. "The other day, I caught him humming. *Humming.* I've been here over a year, and I've never heard him make any noise that wasn't a sigh or a threat."

A warmth spread through me, pushing back some of the cold doubt. "Thanks, Felix."

My phone vibrated. Katie's name lit up the screen, and I sighed, already exhausted.

"Hello?"

"So, don't be mad, but I'm outside your bakery. The one where you work."

"*What*?!" Through the phone, I heard the unmistakable rush of London traffic. She wasn't lying. "Why would you—"

"After that cryptic phone call? Of course I had to come. I told Connor to book us on the first flight."

My stomach plummeted. "*Connor's* here?"

"The girl at Rising Dough said you were off work sick?"

"Emma?"

"Yeah. Though she doesn't believe you. She thinks there's something going on with you and this dangerous stalker? Apparently, the other day, she left you alone with him in the bakery and then ten minutes later the building got broken into?"

"That happened after we left," I said, squeezing my eyes tightly together as if I could magic Katie back to Ireland.

"She said she thinks he could be in a gang." Her voice sharpened. "That he won't leave you alone. That he could be threatening you?"

"Urgg!" *Goddamn Emma and her caring personality!*

Next to me, Felix seemed to be vibrating with suppressed laughter and I kicked his leg. Hard.

"Message me your address," Katie demanded.

I pressed my hand against my forehead. "I'm... not at my London flat. I'm at... a hotel."

"A hotel?" Her voice dropped to a hiss. "Have you gone into hiding?"

"No! It's sort of... *his* hotel. But he's not a dangerous stalker, Katie. Honest."

"So there *is* someone!" She sighed, that familiar big-sister sigh that made me feel about twelve years old. "Look, Flynn, I know the attention of this man probably feels exciting—"

"Stop talking. Now."

"Flynn, you've got two choices. Text me your address, or I'm calling the police. I mean it. You're scaring me."

I glanced at Felix. *Could I give her the name of the hotel? Not without talking to Seb...*

"I'll come meet you. Just let me sort some stuff out. It might take a few hours."

She made a noise of exasperation. "I'll give you thirty minutes to give me a time and place."

I ended the call with Katie. The phone nearly slipped from my grip as I found Seb's contact, heart pounding.

Katie was here, in London. With *Connor*.

Seb answered almost instantly. "Flynn? What's wrong?"

The concern in his voice made my chest tighten. "I'm so sorry, but Katie has flown to London. She's going to call the police unless I come see her."

"That's... not ideal." There was a long pause, followed by a sigh. "Okay."

"Can I go?"

"Not alone, obviously."

I glanced at Felix, watching me with wide eyes. "With... Felix?" The memory of being dragged into that van by deadwalkers flashed through my mind. Maybe Felix was about to get the adventure he never wanted.

"With *me*. I'll be back in an hour. Tell her to meet you at Fat Cat's at 3:00 p.m."

"One more thing..." I bit down on my lip, hard enough to hurt. "Connor's with her. You know... her husband..."

A string of curses crackled through the phone. "I'll be there as soon as possible." He hung up.

With one hand, I typed:

> **Fat Cat's Coffee, Killigrew Street. 3pm. Alone, please. x**

"You okay? You don't look okay." Felix's concerned voice pulled me from my spiraling thoughts.

"Not really. I'll see you later. Unless Katie manages to knock Seb out and drag me back to Ireland, in which case, it was nice knowing you."

I trudged into the main basement, collapsing onto one of the worn sofas. Waves of nausea assaulted me. Seb being there was probably going to make everything worse. What the hell was I supposed to say to Katie about him?

Oh, hi, Katie! I know I only left home a few weeks ago, but guess what? I've managed to get myself marked by a demon and—wait for it—I'm sort of falling for this centuries-old vampire who fights against London's supernatural evil from an abandoned Victorian hotel. He's got witches and werewolves on speed dial, but don't worry, he's really quite charming when he's not being all broody and mysterious. So... how's your flower shop?

Yeah, that was going to go down really well.

Breathe. I pressed my palms against my thighs. *Katie loves you. She'll listen this time. And Seb... Seb won't let anything happen to you.*

The bookcase creaked open less than an hour later. Seb stumbled through. His curls were wilder than normal, tie askew.

"I'm s—"

"Stop. Stop apologising."

"But—"

Seb crossed the room in three strides and pulled me against his chest. The dark spices of his cologne wrapped around me like an anchor. "Let's go."

He started towards the basement stairs. Clearly he'd decided it was fine for us to leave the hotel through the entrance. We passed Dolly, hard at work at her desk, and I gave her a sad wave.

"So," I said. "One warning. Katie thinks you're a member of a dangerous gang, a stalker, completely obsessed with me, and you've locked me up in your hotel."

He shot me a *look*. "So... pretty much entirely correct then?"

I couldn't keep the smile from my face. "And in other news, I texted Katie saying to come alone, so I won't have to deal with Connor face to face."

"Hmm." His face twisted into something unreadable.

"How about you linger at another table?" I suggested. "And I'll introduce you at the end, if it goes well."

"If that's what you want."

Not really. Ideally, he'd sit right next to me, glaring at Katie until she believed me. *Hold on...*

"Rory told me the other day you had mind altering powers?"

Seb frowned at me. "You trust everything he says?"

"So... you can't just make Katie believe me?"

"Compulsion is..." He ran a hand through his curls. "It's not my strength. Some vampires can bend humans to their will as easily as breathing. I've never been particularly gifted at it." His voice held a note of bitterness. "And even if I could, the effects wear off. Your sister would be even more confused and suspicious when she suddenly snapped out of it."

"But you *can* do it?"

"Flynn." The warning in his tone was clear. "You don't actually want to do that to your sister."

I crossed my arms. "Fine."

He was right, of course. The thought of messing with Katie's mind made my stomach turn. But the idea of explaining everything to her? That was equally terrifying.

Outside Fat Cat's, my heart stuttered unpleasantly.

"I can't do this." The words tumbled out before I could stop them. "She'll never talk to me again."

Seb caught my uninjured hand, and squeezed it gently. I stared at our joined hands, fighting back the urge to run. "You've got this. It's almost all over. Remember how you made me be brave, earlier? Well, now it's my turn. And if things do go badly, I'll be right there." He lifted our hands and pressed his lips against my knuckles. "I promise."

The gesture melted every part of me. All the tension drained away, replaced by a warmth that spread through my whole body. It wasn't just the kiss—it was the tenderness behind it, the way his eyes held mine, full of conviction and care.

The barista's face lit up as we entered Fat Cat's. "How's the hotel coming along now?" she asked, and I glanced sideways at Sebastián, curious how he'd answer. I'd laughed when Rory explained they pretended to be painters and decorators slowly renovating the building.

"Still battling with those original fireplaces," Seb replied, which was rich considering the ancient hearths were currently home to so much soot even Freddy stayed away from them.

Seb gave me one last nod, somehow managing to convey both "you've got this" and "I'm right here" without saying a word.

After pouring myself a glass of water from a jug, I slid into a booth near the window, pressing trembling hands against my knees. Two minutes to go. Seb sat three tables away, perfectly still except for his fingers drumming against the surface.

Then I saw him.

Connor pushed through the door first, holding it open for Katie. The sight of him—broad shoulders filling out his coat, that familiar easy smile—sent ice through my veins. Memories of that night on the beach crashed over me: his hands on my shoulders, the salt air, the taste of tears.

"Seb—" Before I could finish, his chair scraped across the floor. By the time I'd locked eyes with Katie, he'd slid into the booth beside me, a solid wall of protection.

"Flynn!" Katie waved, her oversized green coat making her look smaller. Her dirty-blonde hair had grown longer, falling past her shoulders now.

I awkwardly half-climbed over Seb to reach her, letting her pull me into a crushing embrace. She smelled like home—sea air and her lavender soap.

"What have you done to your hand?"

Though she couldn't see, I rolled my eyes. "Cooking accident."

She squeezed me tighter. Connor lingered behind her, with a false smile plastered on his face. I violently avoided eye contact.

"I said to come alone," I whispered into Katie's ear.

She pulled back, keeping her hands on my shoulders. "He just wanted to check you're okay, then he'll go. He's been worried about you."

I'll bet he has, I thought bitterly. *So worried.*

She dropped her grip, shifting away, and Connor moved forward. "Alright there, Flynn? Ye had us worried sick, so ye did."

Connor's arm reached towards me, but I never found out if he meant to hug me or grab my arm. In less than a heartbeat, Seb had sprung from his seat like a coiled snake, pulling me backwards. He positioned himself between us, his stance rigid and protective. The sound that escaped his throat was more growl than anything human.

Katie's eyes went wide. She stumbled back a step, nearly colliding with a nearby table. "Who are you, and how do you know my brother?"

Seb extended his hand, his movements deliberately slow and controlled. "Sebastián Salazar." His accent curled around the syllables of his name. "And let's just say Flynn's sense of self-preservation wasn't what it should have been."

Ever so carefully, I slid into the booth, with Katie taking the seat opposite me.

"I'll sort us out some drinks then," Connor said, his Irish accent heavy in the quiet café. "What're ye all fancying, then? Tea okay?"

As soon as he was out of earshot, I stared down at my water glass, trying to steady my nerves. The table was completely still, yet the surface of the water wasn't—tiny ripples pulsed across it in a steady rhythm, matching the thundering of my heart. I blinked hard, but the pattern continued.

"Seb, do you see—"

"I know you didn't want Connor here, Flynn, but I don't feel like we're safe here without him," Katie said, refocusing my attention on her. She pointedly glanced at Seb, who blinked at her.

"Fine," I snapped. So be it. He could sit here and listen to what I had to say.

"So you've been staying with Sebastián?" She glanced at him. "Why did you tell your bakery that you're sick?"

"I have been sick. With a really bad... chest infection." I rubbed at my cold spot. "My own flat is horribly damp, so Sebastián has been taking care of me."

"And you met…"

"At a bar," Sebastián interjected. "Not the most original of locations, I know."

"Hey, at least we didn't meet on a dating app." I forced a laugh.

Katie's mouth fell open. "So you're *dating*?"

Heat crept up my neck. "Oh, um…" I glanced at Sebastián, who remained perfectly still beside me. "Sort of? Look, I know it seems fast—"

"Fast? It's practically light speed! You run away to London, barely talk to anyone for weeks, and now you're living with some stranger—"

"He's not a stranger." The words came out sharper than intended. "And I didn't *plan* for any of this to happen. Sometimes life just… throws things at you that you don't expect."

Like demons. And vampires. And falling for someone who'd spent twenty years avoiding love because of a broken heart.

Katie's eyes narrowed. "What do you need to talk to me about, Flynn? I'm here now, and ready to listen."

I opened my mouth, but no words came out, because Connor chose that moment to return with a tray full of drinks.

Connor set it down, sitting down next to Katie. "What's the craic, then?"

My throat closed up. Under the table, I searched for Seb's hand, finding his cold fingers and gripping them tight. The chill of his skin helped ground me, keeping the rising panic at bay.

I tried to focus only on Katie's face. "The night I left," I started, then inhaled sharply. "I went with Tom to the pier. And then I sat and cried on the beach."

Katie's face softened with sympathy, but Connor's expression shifted, his jaw twitching.

"Aye, sure. I told Katie all about finding ye that night." Connor's voice thickened like cream. "Though I'm surprised ye remember much at all, what with the state ye were in. You'd had more than a wee bit of that whiskey, hadn't ya?"

Seb's fingers tightened around mine, almost painfully. I could feel the tension radiating from him, though his face remained perfectly composed.

"I wasn't drunk." The words came out barely above a whisper. "You know I wasn't drunk, Connor." Tom and I had shared a few swigs, but by the point Connor found me, I'd almost been stone-cold sober.

"Ach, come on now." Connor's laugh held an edge. "Ye were a right mess that night, weren't ye? All torn up about that lad, Tom."

"Yes, I was upset about Tom. Which is exactly why you—" I took a breath, turning to Katie. "Connor kissed me that night. On the beach."

"What?"

The word hung in the air between us. I watched the change sweep across my sister's face: confusion first, then disbelief, and finally a horrible understanding that drained every drop of colour from her cheeks.

She gripped the edge of the table, her wedding ring catching the light. "No, Flynn, you must have misunderstood—"

"Just like I misunderstood at your party three years ago?" The words tumbled out. "When he cornered me in the kitchen and—"

"Now hold on just a minute!" Connor's fist slammed against the table. Every glass jumped—but my water shot straight up, as high as my face, before raining down on the table. No one seemed to notice, too focused on Connor's rage. "I won't be sitting here listening to these lies!"

Seb rose to his full height. "Then perhaps you should leave."

"Ye can't make me do anything." Connor's face reddened as he jabbed a finger towards me. "And *you*—ye ungrateful little shit. After everything we did for ye?"

Connor's hand shot out, grabbing my wrist. Revulsion coursed through me at his touch, memories of that night on the beach flooding back—his hands, my tears. My whole body went rigid, trapped between fight and flight.

The movement was so fast, I barely registered what happened next—just a blur of motion, the sickening crunch of bone meeting knuckles, and then Connor was stumbling backwards, blood trickling from his nose. Seb had struck with the lethal grace of a cobra, his fist connecting with Connor's face with such devastating precision that the crack echoed through the quiet café.

Behind the counter, the barista suddenly became very interested in cleaning the coffee machine.

"Who the fuck do ye think ye are?" Connor spat, wiping his nose with his sleeve. "Some posh English bastard—"

"I assure you." Seb's voice dropped dangerously low. "I am neither English nor someone you wish to test. You can walk out of here of your own accord, or I can escort you. Your choice."

Something in Seb's expression must have registered because Connor backed away, one hand pressed against his bleeding nose. "Ah, Katie, love. Yer brother was in bits that night, crying his eyes out and drunk as a lord. He's the one who tried it on with me, and I had to push him off, didn't I? Now he's gone and twisted it all around because he's ashamed of himself."

"Just go, Connor," Katie whispered, her eyes fixed on her hands.

Connor teetered on the balls of his feet, and for one horrible moment, I thought he'd never leave, but then he stormed out, door swinging behind him.

A heavy silence fell over the table. My pulse thundered in my ears as I watched my sister, desperate for any sign that she believed me.

Seb's fingers found a lock of my hair that had fallen forward, tucking it gently behind my ear. "He's gone now," he murmured, voice soft but firm. "You won't need to see him again."

My heart stuttered at the tenderness of the gesture—the contrast between Seb's fierce protection and this gentle touch made my heart squeeze. Here was someone who wouldn't let anyone hurt me again—I knew it in my very soul.

Katie watched us closely, her brow furrowing. "Flynn..." She paused, studying how I leaned into Seb's shoulder.

Seb said softly, "Your brother is very important to me, Ms Carter. He's been so anxious about talking to you about this."

Sighing, Katie worried into her bottom lip. "Flynn, why didn't you tell me sooner?"

"Because you didn't believe me the first time." My throat tightened. "Because he's your husband and you love him and I... I couldn't bear to see you hurt like that."

Katie's eyes filled with tears, but there was steel beneath them. "Tell me absolutely everything. From the beginning."

I felt Seb squeeze my hand gently, and somehow I found the strength to start talking.

26

Sebastián

I left Flynn and Katie to their privacy, settling at a table across the café. Of course, their conversation wasn't truly private.

Katie's apologies about Connor poured forth, genuine remorse in her voice. Then their words drifted to memories of his departure, of their mother's tears, of unanswered calls. The weight of abandonment hung heavy between them until Katie broached the subject of Seabreeze.

"You know what, Flynn? I'm glad Mum sold it. Grandad worked seventy-hour weeks. I don't want that for you. Mum never wanted it to tie you down. You know, I'm actually glad you got out of Braymore. You were so young when we moved there... I've always worried it trapped you. Especially when you didn't want to go to uni. But look how happy you are here already!"

"I am."

"But what about Sebastián?" Katie hissed. "You're sure he's not some sort of gangster?"

My pen scratched against my notepad as I feigned deep concentration.

"Does he look like a gangster?"

"No," Katie admitted. "He looks like one of those black and white movie stars. All brooding and handsome. Like James Dean, but hotter."

"Katie!"

"I'm sorry!"

When their laughter died, Flynn asked, "Will you be okay, though? With Connor, I mean..."

"No, it's going to be absolutely awful." Katie's chair scraped against the floor. "But don't worry. I'll be fine, eventually. I'm tougher than I look."

Footsteps approached my table. I looked up to find Katie's lips pursed. "If you hurt my brother, I will cut you."

"Noted."

"Right across your handsome face."

"Where else?"

She smiled, and I felt we had reached some sort of understanding.

"I will protect him with my life. I swear it."

Katie glanced at Flynn, possibly to communicate, *well that was a bit intense.*

Aside from the crunch of leaves beneath our feet, the walk back was silent. Flynn seemed lost in thought, so I let him be.

Eventually, he asked, "Did you see the water? My water?"

"What?"

"My glass of water... It—"

Flynn was interrupted by my phone ringing. *Rory.*

"Boss, where are you?"

"Back at the hotel now. What's wrong?"

"Let's just say Kit and I *might* need to check a guest into room 410 later."

I stopped dead, my fingers tightening around the phone. That room was where we stored dead bodies, on occasion.

"I'll be right there."

Flynn turned to me, brow furrowed. "What's going on?"

"When we get back inside, I need you to go help Felix again."

"*Help* Felix?" His eyes narrowed. "You mean hide in the basement while you deal with whatever scary shit is happening elsewhere?"

I shot him a wide, pleased grin. "Actually, that's exactly what I meant!" I grabbed his head with two hands, kissing him once on the lips.

He was so startled that he didn't argue back.

When we reached Felix's lair, I gave Flynn's shoulder a quick squeeze. "I'll see you later." My eye contact hopefully communicated, *I'll come to your room as soon as I'm back."* Either that or he thought I was experiencing some sort of vampire malfunction. I wasn't entirely sure I'd mastered the art of subtle flirtation. Perhaps in another few centuries.

I moved through the tunnels towards Brixton, following Rory's tracker signal near our earlier search area.

We'd spent the morning chasing leads. Each contact led to another—a necromancer above the butcher's, then a Gifted fortune teller. The pattern repeated: show the photo, watch them pale, receive vague directions. The reaction to Vale's photo was universal—wide eyes, stammered excuses. One shifter had backed away, hands raised. "My pack comes first. Vale's vampires would tear through us."

The message was clear—Vale inspired more fear than loyalty to us. The Brixton supernatural community would rather face my disappointment than his wrath.

Earlier, when Flynn's name had lit up my screen, I'd been mid-rant about my own incompetence, how I should have crushed Vale's influence months ago, when I discovered he'd been vocally opposing my use of bagged blood, deeming it unnatural. Kit had merely raised an eyebrow, weathering my self-flagellation with practiced patience.

The tunnel opened into a derelict toilet. I pushed aside a false panel, wrinkling my nose. Not as bad as Victorian sewers, at least. Brass fixtures, green with verdigris, clung to crumbling tiles.

Rory's signal showed Windmill Gardens, ten minutes away.

Zooming in, his dot appeared over Brixton Windmill, or Ashby's Mill to the locals. The heritage site stood silent, sails motionless against the sky. I remembered when its blades still turned, creaking as it ground the city's grain.

I vaulted the metal fence, ignoring the "PARK CLOSED AT DUSK" sign.

My brogues slid on wet grass as I approached. The brick tower loomed, windows lifeless. The building should have been locked.

The security light flickered on as I drew closer. Rory's signal hadn't moved. I pressed my back against the cool brick, listening intently. Faint sounds were coming from the top—grunts, scrapes. Growls.

The windmill's entrance was a narrow black door set deep in the brick base. A metal plate and electronic lock had been retrofitted beside aged iron fittings. The system's LED was dark—Felix's handiwork no doubt. The handle gave way, so I hurried through, sealing myself in darkness broken only by the faint moonlight filtering through gaps in the wooden slats above.

A louder growl echoed from above—the distinctive sound of a shifted wolf. My shoulders loosened a fraction. If Rory and Kit were still breathing, the situation couldn't be catastrophic.

My ancient blade at the ready, I took the stairs three at a time, the aged wood creaking beneath my feet, and the space soon opened up into the cap of the windmill.

The scene before me crystallised in an instant. My two wolves circled a vampire—Kit's massive grey form prowling with military precision, while Rory's smaller golden shape darted and weaved. Their target, Adrian Knox, was backed against the wooden machinery of the mill.

His buzz-cut hair made him instantly recognisable from the CCTV footage after Greaves's murder, fleeing the scene with Damien. A fledgling—barely two years dead, turned in his mid-thirties.

Adrian's eyes darted between the wolves, then fixed on me. In that split second, he hurled himself toward the stairs. Both wolves sprang into action—Kit slamming into Adrian's torso while Rory, faster and more agile, blocked the escape route. They crashed into the ancient wooden gears, sending a cloud of dust and debris into the air.

Through the chaos, I spotted the brake chain dangling from the windshaft. "Rory, shift back! Get that chain! We'll tie him up!"

The golden wolf hesitated for a split second before backing into the corner. His transformation was anything but graceful—fur receding in patches, bones cracking and realigning with sickening pops. He doubled over, a strangled sound caught between growl and groan. The process took precious seconds we could barely afford.

Still trembling from the change, Rory stumbled towards the brake chain. Adrian lashed out, catching him across the face before he could fully regain his balance. Blood splattered across weathered wood.

At the sight of his brother's blood, Kit's growl turned absolutely feral. He lunged for Adrian's throat, forcing me to physically wedge myself between them.

"We need him alive!" I grappled with Kit's massive form, his protective rage making him nearly impossible to control. Blood-flecked saliva dripped from his jaws.

Adrian thrashed beneath us, clawing at Kit's thick fur. I managed to pin his arms while Rory, naked and bleeding but determined, helped wrap the chain around him. Together, we secured him to the windshaft.

Kit maintained his wolf form, hackles raised as he stood guard. His growls had subsided to a low rumble, but his eyes never left Adrian. His grey fur, marked with darker patches, bristled along his spine. A notable scar traced above his left eye, matching the one he bore in human form. Seeing him like this was always a stark reminder of why wolves were feared, even by vampires.

Rory pulled on his jeans, grinning despite his split lip. "Well, we really *put the brakes* on that situation!"

The terrible pun earned him twin glares from Kit and me, while Adrian tested his bonds with a metallic rattle.

"We chased him here all the way from town," Rory said.

"Nice work." I studied our prisoner's face. "Though I question your choice of venue."

"Blame him."

I circled Adrian slowly, my footsteps echoing in the confined space. "Let's start simple. Why did you murder Alistair Greaves?"

Adrian's jaw clenched, but he remained silent.

"We have CCTV footage of you fleeing the scene with your cambion friend." I leaned closer, studying the defiance in his eyes. "The way Greaves was torn apart... That was personal. A personal attack against *me,* that his family will suffer for."

Nothing. Not even a flicker of emotion.

"Who ordered the hit?" I pressed my palm against the rough brick wall. "Someone must have given you the order. A fledgling like you wouldn't take such a risk without backing."

His shoulders tensed slightly.

"It was Marcus Vale, wasn't it? Your beloved leader? That would make the most sense." The minute widening of his eyes confirmed nothing. "Or perhaps the cambion known as Damien suggested it?"

Kit's growl rumbled through the space as Adrian maintained his silence.

My patience snapped. I grabbed Adrian's throat, fingers digging into cold flesh. "Listen carefully. Your silence won't protect you. You're already dead—the only question is how painful I make it."

He spat in my face.

I wiped the spittle away with my sleeve, then drove my fist into his stomach. The impact rattled the ancient chain. "That was just a warm-up. I can do this all night."

Adrian's laugh was hoarse. "You're pathetic, Black. Trying to play sheriff with your fabricated authority. Trying to force us to repress who we are. We know what you did to Eliza. How you slaughtered her, just because she dared to touch your human pet—"

I seized his right hand, snapping his index finger backward until it cracked. His scream echoed off the wooden beams. But then Adrian's pained expression morphed into a smirk as the bones began knitting themselves back together.

Fucking vampire healing. Always so inconvenient when trying to make a point.

"I can see you need something a bit more..." I reached for the blade at my hip. "Permanent." The dagger glinted in the dim light as I brought it down, severing the finger at the knuckle.

This time, his scream held no trace of smugness.

Adrian's blood poured onto the floorboards as the severed finger twitched, a macabre reminder of vampire biology's persistence.

"Boss." Rory pulled a lighter from his jeans, the flame dancing to life with a metallic click. "Allow me?"

I nodded, maintaining my grip on Adrian as Rory pressed the flame against the bleeding stump—the cauterisation would prevent any chance of the finger being reattached later, or regenerating. The sizzle of burning flesh mixed with Adrian's renewed screams soon filled the tiny space.

"Well then. Shall we continue talking? Or am I moving on to the other nine fingers? Tell me why your clan is working with the cambion who calls himself Damien."

Adrian's laughter turned to whimpers as I bent back another finger. But he still managed to seethe, "You think pain will make me betray Marcus?"

"Everyone breaks eventually." I studied his face, noting the fierce loyalty in his eyes despite the agony. "Though you seem particularly devoted to him."

"He saved me." The words carried a zealot's conviction. "When everyone else abandoned me, Marcus gave me purpose. If you harm me further..." His lips curled into a bloody smile. "The consequences would be severe. I'm special to him."

I stepped back, considering this new information. Marcus Vale was not known for forming attachments to his subordinates. But if Adrian really held such significance...

"You have no idea what Marcus would do if—"

"Actually," I cut him off, turning to Rory. "You could be right. This might be a 410 situation."

Rory's face lit up with savage delight. "Oh, brilliant!"

Kit's low growl suggested approval.

I faced Adrian again, whose bravado had faltered. "If you're so precious to Marcus, then surely he'd be willing to trade for your life."

Adrian's eyes widened with understanding.

"A simple exchange." I gripped his jaw. "Your continued existence for delivery of the cambion who calls himself Damien."

The calculation was clear—with Flynn having mere days on the clock, I needed leverage. Marcus Vale might despise me, might rally against my methods... but *perhaps* he was loyal to his devoted flock. Time would tell.

Adrian thrashed against his chains. "You're making a mistake—"

"The only mistake," I said. "Was allowing Vale to operate unchecked for so long. That ends tonight."

"This is suicide," Adrian spat. "Marcus will tear you apart. He's stronger than you know!"

"Your concern is touching." I straightened my coat. "But I've dealt with far worse than Vale."

I pulled out my phone, and jammed Priya's contact before barking, "Peacock? Bring a van as close to my location as you can." Next was Felix. "Magpie, prepare room 410," I instructed, before sliding my phone away.

"God, I love it when you get all authoritative like this." Rory bounced on his heels. "Makes me feel all tingly inside. Like watching a stern headmaster during assembly."

Kit's wolf form made a choking sound that might have been laughter.

"Rory." I pinched the bridge of my nose. "Your schoolboy fantasies are not appropriate right now."

"Whatever you say, *Daddy*."

"I swear, I will throw you off this windmill—"

"Careful now. Flynn might not like you manhandling other men."

A grey blur catapulted through the air as Kit knocked Rory flat on his back with a thud that echoed through the windmill's beams. Rory squirmed beneath him, laughing breathlessly.

I leaned against the wall, watching them wrestle while our prisoner stared, bewildered. Sometimes I questioned my life choices. Five cen-

turies, and here I was, supervising what essentially amounted to supernatural children.

White had promised me a professional operation when she'd offered
me Killigrew Street. Instead, I had a hyperactive wolf with inappropriate
jokes, his grumpy brother, a tech genius getting sassier by the minute,
and a Gifted witch operating on tea and sarcasm.

And yet... they were mine. My ridiculous, dysfunctional family.

Rory finally managed to wiggle free, his hair full of dust and wolf fur.
"Ha! Victory is mine!"

Kit's tail wagged once.

I sighed heavily. "If you two are quite finished, we have a vampire to
knock out."

27

Flynn

The days slipped through my fingers like sand. Before I knew it, it was the 30th of October.

The team guarded and interrogated Adrian Knox, the vampire prisoner on the fourth floor. The one Seb would trade for Damien, and my life. Messages had gone to Vale's coven about our demands, hoping Adrian's friends would pressure Vale.

There'd been negotiations—though Seb kept me in the dark—but nothing concrete. No deal. No salvation ahead.

So here I was. One day left until the demon magic was due to kill me.

Fun times.

The whole team walked on eggshells around me, their smiles too wide, their voices too bright.

Seb had promised to come find me this evening, but it had already reached 8:00 p.m. With a heavy heart, I pushed off the sofa. My feet carried me up the basement stairs, then the grand staircase, past peeling wallpaper and dusty portraits. Perhaps he'd be in his office, doing something important.

But I needed to see him. To drink in the sight of him, even if just for a moment. Even if neither of us acknowledged the crushing weight of tomorrow hanging over our heads.

I'd only had snatches of time with Seb over the past few days. A flash of his coat in the hallway. The brush of his fingers against mine at any opportunity.

Some nights, he'd managed to slip into my room. We never did much more than lie there, tangled up in each other's arms. Talking a bit, or watching Buffy.

Last night, he'd appeared at my door just before dawn, his face drawn with exhaustion. Without a word, I'd pulled him into bed. He'd wrapped himself around me like a shield, his cool body pressed against my back, his arm draped over my waist. Since yesterday, the ice inside my chest had become a permanent fixture, pumping freezing blood around my permanently cold body. As I clung to Seb, I had to do my best not to shiver, in case he realised he was making me even colder.

Those quiet moments felt stolen, precious. Like fragments of peace in the midst of chaos. We didn't talk about the date. Didn't mention the demon magic eating away at me, or the negotiations with Vale's coven, or the possibility that this—whatever this was between us—might end before it truly began.

Reaching Seb's office door, I knocked. No answer.

"Seb?" I called, as if he might not have heard.

Still nothing.

My hand drifted to the brass doorknob. It turned without resistance. For all his gruff exterior and dark mystique, Seb trusted his team enough to leave his sanctuary open.

A twinge of guilt pricked at my conscience as I slipped inside. The office lay in shadow, illuminated only by the glow of his desk lamp. A notebook lay open, a fountain pen carelessly dropped beside. Though this wasn't his usual notepad that he brought to meetings.

I shouldn't have looked. I really shouldn't have.

But my gaze had already snagged on the words, drawing me in like a hook...

30th October, 2025

Tomorrow is the day. The day the dark magic will have fully incubated within Flynn. I hope to return to my professional records at nightfall with a positive update—that Marcus Vale has agreed to the exchange. As it stands, he is still refusing to negotiate, spreading lies about Killigrew Street to his clan and the wider community.

If the worst does happen—and Flynn dies tomorrow—then I wanted to create a record of him here to look back upon. Presently, I hold the image of him so clear in my mind, and it feels as if he shall always remain that way.

My memories always do, until they fade like watercolours bleached by the sun.

Flynn Carter.

The depth of my feelings for him... They consume me. I feel so utterly unmade. As if he's reached inside me and rearranged everything. I find myself counting the hours until I see him again, cataloguing every smile, every touch, every moment.

What was it that first entranced me, that first night?

Perhaps it was the way he moved on the dance floor—spinning circles around that foul cambion with wild abandon, completely unaware of how he drew every eye in the room.

Of course, a few hours later, he'd driven his knee straight into my groin. I suppose that caught my attention too.

And oh, his stubbornness—his stubbornness rivals even my own. I tried to push him away, warned him of the darkness that follows me, but he refused to listen. He says he wants all of me, even the parts I've spent centuries trying to hide. The blood. The violence. The monster beneath. It's remarkable, really. He looks at me and sees... more. Something worth saving.

He thinks he can save me from my solitude. It is true—my carefully maintained isolation has been undone by his smile, his touch, his unwavering faith in me.

Though now, with tomorrow looming, I wonder if isolation wasn't the safer option after all. A part of me still resists the notion of romantic love, still remembers the crushing pain of James.

Though James feels distant now, like a story I once read. Flynn has brought colour back into my world. He's turned my carefully ordered existence into something chaotic and bright—like those red-chequered pyjamas of his I so adore sliding my skin against, like the way he hums sea shanties under his breath, like the pink sticky notes with smiley faces he keeps leaving attached to my notepad when I place it down.

Tonight, I must

"I've been trying to find y—"

I whirled around, the diary slipping from my fingers and hitting the floor with a dull thud. As if dropping the evidence might somehow erase what I'd done.

Seb stood frozen in the doorway, eyes wide with shock. His mouth opened and closed, no words coming out.

"That's my— That's my private diary!"

Heat exploded across my cheeks. *Fuck fuck fuck.*

Damage control, damage control! "I'm so sorry. The door was open and I was looking for you and—" I gestured helplessly at the fallen book. "I shouldn't have read it. I know I shouldn't have."

Seb's gaze dropped to the diary, then back to me.

"How much did you...?"

I swallowed hard. "I didn't quite finish it."

A peculiar expression crossed his face—somewhere between mortification and resignation. He ran a fraught hand through his dark curls. "Well. I suppose that's..." He trailed off, then bent to retrieve the diary. "I prefer to keep my thoughts private."

"I really am sorry." I took a step toward him. "If it helps, what you wrote was beautiful."

Seb's shoulders tensed. "Flynn—"

"Especially the bit about my pyjamas—"

"Please stop." Though there was a hint of amusement breaking through his stern expression. "This is already excruciating enough."

"You know, I thought you might not be over James yet," I said softly. "I accidentally saw his social media file in Felix's lair. You know, those updates you get him to print monthly."

Seb grimaced. "I ought to tell Felix to stop that now. It's... inappropriate."

"No," I said quickly, even as jealousy twisted in my gut. "If it helps you, then it's a good idea. It's sweet you still want to know. That you care."

Seb's gaze bored into me. "I think that chapter of my life has long since closed." He took a step closer. "I loved him dearly. But I've spent twenty years stuck in the past, and now..." He paused, something vulnerable flickering across his face. "Now I find myself wanting to turn the page."

He took both of my hands in his, pressing his lips first to one, then the other. My burnt hand, now free of bandages, tingled at the contact.

"But I know I'm going to die tomorrow!" The words burst out of me. *Way to kill the vibe, Flynn.*

Seb's brow furrowed. "We never told you an exact date."

I glared at him. "I'm not stupid. You've all been referring to Halloween as if it's some kind of deadline. As if my time will run out." My fingers drifted to my chest, to that spot of permanent ice that had taken root there. "And I can feel it. I can feel it killing me." My voice trembled. "I've been trying to ignore it, but... I'm so cold. So damned cold. And—"

Seb pressed a finger to my lips to silence me as a shiver racked my body, then drew me against him, arms wrapping around me. For once, his cool temperature felt warm compared to the frost spreading through my veins.

"Flynn, I came to find you to tell you the good news. Vale's agreed to the exchange."

The words hit me like a wave breaking against a seawall, the meaning taking time to seep through.

"You... what?" I whispered, my world tilting on its axis. The constant dread that had become as familiar as breathing suddenly felt less absolute, less crushing.

"Tomorrow morning. Even if Damien doesn't tell us who he's working for, we're confident killing him will immediately release your affliction. The dark magic is tied to his life force."

My knees buckled. If Seb hadn't been holding me, I'd have crumpled to the floor right there, the weeks of carefully suppressed terror finally catching up with me.

"I'm not going to die?" The words came out small and broken, like a child seeking reassurance after a nightmare.

Seb's lips brushed my forehead, impossibly gentle. "Not if I have any say in it." His arms tightened around me for a moment before he pulled back, clearing his throat. "But we're not going to talk of such matters right now."

I blinked up at him, thrown by the sudden shift in his demeanor. He looked almost... nervous?

"I've got a surprise for you."

"A surprise?"

"Yes, well." Seb smoothed down his already immaculate shirt. "I thought, given recent events, you could do with something... pleasant."

"Um... okay."

"And you've been saying how you're sick of being stuck in the hotel—"

"We're leaving the hotel?!" I could have cried with joy.

"*Ahh.* Not... entirely. Follow me."

Curiosity officially piqued.

He guided me to the end of the corridor, where a narrow service staircase spiraled upwards. We traipsed up it, all the way to a cramped space with a large metal door, wedged open with a brick, an extension cable running through it.

Seb opened the door, its hinges whining. A blast of cold fresh air hit my face as a small flat section of roof opened up. Two heat lamps glowed amber against the night, illuminating... *a bed?* A double mattress dragged up god knows how many stairs, complete with duvet and pillows probably pilfered from one of the rooms. The warm light caught on the forest of sooty chimney stacks that surrounded us, clay pots silhouetted against the star-scattered sky.

"You've got to be joking," I muttered, even as something fluttered in my chest.

The dormers jutted out from the steep slate roof, creating a bizarre little alcove that blocked the worst of the wind. A small rack of herbs and flowers was wedged against the ancient brickwork, each pot meticulously labelled in Priya's precise handwriting. London sprawled below us, a glittering tapestry of lights and shadows, while above, the night sky felt close enough to touch. As Sebastián took my hand and tugged me toward our ridiculous rooftop haven, I couldn't stop the smile creeping across my face.

"This is either the most romantic or most idiotic thing anyone's ever done for me. Possibly both."

"It wasn't any effort."

I stared at him until his lips quirked.

"Alright, the mattress was an absolute pain in the ass. And it took me thirty minutes to find an extension cable long enough. Felix almost had a panic attack when I tried to unplug one of his." He grinned, then asked, "Are you hungry?" His eyes hopeful as he gestured towards the mattress.

Perched near the edge was a domed silver tray, likely borrowed from the kitchen. I was speechless. If I did die tomorrow, at least I could add, "dined under the stars at London's most exclusive rooftop restaurant" to my achievements.

"I must admit, I haven't cooked in many years," Seb confessed as he settled onto the mattress. "So I kept it simple..."

With a flourish of his hand, he lifted the lid, revealing a plate of grilled cheese sandwiches. But this was no ordinary fare—the bread was artisanal sourdough, worthy of being sold at Rising Dough. It was perfectly grilled to a golden brown, with melted cheese oozing temptingly from the sides. Sprigs of fresh herbs even garnished the dish.

A soft laugh escaped my lips as I reached for one. "And here I thought vampires only knew how to heat up blood in the microwave."

As I took a massive bite, Seb caught my injured hand, examining the healing skin. With an eye roll, I tugged it away. "It looks very similar to yesterday."

He turned away for a moment, then two wine glasses materialised, with a bottle of red wine. I threw him a glance—I'd never seen Seb partake in alcohol, even when Priya and Rory split a pack of beers.

"I can drink it. I might even get a slight buzz if I'm lucky." A wry smile tugged at the corner of his mouth. "My kind often mix it with blood."

A lovely shiver shot straight down my spine.

"Will you be doing that tonight?"

Seb's gaze met mine, steady and intense. "I fed earlier."

Those exact words were now very familiar—he said that phrase every time I offered to feed him.

I hid my disappointment by offering him a small smile as I took another bite. "These are delicious."

He inclined his head, pouring the wine into the two glasses before passing me one. "I'm glad you approve."

A small silence, where we both sipped our wine. Then my next words tumbled out. "Why won't you feed from me?"

Oh god. Why? Why did I have to ask that?

Seb's hand froze mid-sip, wine splashing against the rim of the glass. His eyes snapped to mine, startled.

"I just... I'd like to help. You're always so worried about the blood from Undertone, not knowing where it comes from." My eyes became glued to my crust.

A deep sigh. "I suppose I'm denying myself that privilege."

"What? Why?"

"I promised to save you. And until I've fulfilled that promise, I don't deserve—" He cut himself off.

I set my sandwich down on the silver dome, pushing it aside. With gentle fingers, I pried Seb's glass from his hand, and placed it on the brickwork. I shifted closer to Seb, swinging one leg over his thighs until

I straddled his lap. The heat lamps cast a warm glow across his features, softening the sharp angles of his face.

His hands settled tentatively on my hips, steadying me. The touch sent electricity dancing across my skin, even through the fabric of my jumper.

I reached up, brushing those wild curls back from his forehead. They were beautifully soft, like plush velvet between my fingers. In the warm amber light, his eyes met mine—burnt caramel, so ancient and so human all at once.

"It isn't something that you need to earn," I whispered, trailing my fingers down to cup his jaw. "It's about trust. Connection." My thumb traced his lower lip. "It's about me wanting to share something with you. Something that matters."

"Flynn—"

"Let me finish." I pressed my forehead against his. "It's about letting me in on every part of you. Letting me help you."

"You make everything sound so simple," he murmured.

"Maybe because it is."

His hands tightened on my hips, drawing me closer.

I studied his face—watching the flicker of surrender, his ironclad wall beginning to crumble. The warm light caught on his features like the last rays of dusk dancing over water, transforming everything to molten gold.

"You know, I used to think the ocean at sunset was the most beautiful sight in the world." My thumb traced his jawline. "Turns out I just hadn't met you yet."

His eyes burned into mine with an intensity that stole my breath.

Between one heartbeat and the next, he moved—vampire-fast—sweeping me up like I weighed nothing at all. The world blurred as he drove me across the rooftop.

My back struck the rough brickwork of a chimney stack, and I arched into the delicious friction of Seb pinning me there, his hips cradled between my thighs. A low growl rumbled in his chest as I nipped at his lower lip, tasting the faintest hint of wine.

Then his mouth crashed against mine, hungry and demanding. My fingers tangled in those thick curls, tugging him closer as heat bloomed between us. My cock thickened, pushing insistently against my jeans, his own bulge pressing into mine, and anticipation unfurled in my blood like wildfire.

He drove me even harder against the wall, the rough brick catching at my jumper. That sharp sensation brought me back to myself, even as his tongue swept against mine with maddening tenderness.

"This is so fucking hot," I gasped between kisses. "But it would be a shame to waste that mattress you hauled all the way up here, right?"

The world blurred again—that dizzying speed—and then I was flying, then falling, then sprawled across the mattress, the London sky spinning above me. The delicious weight of Seb pressed me down, down, *down* into the duvet, heavy enough to steal my breath in the best possible way. Almost too heavy, but god, I never wanted him to move, because trapped between him and the bed, I felt so wonderfully, perfectly caught. Held. Safe. Cherished.

Our bodies shifted and melted together as his tongue sought mine, and I answered with frantic hunger.

Hands everywhere. Desperate. Claiming. His mouth cool against mine. Nothing gentle now. Just touch. Raw need. Fingers digging into flesh. Bodies pressed flush. His grip fierce on my jaw. On my hip. Drawing me closer. Closer. Until there was nothing left between us but want.

"I want to take you," he murmured, dark and honeyed, the words ghosting against my skin. "May I have you?"

"Yes," I rasped out, swallowing down my *please, please, please.*

I found the hem of my jumper, and his fingers caught my hand, tugging the garment back down. "Off," I insisted. "I want to feel you." He hesitated only a moment before helping me pull it, and my shirt, over my head. I should have been cold, but between the heat lamps above and the inferno his touch sparked beneath my skin, warmth blazed through me, keeping the demon ice at bay.

I tilted my head, baring my throat. "Bite me," I breathed, beyond caring how desperate I sounded. "I want you to, Seb. So, so much."

"No." The word rumbled from his chest—dark, commanding. "First, I want to show you how good I can make you feel. You'll come from my cock, not my bite."

I tried not to die. *Okay then.*

He stripped off his own clothes, ridiculously fast, each perfect inch of skin revealed, making my mouth go dry. He made quick work of my jeans, kissing the bulge of my dick through my briefs. Catching the material in his teeth, he pulled it down, nose gliding down my thigh.

My dick sprang free, achingly hard and already dripping.

Seb's lips traced feather-light paths along my inner thigh, working their way higher until his tongue found my head. When it brushed against the very tip, licking up what it found there with a soft sound, I forgot how to breathe, every muscle in my body tensing with pleasure. Soon, the careful attention he lavished upon me had me writhing, my fingers twisting in the sheets. His mouth enveloped me with wet sucks, drawing a broken moan from my throat. The vibration of his answering, pleased hum sent sparks of bliss shooting through me.

"Seb, fuck!" The warning was clear in my voice—I was so close already.

He pulled away with an obscene pop, and I whimpered at the loss. His cool fingers wrapped around my cock, giving just a few teasing strokes, and my hips jerked up desperately.

"*Please!*"

He immediately stopped, squeezing the base of my cock hard enough to make me gasp. "Not until I'm inside you."

A groan spilled out of me. "Quickly then!" A sudden thought pierced through my lust-addled brain. "Please tell me you brought the lube up here?"

"What do you take me for, a fool?" He reached over me to retrieve the small bottle from under a pillow. "But first, turn over."

He grabbed my hip, twisting me so I was on my hands and knees. His cool lips pressed against one of my cheeks, then the other. Then his hands guided my thighs apart as his mouth moved lower, trailing kisses against the inside of my thigh.

He brought one of my balls into his mouth.

I cried out, my volume only increasing when he began lavishing it with gentle sucks. He did the same to the other one as his hands smoothed reverently up the back of my thighs. His touch was tender, worshipful, his fingers pressing patterns into my skin. When his breath ghosted across sensitive flesh, followed by the first careful press of tongue, I lost all coherent thought.

My world narrowed to pure sensation. He started with just the rim—gentle, teasing circles that had me gripping the sheets. Gradually, he increased the pressure until I was trembling beneath him. I tried to keep still, I really did, but my body betrayed me, demanding more of his touch. My thighs widened as he worked me with his tongue, each careful thrust drawing desperate sounds from my throat.

My head fell forward into the pillow, muffling my stream of curses as he explored with devastating thoroughness, alternating between broad strokes and precise attention that left me gasping.

This wasn't merely sex.

This was worship.

"Seb..." I managed between ragged breaths, my whole body aflame with need.

The click of the bottle cap made my stomach flip. Cool liquid dripped between my cheeks, making me shiver, but his hands were there instantly, catching the escaping drops and pushing them back up.

"Do you touch yourself?" he asked, and I almost choked.

"*Yes.*"

"While you think of me?"

If only he knew how many times in the last week.

"Yes. Fucking hell, *yes.*"

When the first finger breached me—ever so slowly, ever so careful-ly—my breath caught in my throat.

Seb leaned over me, body blanketing mine to brush his lips across my shoulder blades, trailing gentle kisses along my skin. He pushed deeper, so deep I cried out, but his mouth was there to catch the sound. I sucked on his tongue, matching the rhythm of his finger, losing myself to the dual sensations.

He let my mouth go, and I panted, resting my forehead on my clasped hands.

When he added a second finger, the slight burn made me hiss, but his voice was there, soft and adoring. "My sweet angel. *Mi amor.* You're doing so beautifully."

I melted into the mattress, boneless with pleasure. He shifted to lie beside me, his calf sliding against my leg as his fingers worked deeper, searching. When they found that spot inside me, sparks exploded behind my eyes.

"Now. I need you *now*," I pleaded, because I needed him inside me more than I needed air.

"How do you want this?" he murmured against my shoulder.

"Want to see you," I said breathily. "Need to see your face."

He helped me turn onto my back, settling between my thighs. Looking up at him—at those dark eyes filled with such tender intensity, at the way his curls fell across his forehead—my heart squeezed in my chest. This felt like more than just desire. More than just need. This felt like falling.

The London night sky wheeled above me, stars blurring through my half-closed eyes as sensation overwhelmed me: Seb's voice, low and honeyed, promising to take care of me; the solid weight of him between my trembling thighs; the slick pressure of his cock teasing against me. Then he was pushing in—slowly, so slowly—and everything else ceased to exist except that single point of connection. My fingers scrabbled against his shoulders, seeking anchor as he filled me impossibly deep, each inch stretching me wider than I thought I could take. When I found my voice, it came out broken. "Seb, I can't— It's too—"

He caught my lips with his, swallowing my gasps as he pressed deeper still. The stretch was overwhelming, burning and perfect and too much all at once. I whimpered into his mouth, my body caught between wanting to pull away and wanting to draw him deeper, until finally—finally—he stilled, fully seated inside me. When I managed to open my eyes, the reverence in his expression stole what little breath I had left.

He leaned down to kiss me, then rested his forehead against mine. Though he didn't need to breathe, his chest rose and fell rapidly against mine, as if he was trying to draw me into himself. His breath ghosted across my lips, sweet and cool.

"There aren't words to describe how incredible you feel," he whispered. He rolled his hips—just the smallest movement—and I clutched his shoulders, a broken sound escaping my throat. "So perfect,"—another gentle thrust that made stars burst behind my eyes—"so beautiful." My vision blurred as tears gathered, but I couldn't look away from his face, couldn't bear to miss a single moment of seeing him like this.

"How does it feel?" he murmured, brushing his lips against my temple.

"Wonderfully full," I gasped. Every sensation built upon the last, waves of pleasure crashing through me until the London night seemed to press in around us, pushing us closer together. I'd never felt anything like this—like I might shatter if he moved, might die if he didn't. The universe had condensed to this single moment, to his body against mine, inside mine, completing me in ways I hadn't known were possible.

"This is so intense," I gasped as his crown hit that spot again, my fingernails biting into his shoulders. "Is it always like this?" *Please don't let me go. Not ever.*

"No, Flynn," he breathed against my neck. "It's never like this."

"Come closer," I pleaded, trying to draw him even deeper. "I need you closer."

"I can feel you." His voice was full of wonder. "Every single beat of your heart. You make me feel so alive, like everything before was just leading me here, to you, to right now."

A particularly deep thrust stole my breath, pleasure crackling through every nerve ending. Then the words tumbled from my lips, a wavering rush I couldn't stop: "I think I'm falling in love with you."

He went utterly still above me, those dark eyes searching mine with an intensity that made my heart stutter.

"I *know* I'm falling in love with you."

His hand found my aching cock, stroking in time with his thrusts, each touch tender and gentle. In that moment, I knew with bone-deep certainty that I belonged to him, belonged with him. My body, my heart, my soul—all of it was his now, had maybe always been meant to be his.

"Fly for me, angel," he murmured, voice thick with emotion. "Fall apart for me."

My fingers tangled in his curls as the pleasure built, higher and higher, my body opening to him completely. When it finally crashed over me, I shattered into stardust, euphoria splitting me wide open. Every colour in existence exploded behind my eyes as I spiralled through the darkness, coming undone below him.

Hot cum pooled between us, warm and sticky on my stomach, and when Seb whispered, "Let me taste you," I didn't hesitate. I gathered some on my trembling fingers and pressed them to his lips, watching in awe as he sucked them clean with his quick and eager tongue.

The sight of it sparked something primal in me—a desperate need to give him everything, all of me. "Bite me," I begged, tilting my head back. "Take me. Take all of me." When he hesitated, a wild thought flashed through my mind—that I'd drag my own nail across my throat if I had to—but then his fangs were there, pressing against my skin, and I arched up to meet them.

The sharp sting of his teeth piercing my skin made me gasp, but the fullness of him still inside me and the knowledge that I was sustaining him transformed the pain into something precious. When he latched on and began to suck, my fingers found their way into his curls, stroking down his back.

Every pull of Seb's mouth sent waves of ecstasy pulsing through me. The dual pleasure from both his bite and his continued movement inside me was unlike anything I'd known—it amplified every sensation, and my cock twitched, unbelievably hardening once again.

He drank and drank and drank, and I let him take, take, *take*, floating in a haze of paradise and surrender, each swallow of my blood drawing us closer together until I couldn't tell where I ended and he began.

The stars above me blurred into streaks of light, and my limbs grew heavier with each passing second, as if I was sinking into deep water.

"Seb," I managed weakly. "Let me see you again. Please."

He made a sound deep in his throat as he pulled away. His tongue traced over the wounds with impossible gentleness, sealing them with careful strokes that sent little shocks of pleasure through my oversensitive body, and I was unable to stop the small whimper that escaped my lips.

When his eyes finally met mine again, they were wild, pupils blown wide. "Lord above me, your *blood*..." He sounded utterly undone. "It's like nothing I've ever known."

His hips snapped forward with new urgency.

"You taste of summer storms." *Thrust.*

"Of starlight and salvation." *Thrust.*

"Like everything I didn't know I was searching for." *Thrust.*

"Like mine."

The force of his thrusts drove the breath from my lungs, pleasure bordering on pain in the most exquisite way. My body felt insanely sensitive after coming, after the bite, but I welcomed every savage snap of his hips. The raw possession in his voice made me feel claimed, marked, *owned*—and I wanted it, wanted to belong to him completely. My hands scrabbled against his back as I tried to draw him even deeper, desperate sounds falling from my lips that I barely recognised as my own.

His rhythm turned brutal, animalistic, each thrust threatening to split me apart. "I'm sorry," he gasped against my neck, his control completely shattered. "I can't— God, Flynn, you feel... too perfect... you taste too good, I can't—"

His whole body trembled against mine like a storm about to break. The last scrap of his careful mask fell away, revealing something ancient and hungry and oh-so beautiful beneath—a creature of pure instinct, raw and wild as a midnight sea.

Wrapping my legs tighter around him, I pulled him desperately closer. I wanted this wild, untamed version of him, wanted everything he had to give, even if it broke me.

His eyes locked with mine as his rhythm faltered, a guttural sound tearing from his throat that was half growl, half sob. He crushed his mouth to mine in a bruising kiss as he came, the extraordinary sensation of his cool release filling me, making me gasp against his lips.

He shifted, settling his weight on top of me as he slipped free.

Wedged between us, my cock was still achingly hard, the bite's euphoria singing through my veins. A desperate need seized me—to be inside him now, to claim him as thoroughly as he'd claimed me. I gathered the mess of our combined release with trembling fingers, reaching between us, all the way to his crease.

"Can I?" I whispered against his jaw, pressing a finger against him. "Please, I need— I want to be inside you."

Seb's eyes widened in surprise before darkening with desire. He gasped as I breached him, the tight ring of muscle yielding to my touch. He was gloriously smooth and cool beneath my fingertip, silken marble.

The bottle of lube suddenly appeared in my hand. I squeezed out far too much in my eagerness, the liquid drenching my hand.

I worked a second finger alongside the first, marvelling at how he opened for me, how his breath caught when I curled them just so. His muscles fluttered around my fingers as I stretched him, preparing him with the same care he'd shown me earlier.

"You don't need to be quite so careful with me," he murmured, a hint of amusement in his voice. "Although this is extremely enjoyable, my body is far more resilient than yours."

I needed no more encouragement.

Gliding my fingers out of him, I knew exactly how I wanted him. Wanted us.

"Turn over," I whispered against his ear, gently guiding him onto his side. "Your turn to be little spoon." He huffed a quiet laugh that turned into a sharp inhale as I pressed into him, slowly sliding forward until we were fitted together like waves meeting shore.

I wrapped one arm beneath him, pulling him flush against my chest until I could feel his spine against my heartbeat. My other hand roamed with desperate wonder across the marble planes of his body—chest, ribs, hip—mapping every inch I could reach before my hand found the gorgeous swell of his dick. The contrast between my fever-hot skin and his cool touch made me shiver, like diving into deep water on a summer's day.

I wished more than anything to make this moment last forever, but pleasure was already building, fierce and unstoppable. The exquisite friction, the feel of him—it was too much, already. I pressed my lips against the nape of his neck in a desperate kiss as I came again, my orgasm crashing over me with such force that the world went white at the edges, and I lost myself completely in the undertow.

Distantly, a guttural moan broke through my haze, cool cum coating my fingers as Seb came into my hand.

I drifted in and out of consciousness. At some point, I slipped out of Seb, though I was doing my darndest to stay inside. Seb whispered things into my ear—gentle, lovely things—but I didn't have the strength to reply.

When I surfaced, it was to Seb hovering above me, a frown creasing his forehead. "Are you okay? Did I go too hard?"

"No," I insisted. "It was beyond perfect." I pushed him down to lie on his chest. "You're perfect."

And then it was a quiet symphony of my shallow breaths and our half-formed words. It was us madly clutching each other, foreheads pressing together as if magnetised. Eventually, he leaned up on his elbow, studying my face with an intensity that made my breath catch. His fingers traced delicate patterns—around my eyebrow, down my cheek, across my bottom lip—as if memorising every detail.

"Sebastián." My voice cracked around his name, overwhelmed by the weight of what we'd just shared, what we'd confessed on this starlit rooftop.

"I know," Seb whispered, pressing a soft kiss to my temple. "I know." Then he studied my face for a moment. "Have I told you yet?" he said, rather seriously. "That your eyes are the exact blue of Toledo's sky?"

I tried not to snort. "No, but that's a good line. I'm definitely up for hearing it again."

A smear of crimson caught my eye—my blood on Seb's chin. Without thinking, I licked my thumb and reached up to wipe it away. His eyes followed the motion, as I offered him my thumb. He caught my wrist, drawing it into his mouth. The cool slide of his tongue made me shiver.

"Is my demon blood still demon-ing?" I tried to joke, but anxiety crept in as the post-sex haze faded. The chill in my veins felt more prominent, an icy thread winding through my chest.

Seb released my thumb with a soft pop. "Yes. The effects are even more powerful."

"Ah, so that's why you like my blood so much." I aimed for lightness but failed.

A flash of thunder across his face. "Flynn." He caught my face between his hands, forcing me to meet his gaze. "Your blood sang to me even before you got yourself marked by that cambion. I meant what I wrote in my diary you so boldly peeked at." His thumb traced my bottom lip. "That night at Wilde Card, watching you dance... I wanted you right then. Especially in that ludicrous jumper with all the holes."

"Hey, that jumper was expensive."

"I'm afraid you got severely scammed, angel."

My heart warmed at the endearment, but then Seb's phone, lying near a chimney pipe, vibrated, making me flinch. I almost asked him not to get it, wanting to extend this perfect moment a little longer.

Tutting, Seb reached for it. He held it above him, the notification clear on the screen:

Felix

Can I turn the rooftop cameras back on now? And how about a little warning next time?

A burst of pure, gut-wrenching mortification shot through me before I descended into hysterical laughter, clutching my sides as tears formed in my eyes. "Oh god," I wheezed, rolling onto my back. "How traumatised is Felix going to be? He'll never look me in the eye again."

Seb groaned, throwing an arm over his face. "I should buy him a new computer. Or five."

Seb's laugh rumbled through his chest. I shifted, sitting up to see London's skyline stretching out before us, a tapestry of twinkling lights that seemed to mirror the stars above.

"Come on," he said, pressing a gentle kiss to my temple. "Let's get you into the actual warmth and start grovelling to Felix."

"Fine," I sighed dramatically, but made no move to get up. "But I demand hot chocolate as compensation."

"Hot chocolate," he promised. "And then we'll face Felix together."

"My hero," I teased, but the words felt more sincere than I'd intended.

I tugged my clothes on slowly, trying not to wince as almost every part of my body ached. Then we made our way down the narrow stairwell, my legs still wobbly. The old floorboards creaked beneath our feet, a familiar symphony I'd grown oddly fond of. At the bottom, Seb pulled me close for one more lingering kiss that made my toes curl against the carpet.

"Perhaps we should face Felix first."

"No, definitely hot chocolate first," I insisted. "I need fortification before dealing with that particular horror."

As if summoned by his name, Felix's voice crackled through the ancient intercom system. "I can hear you, you know. And yes, hot chocolate first. I need time to bleach my brain, anyway."

I buried my face in Seb's shoulder, caught between embarrassment and uncontrollable giggles. "Sorry, Felix!"

"No you're not," came the dry response.

"No," I agreed, meeting Seb's dark eyes. "I'm really not."

Seb's answering smile was worth every bit of embarrassment we'd face. Worth everything.

The comfortable silence lasted a mere second, until Seb went rigid beside me, his whole body tensing like a cat about to pounce. His head cocked to one side as he stared down the corridor.

My laughter died in my throat. "What is it?"

"The phone in my office is ringing." His voice was barely above a whisper. "And it most certainly shouldn't be."

28

Sebastián

The phone's ring pierced my skull with crystalline clarity. Flynn's blood coursed through my system, heightening every sensation to an excruciating degree—the mechanical whir of the rotary dial's spring unwinding, the clatter of brass bells striking their dome.

Ring after ring, unrelenting. No one used this line except White. But this wasn't her. I knew it in my very core.

The receiver felt cool against my palm as I lifted it, saying nothing.

"Hello, Salazar."

A male voice. Unknown. My spine stiffened. They'd used my real name, rather than Black.

"How did you get this number?" The line was a ghost—unregistered, untraceable.

"Come now, I thought you'd be pleased to hear from me." A pause, thick with amusement. "Isn't it so much nicer communicating over the telephone, rather than the silly letters we've been exchanging?"

My grip tightened on the receiver. "Marcus Vale?"

"There's been a change of plan, Salazar."

"What change? The arrangements are all in place for tomorrow morning." My voice remained measured despite the rage building in my chest.

"Tomorrow *evening*." The way he emphasised the word made my dead heart twist.

The receiver almost cracked beneath my fingers. Flynn's countdown ticked in my mind—the spreading chill across his chest, the demon magic consuming him hour by hour. By evening it could be too late.

"No."

"Tomorrow evening, *and* you're to bring your pet."

"My what?"

"Don't play coy, Salazar." His tone shifted, honeyed poison. "That delectable human you've become so attached to. The one you slaughtered Eliza over? And then dispatched two of our deadwalkers when they only wanted to *borrow* him for a while. Very rude of you. They're not easy to replace, you know. Oh, and bring the artifact," he added, almost as an afterthought.

My mind raced. "What artifact?"

"The one from Spain. Your silver crucifix." His tone suggested this should be obvious.

The crucifix? How could he possibly know about that? I'd never shown it to anyone outside of Killigrew Street... *had I?*

Unless...

Surely not.

No.

Please, not him. Anyone but him.

I'd long ago stopped tracking Padre Rodrigo's movements. My diaries theorised he'd died in the 1800s. Vampires were tethered to their sires. Surely I'd have felt *something* if he'd been nearby for months?

Yet tomorrow would mark exactly five hundred years since the night he'd turned me. The symmetry was surely too perfect to be a coincidence.

A snarl ripped from my throat, feral and raw. "What are you playing at, Vale? Who are you working with?"

"My, my. Such aggression." His voice dripped with mock concern. "And here I thought we were having a civilised conversation." The line crackled with static, or perhaps it was the sound of my grip threatening to shatter the receiver entirely. "I look forward to finally meeting you face to face tomorrow, Salazar. Do bring the crucifix. Oh, and don't forget your human. I'd hate to have to collect him myself."

The casual threat in those words made my fangs descend, sharp against my bottom lip. The phantom taste of Flynn's blood still lingered there from earlier, sweet and electric.

"*No,*" I hissed, channeling every inch of my fury into the word. "Adrian Knox for the cambion Damien. That was the deal."

"There's no point getting angry at me, Salazar. These aren't *my* instructions. But you'd do well to follow them. See you tomorrow evening. 11:00 p.m. Richmond Park, by Pen Ponds."

The line went dead.

I slammed the receiver down, an icy chill of rage and fear spreading through my limbs, crystallising my thoughts into jagged shards of ice.

Your pet. Your human.

My fist connected with the desk, slightly splintering the ancient mahogany. The pain barely registered—everything felt distant, frozen, as though I'd been plunged into the depths of an Arctic sea.

These aren't my instructions.

Who could he possibly be referring to? The question frosted over in my mind, refusing to form into anything coherent. I pressed my palms against my temples, pleading for the return of rational thought.

The soft creak of hinges broke through my spiral. I lifted my head to find Flynn standing in the doorway, his figure haloed by the dim hallway light. His blue eyes widened, taking in my face, my posture, the splintered desk beneath my fist. A shadow of understanding crossed his features.

"Flynn," I rasped, his name like broken glass in my throat. "I'm sorry."

29

Sebastián

The Halloween revelers had thinned as we drove towards Richmond Park, their garish costumes and fake blood a mockery of the real horrors awaiting us. A full moon hung bloated in the sky, its silver light filtering through wisps of cloud.

Priya's knuckles were white on the steering wheel as she navigated the van through London's outskirts, her lips moving in silent prayer. The dashboard clock blinked 10:37 p.m.

"Take the next left," I instructed, though my attention kept dragging to the rear of the van.

Flynn sat wedged between Kit and Rory, his head lolling against Kit's broad shoulder. Dark veins spread like a web beneath his translucent skin. The shifters' supernatural heat radiated from their bodies, amplified by the approaching moon, yet Flynn's lips remained blue, his breath forming tiny ice clouds with each shallow exhale. The wolves' heat—possibly the only thing keeping him conscious—was a bitter reminder of my own useless cold, sending further spikes of rage through me.

Behind them, Adrian Knox sat bound and hooded, occasional grunts marking each bump in the road.

"Ten minutes," Priya murmured.

The crucifix burned cold in my pocket. I was torn in two—by the desperate urge to know why Vale had asked me to bring it, and the suffocating dread of what it might mean.

The mere thought of seeing Padre Rodrigo again made bile rise in my throat. Five centuries had passed, yet I could still feel his cold hands blessing my forehead, still hear his whispered promises of salvation even as he damned me.

And the notion of Flynn anywhere remotely near that monster...

I was sure I'd feel less panicked if White had answered her phone this morning. Often just the sound of her voice, her clear directives and her simple logic, calmed me. But she hadn't answered.

We weren't completely on our own. Maxwell was going to do his part from a safe distance. Plus, following behind us was another vehicle containing some of Dale and Mags's pack, backup courtesy of Kit's connections with the South London shifters.

The team radio crackled. "North entrance clear," came the update.

A soft whimper from Flynn had me turning again. His fingers clutched Rory's jacket, knuckles white with effort. Rory, uncharacteristically silent, tightened his protective hold around Flynn's shoulders. Another visible breath escaped Flynn's blue-tinged lips, and I found myself counting the seconds between each one. As expected, he had deteriorated throughout the day, drawing ever closer to the moment the dark magic would consume him.

And now you're essentially delivering him hand-wrapped.

But we could only take this chance, or watch him die.

Rain began to patter against the windscreen, the wipers marking a steady rhythm as London dissolved into parkland. Mist crept across the road, thick tendrils steadily inching towards us.

The van's headlights swept across Sheen Gate Road as Priya pulled into one of the lay-bys near the pedestrian entrance. Beyond the locked vehicle gates, the park stretched into darkness, our section of carefully orchestrated emptiness waiting. The weather had worked in our favour—no sane person would choose to be in Richmond Park on a night like this. Still, Dale's pack had spent the last hour patrolling the Pen Ponds area in high-vis jackets, turning away stubborn dog-walkers with warnings about "emergency tree removals."

"Our cameras are all live, boss," Felix's voice crackled in my earpiece. "I've got eyes on all approaches to the ponds. Dale's pack are in position—nothing else out there currently."

Kit was already moving, helping Flynn out of the van. The bitter wind whipped at us as soon as the door slid open. Flynn stumbled, caught between Kit and Rory's steady hands.

Dale's car pulled in behind us, wolves spilling out silently into formation, shedding their clothes.

Kit and Rory were already showing signs of the inevitable change—muscles twitching, shoulders hunching. The full moon pulled at them mercilessly. Kit caught my eye, and I gave a sharp nod.

He and Rory ducked behind the vehicle. After pained grunts and cracking bones, a massive grey wolf joined us. Rory followed moments later, his golden fur catching the moonlight as he shook out his smaller frame.

Flynn took a sharp intake of breath. Despite his weakened state, wonder blazed in his eyes as he watched the wolves. His hand lifted from where it had been wrapped around his middle, reaching tentatively towards Rory, who padded straight up to him.

"They're beautiful," Flynn whispered. His fingers trembled as they sank into Rory's golden fur. Rory pushed his head further into Flynn's palm, tail wagging slightly as Flynn scratched behind his ears.

Kit maintained a more dignified distance, his grey bulk a sentinel presence beside the van. But even he couldn't resist moving closer when Flynn cast an uncertain glance his way, as if seeking permission to admire them both.

Flynn's blue-tinged lips curved into a smile as he ran both hands over Rory's head, examining the way moonlight caught his fur. "So they can understand me like this? Just like normal?"

"More or less," I said, watching Rory press against Flynn's legs like an oversized house pet. "Their base instincts are stronger in this form—the urge to hunt, the urge to protect. But they're still themselves. Still perfectly capable of rolling their eyes at me when I give orders."

As if to prove my point, Kit huffed what could only be described as a derisive snort.

The moment shattered as another violent shiver racked Flynn's frame. Rory whined, pressing closer.

"Let's go," I said. The sooner we got there, the sooner we could face what was to come.

Through the pedestrian gate, Pen Ponds was a distant glimmer through the mist. The twenty-minute walk there was deathly silent. Kit took point, with Rory bringing up the rear, nipping at our prisoner if he slowed. The shifted wolves from Dale's pack melted into the darkness on either side, their presence betrayed only by occasional glints of eyes in the murk.

I couldn't help but attune to Flynn's stuttering heartbeat, growing more erratic by the moment.

The causeway between the ponds emerged from the fog ahead of us. Something caught my eye—a hulking shape in the mist, but not one of our wolves. Those distinctive sloping shoulders, those gleaming yellow eyes...

"Do you see that?" I asked, pointing. But as soon as the words left my mouth, the hyena shape dissolved into the mist.

Kit and Rory moved to flank me, ears flattened against their skulls.

A figure emerged, as if from thin air.

Marcus Vale himself.

Months of cleaning up Vale's messes, of hunting down his feral offspring when they crossed lines, and this was our first meeting.

He stood exactly as I'd imagined him—tall and aristocratic, his silver-streaked dark hair swept back from sharp features. His navy-blue suit seemed untouched by the fog curling around us.

"Sebastián Salazar." His voice carried the weight of centuries, tinged with an accent I couldn't quite place. "How many of my children have you killed now?"

"Only the ones who threatened innocent lives, Vale. Perhaps if you maintained discipline among your progeny, I wouldn't need to."

A smile played at the corners of his mouth. His gaze slid to Flynn, behind me. "I must say, your pet human makes quite the lovely ice sculpture. Tell me, does it hurt watching him freeze from the inside out?"

The surge of protective rage nearly overwhelmed my control. "Shall we move forward with the exchange of Adrian for Damien? Or did you come here simply to trade barbs?"

Vale's laughter echoed across the water, a sound that belonged in an opera house. He spread his arms wide, as if addressing an invisible audience.

"Oh, my dear Salazar. Do you truly believe that's what we're here to do tonight?"

My gaze swept the parkland—the empty causeway, the still waters, the complete absence of Vale's entourage. No Damien in sight. Just Vale, standing alone like an actor on a stage.

"No."

Of course I hadn't. But Vale had left me no choice but to go along with this ridiculous game.

Vale clapped his hands together in mock delight. "I must say, watching you scramble to arrange this meeting has been thoroughly entertaining. The great Sebastián Salazar, dancing to my tune."

"Where's Damien?" I demanded, stepping forward. The fog swirled around my feet, carrying the scent of damp earth and decay. Flynn's labored breathing behind me drove steel into my spine—every second wasted was another moment closer to losing him.

For a fleeting moment, I was back in my office that morning, Flynn perched on my desk as he fixed my laptop. The sunlight had caught in his hair, turning it to molten gold. He'd looked up, caught me staring, and smiled that smile that made me forget what century I was in. "You're doing it again," he'd murmured. "That thing where you look at me like you're afraid to blink, in case I disappear."

I'd told him that I was afraid. I was very afraid.

Now, hearing him struggle for breath in the fog, I'd never meant those words more.

Vale's lips curled into a patronizing smile. "So impatient. Wanting to rush ahead without appreciating the... artistry of a moment."

He lifted one elegant hand, fingers poised, almost lazy. With a sharp snap, the sound cracked across the water like a gunshot.

My hearing picked up the shuffle of multiple feet approaching through the darkness—too many to count. They moved with inhuman grace, their footsteps barely disturbing the wet grass. The sound came from all directions, closing in on us.

A wolf's howl split the night—one of Dale's pack, the sound carrying clear warning. Another joined it, then another, until the air vibrated with their calls. The hairs on the back of my neck rose as the howls shifted from alert to threat, Kit's low growl joining them.

But something else was happening. The mist over Pen Ponds had begun to move against the wind, coalescing into thick, writhing tendrils that crept across the water's surface. The temperature plummeted. Behind me, Flynn's breathing hitched, a small sound of pain escaping him.

Vale's theatrical demeanour shifted. His shoulders dropped, head inclining slightly as he took a step back from the water's edge. Around us, the approaching vampires slowed their advance, their movements almost becoming more ceremonial than predatory.

Something was coming.

Something was coming, and I was powerless to stop it.

The certainty of it settled in my bones like lead. In five centuries, I'd learned to trust my instincts—they'd kept me alive through revolution, war, betrayal. Now they screamed at me to run, to grab Flynn, my team, and flee. But that wasn't an option.

The surface of the pond began to ripple, though no wind disturbed it. Water moved in ways water shouldn't, drawing up towards the sky as though gravity had forgotten its purpose. My fingers felt compelled to tighten around the crucifix in my pocket as each of my muscles coiled with tension. It was as if it was pulling me inexplicably towards the water.

A vampire lunged from the darkness, fangs bared. Kit's massive form spun, slamming them back into the shadows with brutal efficiency, his teeth flashing in the moonlight. More emerged from the mist—ten, twenty, more than I could count. Vale had far greater numbers than we even knew.

Dale's wolves met them with snarls and snapping teeth, but the vampires weren't fighting to kill. They lunged and retreated, fangs flashing but never fully committing. Each strike pushed us further onto the causeway. They were toying with their prey, herding us exactly where they wanted us.

This was choreographed, like pieces being moved into position.

"Hold," I commanded. "Everyone hold."

The vampires pressed closer, and I scanned their faces, finding some familiar. But no, not *just* vampires. There were cambions among them too, which surely meant...

My eyes scanned the crowd until—*there*.

Damien stood motionless among them, his imposing height making him easy to spot. Every cell in my body wanted to lunge forward, to tear him apart with my bare hands.

He was exactly how I remembered from the night I'd tracked him at Wilde Card—the same sharp jaw, leather jacket, silver chain still glinting at his throat. But something was wrong. The casual arrogance I remembered—how he'd smiled at me before scampering up the brick wall—had been stripped away, replaced by an unsettling neutrality.

Behind me, Flynn made a small sound of recognition. Then, despite everything—the ice in his veins, Kit's warning growl—he stepped forward. "Damien!" His voice cracked across the night like a whip. "You fucking bastard!"

But Damien's eyes, like those of his fellow cambions, remained fixed on the pond, waiting.

Each face was blank, reverent almost, as they formed a perfect circle around us.

We'd been played. *I'd* been played. This whole "exchange," just steps in someone else's dance.

All that remained was to see what horror was about to take centre stage.

"Seb," Priya whispered, "something's—"

A pillar of water rose from the pond, twisting impossibly high. The crucifix tingled against my palm as images scratched at the edges of my mind before slipping away like mist through fingers.

A choked gasp behind me. I spun to see Flynn convulsing, frost spreading up his neck like delicate lacework. He collapsed to his knees, and Priya caught him before he hit the ground. Kit and Rory's protective growls died in their throats as they stared back at the pond.

I turned. The water pillar started to take shape.

Time seemed to slow. The crucifix pulsed against my palm in time with Flynn's failing heartbeat, and for a moment I was drowning in half-formed memories. Incense. Laughter. A summer's day. The scratch of a quill on parchment.

From within the twisting water, a figure began to rise. Not swimming, not walking, but ascending. Dark hair plastered to pale skin, white dress billowing in ways that defied physics. Beautiful and wrong, like a painting left to rot underwater.

Vale dropped to one knee. Around us, every vampire followed suit, heads bowed in perfect synchronisation. Even the wolves fell silent, though whether from fear or some compulsion, I couldn't tell.

As her feet touched the causeway, the water sloughed away, leaving her perfectly dry. She moved with the fluid grace of nobility—a memory stirred, something about... dancing lessons, about proper posture.

The woman lifted her chin, and I found myself staring into eyes I knew intimately—the same eyes that had greeted me in mirrors, year after year after year. The recognition triggered an avalanche of buried images, each one tearing through my mind, bombarding me all at once: those dark eyes spying on Father's dinner parties from behind banisters, sparkling with mischief over forbidden books in the library—

I gasped as the fragments hit me, each one burning like holy water in my veins, each one impossible but undeniably real—

"*Hermano mío,*" she said.

The world stopped.

30

Sebastián

"Magdalena."

Her name tore free from my throat like broken glass, centuries of carefully buried grief and guilt rushing up to choke me.

My sister. My little sister.

The heretic I had condemned to burn, my own hand signing the death warrant.

The air grew thick and still, as if nature itself held its breath. Even Vale's smug expression had frozen, his gaze darting between us with newfound uncertainty.

My legs threatened to give way beneath me. "You're... alive." The words scraped past my lips, barely more than a whisper. Every prayer I'd whispered in the dark, every confession I'd made to empty churches, every moment I'd spent trying to atone for her death—all of it crumbled to ash in my mouth.

She stood before me in the same dress she'd worn that final day—plain white wool. Her dark curls tumbled past her shoulders, so like my own. But her eyes... Her eyes now burned with an unholy light I had never seen in life.

Kit and Rory flanked me, hackles raised, but utterly still. Even Flynn's laboured breathing had gone quiet. The night air hung heavy with the scent of grave dirt and stagnant water.

Magdalena took a step forward, her bare feet leaving no impression in the damp grass. The movement was wrong—too fluid, too smooth. Like a puppet being pulled by invisible strings.

A memory flashed—*the hyena*. That impossible creature that had appeared again and again. Outside the hospital, across from Rising Dough, during the van chase. At the time, I'd questioned my sanity, seeing such a beast in London. But now... those unnatural yellow eyes. My mind reeled as understanding dawned: Magdalena had been there all along, watching me.

You're alive, I'd just said. But... was she truly?

"Brother," she said, English now, her voice carrying the hollow echo of a tomb. "Did you truly think death would keep me from you?"

The endearment twisted like a knife in my chest. I had rehearsed this moment countless times in my darkest hours—what I would say if I could see her one last time. But now, faced with this mockery of my sister, words failed me entirely.

"Brother," she said again, that tomb-echo in her voice growing stronger. "Such guilt you've carried. Such *prayers*." Her lips twisted. "I heard every one."

The water behind her rose higher, defying nature. I fought to keep my voice steady. "How did—"

"How did I survive the flames?" A manic, screeching sound—her laugh. "Your precious mentor saw to that. Rodrigo made sure I burned while clutching your crucifix. A final act of *mercy*, he called it." She spat the word. "But he didn't know what that cross had become. What power it held after my lover's ritual."

My mind reeled. The crucifix? *Lover's* ritual?

The diary pages I'd read days ago suddenly blazed with new meaning—how I'd caught her in the woods, my crucifix found in her possession, sitting on her unholy altar. All this time I believed she'd stolen it out of spite, an act of defiance against the brother who opposed her. But no. She'd needed it for something far darker.

"Oh yes, brother. While you were hunting heretics, I found real power. Found *freedom*." Her gaze drifted to Flynn. "But freedom always has a price."

The water twisted into impossible shapes behind her. "Lilith saved me from the flames. But her help came with conditions. Blood magic, at first. Then darker things. Always more, always stronger."

"Lilith?" Horror clawed up my throat. The Mother of Demons. The First Witch. Even humans knew to fear that name, but to creatures like me, she was far more than just a cautionary tale. *The hyena.* Lilith's favoured beasts, her night-stalking hunters.

My sister's eyes flashed. "Who else would understand? A woman cast out for refusing to bow, to submit?" A bitter smile twisted her lips. "You were so busy playing the perfect son, the perfect Catholic, you never saw how they suffocated me. How they stripped away everything I was. Lilith offered me power instead of submission. Choice instead of chains."

The water behind her surged higher. *Lilith.* Lilith, born from the primordial waters before even Eve was created. The first of God's creatures to harness the seas' power. And now Magdalena commanded water—she wielded the very essence of her demonic patron.

"I tried to tell you, brother. All those times I begged you to listen. But you were too busy hunting heretics to see your own sister drowning in their doctrine. Too blind to see that their God had no place for women except on their knees."

The words cut me deep. How had I not seen her suffering? Too wrapped up in my own ambitions, in Rodrigo's poisoned obsession, the Church's iron grip.

My sister's eyes burned brighter. "But Lilith listened. She saw me, saw my suffering. She became my savior." Magdalena's words turned bitter. "For a price. Five centuries, brother. That's what Lilith gave me. Five hundred years before she claims my soul completely." Her voice faltered. "But she's already taking pieces of me. I can feel myself... slipping away."

I stared at her, unable to reconcile this version of her with the young woman I'd once loved, once played with in our garden under the hot Spanish summer sun. The fragment of memory was hazy, but I could still hear her clear voice rising to Heaven, still see the sunlight catching in her dark curls.

"Do you know how many I've sacrificed to keep her satisfied?" When I said nothing, she snapped, "*Twelve.* Twelve so far." Then she smiled, gesturing at Flynn. "He's my thirteenth. My last. And the darkness inside him, it's ready. I can finally break free of Lilith's demands."

Behind me, Flynn made a choked sound. Whether from fear or the spreading frost, I couldn't tell.

The water churned violently behind her. "This is my way out. Thirteen vessels of concentrated dark magic. Thirteen souls prepared by my cambions, their power distilled into something pure enough to satisfy her. To buy my complete freedom."

Vale took his position beside Magdalena. How long must he have been working with her, watching over me, waiting for this moment? Had she bargained with Vale just to toy with me? No, to *find* me. To help reclaim the crucifix. The very cross that had saved her, that she needed for this final ritual.

"Twelve so far." She smiled, an awful thing, too many teeth gleaming in the dark. "The thirteenth sacrifice will complete the ritual, break Lilith's hold forever." Something desperate crept into her voice. "Time's running out, brother. Either I complete this, or Lilith drags what's left of my soul to Hell. Do you want that on your conscience, *brother*?"

The water behind her surged higher, no longer merely defying nature but seeming to mock it. "This thirteenth requires something more. How fitting that the brother who condemned me has brought me the crucifix that started it all." Her sneer pierced my soul. "And of course..." Her gaze slid to Flynn. "Our final sacrifice."

"No!"

Priya's shout cracked through the night like a gunshot. She stood beside Flynn, practically vibrating with defiance, hands raised in a protective stance.

My sister's presence had held me in a trance of horror and guilt, but Priya's cry—and Flynn's face, twisted in terror—snapped me back to reality. The weight of five centuries of remorse couldn't outweigh my duty to protect them.

Magdalena's laughter echoed across the park. "How sweet. The little witch thinks she can interfere." She cocked her head. "Tell me, girl, did your grandmother teach you real magic? Or just pathetic charms?"

"Leave her—" I started, but Magdalena's hand shot out.

Priya's body lifted from the ground as if yanked by invisible strings. She flew backwards, her scream cut short as she slammed into a large tree with a sickening crack. Her body crumpled to the ground.

Kit's wolf form lunged forward with a snarl, but Magdalena's power held him in place. Even Vale took a step back, swagger replaced by genuine fear.

"Begin," Magdalena commanded, and with a flick of her wrist, the crucifix tore itself from my grip, flying across the space between us to land in her waiting hand.

31

Flynn

old. So damned cold.

My pulse skipped and lurched, my heart straining against the ice crystallising in my chest. Each feeble beat felt like ice shattering—sharp, jarring. The natural ebb and flow of life stuttering to a glacial crawl. My lungs too—every breath felt like swallowing shards of metal. But worse than the physical pain was watching Seb, seeing the raw anguish on his face as his sister, the one he'd thought he'd killed, taunted him.

The water rose around us in twisting columns. Some distant part of me recognised its pull, its familiar song, like the waves back home in Braymore Bay. But this water was *wrong*. Corrupted.

Vale began to chant in a language that set my teeth on edge. Around us, perhaps a dozen figures stepped forward. With horrible, wet sounds, they began to shed their human skin like snakes sloughing off dead scales. I watched, unable to look away, as Damien's face—the same handsome face that had entrapped me—split down the middle, peeling away to reveal something ancient and twisted beneath. His new form was sleek, scaled, with too many joints in his limbs. When he opened his mouth to join Vale's chant, rows of needle-sharp teeth gleamed in the moonlight.

I wanted to reach for Seb, to say something, anything, to ease the torment in his eyes. But the water wrapped around me like chains, holding me in place as Magdalena raised the crucifix.

Twelve points of sickly purple light appeared around us. Twelve lights—the harvested power of her previous victims, waiting for me to complete their circle.

The water tightened its grip, and my feet left the ground. Magdalena's voice rose above Vale's chant, speaking words that made my ears ring. The purple lights began to spin, faster and faster, leaving sickly trails in their wake.

The frost had crept up my neck and down my arms. My fingers had gone numb, my legs trembled, but beneath all that piercing cold, something stirred.

The magic cultivating inside me—I felt the moment it was finally, *finally* complete. A visceral thing, like a key turning in a lock, like ice cracking in spring.

The water around me wasn't just water anymore. With every pulse of those lights, I could feel it changing, becoming more like the sea during a storm—wild, untamed. Alive.

And I knew the sea.

God, did I know the sea.

Every summer spent on my grandfather's boat. Every winter watching the waves crash against Braymore's cliffs. Every secret moment alone on the beach, being exactly who I was, not who everyone needed me to be.

The water trembled. Magdalena's voice faltered.

I thought of all the times I'd run away. First from myself, then from my family. From Tom. But here, now, with Seb's anguished eyes on me and a demon's power trying to claim me, I finally stopped running.

I reached out—not with my frozen hands, but with something deeper. Something that remembered salt spray and storm winds and the endless power of the tide.

And the water responded.

The liquid chains shattered. Droplets hung suspended in the air like stars, catching the purple light. For a moment, everything was still—Vale's chanting cut off, the cambions frozen mid-step, Magdalena's eyes widening in disbelief.

Then the water answered my call.

It came surging up from the pond, from the waterlogged earth beneath our feet, from the very air itself. It came with the force of Braymore's winter storms, with the strength of waves that had carved the coastline. The cambions screamed as it slammed into them, their scaled bodies thrown against the trees.

"Impossible," Magdalena whispered. The crucifix trembled in her grip. "Lilith's power cannot be—"

"This isn't Lilith's power." My voice didn't sound like my own. It carried echoes of tide pools and ocean depths, of secrets whispered to empty beaches. "This is mine."

Water swirled around me—not Magdalena's corrupted tempest, but pure and wild and *free*. Like I finally was.

The water roared around us, a tempest of my making. Through the spray, I saw Kit and Rory's massive shapes lunging for the nearest cambions, joined by the other wolves. Relief coursed through me when I found Priya had got to her feet. She had her back against the tree, her blade pointed at a vampire with long silver hair.

I took one stumbling half step towards her, but the power inside me—it was too much. Like trying to contain an ocean in a teacup. My vision blurred, darkness creeping at the edges.

Something warm and metallic filled my mouth. I spat, watching red droplets scatter across the ground. The frost inside me wasn't gone, but somehow fire now burned through my veins. So much fire. Too much. Too strong.

"Flynn!" Seb's voice cut through everything else. He was beside me suddenly, his hands gripping my shoulders. "Your heart's failing. The magic—it's killing you."

I could barely focus on his face, but I managed to lift my hands. The water responded instantly, surging up around us in a perfect circle, creating a barrier between us and the chaos beyond. Inside our private whirlpool, the sounds of battle became muffled, distant.

"Let me help you." Seb's fingers brushed my jaw, tilting my face up to his. "I can drink from you—draw out some of the tainted blood. It might buy us time."

I tried to speak, but I could only manage a wet cough.

Seb's eyes became wild, desperate. "Please, Flynn. Trust me."

The water continued to spiral around us, but each surge felt like it was tearing something vital from my chest. I nodded weakly, already tilting my head to expose my neck.

Seb's fangs sank into my flesh with sharp precision. The initial sting melted into a familiar warmth that spread through my limbs. His grip on my shoulders tightened as he drew the blood from my veins, each pull making the intense pressure inside me ease slightly.

I closed my eyes, letting the muffled sounds of the park wash over me. Metal clashed. Gunshots fired. Wolves snarled. Priya's voice rang out in sharp syllables that made the air crackle. Through it all, the water continued its relentless dance around us, responding to my will even as I weakened. The roar of it filled my ears like the crash of waves against Braymore's harbour wall during a storm.

My fingers found Seb's hand where it gripped my shoulder. I squeezed, his fingers interlaced with mine instantly, and through our connection, I tried to pour everything I couldn't say into that touch.

After what felt like both seconds and hours, Seb's cool mouth left my neck, and he pulled back. When I opened my eyes, the change in him was dramatic. His skin seemed to glow from within, power radiating from him in invisible waves that made the very air vibrate. His eyes blazed like twin supernovas, and when he moved, it was with such fluid grace that he appeared to blur at the edges.

"Flynn," he breathed, and even his voice held new power, resonating in my chest like thunder. "Your blood—"

"Let's go," I said quickly. "Let's find her. Find your sister and end this."

The water barrier collapsed as my concentration wavered, revealing the battlefield Richmond Park had become. Kit had Vale pinned against an oak tree, both of them bloodied but neither yielding. Rory darted between the remaining cambions, a golden blur of fur and fangs. Near the pond's edge, a battered Priya now wielded twin pistols, each shot finding its mark with surgical precision.

But Magdalena herself—my stomach lurched at the sight.

She stood at the heart of it all, her crucifix now blazing with purple fire. The twelve points of light had reformed around her, spinning faster than before. When she saw Seb, saw the power radiating from him, her face twisted into something inhuman.

"Brother," she snarled, but her voice echoed with something else. Something ancient. "What have you done?"

Seb's new power thrummed in the air between them. "I'm ending this, Magdalena. You, Lilith, all of it."

The crucifix's glow intensified as Magdalena lunged for me, her movements impossibly fast. My heart skipped as terror froze me in place—but before she could reach me, Seb materialised between us.

His hand shot out, catching her throat mid-leap. The violent impact created a shockwave that rippled through the air. Magdalena's feet dangled above the ground as Seb held her effortlessly, strength evident in every line of his body, the raw power emanating from him making my skin erupt in gooseflesh.

"You dare—" she choked out, but Seb's grip tightened.

He moved like liquid mercury, spinning her away from me and slamming her into the ground. The earth cracked beneath her, spider-web fissures spreading outward from the point of impact. The crucifix flew from her grasp, skittering across the grass. I tracked its movement, my palm throbbing at the memory of it burning my skin. Now it seemed to pulse with malevolent purpose.

Magdalena recovered instantly, launching herself at Seb with unnatural speed. But he was faster—*so* much faster. In a blur, he dodged her attack, then caught her arm and used her momentum to throw her through the air. She hit the pond's surface with such force that water exploded upward in a ten-foot geyser.

As I watched Seb and Magdalena locked in their violent dance, something twisted painfully in my chest that had nothing to do with the magic ravaging my body. The cruel symmetry of it all struck me with terrible clarity—Seb condemning his sister to death five centuries ago, and now being forced to do it again.

The anguish etched across his face told the whole story—the torment, the regret, the unbearable weight of history repeating itself. The brother who had never forgiven himself. No matter how this ended, Seb would be broken by it. He'd spend another five centuries—or however long vampires lived—haunted by this night.

The water around my feet rippled with my distress. "There has to be another way," I whispered, even as I knew there probably wasn't. But watching Seb prepare to kill his sister a second time... God, it was unbearable.

"Wait. Stop!" My voice was weak, but it carried across the chaos. "I understand, Magdalena."

Magdalena picked herself up and stepped towards me, purple fire still dancing in her eyes. "You understand nothing, *child*."

"You're right. I don't pretend to understand what you suffered—being condemned by your own brother, burned at the stake... it's unimaginable." I swallowed hard. "But I do know something about hiding. About fear. About being trapped by others' expectations."

Something flickered across her face—recognition, perhaps. Or pain.

"They taught me to hate myself too," I said softly. "Not the same way, not with the same consequences. Nothing like what you endured. But I see how desperate you must have been for any escape, any alternative to their cruelty."

The purple light wavered. For just a moment, I saw past the demon-touched creature to the young woman she must have been—before the Inquisition, before Lilith, before her own brother was turned against her.

"Magdalena," Seb stepped forward, his voice breaking on her name. "It was my blindness that condemned you. My weakness. I was so desperate to belong, so caught in Rodrigo's manipulation that I betrayed the one person I should have protected above all others."

"You still know nothing of what they did to us!" Ignoring Seb, Magdalena spoke directly to me. "What their 'God' demanded. While my brother hunted innocents, I watched them burn women for daring to read. For healing. For refusing to bow." The purple light pulsed with her words. "Lilith offered freedom."

"Freedom?" Seb stepped closer. "Look at what that freedom cost. Look at what you've become. Trading one prison for another, trading their cruelty for Lilith's."

She finally rounded on him, water spraying up around her feet. "And what would you know of it? You, their perfect son, their perfect soldier—"

"Their perfect victim." Seb's face softened, leaving him looking suddenly vulnerable. "I was so blind, Magdalena. So caught in Rodrigo's web that I couldn't see..." His voice broke. "I couldn't see he was manipulating me, just as Lilith manipulated you. We were both children," he whispered. "Both so desperate to belong that we let monsters shape us."

"Magdalena, he's spent five centuries torturing himself over what happened to you," I added, praying that the conviction in my voice would get through to her. "It wasn't truly Sebastián who condemned you—it was the Church that twisted him, just as Lilith has twisted you."

Magdalena gaze fixed on me with something like wonder. The purple fire in her eyes dimmed, replaced by an ancient, searching look that seemed to pierce straight through my skin, my bones, down to something deeper.

I couldn't move. Not from magic this time, but from the weight of her scrutiny. Like she was reading every moment of my life—the years of suffocating silence, the crushing weight of expectations I could never meet, desires I could never voice.

"You've carried much pain," she whispered, her voice soft and wondering. "And much guilt."

Pure agony suddenly ripped through my chest, as if someone had thrust their fist between my ribs and squeezed. The darkness inside me resurged—the bitter cold that had been growing and growing, claiming me piece by piece. My vision blurred, the world tilting sideways, and more copper burst onto my tongue as my mouth filled with blood.

I stumbled, my legs turning to water beneath me, but Seb caught me before I hit the ground. His arms were steel bands around my waist, his chest solid against my back. My head fell back against his shoulder as another wave of agony tore through me, and I bit back a cry. Despite everything—the pain, the darkness, the terror—there was something comforting about being held by him. Like finding shelter in the middle of a storm.

But every heartbeat felt wrong now, too fast, too hard, like my heart might explode from the pressure building inside it. I tried to say Seb's name, but my throat seized, the word dissolving into a strangled gasp.

Seb's eyes widened, panic creasing his brow. "Flynn? Flynn, stay with me." His voice sounded like it was coming from the end of a long tunnel, fading in and out.

I clutched at his arms, fingernails digging into his sleeves as another wave of agony swept through me. This one felt different—sharper, more insistent. Like the darkness was no longer content to simply leech away at my life, but was instead tearing into me with vicious intent.

"Seb—" I gasped out his name. My heart jackhammered erratically in my chest, each beat slower than the last. "I... I don't think..."

"No." The single word was a growl, his arms tightening around me in a grip of iron. "Don't you dare, Flynn Carter. Don't you dare leave me."

I tried to speak again, to tell him how much he meant to me, but a fresh spasm of pain stole my breath. Tears burned my eyes as the darkness closed in, blotting out everything but the sound of my faltering heartbeat.

This was it, then. The end of my story.

An unexpected wave of regret washed over me, quickly followed by anger. It wasn't fair—not after finally having the courage to escape Braymore. To start living my life. Not after the gift of Seb's love, brief though it had been. To have it all snatched away like this...

No. I refused to accept it. Digging deep, I pulled together every last scrap of strength and forced my eyes open, twisting my head.

Seb's face swam into view, his expression a mask of anguish. Those fathomless dark eyes I loved so much were awash with unshed tears, his lips pressed into a tight line as if bracing himself.

For what? My death?

The thought ignited a spark of defiance deep within me. With trembling fingers, I reached up and traced the sharp line of his jaw, drawing his gaze to mine. At the look of raw desolation in Seb's eyes, I finally understood the depth of his suffering, the centuries of loneliness and self-denial that had brought him to this point.

"Promise me..." Each word felt like shards of glass in my throat, but I persisted. "Promise you won't go back to how you were before. Alone. Refusing to let anyone in."

"Flynn, I—"

"Promise me," I rasped again, fighting against the rising tide of darkness. "You've suffered enough, Seb. Let yourself find happiness, whatever that means for you. Don't... Don't shut yourself away again. Do it for me."

Bending down, he pressed his forehead to mine, his arms flexing around me in an embrace so tight it drove the breath from my weakened lungs.

"I promise," he whispered, the words containing a torrent of anguish. "Whatever you need of me, I swear it. But stay with me, Flynn. Don't leave me. I... Flynn, I love you. I've existed through five hundred years of darkness, convinced that love was a luxury I didn't deserve. But you... You've brought light into every shadow. I love you with a ferocity that terrifies me, Flynn, and I cannot—will not—imagine continuing this endless existence without you in it."

But even as the words left his lips, I could feel myself slipping away. The pain was fading, the darkness no longer something to fight against, but a soft embrace drawing me down into blessed oblivion.

I let my eyes drift shut, savoring the feel of Seb surrounding me. With the last of my strength, I brushed away the tear that lingered on his cheek.

"I'm sorry," I murmured, the words little more than a whisper on the night breeze. "I'll find you again some day, Sebastián."

The darkness claimed me, sweeping me away into its endless void.

32

El Perdón de la Hereje

He was dead.

The sight of my brother, crumpled over the lifeless form of the boy, stirred something deep within my ancient, weary bones. Over five hundred years had passed since I'd seen Sebastián weep—truly weep—as he did now. His shoulders shook with the force of his grief as he clutched his lover to his chest.

A wolf's mournful howl pierced the night air, a chorus of anguish that matched my brother's pain. How fascinating, that these creatures showed such loyalty to him. Beyond our circle of power, the sounds of battle still raged—snarls and screams as vampire and wolf tore at each other in the darkness.

Flynn Carter lay limp in his arms, pale as marble, those blue eyes that had blazed with such defiance now glazed and empty. What a waste of potential. His power had been extraordinary, the way he'd commanded the water, pure and untainted.

"Hermano mío," I whispered. "Still so weak for love."

Sebastián didn't look up, his fingers threading through Flynn's matted blond hair. After he'd condemned me to burn on the pyre, my darling brother hadn't come to watch. I'd suffered alone. Simply me, and the crucifix.

I clutched the crucifix tighter, feeling its corrupted power pulse through my veins. The sacrifice was almost complete. My thirteenth soul, claimed by Lilith's darkness. Soon, I would be free of her chains.

Yet... something in his broken sobs called to me. Perhaps it was the echo of our shared blood, or a fragment of the loving sister I'd once been. I reached down, my fingers hovering over his trembling shoulder.

The moment I touched him, memories crashed through me—not my own, but his.

Padre Rodrigo's study materialised. The priest's hand rested on my brother's shoulder as he whispered poison in his ear. "God has chosen you, Sebastián. These heretics threaten His divine order." Day after day, year after year, feeding him lies wrapped in scripture until my brother's very soul belonged to him.

Then that terrible night. Sebastián on his knees before Rodrigo, tears streaming down his face. "Please, Father. She's my sister. There must be another way—" The crack of Rodrigo's hand across his cheek echoed through the chamber. "You dare question God's will? Your sister consorts with demons."

The day of my execution. Sebastián locked in his chambers, screaming himself hoarse as they dragged me away. He'd tried to break down the door, bloodying his fists against the wood. "Magdalena! *¡Perdóname, hermana!*"

Later that same night. Rodrigo offering him wine laced with laudanum. "Drink, my darling. Ease your pain." My brother's sluggish confusion as Rodrigo's fangs sank into his throat. The horror in his eyes as Rodrigo forced his own blood past Sebastián's lips.

The hunger that followed was monstrous. In those early days of his transformation, he'd curl into himself, racked with bloodlust and grief. My name was a constant prayer on his lips: "Magdalena, forgive me. *Lo siento, hermana mía.*"

Five centuries of carrying my ghost. Every ten years, reading his journals, torturing himself with the memory of my death. Visiting Spain, standing where the pyre had been, leaving white roses in the ashes.

All this time, I'd thought him my betrayer. But we'd both been betrayed.

My brother had carried such pain, for so long. Until...

As my gaze slid to the dead man in his arms, another wave of memories barraged me—not his anguish this time, but his joy.

Flynn Carter, that very first night. The way his face had lit up at the music, swaying with such abandon. Sebastián had watched from the shadows, transfixed by those graceful movements, seeing something pure and untamed that called to his own trapped soul.

The moment Flynn had looked up at him, terror melting into trust as Sebastián promised to keep him safe. *Keep him safe like he was never able to keep me.* And Flynn had believed him completely, without question. Like a gift freely given.

Flynn in the kitchen with another. Shy, awkward. Making him laugh, drawing him out of his shell. Sebastián's heart had swelled watching them, seeing Flynn's gentle persistence.

His laughter—god, his laughter. Like summer rain after drought, fresh and clean and healing. The sound had washed away decades of my brother's carefully constructed barriers.

Those ridiculous red-chequered pyjamas he wore. Sebastián's fingers itched to touch the soft flannel, to pull Flynn close and breathe in the scent of home that clung to the fabric.

Flynn had done what I was unable to—helped Sebastián face the darkness of his past. Held his hand as they read those damning diaries together. Showed him that even the deepest wounds could heal with enough care and patience.

And their kisses... Those love-soaked kisses. Each one saturated with such tenderness it made my heart ache. The way Flynn would cradle Sebastián's face between his palms... How my brother's eyes would flutter closed, centuries of loneliness dissolving in that tender press of lips.

I stared at Flynn's lifeless form—this bright, beautiful boy who'd made Sebastián whole again. Reminded him the world isn't all shadow and darkness and monsters.

Now dead.

"I thought…" I peered down at my hands, where purple light still danced beneath my skin. "I thought I was choosing power. Freedom. But I'm just another instrument of torture."

A presence stirred in the shadows—vast, ancient, and terrible. *She* had arrived.

Vale stepped forward, his eyes gleaming with desperate calculation. "My lady," he said, voice honey-smooth. "Think carefully. We can find another way. The boy's death need not be in vain—we could harness his power, break your bonds *and* keep your gifts."

"*Sweet child.*" Lilith's voice poured like ice water down my spine. Her presence manifested as a towering shadow, beautiful and terrible. "*Have you forgotten all I gave you? The strength to survive when others would have burned you to ash? The power to make those who wronged you suffer?*"

My hands trembled. "You gave me nothing. You *used* me, just as Rodrigo used my brother."

"*I saved you.*" Lilith's form rippled closer, her touch like frost against my cheek. "*When your own flesh and blood condemned you, I alone showed mercy. And now you would throw away centuries of preparation? For what? A brother who betrayed you and his mortal pet?*"

Vale circled closer. "The Mother speaks truth. Think of what we could accomplish together, Magdalena. No more serving—we could rule. The power you've gathered, combined with what's left in the boy's corpse…"

At this, Sebastián's head snapped up, his grief momentarily eclipsed by rage. His eyes blazed crimson in the darkness, fangs bared in a feral snarl.

"Touch him and I will tear you apart," he growled, his voice barely human. He clutched Flynn's body tighter against his chest, protective even now. "Haven't you taken enough?"

Lilith's presence seemed to expand at his defiance, the shadows around us growing denser, colder. The air crackled with ancient power as my brother and the Mother of Demons regarded each other—predator facing predator across the centuries.

"*You are mine,*" Lilith purred. "*You have always been mine.*"

The purple fire beneath my skin flared in response to her call. For a moment, I wavered. The promise of power, of true freedom, sang in my veins like poison.

But then I looked at my brother, still cradling Flynn's body, and saw the echo of my own past. Another soul twisted by those who claimed to love them. Another life corrupted by false promises.

"No," I whispered. Then louder: "LIES! All of it—LIES!"

The twelve points of light surrounding us pulsed violently as my power surged. Vale stumbled back, his mask of concern shattering into fear.

"You never wanted to free me," I snarled at Lilith. "You wanted to own me. To make me as much a monster as you." I knelt beside Flynn's body, placing one hand over his still heart, the other gripping the crucifix. "But I choose differently now."

Sebastián reached out to touch my knee. "Sister—"

"Five hundred years of a half existence, watching the world from shadows," I whispered. "You ran from your past through endless cities, while I haunted crossroads and crypts. Both of us watching time slip past like water, seeing mortals live and die while we remained frozen. But where you sought escape, I sought power. Creating cambions, corrupting souls, preparing vessels dark enough to satisfy Lilith's hunger."

I looked down at my hands, still bearing the transparency of something not quite alive, not quite dead.

"Five centuries of borrowed time, each decade taking another piece of my humanity. All these sacrifices. Creating monsters to serve a monster." My eyes met Sebastián's. "Just like they did to us. Let me do this, brother." My smile felt foreign on my face, gentle in a way I'd forgotten how to be. "Let me choose to save instead of destroy."

The magic surged through me as I began the transfer, but this time I pulled the power inward rather than outward. Five centuries of collected power, twelve souls worth of darkness, all of it flooding into my own essence. My skin turned translucent, dark veins spreading like cracks across my form.

"*Foolish child.*" Lilith's voice scraped across my soul like winter frost. "*After everything we shared?*"

I poured more power into Flynn's lifeless form, feeling my own existence beginning to fracture. "You never shared anything," I gasped. "You only took. Like them. Like Rodrigo. Like all of them."

The air grew thin as Lilith's darkness coalesced around us. "*Then you choose death? Again?*"

"No." I met her terrible gaze. "I choose life. His life. My brother's happiness." The cracks in my skin spread wider, purple light bleeding through. "I choose to end this cycle of suffering."

Flynn's chest rose suddenly beneath my palm—a sharp, desperate inhale. His eyes flew open, brilliant blue and full of life.

"Flynn?" Sebastián's voice broke on the name, raw with disbelief. His hands trembled as they cupped Flynn's face. "Flynn, *mi amor*?" When Flynn's gaze focused on him, recognition dawning, Sebastián let out a sound somewhere between a sob and a laugh—the sound of a man who had lived only in darkness suddenly finding light.

My brother looked to me. "Magdalena..." He reached for me, but purple flames erupted between us. For the first time, I saw him truly look at me—not the monster I'd become, but the sister he'd loved. The sister he'd mourned. "*Gracias, hermana,*" he whispered. "After everything I did—

"It's alright, brother." Tears left burning tracks down my cheeks as my body began to dissolve. "I'm choosing this. The way they never let us choose before."

As my consciousness scattered into stardust, I glimpsed one final image: my brother, cradling Flynn against his chest, his face transformed. The weight of five centuries finally lifted from his shoulders—the guilt, the self-loathing, the endless penance. In its place bloomed something I'd forgotten existed: hope. The rigid lines of his face softened as he pressed his forehead to Flynn's, whispering words I couldn't hear but understood nonetheless. A promise. A future. The man who had spent half a millennium punishing himself for my death was finally allowing himself to live. And in that moment, I knew my sacrifice had truly set us both free.

Forgive me, brother. And thank you for teaching me how to love again.

33

Flynn

First came the spark—a single, electric pulse deep in my chest. Then the flood: blood rushing, nerves firing, lungs expanding. I breached the surface of death gasping, drowning on air, every nerve ending raw and screaming as sensation flooded back. Seb's arms were the only solid thing in a world that wouldn't stop spinning.

Fragments of reality pieced themselves back together—the damp earth beneath me, the bite of cold wind, Seb's arms around my shoulders.

"Flynn," he said. "Flynn, look at me."

I forced my eyes to focus on his face. Tears had carved tracks through the blood and dirt on his cheeks. His dark curls were wild, eyes wide with disbelief as his hands cupped my face.

"You were dead." His thumbs traced my cheekbones. "You were dead."

Another ragged breath tore through me. My hand drifted to my chest, finally free of the cold chill that had tormented me for so long, my countdown towards death. The relief was staggering—I hadn't realised how heavy that darkness had been. Now I could breathe again, really breathe, without that crushing weight pressing against my lungs. "What happened?"

"Magdalena." Seb's gaze drifted past me.

Scattered purple embers danced on the breeze like ethereal fireflies before blinking out of existence one by one.

"She saved you." He drew a shuddering breath. "For me."

"Why?" The word came out hoarse.

"Because she saw what you mean to me. The depth of my love." His forehead pressed against mine. "She chose to break free from Lilith's hold, even though it meant..." He couldn't finish.

His arms tightened around me, crushing me against his chest as he buried his face in my neck. I felt the tremors running through him, heard the catch in his breathing. Then his hands were running up and down every inch of my body, slipping under my T-shirt to press his hand against my chest, seeing if the chill still marked me.

"Seb—" I swallowed down a lump of emotion. "I love you too. And I'm fine. It's completely gone."

His lips curved into a beautiful smile.

My gaze slipped past him to the pond, reaching out with my mind like I had before. Nothing. The water remained still, lifeless. "I... can't feel the water anymore," I said, disappointment seeping through me.

"It was the dark magic reaching its peak—like a pressure cooker finally exploding."

A sound like breaking branches drew my attention. A figure stepped forward—Damien, but not how I first met him. His scaly skin had turned an oily black, stretched tight over elongated limbs. His fingers ended in curved talons, and when he smiled, rows of needle-sharp teeth gleamed in the moonlight.

"Such a waste," he purred. "All this death, when you could have just given yourself to us willingly." His eyes fixed on me, hungry and cold. "I could have made it pleasurable, your death. Could have shown you ecstasy beyond imagining."

My heart thundered against my ribs, but I forced myself to my feet, Seb beside me. "Like you showed those other victims?"

Damien laughed hollowly. "They served their purpose. And there's still time for you to join them."

As he stepped towards me, a growl rumbled through the air—low, dangerous, promising violence.

"You will die for what you did."

Seb moved so fast my eyes could barely track him—one moment he stood beside me, the next his hand was around Damien's throat. Otherworldly strength radiated from him, an aura of raw power that made the air crackle. Damien's black eyes widened in shock, his talons scrabbling uselessly against Seb's grip.

"You dare touch what's mine?"

Damien broke free, slashing at Seb with razor-sharp claws, but Seb dodged each strike with fluid grace, still possibly feeling the effects of my blood.

Fear flickered across Damien's twisted features as Seb caught his arm mid-swing and wrenched. The crack of breaking bone echoed across the park. Damien howled, black blood oozing from the wound, but the sound cut off as Seb slammed him into the ground.

"*Por mi amor,*" Seb growled, pinning Damien down. "*Por todas las víctimas.*"

The silver dagger appeared in Seb's hand, its blade gleaming with an inner light. Damien thrashed, his confidence shattered, reduced to animal panic. Seb drove the dagger into Damien's heart. Black blood erupted from the wound, turning to ash as it hit the air. His scream cut off as his flesh crumbled away, leaving nothing but a pile of dark ash.

I couldn't take my eyes off Seb as he stood, dagger still clutched in his hand, power radiating from him in waves. Our gazes locked, his eyes ablaze. Perhaps I should have been frightened, but instead I felt drawn to him like a moth to flame. Blood stained his shirt, his chestnut curls were dishevelled from the fight, but he'd never looked more beautiful.

The silver dagger slipped from his fingers, landing in the grass with a soft thud. The rage melted from his features, replaced by something softer—so human, so vulnerable. He took a step towards me, then another, until barely a breath separated us.

His hand cupped my cheek, thumb brushing over my skin as if checking I was real. I leaned into his touch, my eyes fluttering closed for just a moment.

"Flynn," he breathed, and even the way he said my name made my heart skip.

When our lips met, it felt like coming home to a place I'd never been. All the fear, all the running, all the nights spent staring at dark waters wondering about my choices—they crystallised into this perfect moment of certainty. His kiss was gentle at first, careful, like I might shatter. But when I pressed closer, something broke in him. His arms wrapped around me, and suddenly we were drowning in each other, finding air in the spaces between breaths.

This was real. The most real thing. Inevitable. This was falling and flying all at once, and knowing someone would be there to catch you.

When we finally broke apart, I could still feel the ghost of his kiss lingering on my lips, like an echo of everything we could be. Everything we would be.

Seb smiled, that soft, lovely curve I'd only ever seen on his face when he looked my way.

A wolf's howl shattered the moment, and I became aware the night air was filled with the stench of death. Bodies lay scattered across Richmond Park—cambions with their flesh half melted, vampires mauled and bleeding, and near the oak tree, a grey wolf lay motionless, its fur matted with blood. My stomach lurched at the sight, but thankfully it wasn't Kit—he was limping towards us, favouring his right leg. Rory followed, golden fur splashed with dark crimson, but his movements still fluid and strong. Priya was stumbling after them while rifling through a pack around her waist, bandages streaming out.

"Where's Vale?" Seb snapped.

"The vampires slipped away." Kit's voice made me jump. I turned—and immediately regretted it. He stood completely naked, bare to the world. I pointedly snapped my eyes back to Seb's face. Thank goodness for the darkness.

"They freed Adrian Knox and ran for it. With all the wounded, the pack had no choice but to let them go," Kit continued. "They'd already lost one life. No sense risking more bloodshed."

My gaze once again found the dead wolf, surely an acquaintance of Kit and Rory, if not a friend. Pain twisted in my stomach as a nude female pack member pulled the wolf's enormous head onto her lap, whispering something into their ear.

Seb sighed deeply, and I knew he'd already absorbed the weight of the death. "Agreed."

Kit made a grunting sound, and I couldn't help but notice the way his muscles rippled beneath his skin. Fresh scratches marked his shoulders, already beginning to heal.

"You can stay shifted if you need to," Seb said. "If the pull of the moon is too much."

Kit's jaw clenched, another ripple of tension moving through his powerful frame. "I'll manage." His eyes darted between the trees. Something about his stance changed—less wolf, more soldier.

"Kit." Seb's voice was gentle but firm as he gripped Kit's shoulder. "Are you with us?"

Kit's eyes had taken on a glassy quality, fixed on some distant point. His chest rose and fell in quick bursts.

"Talk to me," Seb pressed, stepping closer. The tenderness in his voice surprised me—I'd never heard him speak to anyone that way except me. "What do you need?"

For a moment, Kit remained frozen. Then he drew in a deep breath through his nose, held it, and released it slowly. A ghost of his usual wry smile tugged at his lips.

Kit's hand came up to pat Seb's where it gripped his shoulder. "Nothing to worry about, boss. I'll call Maxwell, get him on this cleanup."

Nodding at Kit once, Seb straightened his shoulders as he shifted into leader mode, barking other instructions. The familiar, commanding tone was back, though his hand kept finding ways to brush against mine.

"Thank you," he told the wolves who'd fought alongside us. With blood-soaked fur, and the full moon illuminating their pained eyes, they pressed tightly together. They'd lost one of their own, whereas we'd gotten lucky. "We couldn't have done this without your support. You've done London a great service. Our children will sleep safer tonight. But my deepest condolences for your lost family member. Killigrew Street will remember this."

Most of them melted into the shadows, leaving just our core team. Tension still radiated from Seb—Vale's escape clearly bothered him. I wished he wouldn't dwell on that failure. We'd won. We'd survived.

I squeezed his hand. "Hey. We did it."

The hard line of his mouth softened. "We did."

We reached the van, and I automatically slid into the passenger seat beside him, shooting him a grin as I clicked the seatbelt in. The engine purred to life, and Felix's voice crackled through the speakers.

"Congratulations on not dying horribly! Also, I've got some absolutely spectacular footage of everything. The bit where Seb went full vampire batman? Pure cinema."

"Felix," Seb growled, then muttered to me, "That kid has certainly come out of his shell. I blame you."

"Just saying, boss. This is definitely going in my highlights reel."

Priya's voice cut in. "Felix, go warm up the milk. I'm making everyone hot chocolate when we get back."

"With marshmallows?" I asked hopefully.

"Obviously. What am I, a monster?"

"So," Rory chimed in. "Am I allowed to give Flynn his codename now? Because I've brainstormed several options. First up..."

I caught Seb's eye, and we shared a smile. His hand found mine across the console, our fingers intertwining like they'd always been meant to fit together.

34

$$Epilogue - Flynn$$

Six Months Later

Braymore Bay's water stretched out before us, a mirror of orange and gold beneath the setting sun. I leaned against the pristine teak railings of the yacht, focused on the perfectly still surface below.

Move. Just... move.

Nothing happened. Not even a ripple.

Beside me, Seb cut an absurd figure against the peaceful maritime scene. While I'd opted for shorts and a light jumper, he stood rigid in his black coat and waistcoat, clutching an umbrella like some Victorian gentleman on a pleasure cruise. The sight nearly broke my concentration.

"You look ridiculous," I said.

"I'm a vampire next to the world's most reflective light source."

"It's sunset."

"UV rays are surprisingly persistent." He twirled the umbrella.

I opened my mouth to mock him some more, but then my phone buzzed.

Rory

We miss you, Selkie. Come back to London. Plus, there's more work for the rest of us if Noctule is skiving on holiday with you. We don't like it.

Hearing my Killigrew Street codename still brought a smile to my face every time. A moment later, another message popped up.

Priya

Ignore Terrier. Keep Noctule away for as many days as possible. God knows that man needed a break after twenty years.

When Seb had booked our flights to Ireland, insisting that he had a surprise for me, I wasn't sure what to expect.

Last night, we'd met Tom for a drink at the pub. Good fortune, really—he was back from the yachting circuit for a month. I'd thought it was going to be super awkward for sure, but it was surprisingly easy. Maybe because Tom couldn't stop grinning at how happy I looked. "You found your person," he'd said later, pulling me into a bear hug that smelled of sea salt and engine oil. "Even if he is a bit... posh." The way he'd whispered that last word, like Seb's skinny tie was somehow scandalous, had made me laugh until my sides hurt.

Then, the next morning, we'd walked the familiar paths of Braymore Bay, past weathered fishing cottages and the old pub where I'd spent countless nights. The late autumn air carried that particular mix of salt and seaweed I'd grown up with, and gulls wheeled overhead, their cries echoing off the cliffs. Everything was exactly as I remembered, yet somehow smaller. Though still as lovely.

The harbour came into view, its ancient stone walls dark with centuries of spray, fishing boats bobbing gently in their moorings like they always had. Except there, gleaming among the working vessels like a swan among ducks, floated a brand new yacht.

I'd almost had fucking a heart attack.

The Selkie's Heart. A Hallberg-Rassy 40C—my absolute dream boat. It was a battle not to wet myself in excitement.

Once I'd stopped crying, we had to leave my new baby to meet Mum and Katie on the beach. Katie's new boyfriend even joined us—she wasted no time after she kicked Connor to the curb, and it was instantly obvious Greg was a massive upgrade.

It had been a lovely afternoon with them, though they were confused by my continued insistence on sitting by the large sea wall that offered shade. Mum had been utterly charmed by Seb—especially when he'd asked for her recipe for her legendary chocolate cake so he could make it for my birthday.

Katie kept shooting me suspicious looks, no doubt wondering how my boyfriend could casually drop half a million pounds on a yacht for me. I caught her mouthing "gangster?" at me behind his back more than once.

Then Seb offered to invest in her florist business, and her whole demeanour changed. Funny that. One mention of expanding into wedding planning and high-end events, and suddenly Seb wasn't a potential crime lord anymore—he was a "savvy businessman" with "excellent taste."

Both of them were slightly sad that it was clear I'd remain in London now, even though they could see how happy I was. But I had plans—proper ones, for the first time in my life. I'd enrolled in a Royal Yachting Association course, working on becoming a fully qualified sailing instructor. Teaching kids to sail on the Thames, passing on that same joy I'd found on the water, was something I was excited to do.

I'd left Rising Dough behind too, though not alone. It hadn't taken much convincing to get Emma to jump ship with me to Fat Cat's. The regular stream of Killigrew Street Hotel customers, with their tendency to tip generously, meant she was earning almost double what she made before. Plus, she got to see Priya most mornings, their lingering conversations and shared smiles becoming quite the entertainment source for the rest of us.

I turned back to the ocean, trying once more to channel whatever spark of power had awakened during Magdalena's ritual. I was determined that my connection to the water hadn't been a fluke, that it had left me Gifted. Though my ability to influence water had been extremely temperamental so far. I was possibly on track for the world's most underwhelming party trick. I could certainly give Priya's teaspoon telekinesis a run for her money.

A small puddle had collected on the deck from earlier. I stared at it, willing it to move with all my might. The surface trembled slightly.

"Did you see that?"

"Might have been the wind," Seb said carefully.

"It wasn't the wind!"

I concentrated harder. The puddle rippled again, definitely this time, and then—

"Ha!"

A single droplet leapt up like a tiny performer, hanging suspended for a heartbeat before splashing back down. My heart shot straight to my throat.

"Definitely not the wind," Seb said, a smile evident in his voice.

I couldn't stop from grinning. After months of trying, something had finally *happened*. Something real, tangible—proof that I still had magic coursing through my veins.

"I knew I just needed to come home!" I said, then caught myself. Because Braymore Bay wasn't home anymore.

The same hotel room I'd stumbled into months ago had somehow become home, my temporary refuge transforming into something permanent when no one seemed keen on me leaving. Even Seb had gradually migrated his things over, one vintage waistcoat at a time, until the wardrobe became an amusing clash of my wrinkled T-shirts and his meticulously pressed clothing.

Still, there were moments—usually late at night—when I'd wonder if I was overstaying my welcome. If the others secretly thought it odd that the random Irish bloke who'd wandered in during a crisis had just... never left. But now? That droplet of water might as well have been a key, unlocking something I hadn't even realised I'd been searching for. I wasn't just the guy dating the boss anymore, or the accidental tourist who'd stumbled into their supernatural world.

I had *magic*. Maybe not the impressive kind that sent demons flying or healed wounds, but it was mine. A gift from the sea itself, echoing the life I'd left behind in Braymore Bay, but transformed into something new. Something that made me truly part of Killigrew Street's peculiar family.

I beamed at Seb, then gestured dramatically at the vast ocean surrounding us. "Now for my next trick—"

"Flynn."

"I shall part the English Channel—"

"Flynn."

"Moses style."

Seb's laugh was wonderful. "Perhaps you'll be able to use your superpower to help with our task?"

Right. Of course. The real reason we'd sailed out here, far from prying eyes.

I helped Seb lift the makeshift raft of driftwood we'd cobbled together into the ocean. His collection of diaries—the ones from his human years, the dark and painful ones—sat in a small wooden box beside us. The silver crucifix lay wrapped in cloth, its presence still making my skin crawl even through the fabric.

"Are you certain?" I asked, watching Seb's face carefully. "These are your only records of... well, everything."

His fingers traced the edge of the oldest diary, its leather binding cracked and worn. "I don't need them anymore." He met my eyes. "They serve no purpose save to cause me pain."

I understood. These weren't just journals; they were chains, binding him to memories of guilt and manipulation, years of forcing himself to relive those memories, punishment for crimes that were never truly his.

Together, we arranged the diaries on the makeshift raft. I held his umbrella over him as he placed the crucifix in the centre, its evil somehow palpable even through its wrappings. It deserved to rust away in the depths.

"Ready?" I asked, holding up the lighter.

Seb nodded, and I flicked the lighter. The flame caught quickly on the sun-dried wood. We pushed the burning raft away from the yacht, watching as the fire spread to the diaries. The pages curled and blackened, their edges glowing orange before dissolving into ash and smoke.

For long minutes we stood in silence, watching his past turn to cinders. The sea air fed the flames, carrying sparks up into the darkening sky. Each diary succumbed in turn, decades of pain transformed into drifting embers.

The crucifix was the last to go, glowing an unnatural red as the flames finally reached it. By then, the heat had taken its toll on the makeshift raft; waterlogged wood finally gave way, splitting apart with a hiss of steam. We watched as the burning remnants scattered and sank, that cursed piece of silver the last thing to disappear beneath the waves.

Seb stood motionless, watching until the last traces of his darkness slipped into the depths. I slipped my hand into his, and he squeezed it gently.

"Thank you," he whispered. "For being here."

"Always," I replied, meaning it with every fibre of my being. *Always.*

A flicker of pain crossed Seb's face at my words, his jaw tightening. The meaning hadn't escaped him—that promise of "always" held different weight for an immortal vampire than it did for my fragile human life.

My heart thundered in my chest. Seb's eyes snapped to my ribcage, confusion etched across his features.

"I mean it." I squeezed his hand tighter. "*Always*, if that's something you want."

He studied my face intently, processing the weight behind those words. The possibility I was offering hung between us like smoke from the burning raft.

"I love you," I said. "And I want to stay with you forever."

"Forever?" His voice caught on the word. "You've never been in love before, Flynn. You're so young. We've known each other barely longer than autumn leaves cling to their branches." Then gently he said, "You can't possibly know how you want to spend the rest of your life."

"My mum and dad met young and got married one month later. They loved each other for twenty years, until the accident that killed my dad." I lifted my chin. "So don't mock me for believing in love at first sight. Don't take away that little bit of magic from the world." My voice wavered. "Unless you... don't feel the same?"

"Flynn." He cupped my face in his hands. "You've brought light back into my world. Made me feel alive again when I thought that part of me had died centuries ago. I love you. I've told you that a thousand times, and I plan to tell you a million more. But..." His thumbs traced my cheekbones. "Do you truly want to be with a vampire? I can't give you a normal life. No growing old together, no Sunday brunches out—"

"Don't be silly," I interrupted. "I'll just eat two portions at brunch."

"But no days spent in the sun," Seb said, his dark eyes fixed on the horizon. "No lazy afternoons at the beach. No—"

"We've got that sorted." I gestured at his ridiculous ensemble and the umbrella. "Besides, I spent ten years living next to a beach. Trust me, they're overrated. Sand gets everywhere."

His lips twitched, but the worry didn't leave his eyes. "I'm half married to my job, chained to that hotel."

"That creepy old hotel feels like my home now." I pressed closer, breathing in the dark spices that clung to him. "And I know you love your job. I'd never want you to stop that. Who else would keep Kit in line? Or stop Rory adopting more zombie pets? Or make sure Felix actually sleeps instead of coding for forty-eight hours straight?"

The tension in his shoulders eased slightly. "You've been thinking about this."

"Course I have. Ever since that night with Magdalena." I traced the lapel of his coat. "Life's too short. Or well, potentially very long in my case, if you'd..."

I trailed off, letting the words hang in the air between us. His hands tightened on my waist.

"Flynn..." The way he said my name, like a prayer and a warning all at once.

"You'll never be alone again," I whispered.

I touched my chest, where my heart beat steadily, pumping blood around my body. If he turned me, it would stop. That thought should have terrified me more than it did. I'd spent so many nights lying awake next to Seb, imagining what it would be like. The stillness. The silence. The hunger.

But wasn't I already changed? Magic flowed through my veins now, that connection to water marking me as something more than human. And hadn't I already left my old life behind, watching it burn and sink beneath the waves? The thought of transformation didn't frighten me half as much as the idea of leaving Seb alone again, of becoming another ghost in his centuries of memories.

"I know what I'm asking for," I said softly. "I know it's not all lollipops and rainbows. But I still want this. Want you."

I pressed my palm flat against his chest. When I'd first listened to the silent stillness of his dead heart, I'd been distraught. Now, I felt a strange sort of peace. Like I was finally steering my boat into the right harbour after years of being lost at sea.

"You don't want an eternity doomed as a monster."

"An eternity with you?" I smiled. "What could be better? We won't need to worry about being lonely ever again."

I could see it in his eyes—how much he wanted that, even if he'd never admit it.

"It doesn't have to be right now," I continued, watching his face carefully. "Not this year, even. I'd like to look a bit older first, actually. My baby face is bad enough without being frozen in time forever."

His lips quirked. "I quite like your baby face."

"I got ID'd buying paracetamol last week."

"Ah."

The last of the sun slipped beyond the horizon, and Seb folded his umbrella up.

I leaned against the railing. "Besides, I still want to sail across the Atlantic. Solo. It's always been my dream. And now with this new water affinity?" I gestured at the sea around us. Being back out here, surrounded by endless blue, felt like taking a full breath after months of shallow ones. The gentle rock of waves beneath my feet, the salt spray on my face... "It feels even more right. Like something I need to do."

"It sounds incredibly dangerous," Seb said, eyebrows furrowed.

"So is dating a vampire." I nudged his shoulder.

He rolled his eyes.

"So?" I looked at him, heart racing. "Will you think about it? Turning me? Letting me stay with you?"

Seb's expression softened. His fingers traced along my jaw, tender despite their cold touch. "Yes. I'll consider it."

Joy burst through my chest like fireworks. I grabbed his lapels, pulling him closer. "Yes! Think of everything we could do together in our eternity! All the places we could visit."

"Flynn—"

"We could sail around the world." I grinned wickedly. "Multiple times. Visit every continent."

"That's—"

"Learn every language. Though you probably already know most of them, you ancient thing."

His lips twitched. "I speak seven fluently."

"Show off." I poked his chest. "Oh! We should renovate the whole third floor. Like, into our own entire apartment. "

"The third floor is haunted."

"Even better! Ghost friends." I wrapped my arms around his neck. "We could solve supernatural crimes forever. Like immortal Sherlock and Watson, except sexier."

"You're ridiculous." But his hands settled on my waist, drawing me closer.

"We could adopt more of Rory's zombie pets."

"Absolutely not."

"Start a zombie petting zoo?"

"Flynn."

"Fine, no zombie zoo." I pressed a kiss to his jaw. "But we could travel everywhere by boat. No more cars."

"I'm not spending eternity on various forms of water transport."

"But imagine the adventures! The romance of it all." I affected a dramatic pose. "Two immortal lovers, sailing the seven seas…"

"You're trying to wind me up now."

"Is it working?"

His answering kiss told me it absolutely was. "No more talking," he said sternly. "Your mouth has more important things to do."

His lips met mine with the gentleness of waves lapping at the shore, each kiss deeper than the last. The sliver of moonlight painted us in silver, and with his arms around me, I felt truly anchored. Not to a place, but to him. To us. His hands cradled my face like I was something precious, and in that moment, with the taste of salt on our lips and the promise of forever stretched out before us, I knew I'd never need another home but this.

The shrill ring of Seb's phone shattered our bubble. He pulled back with a groan, glancing at the screen.

"It's Rory. I'll ignore it."

"No, take it." I straightened his collar. "It could be important."

"Terrier? What is it?" he asked, so clipped that I elbowed him in the stomach.

Because there was a tremor in Rory's voice as he said, "Look, how would you feel about cutting your holiday short? My ex-boyfriend is missing, and I think he could be dead."

Seb's eyes met mine, a familiar spark of determination replacing the tender look from moments ago. "Looks like our eternity retirement plan might have to wait a while."

"That's okay." I grinned, already feeling the thrill of a brand new case humming through my veins. Perhaps Killigrew Street had become as much a part of me as the sea salt in my blood. "Immortality would probably get boring without a few murders to solve anyway."

The End

Don't miss…

I hope you enjoyed Bite Marks & Broken Hearts! If you've got a moment, please leave a rating and/or review. They really do make all the difference to indie authors!

Return of
the
VAMPIRE
Hunter

And now, much more excitingly – do you fancy a (very bloody) bonus chapter?

Join Seb and Flynn for another round of roleplay in *Return of the Vampire Hunter,* a spicy bonus chapter in which the tables are turned. This free downloadable content can be found in 'The Vault' section of my website. **Subscribe to my newsletter** and find the button in the footer of each email.

For links to my other books, newsletter, shop and social media accounts, scan the QR code:

Moonlit Nights
_&_
Northern Lights

KILLIGREW STREET CASE FILE #2025-069B
PRIORITY STATUS: URGENT/HEADACHE-INDUCING
ASSIGNED AGENTS: DI THEODORE MAXWELL & RORY THORNE

Initial Assessment:

One missing werewolf journalist. Two investigators who can barely be in the same room without trying to kill each other. Multiple jurisdictions. A Scottish pack gathering that's definitely a trap. And now I have to send Detective "By-The-Book" Theodore Maxwell and Rory "Never Met A Rule He Didn't Break" Thorne undercover as a couple. May whatever gods exist have mercy on us all.

Primary Concerns:

- Maintaining supernatural secrecy

- Keeping both agents alive despite their best efforts to the contrary

- ~~Preventing Maxwell from having a sexual identity crisis in the middle of an investigation~~

- Preventing Maxwell from arresting Rory (again)

- Stopping Freddy the zombie ferret from feasting on the Scottish sheep

- Preserving what remains of my sanity

Additional Notes:

If anyone needs me, I'll be in my office with a very large bottle of whiskey. Kit has strict instructions to shoot anyone who interrupts unless the building is literally on fire.

And even then, check first.

/S. Salazar
Head of Operations
Killigrew Street

P.S. Taking bets on whether they kill each other or kiss each other first. Current odds favour homicide, but Priya's money is on 'tongue action by day three'.

Acknowledgements

WH Lockwood - Several years and many books later, and we haven't killed each other (yet). It must be true love. Thank you for the tremendous gift you give in helping me with my books, and for all of our Very Important Chats. Your amazing books are some of my favourites.

Sam Northman - Thank you for being the very first to read Bite, and helping me whip it into shape! You are an awesome human and a lovely friend. I can't wait to devour more MM PNR with your upcoming series!

T - Thank you so much for reading the book with your Spanish/historical hat on! Seb thanks you for your service. *Gracias.*

Jordy – Thank you so much for reading Bite! Your continued support of my writing journey is so, so appreciated!

Lauren - Thank you for your eagle eye over an early version of the book!

Evie - Thank you for being top fangirl of Flynn's slutty pyjamas. Your excitement over this book was hugely encouraging and your suggestions were super helpful!

Angela - Your enthusiasm for my characters is always so motivational! Thank you for reading every crazy thing I come up with. Maybe one day I'll write something boringly normal? *(Unlikely).*

www.ingramcontent.com/pod-product-compliance
Lightning Source LLC
Chambersburg PA
CBHW030921120726
47906CB00002B/436